THE MASTER'S APPROACH

In the distance Cissy heard strange, uneven tapping. *Tap-dam, tap-dam.* Graf von Wolfenbach's color deepened, and his handpatting became slightly frantic. He looked back at her, gulped and plastered a forced smile on his face. "I am not...um...exactly the master of the Castle of Wolfenbach."

The tapping sound stopped. "No," a new voice said from behind Cissy.

Her hand slipped from the Graf's grasp. Slowly she turned in the direction of that voice, new and dark and compelling.

The man was tall and as lean as a greyhound. Wavy dark hair fell into his strong-boned face, almost into his burning eyes. A sneer twisted his mouth as he stood in the middle of the vast hall, arms crossed in front of his chest. Cissy's gaze wandered over his body, over his shabby, dusty clothes, over the twist of his hip that rested the weight on his sound right leg and relieved the wooden left.

He cocked an eyebrow at her. "*I* am the master of the Castle of Wolfenbach."

CASTLE OF THE WOLF

SANDRA SCHWAB

LOVE SPELL NEW YORK·CITY

Für Karl Heinbuch,
den besten Opa der Welt, der so oft
mit mir im Schwarzwald spazierenging,
als ich noch ein Kind war.

LOVE SPELL®

May 2007

Published by

Dorchester Publishing Co., Inc.
200 Madison Avenue
New York, NY 10016

ISBN-10: 0-505-52720-0
ISBN-13: 978-0-505-52720-2

The name "Love Spell" and its logo are trademarks of Dorchester Publishing Co., Inc.

Printed in the United States of America.

Visit us on the web at www.dorchesterpub.com.

ACKNOWLEDGMENTS

As you will undoubtedly notice, this is a book about stories. Yet it is also a book about memories: my own memories of a childhood spent in the Black Forest. Even though Kirchwalden and Wolfenbach are fictitious places, I still hope I have managed to convey a sense of place—of the deep, dark forests I loved so much as a child.

I would like to thank the many lovely people who in one way or another helped me to bring this story onto paper and into shape: Gaelen Foley, who unknowingly inspired the story and later on gave me a cover quote for it; Hubert Leuser, who answered my questions about the Palm Sunday procession; Wolfgang Trenkle, who sent me information about the *Bürgerwehr* in Waldkirch and made sure I didn't have the *Bürgerwehr* in Kirchwalden shovel snow; Martin Schupp, Advisor Extraordinaire in all things to do with How to Address the Titled. All mistakes I might have made are my own. (The bad French, though, is intentional!)

As always I'm deeply grateful to the members of the LOL Literary Forum, who critted parts of the manuscript and without whom I probably would have never detected the wolf in the morning-after scene. (Jen, sorry if you read this in the middle of a bookstore again!) Many thanks, too, to Karen, who did some more critting, and to Dorie, who graciously agreed to be my guinea pig.

Last but not least, I would like to thank the two people who believed in and took a chance on this bumbling newbie author and her stories: my editor Chris Keeslar and my agent Stephanie Kip Rostan. Thank you both so much!

CASTLE OF THE WOLF

PRELUDE

The man was walking the ramparts while unseeing eyes followed his progress. Time moved sluggishly for them, and emotions dripped into them slowly. But through the years his despair had filled them, had saturated their very being. Now his desolation churned through them, grinding their hearts just as his.

Alone.

Forever . . .

. . . and ever . . .

. . . and ever . . .

CHAPTER ONE

Water poured from the skies and shrouded the world in gray. Raindrops drummed on the fold-back roof of the old gig, wormed their way through the ancient material and dripped onto the hats of the three passengers. Wetness glinted on the back of the shaggy mare and dye ran down her sides, leaving black oily puddles on the muddy country lane. Huddled in one corner of the gig, her brother's elbow digging into her side as he handled the reins, Miss Celia Fussell wiped another errant raindrop off her cheek. Her sister-in-law's high-pitched complaints grated on her nerves.

". . . could have decked the village in some more *noir*, if you ask me." Dorinda had to speak quite loudly in order to be heard over the rain. "My dear Hailstone, will you look at that?"

Cissy grimaced. So quickly her sister-in-law had internalized the transition from Mr. Fussell to Hailstone. So quickly, so effortlessly. . . .

"My dear Hailstone, I believe your poor sister is crying," the nagging voice continued. "Are you crying, *me chère?* Did I not tell you you had better stay at home? Such *énervement* is surely too much for your constitution. Now, of course, it is too late. But *me dieu,* what shall the people think?" Dorinda wrung her hands in artificial agitation.

What indeed? Cissy ground her teeth. *Puffed-up peagoose!* Upon Dorinda's insistence, the funeral had been postponed so they could send for crêpe, hat bands, and ostrich feathers from London. A hearse had to be built, the little gig painted black and the horses dyed. *Dyed.* Just so the funeral would be pompous enough for the Baron Hailstone.

Cissy's hands clenched into fists.

As if her father had ever been pompous. A shy, bookish man, he had forever preferred the library to the world outside. A pompous funeral with ostrich feathers and mutes and shield bearers was the last thing he would have wanted.

"Hailstone, did I not tell you that your sister should stay at home? A funeral is no place for a woman. I, of course, have to be there. As the *nouveau* baroness I have to inspire new confidence and hope in *toutes les braves gens.*"

Another raindrop trickled down Cissy's neck. "Be so kind and drive on, George," she forced out between gritted teeth. "I assure you, I am perfectly fine."

For a moment her brother turned his round, red-cheeked face and soulful brown eyes to her. "If you say so, Cis."

Forever the lost-puppy look. Inwardly, Cissy sighed. "Do not worry." She patted his arm and wondered, not for the first time, what in all the world George saw in his wife. A thin, pale creature with a thin, sharp nose and affected airs, Dorinda Miller, the Widow Miller's only daughter—but else of dubious parentage—had snatched the baron's son three years ago, soon after she had returned home from a convent in France. *Allegedly* from a convent in France. Her French was a disaster, her blond bouncing corkscrew curls the result of her skill with the curling tongs and probably with bleach, too. But, of course, George, sweet, apple-cheeked George, never saw beyond the carefully constructed façade.

Irritated, Cissy wiped her finger over the tip of her nose, while her sister-in-law's whining voice droned on and on, all the long, long way from the manor house to the village church. The squelching wheels of the gig ploughed on through the mud, and the splash of the horse's hooves sprayed dirt on shoes and clothes. Slowly, steadily, the rain flattened the bundle of ostrich feathers between the mare's ears into an unruly second mane.

The wind picked up and made Cissy shiver, a harsh reminder that the golden days of summer were long gone—in more ways than one. She had to close her eyes for a moment as the pain threatened to overwhelm her. Never again would she find refuge from the world in her father's arms. Never again would she press her face against his soft housecoat and inhale the reassuring scent of mild tobacco and dusty old books that clung to its folds, while his heart beat strongly and steadily under her ear. Never again would her father pat her cheek in his absent-minded manner and leave traces of black ink on her skin.

Cissy slowly inhaled and let her breath go in a heavy sigh.

Never, never again.

And what would become of her now? The new baron's spinster sister, a maiden aunt for his future children. She imagined a lifetime under one roof with Dorinda Miller, and a shudder tore through her.

"Cis?" Her brother's worried voice cut through her bleak reverie. "Are you really all right?"

"Did I not tell you, Hailstone," Dorinda repeated, "that your *sœur* had better stay at home?" Her black veil fluttered in the wind as she leaned forward to cast Cissy a disparaging look.

Abiding like the rain, the woman's whining continued, and even in church it carried on, in whispers and muttered complaints. Trying to shut her out, Cissy stared straight ahead at her father's coffin, which disappeared under black velvet.

Sent for from London, too.

It did not help that she could feel the disapproval radiating from the villagers. Disapproval not because the old baron's funeral had been turned into a farce—no, they had even admired the stupid ostrich feathers, which the rain had transformed into broken, spiky things; had admired the rough-hewn hearse, the blotchy oily and black horses, the tiny old gig that stood in as mourning carriage. As if the attempt at a fashionable funeral somehow raised the importance of the village itself. But what the people, the men, disapproved of was the presence of two women at the funeral. Cissy could not help noticing the frowns, the deploring looks.

All at once, tears welled up in her eyes. She had so hoped they would understand her need to honor her father this last time. Instead, even the vicar shot her dark looks, his face stern and forbidding.

Later, when at last the coffin was lowered into the earth, they all stared at her as if they expected her to break down, to rave and rant against fate, which had stopped her father's heart. Instead, she stood alone under her old umbrella, her eyes burning, and did not utter a sound. Dorinda, meanwhile, sniffed from time to time and prettily wiped her eyes behind her elegant black veil. She had snuggled up to George under his umbrella, the image of sad, sincerely desolate heirs.

To Cissy this sight seemed a vision of her future: standing alone and always apart from the new baron and baroness, forever condemned to a life as Miss Celia Fussell. She had no illusions in that respect. If her father had only been able to afford one London season for his daughter, then the new Baroness Hailstone would hardly agree to waste money on another stay in town. Besides, how could she ever hope to pass muster next to the young, fresh debutantes whose foreheads had never been touched by sorrow and whose mothers spent a fortune on their daughters' dresses and shawls and gloves and reticules? No, Cissy had no illusions: at twenty-seven, stranded in the north of England and thus far from any fashionable town or city, with no prospects of marriage, she was firmly on the shelf. When her father had still been alive, it had not seemed to matter. She had acted as his secretary and librarian; he had taught her Latin and Greek, French and German, and the beautiful languages of the Middle Ages so she could read all his favorite books to him. While he had not been able to afford real travels, he had taken her on the most wonderful journeys of the mind, had shown her the wild beauty of the old North, the mysteries of the Forest of Broceliande, the marvels of King Arthur's court. Most of all, she remembered her father sitting in his worn armchair, puffing his pipe like a merry, oversized dwarf.

Cissy squeezed her eyes shut. "Cwædon þæt he wære wyruld-cyninga, manna mildust ond mon-ðwærust, leodum liðost . . . ," she whispered. *They said that he was of all the world's kings the gentlest of men and the most gracious, the kindest to his people.* . . . Tears seeped from under her closed eyelids and rolled in a searing path down her cheek.

After the funeral, they drove back to the manor, retracing the deep grooves in the mud where the heavy hearse had crushed the wet earth down. And still rain fell, a fine gossamer of water and coldness, rendering the world gray and dreary. It seemed appropriate that even the land should be in mourning for the old baron.

Cissy shivered and huddled deeper into her old pelisse. Once it had been maroon-colored, and with a pang of remorse Cissy remembered its loveliness, how special she had felt when she had worn it during her only season in London. Almost like a princess. And now it was black, black, deepest black, and had lost all hint of its former beauty.

How ridiculous to mourn such a small thing, the color of a pelisse, Cissy thought. But she knew that so much more than the color of a bit of clothing, she mourned the feeling of being cherished. *Never, never again.* She sighed.

"What was that? Was that a cough?" Immediately, Dorinda's high voice took on a quailing quality. "Miss Celia Fussell, did you *tousser?* I have *told* you that you should better stay at home, and now look what has happened! *Une toux!* And you know how frail my constitution is! Oh, *me dieu, me dieu.*" Agitated, Dorinda fanned herself with her gloved hands. "I already feel dreadfully faint. I—"

Cissy could have happily strangled her. "I assure you, I did not cough."

"Well . . ." Her sister-in-law sniffed—a sound of injured dignity. "There is no reason to be so clipped, Miss Celia. One cannot be too careful of one's health, especially if one has such a *fragile* constitution as I."

At that, Cissy barely managed to suppress a snort. *Indeed. You've got a constitution like an ox.* From the corners of her eyes she watched Dorinda primly folding her hands in her lap.

"En outre," the despised voice continued, "it would do you good to start showing some more consideration for those who kindly let you stay under their roof."

Cissy's hands clenched and tightly gripped the folds of her pelisse. She had to bite down hard on her lip to prevent any scathing reply from slipping out.

"Dorrie," her brother protested weakly.

"No, no, Hailstone." Dorinda patted his arm, then slipped her hand into the crook of his elbow. "It is well past time that your *sœur* acts up to her new situation in life." Her voice had a satisfied ring, like a cat's after it had licked up all the cream.

Oh, yes, the Right Honorable Lady Hailstone. How she relished the situation! Cissy turned her head and stared unseeingly at the rain veiled landscape.

The first day of her future life in hell had just begun.

The study, though warmed by a merry fire, seemed full of chills. The large, dark desk was curiously empty, while the thick ledgers stood lined up on the shelves like leather-clad soldiers. No whiff of pipe smoke lingered in the air, and the deep leather chairs, stiff with disuse, were cold and forbidding. The late Baron Hailstone had abandoned this room years ago and had created himself a den in the library instead—a room which always smelled of ink and old paper, where the books stood crookedly side by side like old friends and whispered to each other of old deeds of dare, of stories long forgotten and of ages past. It was a room where you snuggled up in front of the fire, where you sat down with a cup of hot tea when rain beat at the windows and a storm howled around the house.

Now rain was beating against the windows of the study, too, yet Cissy felt cold, so cold inside out, as if she were never going to be warm again. She tried to concen-

trate as Mr. Weatherby, the family solicitor, read out the
last will in his thin, reedy voice. The wrinkles quivered
down his throat, and his wire-rimmed spectacles had
slipped down to the tip of his nose. He spoke slowly and
with difficulty, as if he felt grief, too. And perhaps he
did. Her father had always been fond of little Mr. Weatherby. *"A good man, that. A loyal man,"* he used to say.

"'. . . to my son and heir, the Honorable George
Alexander Fussell.'"

So the house and everything went to George; no surprise there. The surprise was that her father had twice
entailed the estate, meager as its incomings were. Perhaps he had wanted to curb the tendency of his son's
wife to live above their means; perhaps he had hoped
for a more sensible generation of Fussells in the future.

Cissy watched how Dorinda's lips became thin and how
displeasure contorted her face. Even more displeasure
came when Mr. Weatherby read on and made it known that
the late Baron Hailstone had bequested most of his books
to his friends: people who, like him, pursued the study of
mythology or the Middle Ages. Friends whom Cissy had
never met, yet whom she had got to know through the letters she had read to her father in the last few years. It would
be painful to empty the library and pack up all the books,
which had been like a second family to Cissy. Yet she was
grateful that they would be given into good hands, that
they would be treasured and read with pleasure. Dorinda
might have banished them to the attic so she could fill the
shelves with fashionable novels and poetry instead, none of
which she would ever pick up anyway.

Mr. Weatherby went on reading, listing pensions for
the old servants and tenants. "'. . . And lastly . . .'" For the
first time, there was a break in the old lawyer's even pre-
sentation of his late client's wishes. Mr. Weatherby cleared
his throat and stared hard at the piece of paper before

CASTLE OF THE WOLF

him. " 'And lastly, to my only daughter, Miss Celia Fussell, I bequeath the estate of Wolfenbach under the conditions as explained in the letter enclosed. Should she fail to meet these conditions within a period of four months, the estate shall fall to the Altertumsverein Kirchwalden. With this I commend my soul to God. May He forgive my sins and give me His guidance so that after this life I fail not to enter His eternal kingdom. Signed, George Fussell, Lord Hailstone. Fifteenth September, 1825.' "

Cissy blinked.

"A double entail?" Dorinda gave an artful little laugh, which did little to hide the scorn underneath. "How very *curieux*."

A worried frown creasing his smooth forehead, George leaned forward. "Surely there must be a mistake? I have never heard of this Wolfenbach before." He turned to his sister. "Have you heard of it, Cis? Surely you cannot want a place we have never heard of?"

Cissy blinked again, while Dorinda managed a shrill giggle that had even the stout Mr. Weatherby wincing. "Wolfenbach? As in the novel? So it must be a joke, I assume? A very *étrange homme,* your father, Hailstone, full of peculiar jokes like the double entail, *pour exemple, n'est-ce pas?*"

Mr. Weatherby adjusted his glasses. "I assure you, milord, milady, Miss Fussell, that Wolfenbach does indeed exist, and that I here have the papers, drawn up in Miss Fussell's name, to prove it. Miss Fussell?" He cleared his throat and lowered his head so he could peer over the rims of his spectacles at Cissy. "Would you like me to read out the accompanying letter?"

"But . . . but . . ." George spread his arms wide, a picture of genuine puzzlement. "Where exactly *is* this place? Surely our father would not want my sister to own a place we have never heard of?"

"*Exactement.*" Possessively, Dorinda settled her hand on George's arm. "If there is another estate, it is only right and proper that it should go to dear Hailstone."

Mr. Weatherby looked on the couple and sighed, as if the continuous interruptions in the proceedings finally began to annoy him. "Wolfenbach is situated, quite nicely as I have been assured, in the Great Duchy of Baden. In the Black Forest, to be more precise. The letter, Miss Fussell?"

Yet Dorinda was not yet finished. "The *Noire Forêt*?" She shuddered delicately and quite suddenly seemed to have lost interest in acquiring the property after all. "What an odious place! I have heard it is barely civilized. Whatever did your *père* think of, my dear Hailstone, to purchase a house somewhere like that in the first place?"

Mr. Weatherby gave her a bland smile. "Then you should consider yourself lucky, milady, that the castle has been deeded to your sister-in-law. Miss Fussell?" His kind, watery eyes turned to Cissy once more.

A castle?

Who would have thought that her father owned a castle in Baden? He had friends there, for sure, living somewhere near Freiburg, where, as he had told her, small, manmade streams ran through the streets and filled the town with their faint babbling. Each year her father had received a carefully wrapped and boxed bottle of kirsch from the Black Forest. On the cold days of autumn and winter, he had liked to put a glass of kirsch in his cocoa—"to warm his old bones," as he said. Yet her father had not been that old, or so it had seemed to her. Surely not old enough to die. . . .

"Miss Fussell?"

Cissy shook her head to clear the cobwebs from her brain.

A castle in the Black Forest.

"The . . ." She forced herself to concentrate. It would not do to live in the past. If you lived in the immediate past, her father used to say, it was escape. But if you lived in ages long gone, then it was called studies. At the memory, she almost felt like smiling. Almost. "The letter."

"Yes, Miss Fussell." She could hear concern in the lawyer's voice. "Do you wish me to read it out aloud?"

A castle in the Black Forest.

For me?

"To my only daughter, Miss Celia Fussell, I bequeath the estate of Wolfenbach . . . ,"—it seemed to Cissy as if she could almost hear her father's voice, slightly rough and raspy with tabacco smoke—*"under the conditions as explained in the letter enclosed."*

What conditions?

Cissy met the lawyer's gaze. Worry had darkened his eyes. Did he know what the letter contained? She moistened her lips and shot a look at the piece of folded paper he held out to her. Suddenly, her mouth went dry. "If you would be so kind," she managed.

Mr. Weatherby nodded, then broke the wax seal. Carefully, he opened the letter and smoothed out the paper with long swipes of his hand. His eyes flitted over the page, darting back and forth as if caught in the web of her father's spiky handwriting. After a moment, the lawyer cleared his throat delicately, adjusted his glasses once more, and looked up. "Lord Hailstone wrote this letter a few years prior to the existing will. The date given is the twenty-fourth of August, 1820."

"But . . . but . . ." Agitation made George splutter. "That's your birthday, Cis!"

Her twentieth birthday. The day she had resigned herself to the fate of being on the shelf forevermore. For a moment, the memory hurt. Even now. Even after all these years.

"Why would Papa write such a letter on your birthday?" George sounded puzzled.

"*Très morbidé,*" Dorinda commented, obviously piqued because so much attention was focused on her sister-in-law.

Mr. Weatherby chose to ignore her remark. His eyes remained fixed on Cissy. "Miss Fussell? Do you wish me to continue?"

She gave herself a mental shake and straightened her shoulders. "Of course." Pleased, she noted how calm her voice sounded. As if nothing fazed her, not even the memory of that summer after her one and only season in London. Twenty years of age and no hopes for the future. How strange that it had not seemed to matter these past seven years. And how strange that it mattered now, more than ever.

Cissy folded her hands in her lap to prevent them from shaking while she listened to the even voice of the lawyer reading out her father's last wishes:

"'My dearest daughter, when I am no longer among the living and this comes into your hands, I would want you to know how much I have loved you. Indeed, you have brightened my days since the day you were born. Therefore, it particularily pains me that by that day's twentieth return I have not been able to provide for you fittingly, as I strongly fear there will be no more chance for you to mingle with the rich and the wealthy in some fashionable town or other.'"

Cissy blinked, surprised that her father had seen her situation, after all. But she did not want his guilt, had never wanted his guilt, for she, in turn, had understood the family's economic situation.

"How very touching this all is." Dorinda sniffed. "Is this the reason, *peut-être,* for the double entail?"

Mr. Weatherby paused and looked at the new Lady

Hailstone as he would at a particularily nasty insect under a microscope. Suddenly, a thin smile lifted his lips. "I believe, milady, my late client chose that later date in 1825 to rework some points of his will." For a moment his eyes glittered, before he abruptly turned back to Cissy, his face blank once more. "Shall I continue?"

Flabbergasted, she stared at their family solicitor. She could have sworn that for a moment something very much like malicious joy had lit his eyes. As if he held the new baroness in deep disdain. As if her father had indeed changed his will because of George's wife. Cissy swallowed. "Please do."

" 'Several years ago, when I still could do my friends financial favors, I purchased a most beautiful castle in the midst of the Black Forest. I had intended to give it back to my very good friend Wolfenbach upon my death, yet now I give it to you as I am sure you will treasure it just as I did. A castle fit for a princess, a castle fit for my own daughter. And still, it might fall back into the hands of the Wolfenbachs, for I give it to you upon one condition: that if Wolfenbach's son is still unwed you will give him your hand in marriage. Wolfenbach has always been the most decent of men, and I have no doubt that he raised his son to be an equally honorable man. Be happy, my dear. With deepest affection, your father.' "

As he ended the letter, Mr. Weatherby carefully removed his spectacles and set them aside on the desk. "With this, I believe,"—his gaze settled warmly on Cissy—"he thought to secure you a suitable husband after all."

CHAPTER TWO

The tiled stove, a baroque monstrosity in white and gold, filled the sitting room with pleasant heat, while outside the wind howled around the snug little villa at the edge of the small town. Uneasily, Graf von Wolfenbach shifted on his worn armchair.

"Trouble, my dear?" came the soft voice of his wife. Immediately, the knot of anxiety in the pit of his stomach eased. Strange how, even after all these years, her sweet voice affected him, calmed the worst anger or soothed the deepest despair. *His little siren,* he had called her since the earliest days of their courtship so many years ago. In another lifetime, or so it seemed.

He looked up from the letter he had been reading to where she sat at the window, which overlooked the prosperous valley all the way to the dark sweep of the hills beyond. She dyed her hair black—in order to please him, he knew. Yet even with gray hair, white hair, with no hair at all, she would have been the most beautiful woman to him. The only one he had ever loved. The only one who had ever gifted him with children, fine sons, so a part of themselves would live on. He had always hoped the kind of love he and his wife shared would blossom for his sons, too. Yet it seemed as if that was not going to be.

"Ferdl?" A faint line appeared between her brows, and she put her embroidery aside. Her tone and the fact she had used her pet name for him betrayed her worry.

"It's nothing," he hastened to reassure her. "I . . ." He took his glasses off and pinched the bridge of his nose. At her sound of distress, he smiled apologetically. "I am sorry, Anna. It's just . . . I have just received news that my dear friend Hailstone passed away last month."

"Oh, my dear." She rose and hurried to his side, her movements slowed by aged bones and muscles. And yet, when he rested his head against her soft breasts and her hand tenderly stroked what was left of his hair, it seemed as if the years slipped away. And like the first time he had found this heavenly place God had created for him on earth, a warm flood of gratitude and well-being filled his body.

His hand slipped around her waist, while he turned to rest his forehead against the warm flesh of her upper chest. He inhaled her familiar scent, letting it take the sharp edge off his grief. "Do you remember the provisions of the will?" he murmured against her skin.

Her hand on his hair momentarily stilled. She cupped his skull, and he felt the subtle pressure of her fingers. "The mad scheme the two of you cooked up all those years ago? Oh dear." Her fingers relaxed. Her hand glided down to rest on his neck in an oddly protective gesture. "He will not like it. He will not like it at all."

And in accord, both of them turned to look out the window to the hill where the castle nestled amidst the dark trees, the crumbling tower to them a symbol of dying hope and shattered dreams.

*   *   *

"I still don't think this is a wise idea."

Instead of answering, Cissy carefully wrapped one of her tea dresses around her copy of the *Lyrical Ballads* so the leather-bound volume would not come to harm in the travel chest during her journey. She had sent her maid away because the girl had kept blubbering into her big white hankie. That Evie accompany Cissy to Germany was out of the question—a journey to Newcastle would have been enough to make Evie perish on the spot. Yet the thought of losing her mistress seemed equally disconcerting for the poor thing. *Well, I wouldn't cherish the thought of working for Dorinda, either.* Cissy sniffed.

"Have you listened to me at all?" George asked.

Cissy threw a look over her shoulder at George, who sat at her desk and looked mournful.

"Dorinda and I, we would have been perfectly happy if you had decided to continue living at Badford Park. You know that, don't you? We still would. You could still stay here and—"

Her back to him, Cissy rolled her eyes. "We have been through this numerous times in the past three weeks. You will not persuade me, George." She prodded her dress-wrapped book of poetry to find out if it needed more padding. Satisfied, she put it into the chest and reached for the next book and the next dress.

"I cannot imagine what you want to do in Baden." Wood creaked as George shifted on the chair. "There is nothing for you there."

There is nothing for me here. For a moment, Cissy had to close her eyes. Then she shook her head and busied herself with wrapping her book and putting it away. "I am going to have a castle." *Just imagine: a castle. Like a princess.* She took up another tome.

"And marry a man you have never seen in your life."
Suddenly George sounded aggressive. "How our dear father could have come up with such a harebrained
scheme is quite beyond me, I swear!"

Distracted, Cissy frowned and rubbed a thumb over a
scratch in the blue leather cover of her book of German
fairy tales, a present from her father for her nineteenth
birthday. With her forefinger she traced the golden let-
tering: *Kinder und Hausmärchen gesammelt durch die Brüder
Grimm.* "Wolfenbach's son will surely be already married
and bouncing his little ones on his knee," Cissy murmured.

"And if not?" George jumped up. Before she had time
to react, he was at her side and wrenched her around,
hands like iron bands on her shoulders. "What will you
do then, Cis? You know nothing of . . . You cannot know
what . . ." Hot color suffused his face.

His vehemence surprised her, yet she managed a
small shrug, even though his hands weighed her shoulders down. "You have heard what Papa wrote. That
Wolfenbach is a decent man, and that he was convinced
his son—"

"For heaven's sake, Cis!" George shouted. "A man
might be the Archangel Michael personified, and yet his
son might grow into a good-for-nothing! A . . . a rakehell." His voice rose even more. "Dammit, Cis, this is not
one of your blasted fairy tales!" He grabbed the book
she still held in her hands and flung it across the room.
With a dull thud, it hit the wall and fluttered to the
floor, rustling like a bird with broken wings.

For a moment, nobody spoke.

Then another kind of hot color filled George's face. "I
beg your pardon."

"What for?" Her face expressionless, Cissy stared at
her book. "For swearing or for ruining my book?"

Slowly, she raised her eyes to his face, the same apple-cheeked face she had loved all her life. Now it seemed the face of a stranger.

"I do apologize," George said stiffly. "But still—just because Father left you a castle doesn't mean that life has turned into a fairy tale. Life is *not* a fairy tale, Cis."

A harsh laugh escaped her. "And yet you want me to turn into Ashputtel?"

"What?" A puzzled frown marred his smooth forehead.

Of course he would not know. For a moment, she felt tempted to tell him: reduced to a servant in her father's house, to sleep in the ashes of the hearth. Dorinda would love that.

Cissy shook her head. "It's nothing." She brushed past him to retrieve her fallen book. "You will not change my mind in this," she said, her back to him. She lifted the once beautiful book and tried to smooth the crumpled pages with the flat of her hand.

"Cis . . . ," he began.

She looked up. Apple cheeks and soulful brown eyes, and yet the face of a stranger. "Go, George. And tomorrow I will go, too."

Another scratch in the blue leather, one corner bumped. No longer fine and new, but a relic from golden times never to be retrieved.

The door closed with a click.

She was alone.

The next day, for the first time in weeks, the sun broke through the thick, gray clouds and tinted the world in his early-morning hue. Shades of orange and pink touched the trees, the grass and the house, and the road appeared to be strewn with gold. Jubilant birds rose up into the sky to greet the new day.

Standing on the drive in front of the manor, Cissy

took a deep breath to draw it all in—memories that were made of familiar sights and sounds, the smell of damp air that mingled with the rich scents wafting up from the kitchen where Cook was preparing breakfast.

"M-miss?"

Cissy looked around.

Evie stood on the front steps, shuffling her feet and twisting her fingers in her apron. "M-m-m . . ." The maid snuffled. "M-mi-miss . . . yer b-b-b . . ." Her lower lip trembled and then she burst into tears. "Oh, Miss Celia!" she wailed. "How can ye l-l-leave an' go to 'em barbarians?"

Cissy sighed. "Evie—"

"Oooh!" The girl sank down on the cold stone of the steps and buried her face in her apron. Big sobs wracked her plump little body, and the sounds she emitted reminded Cissy of the elephant she had seen at a Covent Garden pantomime all those years ago.

"They are not exactly barbarians." Cissy walked back to the front entrance and gently patted Evie's bent shoulders. "Really, you shouldn't take this so hard, my dear."

Raising her head from her now crumpled apron, Evie blinked up with bloodshot, redrimmed eyes. "Oh, miss . . ." She reached for Cissy's hand. "Can ye not stay?" she whispered.

"Oh, Evie." Cissy sat down on the stairs next to her maid. "You know I cannot. I . . ." She looked down on their linked hands: Evie's pink and plump, her own slender and almost white. "I have this one chance to be something more than mere Miss Celia Fussell, Lord Hailstone's spinster sister." She rubbed her thumb over the girl's knuckles. "Just that one chance, Evie. I cannot forsake my father's gift."

The maid sniffled. "I've always liked ye fine as ye are, miss."

Cissy felt a smile tug at her lips. The girl had a good heart. "And I thank you for it, Evie." She looked up to meet the girl's tear-filled gaze. "But being the baron's spinster daughter was one thing. I could not stand being the baron's spinster sister."

A large tear rolled down Evie's cheek. "I understand, miss. It's just tha' I will miss ye so."

"My dear, sweet Evie." Impulsively, Cissy gave her maid a hug. "I will miss you, too, you know." She sighed. "I wish things would have been different. . . ." Releasing the girl, she stared down the drive toward the street. On and on it went, a gravelly band through meadows and fields. Soon, it would take her away from all that was dear to her, would carry her far away into a new life.

As if she had somehow sensed Cissy's thoughts, Evie suddenly said, "He wouldn't 'ave wanted it, the late master, God bless his soul. He wouldn't 'ave wanted fer ye to stay his spinster daughter forever an' ever. He'd 'ave wanted fer ye to be married with a fine young gentleman and 'ave little 'uns."

With a pang, Cissy remembered the words of her father's will: *It particularly pains me that . . . I have not been able to provide for you fittingly . . .*

"I suppose you are right," she said slowly.

Evie wiped her face with her apron and nodded. "I'm sure . . . I'm sure tha' . . ." New tears welled in her eyes, and her voice started to wobble again. "Tha' he's . . . he's found ye a right nice young man." Swiping her hand over her eyes, the girl sniffed loudly. "Miss."

Cissy stared down the street. "I sure do hope so," she murmured, then suddenly shivered as a slither of ice whispered down her spine.

He prowled the hallways of his home like a beast on the loose. Restless and always searching, searching. . . .

Outside, the storm howled around the casements, hissing viciously through cracks in the ancient walls. The old trees groaned under its onslaught, while overhead, wind scattered the clouds like a distressed flock of sheep. For a short moment, the dark veil was ripped from the moon and a splinter of light fell through the windows, wandered over spartan furniture. Instinctively, the man shrank away from the light. Better the dark, where shapes became obscure and no pity existed.

As if it had suddenly become too heavy, he leaned his head against the door frame, rubbing his leg to ease the pain of overexercised muscles. This was all he had left: darkness and pain. All he would ever be: a ghost, a specter, a fairy tale beast not fit for human company.

A harsh laugh escaped him.

No, not a fairy tale beast. *These* still had hope. In the end, they would always turn back into dashing Prince Charming. But for him, there would be no salvation, no return to a past where he had been fêted as the darling of society, where women had given him smiles full of sexual promise and men had regarded him with respect and envy.

Another flock of clouds hid the moon and plunged the room into welcome darkness.

Bitterness churned in his stomach, a poisonous snake. And yet, together with the pain, it was his only companion in this life that had gone wrong so many, many years ago. He shuddered. No, there would be no turning back to the past for him, no return to innocence, to life in the light. No salvation for this beast. Only loneliness.

Defeated, the man bowed his dark head, accepting the inevitable as he had accepted it all those years ago.

CHAPTER THREE

". . . and then the mice ate the evil bishop up so all that remained was his skeleton," Mrs. Chisholm whispered in her most eerie voice, while peering at the stocky tower from underneath the dripping hood of her oilskin coat. Cissy stood beside her on the deck of the steamer and tried to discern something through the steady drizzle.

Mist whirled around the base of the Mouse Tower and rendered the small island in the midst of the Rhine invisible. More mist, dirty white, poured from the hills to their right and left, and reached out its tentacles to span the expanse of the broad stream. Like an eerie apparition in a gothic novel, the towers and battlements of a castle would sometimes rise above the clogging gray.

Her ears ringing with the never ending bluster of the steamship's engine, Cissy huddled deeper into the folds of her own coat. She blinked. Dampness clung to her lashes like tears. Yet despite the mist and the rain, Mrs. Chisholm had insisted on staying on deck so they could properly admire the splendor of Father Rhine.

Cissy could still hardly believe that she really was onboard a ship heading up the Rhine and bringing her nearer and nearer to a new life. A sense of unrealness shrouded the journey to London with Mr. Weatherby, who had not only organized a passport and the necessary signatures for her, but had also introduced her to Mrs. Chisholm, the widow of a wealthy manufacturer. She liked to spend the winters in the town of Baden-Baden and had agreed to take on Cissy as her companion for the length of their journey. Well versed in the art of traveling at this time of year, she also had insisted on their oilskin coats.

As Mrs. Chisholm stood beside Cissy at the railing, the widow was reminiscent of a rather tall, thin scarecrow. A beaming scarecrow, despite the water which dripped from her nose. She didn't even bat an eye when the ship stopped at yet another customs house, and they had to dig out their passports so they could leave Prussia and enter Hesse-Darmstadt.

"This is surely the loveliest part of our journey!" Mrs. Chisholm exclaimed—as she had kept doing ever since they had left the docks in London. "*Precisely* like the first time my Bernard and I took this route some forty years ago, newly married and *so* in love. Of course, we first had to go to the Michaelmas fair in Frankfurt, but afterwards, my Bernard wished to show me the balls in Baden-Baden. We had the *loveliest* weather that year, only sunshine, sunshine, sunshine, and the balls and amusements in Baden-Baden were still in full swing. At the time, I was still a stupid young chit who had never seen anything of the world, and the glitter of Baden-Baden seemed *so* glamorous to me. I wish I could take you to the balls in Baden-Baden, too, dearie."

Cissy nodded and smiled and looked on as a flag appeared on top of the Mouse Tower, indicating their ship could proceed into the narrow curve of the Binger Loch.

Mrs. Chisholm had wanted to take her to the balls in Baden-Baden ever since they had left the docks in London.

"A few years later," Mrs. Chisholm went on, wiping the water from her nose with the sleeve of her glistening coat, "everybody flocked to Italy. But who needs Italy when you can have the grandeur of German forests, the picturesque towns, the sweetness of Rhinelandish wine and, above all, the majestic Rhine itself!" She threw her arms wide as if she wanted to hug the river. "Oh magnificent, glorious Father Rhine. . . ."

Cissy supressed a smile. Mrs. Chisholm had enthused while the waves of the Channel had tossed their ship about until all passengers had acquired a greenish tinge; and she had enthused all the way from Rotterdam to Cologne when high dykes on each side of the river had intercepted all view, except for a few church steeples which had shyly peered over them. But in Cologne, where the old cathedral, still unfinished even after almost six hundred years, greeted travelers, Cissy had felt it, too—the tingle of excitement, the reverent shudder, the *awareness* of history. Now she felt it again, with each castle, each abbey, each ruin they passed along the way.

Here kaisers of old had erected their residences; Roland, the great hero and nephew of Charlemagne, had built a castle, and Siegfried had fought against the ghastly dragon; here her father's stories took shape and her childhood heroes stepped out of the pages of musty books.

Their ship glided on, and Cissy admired the hills where the fires of Celtic altars had once illuminated the night, where the Romans had erected the Limes and made these hills the rim of the civilized world. They had brought the knowledge of cultivating wine, and still the grapes ripened along the banks of this river. Countless armies had marched through this land, peoples had come and mingled and disappeared, and still their legacy lived on, strong and insistent, and Cissy admired it all, the din of the steamship in her ears.

In Mayence, grown from a Roman garrison town and bearing the Celtic sun wheel in its coat of arms, the two women left the Rhine and traveled on by post chaise on the Bergstrasse to Baden-Baden. While they passed by more ruins and castles, Mrs. Chisholm regaled her with stories about them all, stories of brotherly hate and brotherly love, of star-crossed lovers, of witches and white women.

A little way out of the small town of Heppenheim they finally crossed the border into the Grand Duchy of Baden. From then on, Mrs. Chisholm became quieter and quieter until the stories totally ceased to flow. Now, she only clucked her tongue from time to time and threw Cissy worried glances, which Cissy herself did not know how to interpret.

So, even though she had come to be very fond of the widow, Cissy felt relieved when on their third day on the road Baden-Baden lay before them, nestling between the hills, which formed an offset of the Black Forest. *"Civitas Aurelia Aquensis,"* Mrs. Chisholm murmured absent-mindedly, a deep frown marring her forehead. "Already the Romans appreciated the mineral springs, and you can find altars to their gods all over town. Just like our Bath, really. Only the people are speaking German, of course. Quite curious, isn't it?"

They took up residence in the only real hotel in town, the Badenscher Hof, and Mrs. Chisholm insisted a bath should be brought to Cissy's room just as to her own. "No, dearie, you mustn't protest. I only wish you could stay longer and I could show you the balls. You would like them, I'm sure, just as any young girl would. But in-

stead . . ." The widow pressed her lips tightly together
and the line between her brows deepened. Abruptly, she
threw her arms around Cissy and enveloped her in a
lavender-scented embrace. "My poor girl. My poor,
sweet girl." As abruptly as before, the widow released her
and, blinking rapidly, waved her away. "Shoo, now. Go
and refresh yourself."

The next day, Mrs. Chisholm would not hear of putting Cissy onto the post chaise on her own. Instead, she
hired a carriage for her, and after giving the coachman a
long lecture, they had said a tearful good-bye. "My dear
child. My dear child," the woman choked out, and
pressed Cissy to her heaving bosom. "You *must* promise
to write me and send me many letters. Most uncivilized
this, to send a young girl off all by herself and let her
fare alone in a foreign country. My poor child." She patted Cissy's back. "Do promise to write to me, and if there
is *anything* I can do, don't hesitate to ask for my help."

Finally, Cissy sat in the carriage and waved good-bye
while the coach jerked into motion and rumbled over
the cobblestones. Soon, Baden-Baden lay behind her,
and Cissy was on the road once more. At first the silence
and loneliness seemed oppressive, weighing down on
her. She tried a bit of reading, but soon returned to looking out the window at the country, which became wilder
with each mile they passed. And the farther they went
and the more towns, great and small, with narrow streets
overhung by medieval houses they passed through, the
stronger grew Cissy's feeling of slipping back in time and
into the stories her father had loved so much.

But on the second day, when they had almost reached
their destination, the country changed its pleasant face.
Shortly after they had stopped at an inn along the way to
change horses and to take a small midday luncheon,
dark clouds gathered on the horizon. Cissy watched how

they built up layer after layer of bulging gray, before they sprang up and raced toward the carriage on the lonely road. As if touched by ghostly fingers, the bare branches of the trees to the left and right started to move and wave at the travelers. Dead leaves swirled up, some still colored in bright hues, others already gray with decay and gossamer like spiderwebs, mere skeletons of once green leaves, which crumbled into dust in the breeze. Twilight fell when the clouds overhead reached the carriage. The wind picked up, whistled in the cracks of the coach and made the trees groan under its onslaught. And then the snow descended upon them, first in a thin drizzle, curiously gray in the dimness; but soon thick, fat flakes fell all around. The wind was ominously howling outside, like a large beast on the prowl, out to hunt, and they the prey. . . .

Cissy huddled in a corner of the carriage, wrapped in a blanket she had found under the seat. She remembered all the awful stories of coaches lost in the snow, swallowed by snow storms, not only in the north of Britain; most horrid of all the stories of the great frost in 1814, when nature had held travelers prisoners of wayside inns and farmhouses for days on end. Indeed, it was said that even the Thames had been frozen that year, and an ox had been roasted whole on the thick layer of ice.

If this carriage should disappear, none would be the wiser—nobody expected her arrival, and George would probably not register the absence of mail. He would believe her to be sulking as if she were still a little girl.

Cissy shivered under her blanket.

Should the snow swallow this carriage, nobody would search for it, and they would be found only by chance when the snow thawed. Blue, frozen corpses, the horses caught in midstride, nostrils still flared. And their pale ghosts would haunt this forest forevermore, inspiring fear in the unwary traveler who would venture out at night.

Cissy closed her eyes and shuddered. Perhaps George had been right after all; she did indeed tend to lose herself in stories, believed that fairy tales could become reality. Perhaps this whole venture had not been a good idea. Perhaps she should have stayed at home.

Under one roof with Dorinda?

Her eyes snapped open.

On second thought, she preferred haunting this forest as a pale ghost.

She shook her head and looked outside. The dim light of the coach lanterns did not reach far, yet the snow brightened up the darkness, so they traveled through a world of dim gray. The trees flitted by as dark shadows in the whirling snow.

Later—it might have been hours or minutes, Cissy was never quite sure afterward—it seemed to her she could spot a golden glow in the dimness ahead. With trembling fingers, she opened the window and thrust her head outside, blinking against the sting of snowflakes in her eyes. They were still surrounded by forest, and in the near distance black hills rose up, hovering to their right and left like enormous beasts. But before them, nestled between the hills, a golden halo of light could be seen even through the snow. And Cissy watched, as snowflakes gathered on her hair, how the halo changed form and finally tranformed into the blinking lights of a small town.

"Coachman!" she shouted.

"Ho there," came the cheerful answer. "We've nearly made it, *gnädiges Fräulein.*"

A short time later, the wheels of the coach crunched through the snow that covered the streets of the picturesque little town, just about to settle for the night. Oil lamps, quaintly strung across the streets, defied the whirling snow and cast their soft light about to show the wary traveler the way to the grand pension beside the church. The coach rattled to a halt in front of a great door, brightly illuminated by two lanterns. It opened to emit a flurry of servants. The carriage door opened, and Cissy was handed down under the shelter of an enormous black umbrella.

She turned and stared in wonder at the church, so unlike the ancient gray village church at home, which huddled against the ground as if to seek shelter from the cold winds which blew from the moor. This church rose proudly from the ground, with the bell tower pointing to the night sky like a slender finger. And even amidst the falling snow, the building seemed to shine, all done in white and red, with elegant, sweeping curves and the hint of gold on the toops of the roofs. And in dark niches along the front, saints of stone stood guard over the entrance.

"*Gnädiges Fräulein* . . ."

Cissy turned back.

"*Hier entlang.*" The young footman made a small movement with his umbrella, pointing it toward the waiting door of the inn.

"Yes, of course." Cissy smiled at him and stepped toward the warm yellow light spilling through the open door. As she saw the elegant curves and the red and white repeated in the building before her, her eyes opened wide. "It's like the church," she said in wonder.

"*Fräulein?*"

And she remembered to speak German. "This building," she repeated excitedly, this time in the correct language. "It looks like the church!"

"And no wonder." The middle-aged woman in a

starched white apron, who was waiting for her at the door smiled at Cissy. "This used to be a convent, and St. Margaretha's its church. Good evening, *gnädiges Fräulein*. I'm Frau Henschel, the innkeeper's wife. Welcome to our small town."

The coachman came up to them, carrying Cissy's old, threadbare travel bag. "I thought it best to stop here for the night, *gnädiges Fräulein*," he explained. "In the morning we can then venture to search for the castle."

"The castle?" Frau Henschel started. "Not the Castle of Wolfenbach?"

Instantly the tiredness of the journey was forgotten, and Cissy's heart lifted with excitement. "Yes, the Castle of Wolfenbach, exactly. Do you know it?" she asked.

Frau Henschel's face had lost all color, and she raised her hands as if to ward off evil. "Oh, *gnädiges Fräulein*, you cannot possibly mean to go to that cursed place! He'll get so angry!" She wrung her hands. "He'll rip you apart and tear you to pieces, he surely will!"

Taken aback, Cissy frowned. *Cursed? Why cursed? And . . .* "Who will rip me apart?" she asked.

Owl-like, the innkeeper's wife stared at her. "Who? Who else but the son of our dear *Graf*?" She lowered her voice to a mere whisper, as if afraid he might, like the devil, hear her even when miles away. "He's been roaming that castle some thirteen years, and nobody in their right mind would dare to venture near it. Like a wild beast, he is. Dangerous. And deadly."

Cissy blinked.

Dangerous, deadly, and, it would seem, her betrothed.

When she woke the next morning, the pitch-blackness of night just gave way to a dreary gray morning. From outside came the crunching sounds of snow shovels against cobblestones as the small town got ready to dig itself out of the suffocating layers of white. Dark gray clouds hovered ominously over the surrounding hills, shielding them from view.

Wearily, Cissy stared out of the window. As beginnings to a new life went, this one was not the most auspicious. As she put her hand against the windowsill, she could feel the cold seeping in from outside, as if warding her off.

And when she lightly touched her fingers to the glass, the bite of the ice flowers seared her skin. *Life is not a fairy tale,* they taunted her. *This is no place for you! Go home!*

"No!" In a burst of anger, Cissy slapped her hands against the window. "I will *not* go back to that house where Dorinda is now mistress! I will *not* be the poor relative who just watches life flow by! I will *not* be Aunty Cis and nursemaid to my brother's children forevermore!" Tiny rivulets of water trickled through her fingers as the ice melted away under the warmth of her palm.

Cissy took a deep breath. "This is going to be my new life and I'm going to enjoy every minute of it." She rubbed her wet fingers against her nightdress, turned her back to the clouds and the snow, and started to get ready for the new day.

But when she went downstairs, she was dismayed to find out her coachman had left and was on his way back to Baden-Baden. Frau Henschel assured her it was for the best, that he wouldn't have found the way to the castle anyway, that one of the inn's stable hands would bring her instead. So, after a hasty breakfast and repeated attempts by the innkeeper's wife to make her stay in the valley, Cissy climbed up onto the seat of a small cart. Her battered travel trunk was strapped to the back and her carpet bag was stowed at her feet. Frau Henschel gave her flannel-wrapped hot bricks, a thick woollen blanket, mittens and a woolly cap for warmth, and cast her a last worried look before a surly-looking boy climbed the seat and took up the reins. Clicking his tongue, he slapped them on the horse's back, and with a crunch, the cart jolted into motion.

The boy, a youth of maybe sixteen with a continually dripping nose, seemed uninclined to acknowledge Cissy's existence and stared straight ahead, handling the reins expertly. Cissy decided to ignore him, too, and looked around with interest.

Despite the grayness of morning, the little town looked neat and smart, the half-timbered houses glowing white and black, and a bit of gold glinting over the bakeries and inns. A little chapel of gray stone hid between the houses, far less grand than imposing St. Margaretha's, but still adding to the charm of Kirchwalden. Cissy saw men shoveling snow and clearing the streets, while old women in black stood by and watched. Rosy-cheeked children, straps with books and small slates thrown over their shoulders, ran squealing around and pelted each other with snowballs.

Cissy snuggled deeper into her blanket and let the heat of the hot bricks flow through her body. Soon she would arrive at her castle and everything would be all right. Cozy warmth filled her from without and within, for the ghosts of the early morning had fled, even though the clouds still loomed threateningly nearby.

They seemed even more omnious when the cart left Kirchwalden behind and approached one of the hills, covered not only in clouds and fog, but also with fir trees so dark they looked almost black. *The grandmother, however, lived in the forest, half an hour from the village. As Little Red Riding Hood now entered the woods, she met the wolf. But Little Red Riding Hood didn't know what a bad animal he was, and was not afraid of him. . . .*

Cissy frowned. She was not afraid of wolves either, and she would not be frightened by any heathenish young count who appeared determined to scare the poor villagers witless.

Her eyes narrowed.

Indeed, the Castle of Wolfenbach now belonged to *her,* and having lived under one roof with her horrid sister-in-law, she was determined to keep hold of this property of hers. "But because Little Red Riding Hood was such a clever girl," she murmured, "and saw the evil glint in old wolfie's eyes, she grabbed a thick stick and hit him over the head. Quite, quite hard. And howling loudly with pain, he ran away and was never seen again." Cissy grinned, feeling giddy and just a tiny bit silly with excitement.

From the corner of her eye, she caught the dark scowl her young coachman bestowed upon her. He muttered something she didn't understand and spat into the snow.

After he had steered the cart halfway around the hill, they finally entered the woods, and the horses drew the vehicle up and up and into the fog. To the left and right the trees stood side by side like steadfast soldiers, their lines only now and then broken by craggy rocks. Even though the trees had held off most of the snow, it was still difficult going for the horse and the small cart. More than once, Cissy felt how the wheels slid and the cart skidded in a bend of the coarse road. Grabbing the edge of the seat, she could feel the throbbing of her heart in her ears, its heavy beats against her ribs like a frantic bird trying to break out of its cage.

But finally the trees fell away, and in front of them rose, in all its old, brown glory, a tumbledown castle from the fog.

The cart rumbled to a halt.

With something that sounded like a curse, her driver jumped onto the ground, marched around their vehicle and proceeded to loosen the straps around her travel trunk. With a dull thud it hit the ground.

"And what exactly do you think you're doing?" Cissy asked.

Throwing her another dark scowl, the driver wiped the back of his hand across his dripping nose. Then he pointed with his thumb over his shoulder. "Out!" he snarled.

"I beg your—"

He snarled some more, but Cissy couldn't understand a word he was saying. Somehow he used too many words ending in *le*. Yet even though she couldn't understand what he was saying, she certainly caught the meaning of it, especially since he repeatedly pointed his thumb over his shoulder. Twenty horses would not make him drive into that cursed castle. He had been forced to bring her this far, and apparently he considered this sufficiently heroic.

Reluctantly, she climbed down from the seat. Her old half boots sank into the snow well over the ankle. "Now, look here—"

He strode around the cart and, shoving her roughly out of the way with his shoulder, grabbed her carpetbag and dumped it onto the snow-covered ground. With a last smoldering look, he swung himself up onto the box seat and urged the horse away as if all seven hounds of hell were after him.

Cissy looked over her shoulder at the castle. The tower lay in ruins, and the dark holes of the windows blinked at the her like the empty eyesockets of a grinning skull. Cackling, a raven came flying from the forest, circled overhead and flew inside.

Well, perhaps her reluctant driver knew something she didn't.

"Drat!"

She looked down to where the hems of her pelisse and dress dragged through the snow, and dampness rapidly seeped through the thin leather of her old boots.

"Dratdratdrat!" She gave the snow a vicious kick. *"Drat!"*

Beyond a wooden bridge before her gaped the gate to the castle, dark and mysterious. Certainly too dark to venture in alone. Cissy chewed on her lower lip. She waggled her now icy-cold toes, looked this way and that.

"Drat!"

George would be rather happy to know that she well realized life was not a fairy tale at all. For if it were a fairy tale, this would be a good moment for some sort of otherworldly helper to appear. Or some knight in shining armor.

> *O what can ail thee, knight at arms,*
> *Alone and palely loitering?*

Cissy frowned. Maybe she should drop the idea of a knight in shining armor. Knights were so easily led astray by a beautiful face.

> *I met a lady in the meads,*
> *Full beautiful—a faery's child,*
> *Her hair was long, her foot was light,*
> *And her eyes were wild.*

And as easy as that they would be in trouble up to their necks.

No. Definitely no knights.

Sighing, Cissy reached for the grip of her carpetbag. She hoped she would soon find somebody who would be willing to carry her travel trunk inside. Taking a deep breath, she squared her shoulders, lifted her chin, and marched toward the castle. *Her* castle.

Her steps echoed hollowly on the wooden bridge, which had been cleared of snow. She stepped through the open gate and passed the gatehouse into the outer ward of the castle. The gatehouse appeared to be abandoned, and the castle walls to be missing several stones. Yet the long half-timbered building huddling against the walls of the inner castle looked well cared for, with black wood and patches the color of clotted cream.

Cissy passed by the remains of a first bastion before the path ascended to the upper and main part of the castle. Above her, on the outer wall, she spotted the now roofless ramparts. As she walked along the ward, she couldn't help thinking that this had been the place where in times past the inhabitants of the castle had pelted would-be intruders with arrows and stones before they poured hot oil or pitch onto them. Shivering a little, Cissy peered up the walls on her left, which belonged to the buildings of the inner keep, but all she saw were rows and rows of light brown stone, only broken by arrow slits and a few tiny windows high up.

She passed a second bastion and finally stepped through a small gate onto the courtyard of the upper castle. Her mood immediately lightened. Rows and rows of the light brown stone met her eyes; whitewashed walls and half-timbered third and fourth stories; half-timbered oriels with slate roofs; and windows, both large and small, all with dark red shutters. Even though the color dripped off, they gave the courtyard a cheerful appearance. Her mouth open in wonder, Cissy turned around and around. Yes, the tower was partly ruined and the other buildings all looked battered and must have seen better days, but still. . . .

A castle!

Her castle!

Higher and higher her gaze climbed—until it met the baleful stone eyes of a leering gargoyle.

Cissy started.

Even at this distance, she could see the muscular feline body attached to the ugly head, the long claws that gripped the stone. Her gaze flickered away, only to be caught by the next gargoyle. They lurked up under the roof, hiding behind crooks in the wall. "How curious," she murmured. "I've never heard of a castle with so many of them."

She shook her head and turned to see whether she could find a door. The building on her right lay in ruins; the winter sun shining through the empty windows lent it a skeleton-like appearance. *A skeleton of a house, the bones made of mortar and stone.*

To Cissy's left wooden stairs led up to a gallery, which ran around half of the courtyard, ending at the remains of the tower with a spiral staircase. It ran down to the courtyard and up to a door high in the tower wall. Another gargoyle guarded the entrance to this last bastion of the castle.

Cissy shaded her eyes with her hand against the winter sun. It was hard to tell from this distance, but she could have sworn the gargoyle was silently laughing at her, mocking her. She fought the urge to stick her tongue out at it. Instead, she looked away with emphasized nonchalance and focused her attention on the two buildings at the end of the courtyard. Two doors, both closed, of course, and a yawning black archway to her left.

She chose the archway and found it led to another, smaller courtyard: more buildings, more doors, a wooden gallery above her, but this time no stairs. Sighing, Cissy looked around. Her breath formed small white clouds in the cold air. *"Guten Tag!"* she said loudly.

She waited. Listened.

"Hello-ho?"

Still no answer. The whole place seemed to be abandoned. A ghost castle.

Cissy shivered.

High above her, she detected more gargoyles hiding under the roof. They all had long, wolfish snouts. The Wolves of Wolfenbach.

"Drat."

Cissy turned and walked back to the first courtyard. *"Guten Tag!"* she hollered. "Is anybody at home?"

Eventually she heard a door opening, and then an old woman, small and round, with a tight bun of gray hair on the top of her head peered over the balustrade of the gallery. Her eyes widened and she gave every appearance of having come face to face with a ghost. With a shriek, she turned and hurried back inside.

"Um." Whatever should she do now? "Dandyprat!" Shivering in the cold, Cissy rubbed her hands over her arms. Perhaps Evie had been right after all and these people *were* barbarians.

She sniffed. Whatever they were, she would not freeze to death on the doorstop of her own castle.

Squaring her shoulders, she marched up the stairs, which creaked in the cold, and walked toward the still open door. She saw how the threshold of stone had been hollowed out by inumberable feet—a chain of people stretching back far into the past. She put her foot onto the stone, made herself part of the chain, and stepped through the door.

She came into a wide, high hall. A ribbed vaulting stretched above her, with painted flowers blooming around the center rossettes and in points running toward the walls. Threadbare tapestries and dark portraits of people in clothes from bygone ages adorned the pale beige. On one side stood an empty chimneypiece, on the other a colorful, tiled stove next to a table and a few chairs. Yet despite the furniture, the room appeared empty and chilly. And the four doors on all sides did nothing to improve Cissy's mood.

Her steps sounded preternaturally loud in the silence, and she half-expected to find another gargoyle lurking even in here. Yet there was no trace of another being—be it of stone or human flesh and blood—in sight.

Cissy crossed her arms in front of her chest. Her foot tapped an annoyed staccato on the floor. "What *is* the matter with these people?" she muttered before she cleared her throat several times to holler, *"Guten Ta-hag!"*

This finally produced the desired result: one of the doors was thrown open.

"Miss Celia Fussell!" An older man approached her, in his wake a motherly looking woman. He hurried toward Cissy and, taking her hand, shook it as if he wanted to dislocate her arm. "My dear Miss Fussell," he said, his small horn-rimmed glasses slipping down his nose. "My dear Miss Fussell. My dear, *dear* child." He halted the shaking, and with the forefinger of his free hand righted his spectacles. "You *are* Miss Celia Fussell, are you not?"

Cissy blinked, eyeing him carefully. "Indeed I am, sir."

"Yes, yes." He patted her hand. "You look exactly like your dear papa." His face changed, his features shifting until he reminded her of a sad puppy. "We were so sorry to hear of your loss."

"Thank you, I—"

His face lit up again and he continued the patting. "But we are very happy to have you here, aren't we, Anna." He half-turned to look at the woman behind him.

Cissy could not help noticing that his cheerfulness seemed almost too bubbly, too exaggerated. It was rather worrying, but she aimed at keeping a smile on her face. "Thank you for this kind welcome, sir. So you would be . . ."

He beamed at her and patted her hand some more. "Graf Ferdinand von Wolfenbach."

"Graf von Wolfenbach." She wondered whether she should curtsy, but this did not seem to fit the hand patting and shaking. "So you would be master here?"

With surprise, she saw flustered color blossom on his cheeks. "I . . . er . . . well . . ." He turned and threw the woman behind him an imploring look. "I . . ."

In the distance Cissy heard strange, uneven tapping. *Tap-dam, tap-dam.*

Graf von Wolfenbach's color deepened, and his hand patting became slightly frantic. He looked back at her, gulped and plastered a forced smile on his face. "I am not . . . um . . . exactly the master of the Castle of Wolfenbach."

The tapping sounds stopped. "No," a new voice said from behind Cissy. "*I* am the master of the Castle of Wolfenbach."

Cissy's hand slipped from the *Graf*'s grasp. Slowly she turned in the direction of that voice, new and dark and compelling.

The man was tall and as lean as a greyhound. Wavy dark hair fell into his strong-boned face, almost into his burning eyes. A sneer twisted his mouth as he stood in the middle of the vast hall, arms crossed in front of his chest. Cissy's gaze wandered over his body, over his shabby, dusty clothes, over the twist of his hip that rested the weight on his sound right leg and relieved the wooden left.

He cocked an eyebrow at her. "*I* am the master of the Castle of Wolfenbach."

CHAPTER FOUR

Cissy blinked.

If he was aiming at impersonating the villain from a gothic novel, he was succeeding rather nicely. Of course, the overall effect could still be heightened by, say, a knife dripping blood or a polished skull. *No, that's* Hamlet. *To be or not to be.*

From her thawing toes a sharp pain shot up her body. She surely had envisioned her arrival at her castle differently.

Cissy frowned.

Her castle.

To be or not to be, indeed.

She looked the man straight in the eyes and slowly lifted her brows. "Actually," she said sweetly, "that's not quite true. *I* am the master of the Castle of Wolfenbach now. Or rather,"—she gave him a beaming smile and hoped it would annoy him just as much as her throbbing toes were annoying her—"its mistress."

The rebuttal came in a feral bark. "The hell you are!"

"Fenris!" Graf von Wolfenbach admonished.

Fenris? What a peculiar name! But she had to admit the name fit the man who was glowering at her, his face blacker than a thundercloud. Fenris, the demon wolf of Germanic mythology, of whom the prophecy said would one day swallow the sun and bring about the end of the world.

"Have you invited her here, Father?" The demon wolf rounded on the *Graf*. How such a charming man could have fathered such an ill-mannered son was quite beyond her.

A man might be the Archangel Michael personified, and his son might grow into a good-for-nothing!

Cissy suppressed a shiver as she remembered her brother's words. At the time she had thought his worries about rakehells or worse exaggerated and unfounded, but now she was no longer so sure. However, she suspected that even in the Black Forest rakehells would dress more stylishly than Fenris von Wolfenbach did.

"If you have," he growled, "you can just get rid of her again."

So, no rakehell then, just terribly ill-mannered. A perfect churl.

She sighed. "I believe our family solicitor announced my impending arrival to Graf von Wolfenbach. He also informed him that according to my late father's will . . ." A wave of grief swamped her, and she had to swallow hard before she could continue. "He informed him that I'm now holding the deeds to the castle."

Fenris von Wolfenbach stared at her as if she had suddenly grown a second head. If possible, his expression darkened even more. "What kind of rubbish is this?" he snapped. "This castle has been in the possession of our family for several hundred years."

His mother put her hand on his arm. "Fenris, dear . . ."

With an impatient sound, he shook her hand off and continued to glare at Cissy.

It occurred to her that she would be forced to wed this lout if she wanted to hold on to the castle, if she wanted to start the new life she so craved. Her heart sank. How could she bear to be married to a man who even snarled at his own mother?

An unpleasant smile twisted his lips. "That silenced you, didn't it?" Turning, he snapped at his parents, "Will you please get her out of here!"

Cissy straightened. She had not come this far to be thwarted by a man who didn't even know the basic rules of polite behavior. She took a deep breath and forced her voice to remain calm. "According to the papers I have in my possession, my father came into possession of Wolfenbach several years ago."

His snort broke the uneven sounds of his steps as he walked back toward the door from whence he had come. "Impossible."

"Fenris . . ." his father began.

"He came into possession of it in the autumn of 1811."

That brought the man to an abrupt halt. He whirled around so fast that for a moment Cissy thought he would lose his balance. And then she watched, her heart in her mouth, as he strode toward her, his eyes blazing green fire.

"No!" He grabbed her shoulders, shook her. "No, that's not possible! You're lying!" He breathed heavily, as if he had run a mile, and dark color splashed across his cheeks. "No!" He shook her again, and his fingers gripped her hard enough to hurt.

"Are you mad?" she gasped, horrified by this unexpected reaction. She had certainly managed to rattle him. "Let go of me!" Sudden fear cramped her stomach as she tried to fight against him. But he only dug his fingers deeper into her arm.

"You're lying!" he snarled, and in that moment he indeed looked like a demon wolf, wild and feral and totally out of control.

Panic constricted Cissy's throat. "Let go of me," she whispered.

"Fenris!"

Cissy caught sight of the horrified faces of his parents. They had taken hold of his arms and tried to pull him away from her. Yet the more they pulled, the more he tightened his grip.

"You're lying! Go on, admit it!" He shook her hard enough to rattle her teeth. A vein pulsed at the side of his neck, straining against the skin. "You're *lying!*"

"Fenris!"

"I am not!" she shouted, and shoved at his chest. Her heart hammered in her ears, and tears of shock were running down her cheeks. "I am not!"

Breathing heavily, he finally let go of her and took a step back. He shook his head. "You're lying," he muttered. "Lying!" He brushed the back of his hand across his mouth.

"Fenris . . ." His father put a hand on his shoulder, but he shrugged it off and took another step back.

"You're lying."

"What is the matter with you?" With shaking fingers, Cissy clumsily wiped the tears from her cheeks. "You must be mad! *Mad!*" Shivers gripped her whole body.

"Oh, my poor girl." The *Gräfin* put an arm around her shoulders. "My poor child." She rubbed Cissy's arm. "Everything will be all right, I promise."

Yet Cissy did not avert her eyes from the woman's crack-brained son. "I am the mistress of the Castle of Wolfenbach now," she whispered. "I am."

Fenris's face twisted. "You're lying."

"She is not, son," his father finally managed to cut in. The old man looked sad and tired, as if weighed down by an invisible burden. "We have never told you, but sixteen years ago, Wolfenbach was indeed sold to Lord Hailstone."

Fenris von Wolfenbach's head whipped around. His mouth opened, yet for once no sound emerged. He shook his head.

"Yes, it's the truth." Graf von Wolfenbach nodded and gave his son a sad smile. "Hailstone had no use for the property, so we could continue using it just as before. Just as if it still belonged to our family."

All color drained from the young man's face, leaving it deathly pale. "No," he murmured. "No!" His expression changed, became imploring. "No, Father, *no*. Not Wolfenbach." He looked at Cissy, swallowed. "No, it cannot be." He swallowed again, and something like desperation flickered over his visage. "No." He shook his head.

"I am sorry." The *Graf* patted his shoulder. "I asked my old friend Hailstone for help and he agreed to buy the castle when it was sold."

Which would also explain her family's money problems—the fact that her father could only afford one season for his only daughter, that George had to give up all thoughts of a tour through Europe.

Cissy closed her eyes.

In 1811 her father had bought a castle to help a friend. *Why?*

She opened her eyes and caught Fenris von Wolfenbach's glittering stare. He looked as if he might be sick any moment. Or burst into tears.

Abruptly he turned away, and with awkward strides hurried out of the hall.

Graf von Wolfenbach heaved a deep sigh. He wiped his hand across his brow before he turned to Cissy with a weary expression. "I am so very sorry, my dear. I had not expected my son's reaction to be so . . . so intense." He shook his head. "It has come as a shock for him."

"I would like to go to a room and freshen up," Cissy whispered. Inside, she was still shaking, tiny shivers running through her flesh and bones. Wearily, she closed her eyes. Why did her life have to change? She yearned to seek refuge in her father's library, to bury her face against his housecoat and breathe in the scents of pipesmoke and old books. But . . .

Never, never again.

Cissy shuddered.

She was all alone.

The room she had been given looked as if it belonged in Sleeping Beauty's palace: dust everywhere, and old cobwebs adorned the corners, hung in thin, gray vines from the four-poster bed. In one corner stood a small stove, ashen-colored with dust and dirt. On the floor in front of it, the footsteps of the servant who had brought her to this place were clearly visible. After wrestling with the stove, he had finally apologized and promised to get some firewood.

For now, it was so cold in the room that ice flowers bloomed on the cracked mirror on the wall. They partly hid black splotches of old age, which resembled pressed spiders.

Cissy shivered and wrapped her pelisse tighter around herself. She couldn't help herself—she felt as if she were caught in a particularily nasty gothic novel. A derelict castle, a maniac master—well, ex-master, who had, upon the housekeeper's inquiry, sent his guest to what was obviously one of the most run-down rooms in the whole bloody castle! *The only thing missing now is a skeleton in the closet or a ghost coming through the wall while holding its head under its arm.*

Well.

Even without the skeleton and the ghost it was bad enough. The heavy hangings on the bed were riddled with holes. Here and there were glints in the dark material, as if it had been shot through with golden thread. "Hm." Her interest roused despite herself, Cissy stepped nearer. She could just discern a golden floral pattern in the dark background. But time had destroyed the delicate pattern; the golden thread had become unravelled or had, in places, totally disappeared.

The tip of her boot clonked against china. Cissy looked down.

The chamber pot. Cracked, too, a handle missing. China the color of old ivory, and depicted on it an arcadian scene in pink, which reminded her of French wallpaper. She squatted down.

"I bet it was once a rather nice chamber pot." As she tugged at the remnants of the handle, the pot slid out from under the bed—and revealed its ghastly contents: the remains of a half rotten mouse.

With a shriek, Cissy fell onto her behind and scrambled backward. *Now, here's the skeleton at last.* Sighing, she picked herself up and rubbed her aching derrière.

She scanned the room, tapped her foot on the floor. "How the heck am I supposed to sleep in this hellhole tonight?" Her voice echoed ominously from the walls. "So this crack-brained fellow thinks he can wear me down like this? Ha!" Agitatedly, she brushed an errant strand of hair out of her face.

Once more she looked around the room. She clicked her tongue, wriggled her nose; and then, a slow smile spread over her face. *The cabbage-headed dod wants a fight?*

Gingerly, she sank down on the corner of the bed. *He shall have his fight.* She folded her hands primly in her lap and awaited the servant's return.

Almost an hour later she was shown into a dark-paneled drawing room, to where the *Graf* and the *Gräfin* had retired. The sight of her travel habit caused them to raise their brows. Yet instead of commenting, the *Graf* just cleared his throat and asked gruffly whether she would like some refreshments. He indicated a plate holding a selection of small cakes, and continued, "Wouldn't you like some Prussian coffee to warm you up after your . . . um . . . journey? Rambach, bring a cup for Miss Fussell. Miss Fussell, this is Rambach, my son's butler."

The old, white-haired man sketched her a bow. *"Gnädiges Fräulein."* The way he squinted at her made Cissy suspect he was terribly nearsighted.

She sat down on one of the large red armchairs. Giving the butler a small smile, she folded her hands in her lap. "Rambach, when you get the cup, would you please tell the housekeeper to come and see me?"

"Gnädiges Fräulein?" He looked at her blankly.

Her smile intensified. "The housekeeper. I would like to talk to her."

He threw a cautious glance at the *Graf,* then nodded very slowly. "Yes, *gnädiges Fräulein.* Immediately."

The von Wolfenbachs exchanged a look. When the door had closed behind the butler, the *Graf* cleared his throat and harrumphed several times. "You . . . um . . . wish to talk to the housekeeper?"

"Yes, indeed." Keeping the smile firmly fixed on her face, Cissy reached for one of the little cakes. She had run her father's household for over a decade, and she would be damned if she would now let the servants of her new home get the better of her! *Courage, Celia, courage.*

While she munched on the cake, she forced herself to uphold her cheerful countenance and pretended it was absolutely normal to sit there still in her rumpled traveling clothes. However, the conversation remained stilted. The *Graf* and the *Gräfin* appeared to be embarrassed—and small wonder with such a bugbear of a son! The *Gräfin* asked her about the journey, and Cissy told a little about her time with Mrs. Chisholm.

Eventually, the door opened and the butler returned in the company of an elderly woman. In fact, it was the woman who had run away shrieking when she had spotted Cissy in the courtyard. *"Gnädiges Fräulein."* The butler made a stiff bow. "Frau Häberle, the housekeeper."

Frau Häberle curtsied. *"Gnädiges Fräulein."* Nervously, she twisted the hem of her apron through her fingers.

Oh, this promises to be interesting! Cissy still held on to her bland smile, even though she wished she weren't there all on her own. It would have been nice to have a familiar, dear face to look at, to draw reassurance from. And yet . . .

You're no longer a child, but a grown-up woman. You have to take care of yourself.

Indeed.

And she would start by asserting her authority with her new servants. She subtly straightened her shoulders. "Frau Häberle." She gave the woman an amiable nod. "I believe we've already met, haven't we?" She watched how a soft blush tinged the woman's cheeks, and for a moment she could almost sympathize. But then she remembered the state of the room she had been given and all sympathy fled. Her tone became chillier. "I understand it was you who assigned a room to me?"

"I . . ." Licking her lips, the housekeeper threw a look at the *Graf* and *Gräfin*. What she saw there obviously acted as encouragement, for her hands fell to her side and she lifted her chin. "Indeed. After consulation with the master, *gnädiges Fräulein.*"

After consultation with the master, indeed. Cissy raised her brows. *The lout!* She folded her hands in her lap and smiled some more. "I see. That explains it then," she said kindly. "You were laboring under a misconception. For you see"—she leaned a little forward and lowered her voice as if divulging a great secret—"*I* am now the mistress of the Castle of Wolfenbach. Isn't that so, Graf von Wolfenbach?" She turned to him.

The man cleared his throat, shifted on his seat. "You are quite right, my dear," he finally said.

"See?" Cissy focused her attention on the housekeeper once more and gave her an even kinder smile than before. "And this means that I expect my room to be cleaned and tidied this afternoon and my travel chest brought in. I want to sleep on a clean mattress tonight, with a fresh pillow and featherbed, for I don't care much for mice nests. I'm sure you understand. And make sure the old drapings are taken down, too. If you can't substitute them for something more fitting today, that is quite fine. But else"—she looked the housekeeper up and down—"as I said, I expect to find the room cleaned by this afternoon, else I'm afraid I'll have to look for a new housekeeper—and other servants."

Color came and went in the housekeeper's face. "*Gn-gnädiges Fräulein?*"

"That is all, Frau Häberle."

After the two servants left, the room was very quiet. "Frau Häberle has been in our family's employ for the past forty years." The *Gräfin* finally broke the silence. "I am sure there is no need for such harshness." Gentle reprimand rang in her voice.

Cissy steeled herself to meet the woman's gaze calmly and with no outward sign that her heart was beating faster than normal. She did not want to alienate the Wolfenbachs any more than the servants, but after her inspection of what was supposed to be her new living quarters, she knew it was imperative to take up the reins fast.

Or rather, to wrest the reins from that blunderheaded churl, Fenris von Wolfenbach.

She had to suppress a shudder as she remembered how he had stared at her, snarled at her, how he had gripped her, totally out of control. For a moment she had thought he would actually throttle her. The warning of the innkeeper's wife flitted through her head. "*He'll rip you apart and tear you to pieces, he surely will!*"

Not so fast, she thought. *Not so fast. . . .*

She shook her hair back and met the *Gräfin's* gaze unflinchingly. "Oh, I can assure you it was necessary. Quite, quite necessary."

"She did *what?*" Fenris whirled around to stare at his friend and valet, his anger so intense that he thought his head might burst any moment.

Johann grimaced. Fenris had met him during the war, and they had stuck together during those horrid months Fenris wished he could erase from his memory. When he had returned home, Johann had followed him and stayed on as his valet.

"She threatened to dismiss Frau Häberle. And apparently everybody else, too."

"The hussy!" Fenris growled. "How dare she—"

"Well, if the castle really belongs to her now . . ."

With a vile curse, he turned his back on his valet. Breathing heavily, he leaned on the windowsill and stared outside. The dark bulk of the forest was broken by the bull's-eye pane, and each bulge showed a little piece of snow-covered green with a startlingly blue sky overhead. Closing his eyes, Fenris wearily lowered his head.

"Wolfenbach gone," he murmured. "They even lost the castle because of me. All because of me." Bitterness constricted his throat and viciously cut into his insides like the slow twist of a knife that had been thrust into his belly. *And this time even the legendary Wolves haven't been able to protect their own. . . .*

"Damn it all!" His fists hit the stone. He didn't care that the impact jarred his arms. If anything, he welcomed the physical pain. For if it were bad enough, he might forget the pain inside, the pain and the guilt, which had been his companions for more than a decade. "I won't let her take the castle away from me. In fact . . . ,"—he slowly turned around, and his lips lifted in a terrible smile—"in fact, I will make her regret the hour she set her foot over my threshold."

INTERLUDE

An agitated murmur rippled through the stone. They pricked their ears, listened. Watched. Someone new had entered their realm.

They caught the sharpness of recent pain, but beneath . . . oh, beneath—there was something else. Something they hadn't seen or felt in a long time. Something they had yearned for, hoped for. Something they wanted to keep for themselves.

Stone shifted.

And they *would* keep it.

Would keep her.

Forever.

CHAPTER FIVE

By late afternoon, Cissy's room was moderately clean and warm. The cobwebs had been removed, as had the holey bed drapings and the rodent skeleton. The cracked chamber pot had been replaced by a whole, creamy white pot, and the bedding smelled and looked clean.

For dinner with the *Graf* and *Gräfin*, Cissy could finally change her clothes. While she straightened her wrap-around stays, it occurred to her she would need to hire a new maid soon.

She sighed.

She missed Evie—the easy chatter, the softly rolling Yorkshire accent. She hoped the girl would find a new place instead of staying with Dorinda. There were a number of respectable families in the neighborhood she could work for as maidservant. Or just as a normal housemaid.

Cissy rubbed her forehead.

She should have made sure Evie would get a nice new place. But then, she didn't have any rights in regard to her former servants—her father's former servants. Now they were George's. *George, George, why must you have such an atrocious taste in women?* She shook her head and finished putting on her dress.

The demon wolf of Wolfenbach did not show up for dinner. It was just his parents and Cissy. For some unfathomable reason they dined in the drafty Great Hall, and even though the table stood next to the stove, Cissy could still feel the chill of winter seep through her woolen dress. *Note: Wear more petticoats in the future. Or better, find another dining room!* To prevent another round of awkward and stilted conversation, she subtly steered the dinner talk to the field of mythology. Just like her father, Graf von Wolfenbach was keenly interested in the latest developments in this field. He asked her whether she had heard about the Edda edition and translation by the Arna-Magnaean Society in Copenhagen. He recited some of the Latin translations for her and told her about his plan for a new German translation. "Of course, Herder has already translated some of the songs, as have Gräter and the Grimms, but still . . ." Abruptly he stood, raised his glass and in a deep, booming voice declaimed:

"Up rose Odin,
the old hero,
and saddled
Sleipnir.
Down he rode
to Nifelheim . . ."

He drank from his wine before he gave Cissy a crooked smile. "It is, of course, not terribly patriotic, but I have always loved those old Norse songs best of all medieval literature." He sat down. "Tell me, my dear, which piece of medieval literature do you like best?"

And thus they passed the evening. That night Cissy

dreamt of old prophecies, of divine horses with eight
legs, of heroes riding the skeletons of giant mice, and of
a great demon wolf with glowing eyes, sulking through
the forest and pursuing a little girl in a black hood.

The next morning, Cissy tried to find a new place for all
the things in her travel chest. When she unwrapped her
books it felt like a reunion with old, dear friends. After
they had found a new home on the shelf that adorned
one wall of the room, Cissy thought her own new home
suddenly looked much cozier than before. The finishing
touch was her old blanket on the bed. She left her room
with a smile on her face.

    Yet just as quickly, her smile faded. While the previous
evening a servant had been sent to guide her to the
Great Hall, she was now on her own and soon found
that the castle very much resembled a maze. Hallways
suddenly twisted into different directions or ended in
dead ends, while some staircases led nowhere. With in-
creasing frustration Cissy went from one ghostly silent
room to the next, past faded tapestries and pictures so
dark with old age the lines had been blurred beyond
recognition. The furniture had lost its luster and everything was covered by a thick layer of dust, making Cissy
almost believe it had snowed *inside* the castle. Her
breath formed white puffs of air in front of her face, and
she cursed the fact she had only taken her shawl with
her and not her thick pelisse. *A person might wander
around here for days and never find a way out.* . . . Shuddering, she stepped to a window and looked outside. Far below, she could catch a glimpse of the ward above a rocky
drop enclosed by the unrelenting darkness of the forest.
And even farther below, like a child's toy, she saw the
small town of Kirchwalden. If she were to disappear, nobody would miss her down there. The innkeeper's wife,

Frau Henschel, might eventually spin a romantic tale about a young Englishwoman mad enough to brave the even madder son of the Graf von Wolfenbach. "And she was seen nevermore . . ."

Cissy snorted.

"Oh no, I'm not that easy to get rid of." Determinedly, she walked on and finally found herself in the second, smaller courtyard. Heaving a sigh of relief, she glanced up at the wolfish gargoyles lurking beneath the roof above. On a childish impulse, she stuck her tongue out at them then stomped through the gateway to the main courtyard and up the wooden stairs to the Great Hall.

There she found the *Gräfin* staring at her plate, seemingly embarrassed, while her husband hid behind the previous day's newspaper. At a side table, which hadn't been there day before, Rambach stood waiting, his face devoid of all expression. When the door clicked shut behind Cissy, the *Gräfin* looked up and made an effort to smile. "Good morning, my dear. I'm afraid my son's kitchen does not lend itself to culinary delights as far as breakfast is concerned."

The butler came forward to help Cissy sit down. "Why, thank you, Rambach."

The *Gräfin* wrinkled her nose, but it was her husband who answered from behind the newspaper in a most disgruntled tone. "There's only black bread with butter."

"And cold gruel," Rambach added helpfully.

"Indeed?" Cissy shook out her napkin. *And I am supposed to believe that?*

The newspaper rustled agitatedly. "Who knew what kind of strange diet our son keeps to! It's a shame! A perfect shame!"

The *Gräfin* patted his arm. "Don't upset yourself thus, Ferdinand. We knew Fenris has . . . strange habits."

"Strange habits? *Strange* habits?" The *Graf* started to

fold the newspaper so fiercely it seemed as if he wanted to wage war against it. "He's grown into a heathen, our son! That's what happened! A perfect heathen!"

A lout, a churl, a nidget, a mutthead . . . Cissy cocked her head to one side. "Rambach?" She turned her head.

The butler blinked. *"Gnädiges Fräulein?"*

"Are there some leftovers from last night's roast meat?"

He gave a cautious nod. "There might be."

"Then bring them up." She gave him a beaming smile.

"Y-yes." He gulped. *"Gnädiges Fräulein."*

The thick bulges of the bull's-eye panes of the study softly filtered the light of the late morning sun. Specks of dust danced in the rays of light, which fell across the heavy desk of darkest wood.

"And?" Fenris kept his attention on the treatise on modern forestry he was reading.

Johann shuffled his feet. "Well . . ." He cleared his throat.

At that, Fenris looked up, a frown on his face. "Did it work?"

His valet scratched his head. "Well . . . your parents had black bread and cold gruel for breakfast, just as you ordered." He paused.

"Yes, I admit it." Sighing, Fenris waved his hand about. "That was a bit unfortunate. What did they say?"

"According to Rambach, your father thinks you've become a heathen. Correction: a *perfect* heathen."

Fenris blew up his cheeks and exhaled slowly. Warily, he rubbed his neck. "What's new there?" he muttered. "Go on. What happened then?"

"Well . . ."

"Yes?"

"Then Miss Fussell came and ordered Rambach to bring up the leftovers from last night's dinner."

Fenris groaned.

His valet lifted his hands in a helpless gesture. "Apparently she liked neither buttered black bread nor cold gruel."

"Damn."

"My dear, you cannot possibly stay here." The *Graf* cut off a piece from his slice of cold roast meat. "And mind you, it's not just because my son has turned into an absolute recluse with no manners whatsoever." He waved his fork with the pierced bit of meat at her.

His wife patted his arm. "Don't agitate yourself. It's not good for you." She turned an apologetic smile on Cissy. "You must realize, Miss Fussell, that you cannot stay here unchaperoned and all alone with Fenris. It would not be seemly."

Cissy stared at them. *There's no way I am going to leave this castle. If somebody is moving out it will be your bratty, nutty heir!*

"You are more than welcome to come and live with us at the Villa Wolfenbach, for as long as it takes to sort everything out. Isn't that so, Ferdinand?"

Harrumphing, the *Graf* busied himself with his meat. "Yes, yes. Of course," he mumbled, while a hint of pink crept up his neck, which made Cissy wonder what was wrong this time. After all, when he had become flustered yesterday, the next thing she had known was being face to face with his snarling son.

"This is very kind of you—," she began, but he immediately interrupted.

"Rubbish, my dear." He looked up, and this time she could detect no sign of fluster in his expression. "Your father was a very dear and close friend. And you're more than welcome in our home."

But definitely not welcome in his son's.

No, *her home*. Wolfenbach was hers now.

Of course, she needed to marry the loutish son if she wanted to keep the castle. Yet this was something she did not care to think about at the moment.

"I . . ." Cissy sighed and finally admitted defeat. Fenris von Wolfenbach had not seemed to be the type to be thrown out of a house easily. And short of hauling him out by his collar, which she very much doubted she could actually manage, there was nothing she could do. For the *Gräfin* was of course right: she simply couldn't stay here unchaperoned.

She blinked against a sudden pricking in her eyes.

It was not fair! She had come so far, had endured a hellish snowstorm, a trip on a cart that had made her teeth rattle. She had endured Dorinda's nagging and had watched the witch taking over her home after her father's death. And Cissy had put all her hope in this new life, in her castle. And now she should just leave again until somebody had whacked a little sense in His Churlish Excellency, Fenris von Wolfenbach? She wanted to scream and stamp her foot, but of course, this would not have been seemly for a gently reared young woman.

The *Gräfin* leaned forward. "It is surely for the best, my dear." A frown furrowed her forehead as just then a commotion was to be heard in the courtyard—the slowing tattoo of hooves and the crunch of carriage wheels coming to a halt. "Visitors? Whoever can that be?"

The sound of a carriage door flung open and then: "Oh la, what a picturesque castle!" a familiar English voice exclaimed.

It couldn't be! Cissy rose so quickly her chair nearly fell over. She rushed to the door to the outside gallery and, a little breathless, leaned over the balustrade.

"My dear child!" Mrs. Chisholm's face shone with delight as she caught sight of Cissy. "Oh, my dear child!"

Cissy hurried down the stairs and the next moment found herself enveloped in the widow's lavender-scented embrace.

"My dear girl." Mrs. Chisholm pressed a trembling kiss onto her cheek. "I just *couldn't* leave you all alone among these strangers. How barbarous would that have been? And so I decided to follow you right away." Drawing back, she dabbed at her eyes. Then her gaze scanned the round. "And I have to say . . . I quite adore your castle. It seems a bit tumbledown, though, doesn't it?" She cast a speaking look toward the tower and the ruin next to it before she turned back to Cissy. A beaming smile lit her face. "I can't begin to tell you how *happy* I am to see you, dearie. Tell me: have you already met your intended?"

Abruptly, Cissy's joy evaporated.

"Oh," Mrs. Chisholm said. "That bad, is it?"

In utter frustration, Fenris tore at his hair. "Why? *Why?*"

His valet shuffled his feet. "Well . . . Your parents have left, though." He obviously thought this constituted great encouragement for their cause.

Fenris shot Johann a glowering look. "That other woman . . ." He shuddered just to think of it. Why couldn't people leave him be? All he wanted was a little peace and quiet. *Peace and quiet.* He drummed his fingers on his desk. "Where did *she* come from?"

"Um . . . from Baden-Baden?"

"Damn it all!" Fenris boxed his fist into his flat hand. "Johann, we have to get rid of them. No matter how."

The other man clasped his hands behind his back. "Indeed, we have, for if they continue to stay here, they'll have the servants revolting in no time at all." He gave his master a bland smile.

Fenris narrowed his eyes at him. "What did they do?"

"Well, first they had us all lined up, and then Miss Fussell commented that Lisa needed a new apron, which promptly made the girl burst into tears."

Fenris gritted his teeth. "And then?"

"Then they went away and the older woman chose a room for herself, which Miss Fussell ordered to be cleaned." In a probably unconscious gesture, Johann brushed at the large dirt stain on the sleeve of his jacket. "Thoroughly." He grimaced. "Until this afternoon. And then they . . . um . . . found the normal dining room. And Miss Fussell ordered that from now on meals should be served there."

Fenris's throat felt tight. God, he didn't need this. Didn't need some little miss marching through his castle, through his life. . . .

No, not *his* castle. Not according to his father and that woman. It had never been his, for his family had lost it sixteen years ago, just as they had lost everything else. Because of him.

His stomach cramped. Fenris felt sick.

Sick of himself.

Sick of his life.

He buried his face in his hands, dug his fingers into the flesh until they rubbed painfully over the bone beneath.

"Fen . . ."

"We have to get rid of her." He looked up, hated the worry on Johann's face, the compassion he saw in the other man's eyes. God, what a weakling he was. Fenris shook his head. What a bloody loser. Not only had he managed to wreck his own life, no, he had also wrecked the life of his family. *Hell.* "We have to make her leave the castle." He pushed unsteady fingers through his hair. "We have to make sure she will never want to come back again. We have to win Wolfenbach back." Leaning his hands on the desk, Fenris got up and reached for the lantern sitting under the desk. "Come on, Johann, we're going to the cellars."

His friend's brows creased a little. "The cellars?"

"Indeed, the cellars. Where the rats are."

"I felt a little bit like the evil bishop of Bingen," Mrs. Chisholm confided the next morning over breakfast in the small, comfy dining room they had discovered the previous day. In the corner, a dark green tiled stove created comfortable warmth, while a faded carpet on the floor held off the chill rising from the stone tiles. "Only, of course, the bishop had been eaten up by mice instead of rats." Cheerfully, Mrs. Chisholm took a sip of her coffee, but immediately grimaced. "Oh dear, what kind of brew *do* they drink here? And do look at that color! Like a caramel toffee! This is quite shocking, dearie. Quite, quite shocking!"

"The rat?"

"Of course not the rat! Whatever are you thinking! The—" The sound of the door opening made Mrs. Chisholm turn around. Her eyes widened. "Oh my," she whispered in appreciation.

Fenris von Wolfenbach loomed on the threshold, his dark hair tousled, his eyes gleaming. The harshness of his expression and the wooden leg he again blatantly displayed lent him a dangerous edge, a hint of menace.

And where his frown of hatred darkly fell,
Hope withering fled, and Mercy sigh'd farewell!

A shiver of ice ran down Cissy's spine. Only too well she remembered her own helplessness when he had manhandled her two days prior. She gripped her fork tighter. But she was no longer alone, and she would not let him bully her a second time. Haughtily, she raised her chin and met his glare.

Mrs. Chisholm's face lit up. "Good morning, good morning! You must be Herr von Wolfenbach, no doubt. How *very* lovely to finally meet you! Will you not sit down and have some breakfast with us?"

Momentary confusion flickered over his face. He cleared his throat. "Well . . . good morning." His voice sounded slightly rusty, as if he hadn't used it in a long while.

Or at least not in polite company, Cissy thought nastily. "Rambach," she said to the butler, who stood stonily next to the sideboard. "Since Herr von Wolfenbach is joining us today, do bring up some of the cold gruel he so enjoys." With a smug smile, she turned her attention back to von Wolfenbach. "Or do you prefer buttered black bread?" she asked innocently, and watched with satisfaction how his face darkened even more.

> *That man of loneliness and mystery,*
> *Scarce seen to smile, and seldom heard to sigh;*
> *Whose name appals the fiercest of his crew . . .*

Cissy pursed her lips. *But not me.* She had always thought Byron's pirate somewhat overtly theatrical anyway. And for somebody called Fenris to strut around like a snarling demon wolf was just as ridiculous as, say, for somebody called Darcy to refuse to dance at an assembly.

"I have just told Miss Fussell here"—Mrs. Chisholm patted Cissy's hand, while the demon wolf chose a seat—"about this most horrid rat which came to my room last night."

"A rat?" His dark brows rose. "How . . . unfortunate. These things sadly happen so often in such old buildings." He grimaced a little as the butler put down a small bowl of cold gruel in front of him. "I think I need a mocha with that," Cissy heard him mutter.

Her eyes narrowed. How peculiar that she had spent two nights in this castle and had not even caught an itty-bitty glimpse of a rat tail. "You must have been very frigthened, Mrs. Chisholm," she said slowly, while keeping her eyes trained on von Wolfenbach. And indeed: when he looked up from his gruel, she thought she could detect a glitter of anticipation in his expression.

"Frightened?" The widow laughed heartily. "Oh, my sweet child, not at all! When you're the wife of a merchant and loath to stay at home while your husband travels the world, then you certainly get to see your share of rats!"

Von Wolfenbach's face fell.

"Why, this one took a little longer to kill," Mrs. Chisholm continued merrily, "but there's *nothing* like a pair of good sturdy boots, I tell you!" As happy as a child in a toy shop, she beamed at Cissy, while the butler turned an interesting shade of green.

CHAPTER SIX

The next morning they woke to icy coldness. The water in the ewer was frozen through and through. Shivering, Cissy fastened her wraparound stays over her shift, slipped into two petticoats and decided to wear her woolen dress. At first, she thought it was only the fire in her room that had gone out, yet when she arrived in the dining room, she discovered it had also been transformed into an icehouse overnight. Dressed in a thick coat and with a scarf wrapped around his neck, Rambach stood stoically next to the sideboard.

His bow seemed a little stiffer than normal. "Good morning, *gnädiges Fräulein.* I am sorry to inform you that we've run out of firewood."

"What?" Hardly believing what she had just heard, Cissy gaped at him.

"We have no more wood to light the fires and unfortunately . . . ,"—shifting his weight, he cleared his throat—"the fire in the kitchen has gone out, too."

"I don't believe this," she muttered, and her breath transformed into puffs of white fog. A thick layer of ice flowers bloomed on the windows, and—who knew—by midafternoon there might be icicles hanging from the candelabra!

Anger exploded inside her. How probable was it that a household the size of Wolfenbach suddenly and unexpectedly, virtually overnight, ran out of firewood?

Not. At. All.

Angry heat washed up from her bosom to her face. Cissy gritted her teeth. That devious bastard von Wolfenbach! This was surely just another one of his harebrained schemes to rid himself of her! She took a deep breath and mentally counted to ten before she bestowed a forced smile on the butler. "And since we're surrounded by forest, has somebody gone out to fetch some more firewood?"

Rambach blinked like a large owl. With a red nose. "But, *gnädiges Fräulein*, that wood will be all wet and will need to be dried." He sniffled.

"Bah!" Exasperated, Cissy threw up her arms. "So you think it's perfectly fine that your crack-brained master brings pneumonia over us all?"

"Gnädiges Fräulein?"

"Ah, never mind!" She made to stamp out of the room, but changed her mind. She advanced on Rambach and poked her finger into his chest. "When you next see the fine Fenris von Wolfenbach, you can tell him that he is a devious bastard of the first order!"

And with that, she marched out of the room.

From then on, the day proceeded downward. At midday a young girl arrived, sent by the *Gräfin* von Wolfenbach to be Cissy's maid. Young Marie looked as if she expected to be devoured by a mad beast at any moment. She looked even more horrified when she became aware of the freezing temperatures in the castle. "There's no need to worry," Cissy told her cheerfully, and sent her to

Frau Häberle in the hope the housekeeper would take care of her.

Sighing, Cissy went back to the drawing room, where Mrs. Chisholm, wrapped in a fur coat, sat enthroned on the red settee. The lower half of her face was covered by the collar of her coat, the upper half by a fur cap, which she had pulled down over her ears. Cissy blinked. For a moment she could have sworn that a particularly fat marmot had settled down on the widow's head.

"Hello, dearie," came Mrs. Chisholm's muffled voice from behind the collar. To perfect her outfit, she had thrust her hands into a fur-trimmed muff and now looked ready to brave Russian winters.

Cissy exhaled noisily. "This is so ridiculous!" She sneezed. Even though she was wearing her woolen dress and her pelisse, she was still cold. "That sheep-brained, puerile nodcock! He thinks he can just frighten us away!" Angrily, she stamped up and down the room, in intervals blowing on her icy, mitten-covered fingers. "And of course the servants are all blastedly loyal and support his imbecilic whims!"

"Loyal servants are a good thing, dearie," Mrs. Chisholm mumbled into her furs. "Just regard it as an adventure." The skin around her eyes crinkled as if she were smiling.

"An adventure? We're all going to freeze to death because of that dratted gooserump!" Abruptly, Cissy stopped as something occurred to her. "Is the dead rat still in your room?"

Mrs. Chisholm's eyes widened in horror. "Of course not! I threw it out of the window after the deed was done."

"A pity." Thoughtfully, Cissy gnawed on her lower lip. "Where do you think we might find rats in this castle?"

* * *

When they came back upstairs from their adventure underground, Rambach already awaited them. "There's a gentleman here to see you, *gnädiges Fräulein,*" he said. Warily, he eyed the basket Cissy was carrying.

"Really?" Cissy handed him her lantern. "Who is it?" She started to pat at the dust and cobwebs clinging to her pelisse.

"Herr Geheimrat Haldner of the Altertumsverein Kirchwalden. I understand he is the president of this institution."

"Oh dear, oh dear," Mrs. Chisholm muttered.

Very slowly, Cissy straightened up. "Is he? Is he indeed." The Altertumsverein. She snorted. *So the vultures are drawing in.* "Where is he now?"

"In the drawing room, with the master."

"Ex-master," Mrs. Chisholm corrected kindly.

"Indeed, *gnädige Frau. Gnädiges Fräulein . . .*"

"It is quite all right. I will go upstairs immediately."

"The basket—"

"No. I'll take that with me. Thank you, Rambach." With her free hand, Cissy lifted her skirts a little and went up the stairs.

The scene she came upon in the drawing room didn't look promising. His arms crossed on his chest, von Wolfenbach leaned against one of the windowsills, while an obviously nervous, red-faced man sat on the settee, rustling a pile of papers he had brought with him. At her entrance, his face lit up. *"Meine Gnädigste!"* he exclaimed and rushed toward her. Before Cissy quite knew what was happening, he had taken her hand and, bowing low, bestowed a smacking kiss on the air above her knuckles. "It is a great pleasure to meet you."

"Er . . . likewise." She threw a frowning glance at von Wolfenbach. A mocking smile played around his lips.

He lifted his brows. Hastily, she turned her attention back to the man before her. "Herr Haldner."

He straightened. His face fell. "Geheimrat, *gnädiges Fräulein.*" He cleared his throat. "Well, I believe as a foreigner you will not be familiar yet with our customs. . . ."

Irritated, Cissy freed her hand and pointed to the settee. "Won't you sit down again?"

"Oh, yes, yes." Cackling, he rubbed his hands. "I dare say we have a lot of things to discuss." He blew on his hands, which had already turned red with cold. "It is somewhat chilly. . . ."

Cissy shot a glowering look at von Wolfenbach. "We have got a small problem with the firewood." At von Wolfenbach's answering smirk, she gripped her basket tighter and fought against the urge to fling the contents at his head then and there. With an annoyed grunt, she plopped down in one of the armchairs. "Now, how can I help you, Herr Haldner?"

"Geheimrat." With a pained expression he sank back on the settee. "I have to say, Miss Fussell, the Altertumsverein is rather delighted about its imminent acquisition of the Castle of Wolfenbach."

"Imminent . . ." Cissy started to protest, yet he continued unperturbed.

"Back in 1811, when the government auctioned the castle off after the family had unfortunately lost all rights to it, some of the later members of the Altertumsverein were already very interested in the object. You know, to make sure that such a historically important building remains the property of the town. But of course, your father beat them to it." Cackling, he shook his finger at her. "I have to say, that must have been set up rather craftily. A foreigner, an enemy even! Buying such an important historical object from the government of Baden!"

Cissy gaped at him in utter astonishment. Her annoyance had fled long ago. "The auction was done by the state? I thought the Wolfenbachs sold it." She looked at Fenris—and her heart missed a beat at the transformation that had come over him. The sneer had been wiped off his face, which had darkened ominously. His lips had flattened into a thin, bitter line, and where his hands curled around the edge of the stone windowsill, his knuckles pressed white against the skin.

"Sold by the Wolfenbachs? Oh dear, not at all." Haldner gave a half-smothered cackle. "No, no, everything had fallen to the state, of course, after . . . um . . ." He coughed delicately.

"Yes?"

"Well . . ." Haldner licked his lips, shot a look at von Wolfenbach, and erupted into a series of embarrassed cackles.

Von Wolfenbach pushed himself off the sill and sauntered over. Despite the sound of his uneven steps on the tiles, his movements possessed a feral grace. Rather than diminishing the danger he emanated, the wooden leg heightened it; a wild wolf was not any less dangerous because of a vicious scar—he presented an even greater menace, for the things he had survived had made him stronger and more cunning.

"What the Herr Geheimrat wishes to say, is . . ." He raised an eyebrow at Cissy. His voice was smooth as silk, yet at his sides his hands had curled into fists. "Due to my youthful error of judgement, the family of Wolfenbach lost all of their privileges: the rights of the land, jurisdiction, administration, you name it. And the rights to the castle, it would seem." His mouth twisted.

With wide eyes, Cissy looked from one man to the other. Her heart thudded with sudden apprehension. "An error of judgment? What are you talking about?"

"Er . . . well . . ." Cackling, Haldner fumbled with the buttons of his coat and drew a large handkerchief out of his jacket, with which he proceeded to mop his brow.

His green eyes glittering, Fenris von Wolfenbach watched, and a cynical smile lifted his lips. Abruptly, his gaze shifted and his eyes met Cissy's. "When I was nineteen, I betrayed my country and ran away to join the British army to fight against Napoleon."

Something worse than just the wintry cold chilled Cissy's heart. Almost still a boy and he had gone to join the war? Her eyes dropped to his leg. Was this a wound he had incurred in battle? So he had fought for the freedom of Europe, had sacrificed his well-being, and in turn his family had lost everything? Suddenly his intense reaction when they had met made awful sense.

"Quite rash, if I may say so," Haldner muttered. "Such a betrayal of all patriotic sentiments."

Fenris von Wolfenbach lifted his shoulders a little and turned his back on them.

Cissy considered banging the contents of her basket into the face of the slimy, arrogant Geheimrat. "Betrayal of patriotic sentiments? How so?" she asked in her iciest voice. "When Baden had been under the thumb of Napoleon? And did not your government finally decide to join the alliance two years later?"

Haldner ran his hand under the collar of his shirt. "Yes, we did, but—"

"So how can it be a betrayal to his country, when Herr von Wolfenbach went and fought heroically against the man who threatened peace and order in all of Europe?"

"I—"

"This is quite enough," von Wolfenbach's voice cut in like a whiplash. He turned around, his face a stony mask. "Didn't you want to tell us why you have come here, Herr Geheimrat?"

"Oh yes, yes." Clearly relieved, Haldner dabbed his forehead with his handkerchief. He took a deep breath; his chest swelled. "In view of the imminent acquisition of the castle by the Altertumsverein, I thought it best if we could already have a look at the ledgers. For reasons of preparation, so to speak." He regarded them expectantly.

Cissy folded her hands in her lap to hide that they were trembling with anger. The nerve of that man was unbelievable! Yet before she had even opened her mouth for a scathing reply, von Wolfenbach asked very quietly: "What makes you think the castle will go to the Altertumsverein?" His voice sent a shiver down her spine. "When it is Miss Fussell who holds the deeds to the castle?"

"Well . . ." Haldner looked from one of them to the other. His forehead wrinkled with confusion. "I thought this was obvious, given there has been no news of your impending nuptials." He smiled.

"My *what*?" von Wolfenbach spat, his eyes glittering with fury. He took a step nearer, and Haldner shrank back on his seat.

"I th-thought you knew," he squeaked.

At the same time, Cissy asked, "Didn't you know?"

"Know what?"

Haldner gulped, his eyes bulging from the sockets. He obviously would not be capable of an intelligible explanation. Cissy sighed. "It is true: I hold the deeds to Wolfenbach—for the moment." She gave her intended a bland smile. "But my father's will stipulated that if I don't marry the son of his old friend Wolfenbach within four months, then the castle will fall to the Altertumsverein Kirchwalden."

Haldner coughed. "Indeed, indeed. Which seems only fair given that Mr. Fussell—"

"Lord Hailstone," Cissy corrected automatically. It seemed that the Geheimrat had regained his composure—or, what was more likely, she reconsidered after glancing at von Wolfenbach's thunderous expression, that he had completely taken leave of his senses.

"I do apologize, my dear Miss Fussell," he continued sunnily. "Given that *Lord* Hailstone snapped up the castle in 1811, don't you think so, too?" He beamed at von Wolfenbach. At the expression on the other man's face, his own cheerfulness subsided. "Er . . ."

Von Wolfenbach's voice was very, very quiet, when he said, "You will take your papers and leave my castle immediately." And then he simply exploded. "*Out!* Before I see my castle fall to you bunch of cackling hyenas, I will set fire to it myself!" He steadily advanced on Haldner, who hastily scrambled to his feet and fled the room in a flurry of rustling papers.

Breathing heavily, von Wolfenbach leaned his hand on the open door and watched the Geheimrat stumble down the stairs. Cautiously, Cissy rose from her chair and went to him. "Do you think he will be back?"

He barked a laugh. Yet when he turned his head to look at her, his face was once more void of all expression. "The next time you talk about the war," he said pleasantly, "do not spout such utter rubbish about heroism and glory and whatnot."

"But—"

His tones became chilling. "There is nothing glorious about war. It turns men into beasts, intent on slaughtering each other." He raised one brow. "But what would a silly country chit like you know about it, hm?"

For a moment Cissy simply gaped at him. "God, you're such an arrogant bastard!" she hissed. She marched back to the armchair in order to fetch her basket, and her boots clicked an angry staccato on the tiles. Her head held high, she stopped in front of von Wolfenbach. With jerky movements, she pulled out the basket's heavy content, wrapped in a now dirty napkin, and plonked it into his hand. "It seems that you've forgotten something in Mrs. Chisholm's room." She lifted her lips and showed him her teeth. "Don't do it again."

And with that, she left the room.

"She gave you a dead rat?"

"Wrapped in a napkin." Fenris rested his chin on his folded hands and regarded his valet. "It looked a bit . . . mushy." He had to bite his lip to suppress the betraying twitch. "It's been stomped to death by the good Widow Chisholm."

"Dear God, Fen." Johann momentarily closed his eyes. His Adam's apple bopped up and down. "These women are—"

"Wild." Fenris poked his tongue into his cheek and then raised his brows. "I know."

The two men looked at each other.

The valet blinked. "Rambach said he had to fetch them a lantern so they could venture down into the cellars."

"To terrorize the rats."

The men exchanged another long look before they finally burst out laughing. Fenris wiped his eyes. "And did you see what they've been wearing today? One looked like a bear, the other like . . ." His voice trailed away.

"A plucked crow?" Johann suggested.

Fenris's smile faded. "Yes. Yes, exactly like a plucked crow." He stood up and went to the window. The bulges in the bull's-eye pane distorted the view of the outside world, and the flaming colors of the evening sky appeared as if mirrored in a prism. Beneath lurked the dark bulk of the forest, black and impenetrable, hoarding secrets and fears. He had always loved the solitude the forest offered, the darkness behind which the world retreated. His fist lightly touched the window frame.

But now his solitude had been disturbed. Never to be regained, it seemed. A young woman, as lively as a whirlwind, with oh-so expressive eyes and courage in her heart. And with all the naïve ideals of youth still intact.

He snorted.

And yet . . . And yet, when she had plopped the dead rat into his hand with that strange mixture of triumph and exasperation, something in his heart had wrenched.

Just like that.

And for a moment he had yearned for that same naïveté, that same innocence and fire. *So much fire.* Closing his eyes, he leaned his forehead against the cool stone. His own fire had been extinguished long ago, and all there were only ashes left. There were only darkness and guilt.

He had seen how shabby and old-fashioned her clothes were—another weight to his burden of guilt. It seemed his youthful folly had not just ruined his family, but also hers—at least financially. There was no way he could ruin her life even more, burden her with a husband whose body would remain crippled forever after. With a husband whose body could ever only evoke disgust in a woman. He should know. After all, it had happened before.

"I cannot marry her," he said very quietly.

For a moment, Johann was quiet. "If you say so. But we can light the fires again, can't we?"

Fenris smothered a laugh. "Yes, you can." He turned his head to look over his shoulder at his valet. "There's no need for all of it any longer, is there?"

The firewood reappeared mysteriously, and no rats could be found in the upstairs rooms ever again. In addition, Frau Häberle apparently managed to convince Cissy's new maid that, except for the demon wolf, no beasts lurked in the corners of the Castle of Wolfenbach. As a result, young Marie stayed on despite any initial misgivings she might have had. Cissy was glad, for she missed Evie, her maid at home in England, and their intimate chats in the privacy of her bedroom. She had always loved to giggle over the latest gossip and scandal with Evie, and she was delighted to find that Marie was not adverse to doing the same, albeit with the latest Kirchwalden talk. Furthermore, she introduced Cissy to the intricacies of the Badener dialect, and soon Cissy knew how to say "thank you"—*vergelt's Gott*; "goodbye"—*adee*; "would you please"—*dädsch*; and, most importantly, "moron"—*dummi Nuss*.

The latter was certainly an apt description for von Wolfenbach, who turned into even more of a bugbear than before: he usually wore the most thunderous expression, his brows drawn together in a perpetual frown. His moodiness soured the atmosphere at meals and his contribution to conversation consisted of monosyllabic snarls.

No, Cissy did not want to see the castle fall to the Altertumsverein and the horrid Geheimrat Haldner, but on the other hand, she most certainly had no wish to marry a snarling demon wolf without even the hint of basic good manners.

She started to pray for a miracle.

And then the miracle happened.

CHAPTER SEVEN

One morning in early November, when Cissy came to the dining room to have breakfast, she found him sitting—no, *lounging*—on one of the chairs in all his golden glory, one leg thrown nonchalantly over its arm. His teeth flashed white in a broad smile when he turned and caught sight of her. Green eyes, like von Wolfenbach's, but sparkling with life and laughter, regarded her from under tousled blond curls. *"Ma chère."* Lithe and graceful, he swung his leg to the ground and stood, his fashionable clothes slightly rumpled, his necktie loosened, and a faint golden stubble covering his jaw. And still, he looked so beautiful Cissy's breath caught in her throat.

Like a golden Greek god, deliciously mussed up . . .

Mussed up?

Heat spread over Cissy's face.

"Ma chère." He came toward her and bent over her hand to kiss it, while he flashed a mischievous smile up at her. Hot tingles raced up her arm. "You see me thoroughly enchanted. You must be the daughter of our dear father's old friend."

"Miss Celia Fussell." Automatically, she bobbed a small curtsy, then became aware that he was still holding her hand.

Her blush deepened.

What did a rumpled golden god want with the likes of her? Next to him, his stylish jacket and the gayly colored waistcoat, she felt drab and uncomfortable in her old dress of bleakest black.

As if he could read her thoughts, a small smile flickered across his face, and he released her hand to throw his arms wide. "I am truly enchanted." Then he executed an exact, formal bow. "Leopold von Wolfenbach, your servant."

Leopold? Cissy frowned. After Fenris, she would have expected something more . . . exotic.

This time, ruefulness tinged his smile. "Actually, it is Loki Leopold von Wolfenbach." His eyes twinkled merrily, inviting her to share the joke. "But who would want to run around with such a ridiculous name as Loki?"

Tap-dam, tap-dam, tap-dam.

His smile twisted into a grimace. "Well, let's say who except my big brother?" he conspiratorially whispered to Cissy. With a sigh he straightened, just as the aforementioned party walked into the room.

Fenris von Wolfenbach stopped dead, and Cissy thought his face became even stonier than usual. "Leo."

"Fen." The man beside her nodded and bobbed up and down on the balls of his feet.

"What are you doing here?" Von Wolfenbach's voice was devoid of any inflection.

With a hint of a defiance, the younger man thrust his chin forward. "Gee, I'm so happy to see you, too, big bro."

Von Wolfenbach's brows drew together into an ominous line.

And then it finally registered with Cissy. *Brothers!* She gasped. "Brothers?"

Both men looked at her—the older clearly annoyed, the younger with surprising grimness. "So, they haven't mentioned me, have they?" he asked bitterly, as if he already knew the answer.

Numbly, Cissy shook her head. If they were brothers . . . if Graf von Wolfenbach had more than one son . . .

Leopold barked a laugh as he turned back to his brother. "And isn't this nice and dandy?"

Fenris's eyes narrowed. "I ask you again. Where have you come from, Leo? And why are you here?"

"I was in Freiburg, where else?" Leopold intently regarded his sibling. He licked his lips. "At Contessa Czerny's ball. You remember the *contessa*, Fen, don't you?"

With a jolt of surprise, Cissy watched how the older von Wolfenbach brother broke eye contact and slowly walked to the sideboard, where breakfast was set. It seemed to her that he walked more slowly than usual, and with a more pronounced limp, as if his old wound had suddenly started to hurt again. "Of course I still remember the *contessa*," he finally said, with his back to them.

Again, Leopold von Wolfenbach's tongue sneaked out to lick his lips. "She has grown into a lovely woman, the *contessa*. Marriage . . . becomes her." A strange smile played around his mouth, while his gaze remained glued to his brother's back.

Yet whatever he had expected, the other's voice was rock-steady when he answered. "Then I wonder why she isn't in Vienna with her husband." He turned, a plate full of food balanced on one hand. Slowly, he raised a brow. "If marriage so agrees with her."

Leopold threw his head back and laughed. "God, Fen, you're priceless! Don't you know? Don't you . . ." He calmed down, wiping tears of mirth from his eyes. And then his teeth flashed once more. "Yes, marriage agrees with her. She's got a rich old husband and plenty of . . . time on her hands."

As his smile deepened and his brother flinched, Cissy wondered which parts of the conversation she was missing. The air simmered with hostility. It seemed only a question of time until the two men were at each other's throats.

Fenris's eyes darkened. "Are you sleeping with her?" he snapped.

Or perhaps they already were.

Heat exploded in Cissy's cheeks, covered her whole body with a painful flush. God, did the large lout know no shame? She took a deep breath. "I believe it is well past time for me to leave. Gentlemen . . ." Of course, at least one of them was definitely no gentleman, but an uncouth barbarian!

Yet before she had even taken a step toward the door, a hand had grabbed her wrist. "Please stay." Leopold's voice softened. "You must excuse my brother. He's locked himself away in this castle for over a decade and apparently lost all his social skills."

Fenris snorted, making his brother laugh again.

"So they haven't told you about me, my dear Miss Fussell? Well, then I must call it a happy turn of events that at Contessa Czerny's ball a small bird whispered the latest Kirchwalden news into my ear."

With a clang, Fenris's plate landed on the table. "So you *are* sleeping with her."

"Of course not. Or do you think I'm following in my big brother's footsteps?" The brothers exchanged glittering glances, while Cissy gnawed on her lip. Nobody had ever discussed their intimate connections in her presence, and she sincerely hoped people would refrain from it in the future. Or perhaps they could just give Fenris von Wolfenbach a good whack over his loutish head.

All at once, Leopold chuckled and patted Cissy's hand.

"Don't let him scare you away, Miss Fussell. My brother has become famous for his incivility. Indeed, I believe down in Kirchwalden they're telling their children he will come in the night and swallow them up if they don't behave. My brother, the bogeyman—isn't this the most delicious joke? Can I get you some breakfast, Miss Fussell?"

Cissy blinked at him. She glanced at Fenris and saw the dull color staining his cheeks. Was he embarrassed? She frowned as she remembered the words of the innkeeper's wife all those weeks ago. *"He'll rip you apart and tear you to pieces. Like a wild beast he is. Dangerous. And deadly."* Well, if he behaved like such an uncivilized barbarian that the children were afraid of him, not to mention engaging in the most shameless conversation, then he had all the reason in the world to be embarrassed.

Leopold gave her a charming smile and a slow, droll wink, which made her smile back at him. "Yes, some breakfast would be nice." She let him hand her into a chair before he went to the sideboard to get a plate for her. Only then did she notice the absence of the butler. "Where's Rambach?"

Leopold airily waved his hand through the air. "I sent him away. The old chap makes me nervous. He keeps throwing me those stern glances." Looking over his shoulder, he winked at her. "I fear the stout Rambach doesn't like me, Miss Fussell. So . . . they didn't tell you about me, but did they tell you at least about the treasure?" He poured her a cup of caramel-colored coffee.

"Treasure?" Mrs. Chisholm entered the room. "Oh, and whom have we here?"

Fenris von Wolfenbach heaved a sigh. "Mrs. Chisholm, may I introduce my younger brother, Leopold von Wolfenbach."

Leopold bowed. "Enchanted, *gnädige Frau*."

Mrs. Chisholm giggled like a schoolgirl. "My, my, and aren't you a charming laddie?" She beamed at the younger man. "I believe you were talking about a treasure?"

Fenris rolled his eyes. "There's no treasure," he growled.

Mrs. Chisholm put her hands on her hips and bestowed upon him a look full of reproach. "You didn't tell us anything about a treasure. Or did he, dearie?"

"He did not." Cissy found she enjoyed seeing Fenris von Wolfenbach totally exasperated. If she could not give him a whack on the head, she could at least needle him in other ways. She raised her eyebrows and gave him an expectant look.

He did not disappoint her.

His glower held daggers. "Because there *is* no bloody treasure," he forced out between gritted teeth.

"He's doing it again." Leopold sighed. "You should apologize to the ladies, you really should, Fen." But then he focused his attention on Mrs. Chisholm again. "Which treasure you ask, *gnädige Frau?* Well, the famous Wolfenbach Hoard, of course!" He beamed at the widow. When he turned toward Cissy, she noticed the dimple in his cheek. For a moment, she actually forgot to breathe. Leopold von Wolfenbach looked utterly charming. Leaning closer to her, he whispered: "Our forebears were unscrupulous robber barons, you know. For many decades, they terrorized this area and robbed thousands of people, rich and poor, young and old. And they hid the loot somewhere in this castle. There it still rests today, gold and gemstones, the whole Wolfenbach Hoard."

"How delightful!" Mrs. Chisholm clapped, her eyes sparkling. "A real treasure!"

Cissy listened with openmouthed wonder. She felt how her heart thumped heavily against her ribs. "A hoard," she whispered back, swaying toward him. "A real hoard?"

"Oh, yes." Leopold's warm breath carressed her face. "Golden coins shining like tiny suns, and fiery rubies and gleaming emeralds. Golden and silver cups. Jewelry. All hidden somewhere here in this castle."

"Don't be ridiculous," his older brother growled. "If there's ever been a hoard—and that's a big if—then other forebears of ours would have found and plundered it long ago."

Leopold shrugged and straightened. "Which only shows that my brother has no imagination." He grinned at Cissy and Mrs. Chisholm.

Indeed. Cissy couldn't help grinning back. Fenris von Wolfenbach was an uncivilized lout. And then she laughed aloud when she again realized that she didn't need to marry the churlish von Wolfenbach in order to permanently gain her lovely castle. She could marry his brother instead! His brother, who obviously loved stories just as much as she did. His brother with the sunny smile, who looked like a Greek god.

What a happy turn of events!

"A rather charming young gentleman, Leopold von Wolfenbach," Mrs. Chisholm mused. With pointed disinterest she looked out of the carriage window at the winter-gray trunks of the trees outside. "Don't you think so, dearie?"

Biting her lip, Cissy folded her hands in her lap. "Truly charming," she agreed.

Mrs. Chisholm half-turned and shot her a conspiratorial smile. "And very handsome, too."

"Very!"

Cissy's heartfelt sigh made the widow chuckle. "He reminds me of one of those mischievous cupids you see in old paintings. All golden curls."

At that, Cissy couldn't help laughing. "A rather large cupid!" But then she remembered that the little Roman Cupido was the accomplice of the goddess of love. That he went around and shot his arrows into human hearts. That he delighted in watching humans fall in love. Cissy sighed. How easy this particular golden god would make it to—

"A large cupid, indeed." For a moment, a thoughtful expression crossed Mrs. Chisholm's face; then she chuckled once more. "But have you seen the little devils in this one's eyes, dearie? Coming halfway undone in the breakfast room." She clicked her tongue. "A dangerous one, I should think."

"Oh." Cissy cuddled into the blankets that kept them warm during the drive into the valley. "But so much more charming than his brother. You said it yourself, Mrs. Chisholm."

With faint surprise, she watched how the smile left the widow's face. "Fenris von Wolfenbach is a very troubled man, dearie."

"He is an uncivilized beast," Cissy insisted. "Have you forgotten what kind of language he used this morning? It was shocking indeed!"

Mrs. Chisholm's lips twitched. "I fear I have heard worse on the London docks. Of course, for a chick-a-biddy like you, this is all quite foreign." She reached for the straps as their carriage rumbled over an unevenness on the road. "Aren't these German roads a horror?" she murmured and shook her head. "I've always thought," she continued more loudly, "that the sheltered upbringing of young girls harbors serious disadvantages. It certainly does not prepare you for the realities of life, for one thing."

"Oh, but I am well acquainted with the realities of life!" Cissy protested.

Mrs Chisholm clucked her tongue. "Tut-tut, dearie. Of course you are not. You might devour young Leopold von Wolfenbach with your eyes, but once a subject of any indelicate kind is mentioned, it makes you blush like a peony."

Disgruntled, Cissy wrinkled her nose. Yet sure enough, she felt her cheeks heat. It was most aggravating!

Chuckling, the widow reached out and patted Cissy's knee. "You will grow out of it, never fear, dearie. But for now believe me, swearing doesn't tell you anything about a man's worth. If he has really shut himself up in the castle for these past years, it stands to reason that Fenris von Wolfenbach has . . . let us say, temporarily forgotten his manners." She shrugged.

Cissy gave an indelicate snort. "He is abhorrent, that's what you mean. Intolerably rude. And wouldn't he love to see the last of us. Ha!" Arms crossed in front of her, she leaned back. "But I won't give him this satisfaction. The Castle of Wolfenbach belongs to me now."

The older woman gave her a strange look. "That it does, dearie."

"And don't you think . . ."—eagerly, Cissy leaned forward toward the widow—"don't you think that Leopold von Wolfenbach would make a lovely fairy tale prince?"

Mrs. Chisholm grinned. "Kissing Snow White?" she suggested, her eyes twinkling. "How terribly forward!"

Cissy shrugged and giggled. "Well . . ."

"My dear, I can perfectly understand how a young girl would be smitten with such a dashing man as Leopold von Wolfenbach. But still, you should not make any hasty decisions."

Now, this came as a surprise. Cissy frowned. "Do you really think I would want to marry his brother? A man whose chief means of communication are growls?" She shook her head.

If anything, it only increased Mrs. Chisholm's amusement. "It comes with the name, don't you think? Still . . ." She sobered. "Please do remember all is not gold that glitters."

Utterly astonished, Cissy lifted her eyebrow. "I thought you liked him!"

"Oh, I do, I do." She patted Cissy's knee some more. "But I also reckon that he can be a rather dangerous man. Now let us speak no more of these young men. Tell me, what book did you want to look for?"

"The last time we went to the printer, Herr Ellinger told me about a collection of Hoffmann's tales. *Die Serapionsbrüder*, it is called, I believe."

"Ahh, Herr Hoffmann of Berlin? Did he not die a few years ago?"

INTERLUDE

A disturbance rippled through the castle. Unease whispered in the ancient stones: the Other had entered their realm.

They bore no love for him, for he was a threat to their world.

Stone sighed, shuddered.

And yet, caught fast, all they could do was watch and wait.

Watch and wait . . .

Forever.

CHAPTER EIGHT

"So your ancestors were robber barons?" An icy wind blew past Cissy's nose as she stood on the remains of the castle's tower a few days later and admired the view of the snow-covered landscape. Here and there a hint of dark green shone through the white caps of the great trees, while down in the valley, the houses looked like toys, all sparkly and shiny. The sun glinted off the cross on top of St. Margaretha's and transformed it into a tiny star.

"Oh, yes." Beside her, Leopold chuckled. "They probably stood here, too, and looked out over the country they held in their thrall." He widened his stance. "All this you see was once Wolfenbach property."

"Was it?" Curious, she looked at him. His voice had taken on a strange tone. "And now?"

"Now?" He gave a sharp laugh. "Now it's..." He shook his head. "It no longer belongs to our family." His lips pressed together, and Cissy felt the sudden, unexpected urge to touch his arm in reassurance.

Like a wanton. Her face flamed, and she was uncomfortably reminded of Mrs. Chisholm's words: *Once a subject of any indelicate kind is mentioned, it makes you blush like a peony.* How unfortunate that it would appear an actual mentioning was not even needed; mere thought was quite sufficient. Aggravating indeed! She took a deep breath. "As a result of what happened in 1811?"

He shot her a look, one golden eyebrow quizzically raised. "So they've told you about this at least?"

"Not really." She clasped her hands in front of her, twisted her fingers together.

Shaking his head, he turned back to contemplate the land spread below them. A furrow marred his forehead. "How did you find out?" He was watching her from the corner of his eyes.

"Herr Haldner . . . *Geheimrat* Haldner called a few days ago." She lifted her shoulders a little. "The Altertumsverein is apparently very interested in acquiring Wolfenbach. They hope it will fall to them should . . ." She stopped. Gnawing on her lower lip, she pondered which words to choose to make it sound more delicate. "It's because of the condition which was named in the will. Have you heard about the . . . er . . . condition?"

Chuckling, he turned his back to the view and leaned against the balustrade. "Everybody and their auntie have heard about that condition by now, *Liebchen*." The corners of his mouth lifted and his eyes twinkled.

Liebchen.

He had such beautiful eyes. Green like the forest, green like the trees whispering in the wind.

The breeze lifted a strand of Cissy's hair and blew it across her cheek like a lover's caress. What she imagined a lover's caress to be like. She shivered.

Leopold's smile widened, then he reached out and carefully placed the stray lock of hair behind her ear. His knuckles brushed over her cheek. Gasping, Cissy took a step back. Painful heat flooded her face, and her breasts. . . . Again, she shivered.

Her breasts tingled and strained against the confinement of her stays. Was it only a few days ago that she had told Mrs. Chisholm that she was quite aware of the realities of life? Nothing, *nothing*, had ever felt like this.

"Don't," she croaked, but wasn't quite sure whether she was telling her misbehaving bosom or the man in front of her. "Don't." How vulnerable she suddenly felt! Delicate. As if she were made of fine glass.

Leopold's smile dimmed. "I apologize, I . . ." He spread out his hands, and for a moment he reminded her of a sad puppy. "I was taken away by your beauty, the sweetness of your face." His voice lowered. "Your loveliness." He breathed gently, softly, and Cissy felt her heart melt.

These were the sweetest words a man had ever said to her. He had called her beautiful. *Beautiful.* A tousled Greek god, who surely was besieged by countless women—sophisticated women, not brown Yorkshire mouses like her—this golden god thought her beautiful.

And suddenly, she *felt* beautiful, despite her drab, black dress with the old-fashioned cut. Her heart lifted, jumped, as if it could fly straight out of her breast. She could no more stop the loony smile spreading over her face than stop breathing. "I forgive you." She held out her hand to him. "Friends again?"

His face lit once more. He took her hand, and through the glove she could feel the heat of his skin, the strength in his fingers. "Friends," he agreed. But then he turned her hand so it was facing palm up, and with deft fingers undid the first button at her wrist. Her breath caught in her throat when his thumb stroked her sensitive skin. "Friends," he repeated. "For now." With a mischievous smile he raised her hand and pressed his lips to the small strip of skin he had exposed.

Tingles raced up her arm, spread through her body and made her bones sing. "Oh my," she breathed, and all thoughts of impropriety fled.

"Lovely," he murmured against her wrist, and his words vibrated along her nerves to the marrow of her bones.

Gasping, she pressed her wrist to his mouth, and with a soft laugh he bestowed a last, lingering kiss to her wrist before he straightened and buttoned her up again. He looked at her, and she drowned in the green of his eyes. *So, so green* . . . She swayed a little, trembling like a fragile leaf in the wind.

Not prepared for the realities of life . . .

She inhaled sharply to clear her head. Leopold's cheek dimpled.

"The lovliest woman I've ever seen."

Over the next few days Leopold showed her around the castle, and she felt more and more comfortable in his presence. He showed her all the nooks and crannies she had seen before, but through his eyes. He told her about the duel that had been fought on the central staircase in the pallas, brother fighting brother, until they both had lain bleeding at the foot of the stairs. He told her how each year, on a special night in May, the two could still be seen fighting on the stairs, and how the clang of their ghostly swords would reverbrate from the walls of the darkened castle.

He showed her the entrance to the secret passage in the library, where the air was heavy with the smell of dust and old leather and paper that had turned yellow with age. Outside, he pointed out to her the place where spikes with the bloody heads of Wolfenbach's enemies had once crowned the gate until the ravens had come to pick the dimmed eyes, to tear the flesh from the bones.

She couldn't suppress a shiver as a raven cawed overhead. She looked up to follow its flight, and her gaze was
caught by a snow-covered gargoyle looming on an over-
hang above her. Again, she shivered. The dead stone
eyes regarded her stoically.

"All the gargoyles," she murmured.

Leopold followed her gaze. "Aye. Nasty old buggers,"
he growled. "One of our ancestors apparently had a
penchant for the grotesque. Never liked them myself,
though." He shrugged.

"They always surround you," Cissy said softly and
looked around, spotting more of the stone beasts clinging to the roof or thrusting their heads through the wall.
"Watching you." She hugged her pelisse tighter around
herself.

Leopold chuckled. "Awww, no, not with these dead
eyes of theirs. Do you see that one over there?" He
pointed. "See how parts of his eyes have crumbled away?
This fellow is watching no one ever again." Again, he
chuckled, but Cissy shivered in the cold breeze.

"Let us go back inside," she pleaded. "It's eerie out
here."

Offering her his arm, he led her to the nearest building. Their steps sounded loud on the stone tiles of the
empty rooms and corridors. He showed her the
weapons room, where old swords rusted on the wall and
suits of old armor stood in the corners like soldiers
made of tin. In the middle of the room, the empty shell
of half a steel horse stood waiting for battles long past.

Leopold next showed her staircases that led nowhere
and doors that hid stone walls. Generations of Wolfenbachs had built and remodeled the castle, had added
new buildings and turrets, new stairs and hidden re-
cesses, and thus had made the castle into a stone maze.
Leopold talked of the many secrets the castle still held

even from him. "So the Wolfenbach Hoard can be any-where," he said. "There's even a secret door down in the well."

"How do you know about the hoard in the first place?" she asked, curious, while she admired the painted ceiling in one of the state rooms—a sea of golden stars against a dark blue backdrop.

Leopold shrugged. "There were always legends. Our old nanny told us many tales and myths about this area. There isn't a stone in this land that doesn't tell a tale."

"I have always loved old tales and legends," Cissy confided, glancing his way.

"Ah well, most of these tales are, of course, simply superstitious rubbish. But I've also read a bit from the town annals." He grimaced. "It was mostly gibberish to me, that old German. The Latin wasn't much better, really." He bit his lip, and his face filled with remorse. "I was never much of a scholar," he admitted.

With his blond curls and rueful expression, he reminded Cissy of a little boy. God, he was adorable! She gave him a smile and nodded, encouraging him to go on.

He hooked his thumbs into the pockets of his waistcoat and rocked back and forth on his heels. "From the little I could piece together, I learnt a bit about the fate of the last Wolfenbach robber baron. How the villagers down in the valley eventually revolted against his tyranny and one day killed him when he took a ride through the forest." He shook his head. "It must have been quite a fight. First they pelted him and his horse with stones, and then they came after him with hayforks and flails."

Cissy's stomach lurched. "Did they harm the poor horse, too?" she asked, aghast.

He shrugged. "I don't think so. To be honest, I was more interested in reading about what they did to the castle. They looted it, of course."

"Of course," Cissy murmured, her thoughts still with the poor horse.

"But the annals don't mention a treasure." Excitement crept into his voice. "And this means it must still be here!" He made a wide, encompassing movement with his arms. "Somewhere in this castle. It was reclaimed by Wolfenbach's son several years later, you know. He had managed to flee, and joined the Crusade in repentance of his father's sins. A real paragon of virtue, that chap. And probably a bit soft in the head, too. Why, there is even this silly story of how he spared some wolf or other during a hunt. Spared a wolf! Can you believe the stupidity?" He rolled his eyes dramatically, which made Cissy giggle. "But, of course, later generations of the family made a great hullaballoo about it and even created this fantastic tale about the spirit of the wolf protecting the castle and the Wolfenbachs forevermore." He snorted, then gave her a broad, boyish smile. "Anyway, ever since that crusading fellow entered the scene, the Wolfenbachs have been model knights. No more robbing for us." He winked at Cissy.

She hid a grin behind her hand. "I am so glad to hear it," she said, and managed to keep a straight face, even though, for no discernible reason, her heart sang in her chest and she yearned to whirl around and around under the golden stars on the ceiling. "I would very much like to read these annals one day. Do you think that would be possible?"

"You?" For a moment or two he simply stared at her in surprise before he burst out laughing. "*Liebchen,* you're priceless! What a delicious sense of humor you have!"

Cissy frowned. "I was not joking."

Abruptly the laughter stopped. "You weren't?" Something like suspicion entered his eyes.

She shook her head. "My father taught me to read

Latin. I used to read to him often in the past few years."

"How . . . peculiar." He cleared his throat. "Well, then. Would you like to continue the tour?" He held out his hand. "There's more to discover."

Yes, so much more to discover: the tapestries along the walls, the unicorn about to lie his head on the maiden's lap while the hunter hid behind the nearest tree, an arrow already cocked in his bow. In another room, the large wallhangings depicted the four seasons. And while the scenery changed with each tapestry, in the background there was always a castle on a hill. "The Castle of Wolfenbach," Leopold said proudly. He touched one of the tiny castles with his forefinger, giving Cissy a chance to admire his wide, graceful hand, the long, blunt fingers with the short-clipped nails. Warmth blossomed low in her belly as she remembered how on the crumpled tower he had touched her cheek with this same finger. And she marveled at the fate that had brought her to this moment, into the company of this man, her golden knight.

She smiled at her own fancy, but the tiny flutters in her stomach did not stop.

Next he showed her the tapestry his great-great-great-great-grandmother had woven, a hunting scene in the forest, where the hunters had just cornered their prey, a proud stag. And he told her how his distant grandmother had given one of the hunters the face of her secret lover. The vines and flowers surrounding the man on his great stallion curved and twisted and revealed their secret only upon a closer look: *Te amo.*

Blinking away sudden tears, Cissy traced the faded green lines with a gentle forefinger. *Te amo.* She touched her heart.

When she turned, she caught Leopold watching her, his head cocked to one side. The dimple appeared in his cheek. "It's very romantic, is it not, Celia?" He paused, then added in a murmur, *"Liebchen."* A mere whisper of sound, but her cheeks warmed nonetheless.

Once a subject of any indelicate kind is mentioned, you blush like a peony.

Confused and breathless, she stepped past him. Even if it was improper, these whispered endearments excited her. Whenever he looked at her like that, his green eyes dancing like wood sprites and the sweet dimple denting his cheek, her whole body tingled and shivers raced along her nerves. She wished she were brave enough to bare her wrist for him to kiss the skin there once more. She wondered what it would be like to be close, without a breath of air between them, oh so close to all his golden beauty, to have his hands carressing her face once more, and his lips . . . his lips . . .

Cissy laid her hands against her burning cheeks. Quickly she reined in her wanton thoughts. She felt as if she were going up in flames.

Chuckling, Leopold reached out and lightly drew his finger over the back of her gloved hand. "What delightful innocence. I am quite smitten by your blushes." His lips twisted with amusement. *"Liebchen."*

He laughed as she tried to hide her flaming cheeks. "No. Don't be embarrassed. You are charming—truly charming." He offered her his arm. "Come, there's much more to see."

His inner restlessness drove him to walk the ramparts at night, when the wind blew icier than ever. Fenris welcomed the bite of the wind, which brought tears to his eyes; sometimes the pain was enough to chase away unwanted thoughts, to dispel impossible dreams.

Yet sometimes, the light was still on in her room high above him, and every dream he ever had came rushing back. On some nights the pain was bad enough to bring him to his knees.

Fortuna must be laughing spitefully down at him to bring somebody like her to a place like this. To have her disrupt his self-imposed solitude and shred all his acceptance of his fate. His hand crept to his chest, where his heart burned with impossible longings.

Wearily, Fenris closed his eyes. No, there would be no redemption for this beast. He would forever remain in this form, would forever be caught in a crippled body. Redemption had become impossible long ago, when the cannonball had exploded next to him and blasted his leg away. Curiously, it hadn't hurt at first. He had lain on his back on the muddy ground and stared up at the sky, his eyes burning with gunsmoke. One last time—he had wanted to see a bit of blue sky one last time. He had hoped for one last glance of brilliant, untarnished blue. But there had been only acrid smoke, the rolling thunder of cannon, the screams of men and horses, and the sickly smell of burnt flesh and blood. They had soaked the earth with blood, men and mere boys sacrificed to the God of War.

Was it any wonder that he had lain there and hoped in vain? And then, finally, a red veil had been thrown over the world and he had sunk into a sea of endless pain.

Fenris gave an unsteady laugh.

A sea of pain it had been, from which he had emerged as a fairy tale monster, no trace left of the man he had been. And like a fairy tale beast he had taken possession of this castle—only to have his life disrupted once more by his very own Belle. An intelligent, funny, brave Belle, with a temper quick to rise to his baiting.

He smiled a little.

Yes, she could get so angry that she looked ready to spit nails. And how her eyes glittered hotly! A regal queen of the Amazons, who would probably enjoy running him through with a long, sharp spear.

Chuckling softly, he shook his head. She was an exceptional Belle indeed.

She was also a Belle to which he had no right. No right at all. His amusement ebbed away, left him choked with longings and yearnings and bitterness, so much bitterness. When he stumbled back to his room, frozen to the bone, a sleepy Johann was waiting to help divest him of his clothes.

"I told you, you don't need to stay up for me," Fenris said gruffly.

His valet gave him one of those unfathomable glances he was so good at, and continued unbuttoning his coat. "I daresay if I didn't stay up for you, you would fall into bed still fully clothed. Dear God, Fen, your hands are frozen stiff! Can't you at least wear a scarf and mittens when you venture outside in the middle of winter? I swear, you're one of the most pigheaded people I've ever met!"

It stung. "Well, then . . ." Shrugging, Fenris looked away. "Nobody forces you to remain here. You could easily get work somewhere else."

"Oh, yes!" Snorting, Johann helped him out of the coat. "With that vain peacock of your brother, perhaps? After all, you already seem bent on seeing that the castle falls to him." Grumbling, he started working on the buttons of the jacket.

Fenris blinked. "What are you talking about?" Looking down at his valet's head, he could just imagine Johann rolling his eyes, even though the man didn't look up.

The answer, when it finally came, was softer than before. "I simply don't understand why you leave the field to your brother in this. You will lose the castle, don't you see that?"

Fenris raised his shoulders as if such an occurrence wouldn't touch him in the least. "So?" He shuddered a little as Johann helped him out of his jacket. God, he was cold, so cold. His very bones hurt with it.

Johann impatiently tugged at the strings that secured the cuffs. "Can't you just try at least? Be a little nicer to the girl?"

"And what for?" Fenris stilled his friend's hands on his wrist. He waited until Johann met his gaze. "What for? What right do I have to . . . to court somebody like her? What right would I have to drag her into my darkness?" He shook his head. "Leave it be, Johann."

The other man searched his face, then sighed. "As you wish. But I think you're wrong."

The weariness that descended upon him was worse than the pain of the winter cold. "Just leave it be."

And so, during the days, Fenris kept away, watched from afar how his brother courted her, dazzled her with his charm. Charm came so easily to Leo. It had once come easily to Fenris, too. Once, in a distant past.

But that was before his life had been literally blown to smithereens, before he had in turn destroyed the lives of the people he cared for most, before it had been made clear to him how utterly, utterly undesirable he had become as a man. Before he had seen revulsion in a woman's eyes as he bared his body to her gaze.

Never, never again.

So, yes, he kept away from her during the days. But at night, he would stand on the ramparts and look up at the light in her room. Or, when the cold became too intense and his longing too bitter, he would walk the hallways instead. And just a little ways from her room, he would stop and lean his head against the cool stone and remember the sound of her laughter.

But not for him, of course.

Never for him.

CHAPTER NINE

The castle was vast. There was so much to see. Yet when they finally came across the grandfather clock, Cissy wondered why she hadn't noticed it before. But then, it stood almost hidden in a small niche, rising up in warm honeyed tones against the cold gray stone. The afternoon sun slanted a lonely beam of light across the wood and lent it a reddish tinge.

Entranced, Cissy stopped in her tracks. "Oh, it's beautiful," she breathed.

"What?" Leopold turned to follow her gaze. "That?" He gave a laugh, then flashed his sweet dimple at her along with a broad grin. "It's just an old clock. One of the oddities my brother loves to accumulate."

"Is it?" For once his dimple failed to charm her. She was much more interested in this clock, which stood taller than a man. Graceful, slim pillars framed the three levels of the timepiece—a lower compartment where the counterweights would be, a mysterious middle compartment with a curved double door, and a glass-covered upper section, which held the face, faintly yellowed with age, and a curious, dark blue half disk.

Stepping nearer, Cissy peered up at this last element. Royal blue, with a stormcloud face to the left and a smiling sun on the right. And in the middle before them . . .

Cissy blinked. "Is this a sheep?" When she didn't get an answer she turned, and only then became aware of the tapping of Leopold's foot on the stone tiles. Impatient? She frowned. "Sheep?" she repeated, making her voice more assertive than before.

"Sheep? Where?" Leo looked around as if he thought a live sheep were running bleating through the castle.

She felt her frown deepen.

Her irritation increased. Whatever was the matter with her charming golden god? "There. On the clock." She pointed, even though that was supposed to be unladylike.

Leopold rolled his eyes. "Geez, that old thing. What's the attraction? A pile of rotting wood and an old music box which will be forever out of tune."

Her heart gave an excited thump against her breastbone. "There's a music box, too?"

He shrugged. As she continued to stare at him expectantly, he finally heaved an exaggerated sigh. "Oh, all right, it's got something to do with gnomes, dwarves, or whatever you call the little buggers." He pointed to the middle section of the clock. "That's where they are."

"But, why is there a sheep at the top?"

With an expression of exasperation, he threw up his arms. "How should I know? It's probably there because the clockmaker was a loony or—"

To their right a door was thrust open with enough force to make the hinges creak in protest. "Do you plan to raise the dead with all your screaming and shouting?" Fenris von Wolfenbach growled.

Cissy quickly stifled a startled squeak behind her hand.

Fenris shot her a murderous glance. "What?" he snapped.

She marveled; he looked as ferocious as his namesake. His expression was angry, his hair dusty and sticking up in odd tufts as if he had repeatedly run his hands through it. A thin trace of black ink marred the corner of his mouth. *Like black blood dripping to his chin.* Cissy shuddered.

"My, my," Leopold drawled. "Aren't we testy today?" He had hooked his thumbs in the pockets of his waistcoat, and, smirking at his brother, rocked back and forth on his heels.

Von Wolfenbach's black brows drew together and he muttered something unintelligible while apparently trying to murder his brother with his gaze. If he would but lift his lips and reveal his teeth and growl some more, he would look exactly like a mad dog, Cissy thought.

Or rather, like a mad wolf.

She shook her head. Whatever. She'd had enough of these antics.

"What are you doing here?" she asked loudly.

He turned his dagger-like glare on her. "This," he said clearly and slowly, as if talking to a particularly daft child, "is my study. Where I work."

Leopold leaned forward to whisper: "His den." His breath whispered initmately over her ear. "As in, the lion's den. Where the beast resides." He winked at her.

His brother grimaced in distate. "You always had a horrible sense of humor, Leo."

"Better a horrid one than none altogether."

Cissy rolled her eyes. The men reminded her of snarling dogs.

And then she heard the melody.

Whirling around, she faced the old clock. After the first few notes a clicking sound joined in, and the door to the middle compartment opened to reveal a group of dwarves hacking away in their mine. *Click-clack, click-clack*.

"Oh!" Delighted, she stepped nearer. They were perfect, with little caps and hammers and long beards.

Click-clack, click-clack.

Eventually their work slowed down, then stopped altogether, just as the last few notes of the little melody sounded. A creaking and whirring started, and on the face of the clock the eight turned inward and a man with a flowing cap and starry cloak appeared at the window.

The clock struck the hour in clear, almost musical strokes. And all the while the tiny man looked yearningly up toward the sheep on the disk above him, looked and looked, until the last stroke had sounded and the door to the dwarves' mine closed. Slowly, the cloaked man turned away, too. The window closed, and the big hand slipped to one minute past four.

"Oh," Cissy said again. "How lovely!" Behind her, she heard Leopold's long-suffering sigh. Not paying him any attention, she turned toward the other brother. "What *is* this?"

He looked her up and down, then raised a mocking brow. "A grandfather clock."

Cissy briefly considered hitting Fenris over the head. In her eagerness, she had forgotten what a grumpy old wolf he was. A wolf who surely loved to devour small Little Red Riding Hoods.

Not that she saw herself as a Little Red Riding Hood. She hoped to have far more sense than to let herself be devoured.

She decided to ignore his testiness for once, and waved in the general direction of the clock instead. "Of course this is a grandfather clock. For what kind of moron do you take me?" She allowed herself a momentary glare before she went on. "But what about the sheep?

Why is there a sheep up there? And why was that mannikin staring at the sheep?"

Von Wolfenbach shrugged. "She's a fairy princess."

"A fairy princess?" Cissy could hardly believe her ears. "It's a sheep!"

Von Wolfenbach's long-suffering sigh sounded almost exactly like his brother's. "Because she is an *enchanted* fairy princess. She is . . ." He pointed toward the clock and stepped nearer. "It's a punishment for . . ." Another step nearer. "She has been cursed." And then the story caught up with him. Cissy watched how he lost himself in it, how it lit his face and eyes, and she marveled at the transformation that came over him. "She's been cursed because she fell in love with the King of Dwarves." He pointed to the face of the clock. "He comes out every hour, waiting for her, hoping to catch a glimpse of his beloved. But she only changes when the clock strikes twelve. And for the span of the twelve strokes, she lights up the starry sky with her radiant beauty." His voice trailed away.

"How sad," Cissy murmured. "The poor princess. And the poor king!"

Von Wolfenbach blinked, as if only now he became aware of what he had been doing. Astonished, Cissy watched the flare of dark color that rose from beneath his collar. For a moment, he looked almost adorable; then his features shifted, tightened into a fierce scowl once more.

She sighed with disappointment.

"Sad?" Leopold scoffed behind them. "It's pathetic! The King of Dwarves in love with a fairy princess! He should have been the one to be punished. After all, what right does he have to court a fairy princess in the first place?"

"What do you mean?" Cissy turned toward him.

"Oh, come on." Clearly exasperated, he rolled his

eyes. "He's just an ugly old dwarf, after all. The likes of him shouldn't go around courting fairy princesses. Or any princesses, come to think of it."

Leopold's obvious annoyance astonished her. "But . . . but he's *in love* with her!" It was romantic and tragic; lovers caught between their two worlds. Like Romeo and Juliet, really.

"Love? Geez." Leopold huffed. "He isn't even worthy of looking at her! If she ever spares him so much as a glance, it will be out of sheer pity."

Aghast, Cissy stared. "I can't believe you've just said that."

"Why?" Leo threw up his arms. "He's a dwarf. A D-W-A-R-F." With his thumb and forefinger he showed her how small he considered a dwarf to be. How insignificant. "And besides,"—putting his hands on his hips, he narrowed his eyes at her—"this is just a silly old story, anyway. A *fabricated* story."

Fenris gave a grunt that sounded very much like disgust.

Unperturbed, Leopold continued. "I thought you were interested in reality! This is not real. What difference does it make whether he loves her or not? They're both not real!" Breathing heavily, he stared at her as if he expected something.

Baffled, she could only reply, "Of course it's not real. It's a fairy tale." What was his point?

"Bah!" He snorted. "All my life I've heard nothing but fairy tales and legends and all this mythological crap. I'm sick of it! *Sick*, do you hear me?" His fair face slowly turned a mottled crimson, and he no longer looked quite like a golden god.

"Oh, I'm sure she's heard you." His arms crossed on his chest, the older von Wolfenbach leaned one hip against the wall. "Actually, I believe they've heard you down in Kirchwalden." And he smiled. It was far from attractive.

At his brother's taunting words, Leopold's color deepened. "You!" Enraged, he advanced on his sibling. "You adore all this fairy tale nonsense, don't you?" He leaned in, crowding his brother. "You enjoy twisting reality for your own purposes. And our parents support you, of course. Our great wartime hero!" A feverish light glittered in his eyes.

Casually, Fenris von Wolfenbach shifted his weight and straightened to his full height. He easily towered over Leopold. "You talk rubbish, little brother," he said, very quietly. "And perhaps you shouldn't forget that this is my home. . . ." Letting his voice trail away, he lifted a brow. He certainly liked these taunting little gestures.

Cissy cleared her throat. She waited until both brothers looked at her, both wearing similiar expressions of annoyance. "Actually," she said sweetly, lifting both brows "this is *my* home now." She gave them both a beaming smile. "Or have you forgotten?"

Leopold visibly pulled himself together. With an effort, he wiped the surly expression from his face and managed a tight smile instead. "My dearest, I apologize. I am mortified." He went to her, took her hand and made as if to lift it to his mouth. But halfway there, Cissy snatched it back. After all, he had behaved like a perfect churl. Why, he had even yelled at her! She saw how he gritted his teeth. But then he sketched her a bow. "I am deeply ashamed I have let myself go like this. Be assured it will not happen again. Let me make up for it. Shall I show you the state rooms? They're quite wondrous."

Again he reached for her hand, but again she evaded him. This time she could hear the crunching sound of his teeth.

"Thank you, this is very kind, but I believe I prefer freshening up before dinner. Perhaps—"

He turned purple. He actually turned purple. A blue vein pulsed across his forehead. "Well then," he snapped. "Do whatever you like." And with that he turned and stamped away.

Blinking, Cissy stared after him. "Whatever set him off like that?" she wondered aloud.

The sound Fenris von Wolfenbach made was something between a snort and a laugh. "Well." He shrugged, and again a mocking smile twisted his lips. "My brother doesn't like fairy tales." He raised his brow. "Obviously."

Leopold apologized at dinner, while his brother and Mrs. Chisholm looked on. He even produced a little box, which he gave to Cissy, and when she opened it, a singing tin cat rolled out.

"Awww." Mrs. Chisholm clapped and looked rather touched. The older von Wolfenbach brother just gave an indelicate snort and drank his wine.

Flustered, Cissy didn't know what to say. "It's lovely," she finally managed. A singing tin cat? In cadmium green?

Leopold's face lit. "I knew you would love it. Young ladies always enjoy these silly little things." He positively beamed at her, and Cissy didn't have the heart to disappoint him by saying she had no idea what to do with a singing tin cat in cadmium green.

The next day she let him continue the tour of the castle and listened to his tales about the Wolfenbach Hoard. He was as charming as she could wish for, and over the next few days his churlish behavior began to appear like a thing of the distant past, something to be easily forgotten.

Almost.

INTERLUDE

The Other was taking over their realm. They watched him strut across the stones that formed their world, watched him charm an innocent maiden, their hope for the future. Like poison, worry dripped into them. The Other had a sunny smile, yet the heart of a viper, they knew. But caught in stone, there was not much they could do to reveal a heart of human flesh and bone.

Agitated, they muttered amongst themselves until their humming filled the dark night like a swarm of bees. Whispers wound through the foundations of the castle, sprang from stone to stone.

A thing to reveal a human heart.

A thing to invoke fear in a maiden's heart.

And they searched and searched, and when they had found what they were looking for, all it needed was a little nudge.

Then they watched and waited some more.

CHAPTER TEN

The rattling of the shutters was what alerted her first. Slowly she came awake, blinking in the dark room. Snuggled up in an enormous featherbed, Cissy liked to keep the window open at night so the fresh crisp smell of the forest would accompany her even in her dreams. But the shutters she always partly closed. *The rattling of the shutters* . . .

She rubbed the rest of the sleep from her eyes and then lay still, listening. For a moment, there was nothing. But then . . .

Flop-flop.

Flop.

Cissy shot upright, her heart hammering in her ears.

Flopflopflopflopflop.

The sound of agitated wings. Something was flying around her room—with large wings. Not tiny and soundless like a fly's.

Cissy swallowed hard. What could it be? A large insect, a moth perhaps? She imagined how whatever it was would flap against her and cling to her nightgown, and she shuddered with revulsion.

Hastily she scrambled out of bed and searched for the flint box. Her candle flared up and cast the room in mellow golden light. Cissy grabbed a shoe and looked around. If it was a moth, she could kill it. True, that would probably leave a stain on the wall, but she considered such a stain preferable to sharing a room with a monster moth.

Only it wasn't a moth. . . .

Flopflopflopflop.

She saw a dark body, a blur of skinny wings.

"Iiiiih!" Cissy shrieked, grabbed her candle and, still screaming, fled the room. Safely arrived in the hallway, she banged the door closed behind her and stopped shouting. Leaning against the old wood, she took a deep breath. "Drat," she said. "Drat! Drat! *Drat!*" And she kicked the door frame. "Ouch!" She yelped as she found that kicking a stone door frame with bare feet was not a very wise idea. "Dang my buttons!"

"I was not aware that gently reared young women would even know such words," drawled an amused male voice behind her.

Cissy whirled.

Leopold stood, one shoulder leaned nonchalantly against the wall. His mouth curved upward in a mischievous smile, and the dimple appeared in his cheek, while the light of his candle transformed his fair hair into a halo. He looked utterly charming.

While she . . .

Cissy's gaze fell to the shoe she was still holding. She hastily hid her hand behind her back, feeling very much like a naughty child who had been discovered stealing a biscuit. Heat rushed into her face. Flustered, she raised her eyes to his. "I . . ."

She saw how his gaze ran over her, and became aware of how scantily clad she was. Just a nightgown. Not even a robe. Her blush deepened, and his smile changed.

"What amazing things one finds when staying up late for a little game of billiards. Did you know my brother keeps a billiard room in this godforsaken castle?" He pushed himself off the wall. "What a truly charming figure you cut. Exquisite." Slowly he came nearer, like a panther on the prowl.

Or more like a sleek, golden leopard.

Cissy bit her lip. "I know you must think this highly unusual—"

"Highly." He halted in front of her and reached for the arm she hid behind her back. He slowly drew it around and forward, running his hand from her upper arm to her wrist. "But very, very charming." Her shoe fell to the floor with a thunk, when, with gentle force, he pried her fingers open. He bowed over her hand and kissed her knuckles.

"Oh." *Finally.* To feel his lips on her skin again. It was terribly improper, of course. A gently bred young woman should not invite a man to take liberties with her person, yet . . . Forbidden but oh-so-pleasurable tingles spread up her arm, and her knees weakened a little.

Leopold looked up at her. "Enticing," he breathed against her hand, and the sweet aroma of port drifted up to tickle her nose. And then she felt his warm, wet tongue sweep into the crease between two fingers.

His tongue?

With a gasp she snatched her hand away. Mortification made her cheeks burn. Surely this was too intimate, too—

Laughing, Leopold straightened. "And shyly virginal, like freshly fallen snow."

"What?" She gaped at him, hardly believing her ears. A spark of anger joined her mortification. This was not her charming golden god!

"Don't be such a prissy little madam." He trailed his knuckle over her cheek and laughed again when she twisted her head away. "It does not fit your dishabille." Again, the smell of port wafted to her.

Cissy narrowed her eyes. He was befuddled. He must be befuddled. How else to explain the feverish glint in his eye and the indecent talk? Straightening her shoulders, she glared at him. "I, sir, was awakened by a bat flying into my room. So I would be most obliged if you would go into that room and remove it."

"A bat?" He gawked at her for a moment or two before throwing his head back and roaring with laughter. "A bat in the middle of winter? You English have the most fertile imaginations!"

He thought she had made this up? Cissy stared at him disbelievingly. Into what kind of dunderhead had he turned? *A foxed dunderhead for sure,* she thought, and wished an enormous blob of wax from his candle would drop onto his hand and scorch that moppy laugh off his face. Perhaps it would also scorch some sense back into his brain.

"Yes." She rudely poked a finger into his chest, determined to make him solve her problem. "Now, would you kindly go and remove it from my room?"

He stopped laughing and chose to giggle insanely instead. "It's winter. How can there be a bat in your room?"

Cissy shrugged impatiently. "How should I know? All I know is that there *is* a bat there. Now, would you please do me the favor of removing it?" Dear heavens, what was the matter? He couldn't be so far gone that he had lost all sense of chivalry.

"A bat." The giggles stopped and a speculative glint entered Leopold's eyes. He swayed toward her. "And what favor would you grant me in return, *Liebchen*? A kiss perhaps?"

"I—"

"Or more?" The look he gave her could only be described as a leer. His eyes dropped to her bosom, where her nipples, puckered with the cold, poked through her nightgown. He licked his lips, very, very slowly.

For the first time Cissy felt a shiver of real fear. No, this was not the charming young man she had got to know. Instinctively, she took a step back. It made him chuckle.

"Look at you. Those sharp little tits, begging to be kissed. You're hot for it, aren't you? Such a randy little—"

Cissy gasped with outrage. Without thinking, she slapped him, hard and fast. His candle clattered to the floor, rolled over the stone tiles.

"Why, you . . ." He held a hand to his cheek. "You . . ." His expression shifted, darkened.

Her breath heaving in her chest, Cissy eyed him warily. Suddenly, she felt cold. The temperature of the stone, which she had not noticed before, now bit at her bare feet, clenched her heart. A gentle breeze seemed to stir in the hallway. The flame of her candle flickered. Shadows sprang up from the walls as if in warning.

Dear God, what have I done?

She wondered whether she should run. Run and scream. But who would hear her in this wide and empty castle? Just the stones, only the stones. Cissy shuddered.

Help me! Oh, please help me!

"You little . . ." Leopold's face twisted, became an ugly mask. He was a beast, was no longer human, no longer a charming golden god.

She took a step back as he raised his hands, fists.

Please.

She took another step back. "I did not ask you to grope me," she said. Despite her sudden fear, she laced her voice with coldness.

For an answer, he growled.

She took another step back. He took a step nearer. And then . . .

Tap-dam, tap-dam, tap-dam.

"What exactly do you think you're doing?" Fenris von Wolfenbach asked, his voice as cool as the stone itself.

Cissy sagged against the wall with relief.

His eyes flicked over her, lingered briefly on her heaving bosom. Her face flamed. Hastily, she put her free hand over her chest. His expression subtly changed: his lips became thinner, his eyes darker. Wordless, he shrugged out of his coat and gave it to her. Her hands trembled so much the garment nearly slipped out of her grasp.

"Fen." Blotches of bright color bloomed on Leopold's cheeks. He licked his lips. "Well, whatever should be the matter? Miss Fussell here and I, we were just talking." Sweat beaded on his upper lip. "Isn't that true, Miss Fussell?" Leopold wiped the back of his hand over his lip and shrugged.

Feeling so numb and cold she wondered whether she would ever warm up again, Cissy huddled into Fenris's frock coat. A soothing smell of sandalwood rose up from the material, and she felt as if enveloped in a warm embrace.

Leopold's words had been just the slightest bit slurred—enough to make his brother's eyes narrow. "You've been drinking again." Disdain laced his voice.

Leopold's nostrils flared as he stared at his older brother. Then he threw his head back and laughed, a hard and ugly sound. "You're such a bloody hypocrite, Fen. As if you were a saint in this respect! I seem to remember a time when you couldn't get enough of drink—and women." His eyes glittered. "You fucked yourself through the beds of Freiburg's fair world, my randy big brother, the darling of society, fêted and bedded. . . ." Leopold made a suggestive movement with his hips, back and forth, while an ugly smile twisted his mouth.

Cissy felt how shock drained all color from her face. The shadows in the hallway seemed darker, denser. An icy gust whirled around them all, made her shiver. *Dear God. Dear God . . .* She pressed her hands to her mouth so she wouldn't cry out. Yet when she dared a look at Fenris's face, she found that his expression had not changed. Stoically he regarded his brother, his features as hard as the stone itself.

Another laugh, wilder than before. "Perhaps you don't remember, Fen? Did they shoot off your cock with your leg?"

"Stop it!" Cissy croaked, forcing the words through her constricted throat. How sick could one man be?

"What?" Leopold's eyes swiveled to her. His hand not quite steady, he brushed the hair from his forehead. "What?" He giggled. "Oh, the demure maiden is speaking up." Quick as a viper, he grabbed her arm, thrusting his face into hers so that his hot, moist breath tickled over her skin and she could smell the alcohol he had consumed. "And later, did you know what happened later?" he asked softly, cocking his head to the side while his eyes caressed her face.

Cissy shuddered with revulsion. "You, sir, are disgusting." She tried to twist free, but his grip only tightened like a painful vise around her arm.

He grinned, lowered his voice to a conspiratorial whisper. "Later, when he came home after he had ruined our family—oh, you should have seen him then, Fenris of Wolfenbach, the former darling of society, drinking himself into a stupor night after night." Leopold giggled again. "The whole castle reeked of alcohol. A den of iniquity."

Cissy shoved at his shoulder, but Leopold just laughed. "He drank to forget, but he couldn't—as was only right when he had made his whole family miserable."

A large hand closed over Leopold's shoulder and the older von Wolfenbach pulled him away. "You talk too much, little brother," he said. His voice was just a lazy drawl, yet when he shifted, his body was between Leopold and Cissy. "And you're dead drunk. Go to bed."

He's shielding me, Cissy realized numbly. *He's using his body as a shield for me.* On top of everything else, this was simply too much. Tears welled in her eyes, and she had to bite her lip hard to prevent them from overflowing. While she watched the play of the muscles of Fenris's broad back underneath his lawn shirt, she suddenly felt the urge to step nearer, to put her forehead against that expanse. . . .

This time, she bit her lip to suppress her shaky laugh. He would loathe it. How he would loathe it!

"Go to bed, Leo." Steel had slipped into Fenris von Wolfenbach's voice.

"Go to hell, Fen."

Von Wolfenbach advanced on his brother until the two men stood chest to chest, illuminated by the candle Fenris carried with him. One light, one dark. One with a smooth face, one with stark lines etched into his skin. The hair of one was like a halo, the other's hair black like a raven's wings. Black like Merlin's hair, spawn of the devil, and yet . . . and yet . . .

"Go to your room, Leo," Fenris said very quietly. Yet

Cissy could hear the underlying edge. "Or better, go outside and push your thick head into the snow to sober yourself up."

"I—"

"Go *now.*" His voice was sharp.

Cissy watched Leopold's face turn glum. He thrust his lower lip out into a small boy's pout. He snarled a word Cissy had never heard before, then stormed off. She shivered.

Fenris von Wolfenbach waited until even the echo of his brother's steps had died away before he turned to Cissy and scanned her with his gaze. "Are you all right?" he asked in a completely different tone: soft, as if she were a doe, as if the smallest movement, the slightest harsh sound, might frighten her away.

Cissy lowered her head and stared at the flame of her candle. How it danced! So merrily, as if nothing had happened. A shudder ran through her. "I am fine," she whispered. "I woke up and there was a bat in my room. I thought it might be a moth, but it was a bat. So I ran outside and hoped . . . and hoped . . ."

"A bat?" She looked up and saw him lift an eyebrow—but for once she couldn't detect any sarcasm or mockery.

Biting her lip, she nodded. "A bat. I didn't want to . . ." She looked away and swallowed painfully. "I thought . . . I thought he would help me."

Fenris caught her chin with two fingers and gently turned her head so she had to look at him. "He has not hurt you, has he?"

She shook her head. "No."

"I'm glad." His thumb stroked in soothing circles over her temple.

She stared at him blandly. "Why?" She shook her head. Exhaustion crept over her, made her sway on her feet. "Why did you come?"

His face became inscrutable again. "I heard a commotion in the hallway. Would you like me to remove the bat from your room?"

"Oh yes. Yes. Please." Cissy shivered despite his coat around her shoulders. How she longed to crawl back under the duvet, seek the cozy warmth of her bed and pretend this all hadn't happened. That it had been a bad dream, only a bad dream.

"I won't be long," he promised, and with a final lingering glance, he stepped into her room.

Cissy heard how the door clicked behind him, and with a weary sigh she sank against the wall. As she pressed her face against the cool stone, Leopold's ugly insinuations came back to her—the horrid things he had said, how he had made her feel soiled. She shuddered. And even uglier and more hateful still were the words Leopold had flung at his own brother. *"Did they shoot off your cock with your leg?"* So cruel, so unbearably cruel . . .

A tear trickled over her cheek.

Cissy closed her eyes and fought for composure. Von Wolfenbach surely wouldn't like it if he found her in tears when he came out of the room. But how he must hurt. So much hurt . . . She bit her lip.

A few minutes later, he stepped into the hallway. "That bat should have been hibernating." He looked into Cissy's face. Frowning, he reached out and lightly touched her arm where his brother had gripped her. "You are certain he hasn't hurt you?" Concern made his voice gruff.

Concern. All these weeks he had tried to scare her away, and now he was concerned for her. Cissy blinked away the tears. He would not want her tears. "I'm fine." She managed a smile, a quick lifting of her lips. "Is the bat gone?"

"Quite." Yet he did not budge, and still regarded her,

his frown deepening. "You will not hold it against Leopold, will you? Drink makes him aggressive. But he's not. Normally."

That he would defend his brother grated on her. "Then he should stay away from alcohol in the first place," she said sharply.

Fenris flinched. The lines in his face made him look haggard and older than his years.

Contrition came immediately. He had, after all, saved her and did not deserve more harsh words. "It is all right." She touched his hand, the big rough knuckles. "I am fine. Really. Thank you for all you did tonight."

His face changed, became blank as the stone walls themselves. "Well, yes . . ." He straightened, took a step back. "Don't think about it. And in the future—don't be so foolish as to walk the hallways at night. It's dangerous." And with that, he walked away.

CHAPTER ELEVEN

The next day, Leopold came to apologize, a sheepish smile on his face—as if the incident in the hallway had been a mere trifle, as if his charming dimple and his striking good looks could make her forget the hateful things he had said, the unleashed beast she had seen. As if, just like that, he could make her forget the fear that had clutched her heart.

God only knew what he would have done to her had his brother not arrived on the scene. She still could not fully understand what von Wolfenbach had been doing in this part of the castle—but oh, how glad she had been to see him! Who would have thought it: that she would one day welcome the sight of the demon wolf of Wolfenbach! And even though he *had* manhandled her at their first meeting, she had never felt a need to fear him the way she had feared Leopold the previous night. For it hadn't been so much the violence that had frightened her, but the sexual intent beneath. To be at a man's mercy like that, to know he could easily overpower her and do . . . things to her . . .

Cissy shuddered. She remembered Mrs. Chisholm's warning on that first day: All is not gold that glitters. She would be very, very careful around Leopold von Wolfenbach from now on. When she thought about what liberties she had allowed him, she felt ashamed of herself. A pea-brained mooncalf she had been, falling for a pretty face and a few pretty words.

And so, while she coolly accepted his apology, she did not choose to accompany him on further tours of the castle. Two days later he threw a fit over her "lack of understanding." His face mottled with anger, he called for his curricle and drove away in a huff. *On to greener pastures,* Cissy thought cynically. *Probably back to the delights of Freiburg.*

It was strange—when she thought about her London season, about the lure of life in the big city, what she remembered most was how unreal this life had seemed: a glittering surface without any substance. Even though she had had to do without most fineries, she had enjoyed her life as her father's secretary and companion. The worlds he had opened for her had been utterly fascinating. This was also true for the last world he had gifted her with—the Castle of Wolfenbach. She loved the smell of cool, old stone, the feeling of timelessness that enshrouded the castle. By now she even liked the gargoyles peeking down on her from the castle walls whenever she ventured outside, as if they were standing guard over her. On the ramparts she would sometimes pat their heads or form fantastic snow caps for them. Their ferocity presented an intriguing contrast to the finer things inside the castle. The grandfather clock with the sad King of Dwarves never failed to bewitch her, and she simply adored the ancient tapestries.

Every morning on her way to the room where breakfast was served, Cissy passed the tapestry of the hunting party with its secret declaration of love. Each morning, Cissy stopped to admire it. She loved the intricate floral design surrounding the men and animals; the curving lines which cleverly hid the *Te amo.* And she wondered about the woman who had created this tapestry. How unhappy she must have been, married to one man but in love with another. So much in love that she had even left a secret testimony of it. And though she and her beloved were now long dead and had fallen to dust in their graves, the proof of her love survived the ages.

With a gentle forerfinger Cissy touched the letters. Lowering her voice to a mere whisper, she told the man forever caught in the fabric: " 'O I will love thee still, my dear, / While the sands o' life shall run.' " Smiling at her fancy, she let her gaze wander across the tapestry and caught the many places where the thread had thinned, and the spots of slightly brighter color where the fabric had been repaired. One of the lower corners was frayed, and it would need a few stitches to keep the whole from unraveling.

Cissy carefully lifted the damaged corner to take a closer look. Her thumb stroked the frail threads while she imagined what kind of stitches the repair would take. *I won't let your legacy fall apart,* she promised the long-dead woman, and a sudden, strong feeling of kinship for her welled up inside Cissy. A labor of love this tapestry had been, just like Cissy's own work in her father's library. And while she knew more about books than about anything else, she knew enough about needlework to fix the corner and thereby make sure that the woman's declaration of love would survive the next few years.

Her smile deepening, Cissy let go of the fabric. Just as

she turned to go to the dining room, the deep sounds of male voices at the top of the stairs drifted down to her. She looked up and saw Fenris von Wolfenbach engaged in deep conversation with his valet. It was strange, Cissy thought; even now, von Wolfenbach's face was set in harsh lines as if he never quite allowed himself to relax. Unnoticed, she watched how he walked down the stairs, wondered if he knew what a powerful aura he emanated. Grace and strength, mixed with a strong will and determination.

His wooden leg clacked on the wood of the stairs.

Cissy was certain there were possibilities other than just a wooden stick. Yet for some strange reason, Fenris von Wolfenbach seemed determined to flaunt his missing limb in the face of the world. As if he didn't want others to forget that he was different. Or . . .

Cissy frowned.

Or as if he didn't want *himself* to forget that he was different. But not that much different. Cissy remembered the night he had used his body as a shield for her. How easily he had towered over his brother, how easily he had dominated him. How safe she had felt standing behind him.

Cissy sighed.

An awful crunching sound came from the stairs. Her head jerked up. Time seemed to slow down as she watched how von Wolfenbach stumbled, how his hand shot out to grab the banister and his fingers brushed the wood—and how they slid away as momentum dragged him on and on, down the stairs. The startled look in his widened eyes. The thuds as his body hit the stairs again and again, tumbling down head over heels. And the awful quiet as he finally came to a rest on the landing.

For a moment, Johann the valet remained frozen on the spot, then he gasped and hurried down toward his fallen master. Only then did Cissy realize she had pressed her hands against her mouth to keep back a scream. Oh God, was he dead?

"Help!" she shouted. "We need help!" She ran toward the stairs and up to where Johann, his face drained of all color, was bending over von Wolfenbach. Fenris lay there, pale and still, his mouth slack, blood oozing from a gash at his temple and running into his hair.

Her blood pounded in her ears. Cissy fell to her knees next to the two men. "What is it? Is he dead?" With the breath wheezing in and out of her lungs she barely managed to form the words.

Johann's mouth formed a tight line as he fumbled with his master's necktie. He finally managed to loosen the knot and pull back the starched white collar of the shirt so he could check the pulse in the hollow of the neck. His head sank forward; his shoulders dropped.

"What?" Cissy felt how her own throat tightened painfully. "Is he . . ."

"He's alive." Johann straightened. Relief made his eyes shimmer wetly. "Thank heavens, he is alive." He sank back on his haunches and, for the first time, really seemed to register Cissy's presence. For a moment he closed his eyes, then wiped his arm across his forehead, which shone with sweat. "His leg— it just broke away from under him."

"His leg?" Cissy looked down at the still body.

"His . . . *other* leg."

The sounds of hurried footsteps made Cissy turn toward the bottom of the stairs. Servants came running, a maid shrieked.

"Quick!" Johann's strong voice easily carried over the sudden din in the hallway. "Somebody fetch the doctor from Kirchwalden!" He bowed his head. "It will take hours to get the doctor here," he murmured tiredly to Cissy. She swallowed hard.

The wound at von Wolfenbach's temple still leaked blood, a steady red trickle, which had already formed a small puddle on the wooden stairs. Cissy reached out and pressed her sleeve against the wound. With her free hand, she gently stroked his forehead. *A ferocious wolf no more*. The thought stabbed at her heart.

"Do you think we can move him?" she asked quietly. "We cannot let him lie here for hours."

"You're right." Johann nodded. "We should get him into a bed . . ." He gazed at his master. "And search for more injuries. Hey, there!" he shouted. "Come somebody and help me carry him upstairs!"

More injuries? Cissy shuddered. Perhaps broken bones. She could only imagine how bad it would be for Fenris von Wolfenbach to be even more restricted in his movements. She knew that fate could be cruel, but it seemed terribly wrong that he should endure even more than he had. A missing leg.

How curious that his wooden leg had snapped like a twig. Cissy bent forward.

The butler came up behind her. "You should move now, *gnädiges Fräulein*."

"Yes." She stood to make room for him and watched how Johann and Rambach lifted von Wolfenbach up. His legs dangled from their arms; the wooden stump looked grotesque.

Her gaze was drawn to the broken wood.

There was something . . .

Frowning, she leaned nearer.

Something not quite right . . .

Now she could see the broken wood clearly, only it wasn't broken at all. It was . . .

Cissy gasped. She straightened so quickly that for a moment she felt dizzy.

Johann caught her gaze, and suddenly she knew that he

had seen it, too: the wood had snapped cleanly. A sliver of ice touched her heart. This had been no accident.

Cissy clutched the banister. Dear God, who would do such a thing? To saw at a wooden leg to make a proud man fall, to humilate him . . . to kill him?

She looked after the servants carrying von Wolfenbach upstairs.

A wave of anger washed over her. To attempt to kill a man in her castle! *Her* castle! She would be damned before she saw that happen. Determinedly she stomped up the stairs after the men. She would not depart from von Wolfenbach's side until the doctor arrived.

On the threshold to his room, Mrs. Chisholm caught up with her. Breathing heavily the older woman put a hand to her heaving bosom. "The stableboy has gone to fetch the physician. And von Wolfenbach's parents." She threw a sympathetic glance to the man who was being laid out on the bed. "The poor lad." She sighed. "I hope that teaches him to refrain from walking around on a mere stick in the future." Before Cissy could reply, she'd marched past and into the room, gesticulating to the servants. "Gently, gently, gentlemen."

Cissy followed and stepped up to the enormous four-poster bed. Von Wolfenbach's face had taken on a grayish tinge, except for the dark blood at this temple. "We need towels to stop the bleeding," she said.

Johann tugged at the cloth that still encircled Fenris's neck. "Here." He turned. "Take this tie for the moment."

Cissy lifted the corner of a pillow and sat down on the bed to press the pristine white cloth against the wound.

"It doesn't look as if he's broken any limbs," Mrs. Chisholm commented, surveying the scene from the foot of the bed.

"No." Johann frisked his hands over his master's body.

"But he might have broken some ribs." He exchanged a look with the widow. "There might be internal injuries."

Cissy bit her lip.

Mrs. Chisholm frowned. "No stab in the lungs, though. No, not that. But you should loosen his clothes, dearie." She turned to Cissy. "These modern waistcoats and jackets are quite horribly tight. I don't know how a man can breathe in them at the best of times. Rambach, be a dear and fetch us some towels and warm water." She clicked her tongue. "And kirsch," she added as an after-thought. "Johann?"

"Kirsch?" Cissy lifted her eyes. Incredulity made her voice higher than usual.

"To swab at this nasty bump." Mrs. Chisholm went around the bed. "Shoo, Johann, whatever are you wait-ing for?" With obvious reluctance, von Wolfenbach's valet left the room.

"Now, dearie"—switching to English, Mrs. Chisholm rolled up her sleeves—"let us take a look at this." She nudged Cissy and, when Cissy stood, took her place be-side von Wolfenbach's head. "You go on and open his clothes."

"Me?" Cissy flushed hotly at the thought of undressing a man.

"Of course you!" Mrs. Chisholm gave her a suprised look. "Do you see anybody else in this room at the mo-ment? Don't be so squeamish, dearie. Have you never seen any of those Greek sculptures? It's exactly the same thing, I assure you." Frowning, she bent lower to exam-ine Fenris's wound more closely. "A nasty gash," she murmured and clicked her tongue some more. She prodded the surrounding flesh. "But no broken skull. Got a thick head, this one. Dearie, do start, will you?"

Gingerly, Cissy lifted a knee onto the bed and bent over the prone figure. She tried to ignore the queasy feeling in her stomach as she pulled back the sides of his coat. Where Johann had removed the cravat and loosened the neck of the shirt, some curly black hair peeped out over the top button—as if inviting her to stroke it with the tip of her finger. She gulped and focused her attention on the buttons of his waistcoat. In contrast to the men she had met in England, he never wore bright colors, seeming to prefer shades of brown or drab gray. *Like a wolf.*

The last button came undone and she pushed back the sides of the waistcoat, too. Now his shirt . . . Cissy licked her lips.

As she opened the top button, her fingers brushed against the springy dark hair at his throat. Her fingers tingled with this new sensation, and she had to swallow hard before she could go on.

Her face flaming, she worked on the rest of the buttons. Bit by bit she revealed pale, smooth skin, the heavy muscles of his chest, which were sprinkled with dark hair, and the hard ridges of his belly. Yes, she had seen Greek sculptures in the British Museum in London, beautiful bodies in white marble, but this . . . this was different. Quite, quite different. Von Wolfenbach's skin was warm to her touch and satiny soft. The contrast between that smooth skin and the hardness of the muscles underneath fascinated her. Just visible over the waistband of his trousers was the top half of his navel, surrounded by a whirl of black hair. It looked . . . delicious.

"So I was right." Mrs. Chisholm's voice cut into her thoughts. "A nice laddie, this one. Well made."

Cissy felt as if she were about to go up in flames of shame because of her wanton thoughts.

Her friend just chuckled. "No need to be bashful, dearie. I'd look my fill, if I were you. 'Tis not often that a woman gets to see such a lovely specimen of a man. No blood, is there?" Unceremoniously, she drew her hands down his sides. "No broken ribs either, it seems. Just some ugly bruises." She touched a dark discoloration at his waist.

"How do you know about broken ribs?" Cissy asked.

"I've raised six boys. Let me tell you, boys tend to fall off and down a lot of things. All the time, practically. And if they don't fall off things, they get into fights. So it's always a scraped knee here, a scratched elbow there, a bump here, a loosened tooth there. Ah, Johann, there you are." She switched back to German.

The valet brought her towels and a bottle of kirsch. She poured a liberal dose of alcohol onto one of the towels and swabbed the wound with it. Von Wolfenbach groaned and tried to lift his hand.

"Ah, here he is." Mrs. Chisholm sounded like a satisfied cat after it had licked up the cream. "That woke you, laddie, didn't it?"

He blinked up at her. "What . . . ?"

Mrs. Chisholm patted his hand. "You took a nasty fall and bumped your head on the stairs. You'll probably feel a bit sick in the next few days just like Dickie, my eldest, when he fell off the great oak on the village green." She beamed at him.

He stared at her, his gaze still clouded. Then his eyes narrowed. "I take it I didn't fall off an oak tree, though."

"On the staircase?" Mrs. Chisholm snorted. "Not very likely, is it?" She patted his hand some more. "My dear boy, you really shouldn't walk about on a mere stick, you know. The thing broke and you fell."

"My . . ." Dark color surged up from his neck. Grimacing with pain, he slowly lifted his head a little to look down his body.

Cissy saw the expression in his eyes before he closed them, and in this moment her heart broke for him. Fenris, this ferocious wolf, was fettered by something worse than dwarves' chains.

Quietly she stepped back from the bed. So far he had not seemed to notice her, and she wanted to spare him the realization that she had witnessed his humiliation. Or that she had seen him half-naked. She had touched his skin, had felt the warmth of his body, the crispness of the hair that covered his chest—how could she look him in the eye again?

Vividly she remembered the strength he had emanated as he had stood before her in the darkened hallway. The wolf might be fettered, but his power was most definitely still there.

The doctor came in the Wolfenbach carriage together with the *Graf* and *Gräfin*. It did not take him long to ease their fears: he found no serious injuries. He suspected one or two ribs to be cracked but not broken, and a tight bandage around the torso was all that was needed. By then, Fenris von Wolfenbach insisted on leaving bed anyway, and hidden by the people milling around, Cissy slipped out of the room unnoticed. He was, after all, in safe hands now.

Yet her exit was not entirely unnoticed.

"*Gnädiges Fräulein?*" Von Wolfenbach's valet came hurrying after her.

"Yes?" Surprised, she turned.

Johann lowered his voice. "You've seen it too, haven't you? The way the wood broke?" At her nod, he cleared his throat. "I've been thinking—perhaps it wouldn't be good to talk about it. If the culprit hasn't left any traces in my master's bedroom, then there's not much we can do. Yet should one start to ask questions . . ."

Cissy nodded thoughtfully. "They would know that *we* know."

"I will . . ." He lifted his arm, let it fall again. "I'll make sure my master is safe. I'll be prepared from now on."

"Yes. I quite understand." Cissy watched as he bowed and went back to von Wolfenbach's bedroom.

Slowly, she walked on to the great staircase, where on one of the steps above the landing the lower part of the wooden leg still lay. She bent down and picked it up. For a moment she could only stare at it, stunned once more by the viciousness of the deed. She rubbed her thumb over the clean section where the person had cut into the wood. Thoughtfully, she gnawed on her lower lip. Who would do such a thing? And what was the purpose of it? It did not seem to make sense; if somebody wished to kill Fenris von Wolfenbach, there were other, more surefire ways to accomplish it. Or had it just been about the humiliation? If so, they had most certainly succeeded.

Cissy closed her eyes as she remembered the expression in von Wolfenbach's eyes when he had realized what had happened. Whoever had done this, he had attacked Fenris's greatest weakness and thereby cut him to the quick.

Her heart clenched painfully.

At that moment, she heard steps on the stairs above. Blinking rapidly, she slipped the piece of wood into her pocket and quickly wiped her eyes before turning around.

"Ah, there you are, dearie," Mrs. Chisholm said. "What do you think about telling Rambach to bring some fresh cocoa and coffee to the dining room? After that big fright we could all do well with a good, hearty breakfast, don't you think?" She reached the step on which Cissy stood and put her arm around her shoulders. "And our laddie is already up and around again, too. Quite a robust young man, I have to say, when not even a bump on the head will stop him." She paused. "Well, I daresay he will feel quite sick this afternoon, just like my Dickie did. But, of course, he won't heed the doctor's advice to stay in bed. Stubborn as a mule, that lad. Ah well, boys will be boys, I guess—don't you think so, too, dearie? And the older they are, the more pigheaded they become." She heaved a sigh. "It's a shame."

CHAPTER TWELVE

Despite their son's protests, the *Graf* and the *Gräfin* decided to stay for a few days at the castle to make sure he didn't suffer any aftereffects from his fall. The company made Cissy edgy. The attack on von Wolfenbach deeply bothered her. Should she suspect the servants? But when their master had undertaken the most imbecilic attempts to get rid of Mrs. Chisholm and herself, they had all proved to be loyal to him—even to the point of risking pneumonia. So how could she suspect *them*? But who else was there? And was Johann really right that it was safer not to talk about it to anybody else?

At this point, her thoughts always started to run in circles. To escape brooding, if only for a little while, she would withdraw into the castle library and—like so many times before—seek the solace of fictional worlds and people.

The library was surely one of the prettiest rooms in the castle, Cissy thought. It had been refurbished seventy or eighty years before, probably by the father of the current *Graf*, and featured white walls, a white ceiling with stucco adornments and a golden-framed center image of Apollo surrounded by the muses. Depictions of allegories of the old four continents hung resplendent in the four corners of the room. Strangely enough, each continent was a woman wrapped in some diaphanous material or other. The white walls contrasted nicely with the dark wood of the bookshelves.

Cissy was sitting in one of the deep window alcoves and reading the first volume of a Hoffmann novel she had found on the shelves. The strange story, an autobiography of Murr, a tomcat with literary aspirations, interspersed with the biography of the music master Kreisler, enthralled her. It was a novel unlike any other she had read before, a riddle, like so much in the castle appeared to be. Most puzzling of all, though, she found the man who had obviously bought the book. She tried to envision Fenris von Wolfenbach reading such a fantastic tale—and failed. How to combine the snarling, angry man with this? But then she remembered how he had lost himself in the story of the grandfather clock.

Bemused, she read on, and smiled as Murr ripped the books he attempted to study.

"What a beautiful image you make, my dear."

Starting, she looked up and saw Leopold von Wolfenbach leaning against the nearest shelf. He presented a slightly rumpled appearance, with his necktie loosened and his golden hair ruffled. As she watched, the familiar charming smile dimpled his cheek. Leaning forward, he asked in a conspiratorial whisper: "Have you missed me?" He gave her a slow wink, as if he already knew the answer to his question.

So sure of himself. Frowning, Cissy marked the page she was reading and shut the book. "No," she finally said, turning her attention back to him. "I'm afraid not."

"Ouch." He straightened and wrinkled his nose. "I

would have thought, for a young woman like you, shut up in a dreary old castle such as this . . ." He shrugged.

"Yes?"

"I would have thought you would welcome distractions." Again, he magicked a smile onto his face. "Like my company, for example?"

"I am quite happy with my life at Wolfenbach. Thank you." And because she remembered the night she had most definitely not enjoyed his company, she stood up and tried to slip past him.

He followed.

"Where have you been these past few days?" she asked to distract him.

Satisfaction flickered over his face. "So you *have* missed me. I was in Freiburg." A few long strides carried him around to her front. He leaned his elbow against the shelf before her, thus blocking her way. "Wouldn't you like to live in Freiburg? Just imagine—balls and parties and—"

"I've been to the balls in London."

Unperturbed, he continued smiling at her, his green eyes twinkling merrily. His nerve was really quite beyond the pale. "So, wouldn't you like to visit some balls again? Fashionable people, fashionable clothes, champagne, the best food . . ." He raised his brow in a manner which eerily reminded Cissy of his brother. "Wouldn't you like to buy new dresses? The latest fashions from Paris?" His voice dropped to a seductive burr. "Just think of it, Celia, how your beauty would be enhanced by such clothes, how you would shine like a diamond among all the fashionable ladies."

Oh, indeed? Did he really think she would fall for his flattery after—

Cissy shook her head.

Of course, she did long to buy new clothes, dresses

with low waists so people would no longer see how old her garments were. But she didn't want ball gowns; she much preferred the simpler dresses, things she could wear and feel pretty again. She looked down at the black dress she was wearing. She no longer remembered what color it had been before the dyeing. The dye had already become washed out at the hems and seams, making her feel even more drab. Yes, of course she longed to feel pretty again.

"If you marry me . . ." When she looked up, Leopold's face was near her own, his eyes two clear pools of green. He smiled. "I will take you to Freiburg and you will always have new clothes. After we've found the hoard, we will sell the castle to the Altertumsverein and it'll never burden us again. Think of it, Celia."

Sell the castle? "What are you talking about?"

He looked taken aback. "Don't you need to marry a Wolfenbach son?"

"Why are you talking about marriage now? *Now!* When your brother is still black and blue from his fall?"

Leopold's expression changed, annoyance entering his eyes. "You cannot seriously think of marrying Fen! Not after all that has happened!"

Everything went still in Cissy. "After all that has happened?" she echoed

"He fell. Dear God, Celia, do I have to spell it out for you?" He ran both hands through his hair. "How can you even think of choosing him when he is not even . . . whole." He grimaced in distaste.

"You mean his leg? What has that to do with anything? I can't believe you're saying this. He is your brother." And, it would seem, he'd been spectacularly wrong about Leopold: his sibling was an odious cad even when stone-sober.

Dark blotches appeared on Leopold's cheeks. He

snorted. "Brother?" he spat. "After he ruined our family?" He advanced on her and she backed away. "After he came from the war, shot to pieces, how they commiserated! Poor Fenris! Oh, yes," he snarled. "What is his life worth now? Nothing! Nothing! Oh yes, the erstwhile darling of polite society—but what woman would ever spare him more than a look now? None!" He leaned in on her until his hot breath seared her cheek.

Cissy shuddered and tried to twist away, but his hand shot up. His fingers gripped her chin tightly, while his gaze slithered over her face. "Tell me, *Liebchen*." His voice had dropped to an intimate whisper, which made the fine hairs on her neck stand on end. "Would you enjoy lying in his bed?"

"You, sir, have lost your mind." She pushed her hands against his chest, but Leo would not budge. "Let me go. *Now!*"

He only chuckled and brought his mouth nearer to her ear. "Oh, sweet Celia . . . My brother would have to make you shut your eyes when he wanted to shag you."

"Are you totally mad?" Again, she tried to struggle against him.

"Make you shut your eyes tightly enough he could disregard the pity in them," he continued in a horrible sing-song voice. "Think of it, Celia. What a miserable marriage bed it would be for a pretty girl like you."

"You *are* mad. All because he is missing a leg?"

He gave an angry hiss, and his hands fell away from her. "Because he is a goddamned cripple! A freak!" he yelled.

"Oh, Leo," came a new voice. His head whipped around.

His mother stood there. Tears were running down her cheeks, disappearing between the fingers she pressed to her mouth. His father, ashen with shock, supported her with a hand under her elbow. Mrs. Chisholm's eyes had widened with what Cissy suspected was horrified fascination. Fenris alone showed no reaction whatsoever to his brother's slander. He might still be a little pale, and a bruise blemished one side of his face, but he stood upright and his expression seemed carved from stone.

Leopold breathed heavily. "I am just telling her the truth. How could she live with a—"

"Don't say the word," his father thundered. "I warn you, Leopold. Don't say it. He is your brother!"

"And half a man," Leopold taunted.

Cissy tightly clasped her hands together to keep them from shaking. "Well . . . ,"—she cleared her throat—"he is certainly more man than you could ever be." And then she walked over to stand beside Fenris von Wolfenbach. She remembered the night he had stood in front of her, shielding her. She remembered the feeling of his skin under her fingertips, the alluring whorl of hair around his navel. Fate might have fettered this particular wolf, but, oh yes, the power was still there, she was certain of it.

She reached for his hand, which hung limply at his side. His fingers jerked against hers, but she held fast. "As you said, I need to marry a Wolfenbach son. And I am going to marry Fenris."

CHAPTER THIRTEEN

The wind whistled sharply around the castle and blew away the caps of snow winter had bestowed upon the gargoyles. It also snatched strands from Cissy's braided hair and blew them around her face, while she stood on the remains of the tower and stared glumly into the valley, where the bells of St. Margaretha's pealed the Angelus.

Cissy heaved a deep sigh.

Only three months before they had pealed for her wedding—merrily, joyfully—and for once, she had felt really beautiful. Mrs. Chisholm had insisted on buying her a wedding dress after George and Dorinda had sent their congratulations and a pair of pearl earrings that had belonged to Cissy's mother. Cissy wore them, and the wedding dress of unadorned ivory-white silk. Mrs. Chisholm had chosen a simple cut as a foil for a beautiful veil: a basis of machine net of a texture as fine as a spiderweb, decorated with handmade Devon lace. Tears were swimming in Mrs. Chisholm's eyes as she kissed

Cissy's cheeks before she finished arranging the veil. "Be very happy, my dear child," she'd whispered.

And indeed, when Cissy saw the expression on her bridegroom's face as she walked up the aisle to him, she could almost believe that happiness could really be hers. The yearning she saw in his eyes tugged at her heartstrings, and when they walked out of the church, husband and wife, to the joyful cheering of the crowd, her hand slipped into his and held on tight. His fingers curled around hers so perfectly it was as if God had created them with the specific measurements to cradle her hand. *And two shall become one* . . .

Yes, as Cissy stood smiling in the crisp wintry air, with the clear blue sky above her and the sun smiling down on her, at that moment she had felt so very, very blessed. Yet that night had found her alone in her old bed, staring up at the canopy and wondering why her husband did not come. Nothing had changed.

"Give him time," Mrs. Chisholm had said to try to cheer her up later. "Have a little patience."

Patience . . .

The days had flown by. Cissy and Mrs. Chisholm organized the cleaning of the castle; the dust and dirt slowly disappeared, beeswax lent the old furniture new luster, and Cissy started to mend the tapestries. Still, the two women drove down to the valley every so often to look for new prints, books, or magazines. And thus, Christmas drew near.

In the first volume of Hoffmann's *Serapionsbrüder* Cissy and Mrs. Chisholm had found a Christmas story about the nutcracker who fought against the seven-headed king of mice and then took little Marie to his land of toys and sweets. But more than Marie's wonderful adventures, it was the description of a Christmas tree that fascinated Cissy and Mrs. Chisholm. "Yes, indeed, it's a dear, lovely German custom, these small fir trees decorated with apples and sugar almonds and whatnot," the widow commented. She exchanged a look with Cissy. "I always thought it would be most exciting to have such a Christmas tree of my own." And they smiled at each other like a pair of crafty conspirators.

The morning of December 23 dawned bright and clear, extraordinarily perfect for their plan to gather their Christmas tree hunting forces. As always, Cissy stopped to admire the tapestry with the hidden message of love. She waited until Mrs. Chisholm came downstairs, too, and together they proceeded to the dining room. Fenris already sat at the table, studying yesterday's newspaper so intently that his greeting constituted a mere grunt. Cissy waited until the butler poured her a cup of steaming hot Prussian coffee. "Rambach?" She gave him her sweetest smile. "When is the Christmas tree for Wolfenbach brought in?"

"Ch-Christmas tree?" He was so astonished he nearly poured the coffee into her lap.

"Yes, Christmas tree." Cissy threw a glance at the top of her husband's head, which was just visible above the paper. "The castle does get a Christmas tree, doesn't it?"

The old man regarded her quizzically.

The paper rustled as another page was turned. "Humbug," the demon wolf growled from behind it. "Wolfenbach has *never* had a Christmas tree!"

"Oh, such a pity," Mrs. Chisholm exclaimed and clutched her bosom as if a dagger had pierced her heart.

The upper corners of the newspaper trembled a little.

"I have so looked forward to a Christmas tree," Cissy said mournfully. "With golden flitter and apples and nuts and sugar almonds . . ." She ran out of ideas. Annoyed with herself, she rolled her eyes at the newspaper.

"And gingerbread and straw stars and blinking lights?" Rambach added helpfully.

Cissy's head whipped around.

The old man's bushy eyebrows rose, and then, very slowly, he winked at her. Equally surprised and delighted by this unexpected support, Cissy grinned back.

The newspaper rustled.

Watching expectantly, Cissy gnawed on her lower lip. Yet, nothing more happened. Mrs. Chisholm shrugged. Rambach mumbled something unintelligible.

Well then, Cissy thought, *it's time to play the trump card.* She took a deep breath. "I've so wished for a Christmas tree." She lent her voice a plaintive little tremble. "My first Christmas tree for my first Christmas in my new home."

Mrs. Chisholm nodded in pleased delight. "Brava!" she voiced soundlessly.

For a moment, the newspaper remained absolutely still. Then the demon wolf heaved a deep sigh. "All right," he growled. The newspaper was folded together with obvious reluctance and finally revealed her husband, his black hair deliciously tousled and a dark scowl on his face. "When do you want to leave for the forest?"

Cissy's answer was a beaming smile.

That very afternoon they went on a Christmas tree hunt, Fenris dragging an axe and his valet into the forest, and he gamely went from tree to tree until Cissy and Mrs. Chisholm had finally found the perfect one. The next morning the two women drove to Kirchwalden to buy a small basket full of ornaments for their tree: ribbons, flitter and small candles from the haberdashery; *Springerle,* white cookies depicting fairy tale characters, and gingerbread stars on delicate ribbons from the bakery. From the trunks of treasures in the attics of the castle, Frau Häberle produced a metal stand for the tree, which they put up on a small table in the Great Hall. Now the whole household stood in front of the Christmas tree and watched it rotate on the stand, while the built-in music box tinkled the sweet notes of "Stille Nacht, heilige Nacht." Deeply moved, Frau Häberle dabbed at her eyes. "Who would've thought we were going to have a Christmas tree this year?" she murmured.

Fenris gave his housekeeper a strange look. His brows drew together in a perplexed frown, and Cissy bowed her head to hide her smile. She thought she could also hear underlying amusement in Mrs. Chisholm's voice, when the widow said, "Rather lovely, indeed." She delicately cleared her throat. "Perhaps the decoration of the tree should be done by the master and mistress of the house alone."

Cissy's smile widened even more as her friend ushered everybody out of the Great Hall. Soon only she and her husband remained. With a slightly flabbergasted expression, Fenris looked from the tree to the door and then to her. "What just happened here?" he asked.

Biting her lip, she regarded him from underneath lowered lashes. "I believe they want us to decorate the tree for the evening."

He scowled at her, as if decorating a Christmas tree somehow equaled mucking out the stables of King Augeas. Cissy could only just prevent herself from rolling her eyes. Gosh, he was a dolt, after all!

The line between his brows deepened. "I already helped get that thing!" he complained.

"Fine. And now decorating the tree won't hurt you, either," she snapped, and she slapped the basket with the decorations against his chest.

Sullenly he stopped the rotating of the tree, then

picked an assortment of white ribbons from the basket and tied the first one around a branch. "Perhaps we can ask your dear friend if she doesn't want to contribute some mushed rats," he said nastily.

She glared at him. "Are you such a bugaboo on purpose, or is it just incidental?" she asked in English.

One black eyebrow shot up. "A bugaboo?" he echoed, his voice mocking. "And what's that supposed to be, if I may ask?"

Cissy jammed a gingerbread star onto a twig. "Something that scares the wits out of children."

"Ah." With exaggerated care, he tied a bow around another twig. "Well, then . . ." He shrugged. "It's unavoidable, I should say."

Indeed. With that black scowl and all that snarling, it's no wonder the children of Kirchwalden think he's going to devour them at night. Exasperated, Cissy shook her head. "It can hardly come as a surprise," she mumbled.

He shot her a sharp look. "Yes."

Turning his head away, he busied himself with the next bow, while Cissy continued to maltreat more gingerbread. For some time they worked in smoldering silence.

This was surely not how decorating a Christmas tree was supposed to be! It was intended to be a joyous event, full of merriment and family spirit.

From the corner of her eye, Cissy glanced at her husband. He fumbled with the ribbons and muttered oaths in between when the needles stuck his fingers. The sight of her tall spouse doing battle with the fine, silky ribbons made her smile—until her gaze fell onto his lopsided, crumpled creations. Her heart melted. She reached out and touched one of the bows with her finger.

"What?" he snapped. "Aren't they good enough?"

Heaving a sigh, Cissy rolled her eyes heavenward. But

she kept her voice light. "Do you *really* always have to be such a bugbear?"

Frowning, he finished the bow he was tying. "Is that the same thing as a bugaboo?"

She nodded.

"Then yes."

She waited for some elaboration, but none came. Thoughtfully, she wrinkled her nose. "Is there a purpose to it?"

He glanced at her. His eyes, she saw, were very green. "Yes," he said.

"Hm." Cissy twiddled the ends of one of the bows he had made. "What is it?"

The scowl returned to his face. "You wouldn't want to know."

Indignant, she let the bow be. "Of course I would!"

"Believe me, no." And as cool as you please, he proceeded to tie his last ribbon onto the tree.

Cissy narrowed her eyes and looked daggers at him. "Yes. I. Would."

He snorted.

She tapped her foot on the floor.

He glanced at her foot, then at her face. Very slowly, he turned his body fully toward her. He raised a brow. "You want to know why?" Another snort. He shook his head. "Well, it's very simple," he finally admitted. "It's so I won't do *this*." And with that, he leaned forward and, cocking his head to one side, kissed her.

Everything in Cissy froze.

Fenris's lips moved gently over hers, and one of his hands cradled her jaw as if she were made of fine glass. She had not noticed before how very large his hands were. Large and strong, but with the strength leashed, held in check. His thumb rubbed over her cheek, just as she could feel the tip of his tongue tracing the seam of her lips. Her skin prickled where he touched her. Unfamiliar feelings rushed through Cissy's body and made her shiver. She arched her neck—

But he had already drawn back. His thumb glided over her lower lip, but then he let his hand fall to his side. Straightening, he searched her face. Cissy's whole body seemed to be afflicted with a strange sort of numbness, and so she could only stare at him. A sad little smile lifted his lips. "*That's* why. I think it would be better if you finish decorating the tree alone." He turned and, with measured steps, walked toward the nearest door. Without a single backward glance, he left.

The day proceeded downward from there. When she saw him again, he was moody and aloof once more, hardly sparing her a glance. She could almost believe that kiss under their Christmas tree had never happened. Stonily he watched the exchange of presents, saw to it that the servants all received their little bundle. But that done, he left again.

A hush fell over their little assembly, but with a few words and Mrs. Chisholm's help, Cissy managed to restore the castle's cheerful atmosphere. It was much later, when everybody had gone to their beds and she checked that none of the candles in the tree was still burning, that she discovered another package, lying half hidden behind the silver stand: a small box, held close with a ribbon tied in an eerily familiar bow. "To Celia," she read aloud from the neat label. She rubbed her finger over the letters, smearing the ink a little.

How to understand this husband of hers?

Her heart felt heavy as she tugged the bow loose and lifted the lid of the box. Two small leatherbound books rested on a patch of green velvet. She took one out of the box, turned it in her hands. Golden, square leaves on the spine. Amidst a field of burgundy-red, the title:

Wolfenbach. Her heart thudding unsteadily, she flicked the book open, read the title page.

Castle of Wolfenbach
A
German Story
In Two Volumes
by Mrs. Parsons

A gothic novel set in another Castle of Wolfenbach, probably full of cobwebs and rodent skeletons, too. Cissy's chuckle turned into a little sob. She closed her eyes. He had given her a most curious, funny and thoughtful present. And he must have sent for it several weeks before.

Why, then, was theirs not a real marriage?

A crow cawed overhead. With a jolt, Cissy came back to the present, to this ruined tower of the castle, where she stood, where the wind blew sharply. No, she did not understand her husband. After Christmas he had never again taken a meal with her. It did not help that Mrs. Chisholm had left for Baden-Baden before the New Year and that Cissy was again all alone. By now she had not seen her husband for weeks. Sometimes, though, when she looked out the window in the evenings, she saw a flickering light dancing along the ramparts. Surely this must be him—for who else in this castle would sulk along the ramparts in the darkest hours of the night?

All that was left to her was fleeing into the reassuring world of stories, to lose herself in the lives of fictitious people.

She sighed.

The wind blew so cold: it was time to go back inside.

CHAPTER FOURTEEN

Cissy wandered along the hallways, deeply engrossed in her book, a collection of modern fairy tales she had found on the shelves of the Wolfenbach library. She had started to read it in her room, yet the chair there wasn't comfortable enough to curl up in and spend an afternoon reading. So she had decided to move back to the library instead.

Waldeinsamkeit,
Die mich erfreut,
So morgen wie heut
In ew'ger Zeit,
O wie mich freut
Waldeinsamkeit.

Woodsolitude,
Brings joy to me
Now and tomorrow,
Forevermore,

> *What joy to me,*
> *Woodsolitude.*

Cissy sighed happily. Oh yes, she could well envision the little hut among the birch trees, the small dog running toward the wanderer in greeting, and the magical, beautiful bird which sang of woodsolitude all day and night.

> *Woodsolitude,*
> *Brings joy to me . . .*

And to me. A bright smile lit Cissy's face.

Indeed, she had come to love the hum of the trees at night, the dark, mysterious forests of her new home country, where old castles held old secrets and told of strange stories.

> *What joy to me,*
> *Woodsolitude.*

Eagerly, she read on about how Bertha came to live with the old woman in the forest and how she cared for the little dog and wonderful bird. She almost walked past the door to the library. Without taking her eyes from the letters in the book, she fumbled for the door handle and pushed it open—and held her breath. For now Bertha discovered the secret of the bird: it laid eggs which—

"*Ouch!*"

The door had clicked shut with one of Cissy's fingers still in between.

Her book fell to the floor. Cissy yelped and cursed and finally managed to free her finger. "Oh drat! Oh drat! Oh *drat!*" Flames of pain licked up her arm and made her breath catch in her throat. Whimpering, she cradled her hurt hand and bit her lip to keep from crying.

"Celia?"

Breathing heavily, she turned. Her husband stood in front of her, a frown on his face. His features swam in and out of focus as tears obscured her vision. How vexing to see him again like this, just when pain was making her feel queasy.

His gaze dropped to her hand, then rose back to her face. "Have you hurt yourself?"

"I . . ." Cissy's lips trembled. "The door . . ." She raised her elbow and pointed, yet suddenly a wave of dizziness assaulted her. Her stomach lurched, and as she sagged to her knees a deep humming filled her ears.

She gasped.

A strong arm had snaked around her waist and hauled her up—up against her husband's tall body! Her cheek came to rest against his hard chest. Sandalwood-scented warmth rose to engulf her, and the strong, steady beat of his heart mingled with the whistling in her ears.

"Don't faint on me, sweetheart," he said.

It was strange, she thought dizzily, to hear his voice rumbling in his chest and to have the resonance of those deep tones tickle her ear. Then her world lurched again as he hoisted her in his arms and carried her over to the settee.

"Just close your eyes," he murmured with strange gentleness.

Everything was whirling around her, and the humming in her ears grew louder and louder, but—had he really just brushed his lips over her temple?

Carefully, he placed her down on the settee. He reclined beside her, and the next thing she knew was that her head rested on his thigh, while he held up her legs with her ankles—and, thankfully, the hem of her dress— gripped in one of his hands.

With a squeak, she opened her eyes. "Fenris . . ."

"Shhh." His free hand cupped the side of her face.

"Close your eyes and relax. You'll soon feel better." His thumb stroked in soothing circles over her temple and sent delicious shivers through her whole body, despite the throbbing pain in her finger. Indeed, she almost forgot all about her finger as she relaxed against him. With a small sigh, she sank into a sea of new sensations: the hardness of his thigh against her head, the feeling of his hands holding her. They were so large and strong! She could easily feel their strength, a curious contrast to the tenderness of his touch.

His body emanated cozy warmth, and if it hadn't been for the dull pain, she could have lain like that forever. So comfortable, and yet exciting.

Her heart did a curious little jump. Her breath caught. She moved her head restlessly against his thigh.

"Shhh." His fingertips lightly stroked her brow, her cheek, while his breathing grew a little ragged. As if in answer, her breasts started to tingle.

"Ohh." She sighed and subtly arched her back.

The caress of his hand stopped. Fenris cleared his throat. "Are you . . . feeling any better?" he asked.

"Marvelous." She blinked and smiled up at him. Oh, he was terribly handsome, this husband of hers—in a dark, deliciously rugged way. A hint of color accentuated his cheekbones. His gaze skittered away.

"Well, then . . ." He helped her sit up. "What exactly happened, anyway?"

"I crushed my finger in the door." She raised one shoulder and rubbed her chin against it. "I was reading and didn't pay any attention." Smiling wryly, she looked up at him, willing him to share the small joke. He gazed fixedly at her hand.

"Does it hurt a lot?"

"Oh, well . . ." She held up her hand to inspect her finger. What she saw made her grimace. "Eww." Half of her nail was crushed, and a little blood had welled up.

"Let me see." He cradled her hand in both of his. "Och, your poor finger," he murmured, his voice gruff. And then he bent his head and, very, very carefully, kissed it.

The world rumbled to an abrupt halt. The moment lengthened until it seemed to stretch into eternity.

In utter astonishment, Cissy looked down at his bowed head. She could see where his hair lay in black curls against his nape. His lips were soft on her skin. They opened, and his warm breath whispered over her knuckles. He made a small sound deep in his throat, and then he turned her hand around and pressed a lingering, moist kiss into the center of her palm.

Cissy's heart jumped. The world resumed its normal pace, quickened even, and the blood still whirled in her ears.

Fenris's lips wandered to her wrist, found the thin, delicate skin over blue veins. The nick of his teeth made her breath catch in her throat.

"Fenris." A whisper of sound. Her whole body tingled, and she yearned for . . . she knew not what. "Fenris."

But then, he simply stopped.

He kept his head bent over her hand. Cissy looked down on his tousled black hair, watched how his shoulders moved with his ragged breaths. For a moment this was the only sound to break the silence.

Finally, he exhaled a long sigh. He pressed another, but fleeting, kiss on her palm and raised her hand to hold it against his cheek. Her fingers curled a little. Their tips rasped over his stubbly skin.

"Forgive me," he whispered.

And with that, he stood and hurried out of the room.

* * *

Stumbling, Fenris rushed up the stairs, away from his wife, away from temptation. God, he had done it again. He had again lost control and kissed her, touched her. Gasping, he halted in front of his study and leaned his face against the cold wall, the coolness of the stone soothing his hot skin. He closed his eyes. Lust drummed a wild beat inside his temple.

The delicious weight of his wife's head on his lap, her silky soft hair spilling over his thighs. The vulnerable arch of her throat, creamy white skin, so very fragile. And—oh—the gentle swell of her breasts.

How he had wanted to close his hand around one smooth globe, to free it from the restraint of her stays, to test the weight of it in his palm. What color would the nipple be? Would it be large and pale, or small and dark like a cherry? Sweet like a cherry . . . ? Fenris softly groaned.

God, how long had it been since he had touched a woman? Nine years? Ten? Too long, certainly. Too long.

A sweet little melody cut into his reverie. He opened his eyes and slowly turned. In the middle compartment of the grandfather clock, the dwarves were merrily hacking away in their mine. *Click-clack, click-clack.* The melody stopped, and the dwarves halted their efforts. With a whirring sound, the eight on the face of the clock turned inward and revealed the King of Dwarves looking yearningly up at the sheep while the clock struck three. Long after the king had disappeared and the door of the middle compartment had closed, Fenris still leaned against the wall and stared.

Ten years. It had been ten years since he had last touched a woman. And she had been a whore with disgust in her eyes. His body had repulsed her, and despite the money he had given her, she had not been able to hide it.

He gave a strangled laugh.

What had his brother said? What right did the King of Dwarves have to court the fairy princess? *"He's just an ugly old dwarf, after all. The likes of him shouldn't go around courting fairy princesses."*

The likes of him.

Wearily, Fenris closed his eyes.

No, he had absolutely no right to bother a fairy princess. Not when all he could hope for from her was pity.

"All right, so first he pretends he wants to eat up my hand and then he mumbles an apology and races out of the room? Like he kisses me and then races out of the room and avoids me like the plague forevermore. Argh!" Cissy threw up her hands while she marched up and down in her room. "It doesn't make sense! *He* doesn't make sense!" With a sigh, she stopped. "Drat that foolish man!" Impatiently she rubbed at her finger, which— apart from a curious numbness in one spot—no longer displayed any unpleasant reminders of its encounter with the door a few days ago. Which was more than could be said for her peace of mind. *That* had been completely shattered by the event. Or rather, by what had happened afterward. Even more so than by the light, fleeting kiss he had given her under the Christmas tree.

Exasperated, Cissy blew an errant strand of hair out of her face. No, the incident of the settee had more than shattered her peace of mind; it had turned her into a goosecap! Into a hare-brained ninny!

She shot a guilty look at her wardrobe, the deepest depths of which hid the dress she had been wearing that day. The *unwashed* dress. The dress to which still clung— given, very faintly—the scent of sandalwood.

Groaning, Cissy buried her face in her hands. "A maggot-headed loony, that's what you are!" she mumbled.

She had hidden the dress carefully, so Marie the maid

wouldn't find it and give it to the washing. She had hidden the dress so she could scramble out of bed at night, tiptoe to her wardrobe, take the garment out and bury her nose in it to inhale that sweet, elusive scent.

"Ooooh!" She let herself fall back on her bed. "Henbrained pea-goose!" she told the canopy.

But oh, how he fascinated her, this husband of hers. She even liked the growling part, when he was bristling with anger and looking very much like a real demon wolf. Yet she had also caught glimpses of a gentler side. Her favorite memory was probably the Christmas tree hunt, when he had trudged patiently through the snow, an axe thrown over his shoulder, while Mrs. Chisholm had ordered him and his valet from tree to tree. They had all looked like snowmen themselves, bundled in thick layers of clothing, caps drawn down over their ears, and their cheeks bright red with the crisp wintry air. And despite his nondescript, rather shabby black coat and woolen cap, Fenris had looked so dashing. Cissy heaved a sigh.

How he had strode through the forest, handling that axe as if it weighed no more than a feather. Tall and dark, he had walked like Thor himself.

She frowned.

Well, if Thor had been dark-haired and handling an axe instead of a hammer, that is.

"Hmm." She wrinkled her nose. Earnestly regarding the canopy, she put her folded hands on her belly and pondered this particular problem. Tall, with raven-black hair like . . .

. . . like . . .

Her face lit up.

"Lancelot du Lac!" Triumphantly, she rose up to lean on her elbows.

A moment later her face fell.

Lancelot du Lac, who betrayed his king with the queen.

She groaned and flopped back onto the pillows.

No, not Lancelot.

Merlin?

No, Merlin had ended up being caught under a hawthorne tree because he was so bedazzled he didn't see through Nimuë's treachery.

Cissy rolled her eyes. Perhaps men were totally jolter-headed beings in general.

Which would account for the fact that she hadn't had a wedding night yet, and that her marriage was not a real marriage. Since it was the only one she was ever likely to have, however, she wanted to make it work. Yes, this was not a love match, but surely some sort of companionship was not too much to ask for. Yet she would get neither wedding night nor companionable marriage if all she did was lie around and think up ridiculous similes. Inappropriate, ridiculous similes on top of that!

Cissy sat up.

No, she would not languish like one of those insipid storybook heroines waiting for a large bell to fall on her head. Or for the wicked uncle to come chasing her with a wickedly sharp knife. No, she would take a large frying pan and bang it over the wicked uncle's head—in a manner of speaking. She would take *action*.

Determined, she scrambled down from the bed and shook out her skirts. If she wanted to get her wedding night, it stood to reason she needed to find out what generally happened on wedding nights. Not that she didn't have a vague idea. After all, she had lived in the country for most of her life—she hoped, though, that intercourse between people did not too much resemble the mating of sheep. Having somebody jump about on your back must be terribly uncomfortable, and as far as she could tell, the female sheep had always looked utterly bored by it all. As if they couldn't get back to grazing soon enough. Poor sheep.

Cissy took a deep breath. Yes, she had a general idea of what happened on weddings nights. But she was more interested in the details, the . . . trappings, which it seemed that she couldn't count on her husband to take care of either. Of course, her forwardness might be considered terribly improper. In cases such as hers, however, impropriety seemed to be a much better option than, say, a bell on the head. Indeed, one might even go so far as to say it was her wifely duty!

"So . . ." She rubbed her hands. She knew where she would start looking: the library. For each library—as everybody knew quite well—stocked certain books which usually remained hidden from curious eyes. Several years ago, she had found one such book under her brother's bed. It had been in French, which had had her wondering, because her brother's French was not fluent, to say the least. But then she had seen the illustrations and had realized her brother didn't hide this book under his bed for its literary merit. Unfortunately, somebody coming up the stairs had seen her shove the book back under the bed before she'd had time to study the pictures properly. The next time she'd looked, the book had vanished and she had never found it again.

In a library as big as Wolfenbach's there should be *something* to make up for it.

Cissy marched to the library.

For two days, she searched the shelves. She found a treatise on the diseases of sheep; a copy of Kristian Franz Paulini's *Heylsame Dreck-Apotheke*—who would have thought that the stuff apothecaries sold as "White Gentian" was in truth dried doggie poop?—a book called

Helle Barden—was this about bards, or about weapons and the author orthographically challenged?—and, wrapped in a bit of sackcloth, a late medieval tome totally covered in mold. But there were no hidden compartments, no interesting French books with even more interesting illustrations.

On the third day, Cissy finally admitted defeat. Wherever the men of the House of Wolfenbach hid their secret books, it was not in the library. Thoughtful, Cissy tapped her finger against her cheek.

No doubt, she needed help. And there was only one person whom she could ask.

She hurried back to her room and got out quill, ink and paper. *Dearest friend,* she wrote. She tickled the end of the feather over her nose. The wording needed careful consideration, for who knew who else might read these lines? After all, she didn't want to provide amusement for any fool at some German censor's office. She sighed, and eventually continued, *I hope this letter finds you well. I have abided by your advice, yet the circumstances of my life here are no different from what they used to be before your departure. I am impatient for change, however, and eagerly await your further advice on the matter. Yours &c.*

Carefully, she sanded and sealed the letter, before she wrote the address in sweeping lines on the back. *"Voilà."*

Softly humming under her breath, she went in search of Rambach and gave him the precious letter to put into the mail.

A week later, a package arrived from Baden-Baden. Gleefully Cissy brought it upstairs to open it in the privacy of her room. Even though, of course, it would have been difficult to find many prying eyes at Wolfenbach, still it was better to be safe than sorry. She recalled the tale of the farmer knight who took only half the dragon's hoard, so he wouldn't get a curse laid upon it. Of course, with dragons' hoards it was safer to keep wholly away. After all, the theft of a single golden cup caused the downfall of a whole nation.

Sinking down on her bed, Cissy started to pry open the knots of string. Eagerly, she ripped open the paper—and a small red box fell into her lap. Taken aback, she turned it around. This was certainly too small to hold a book! No, it held—eagerly, she opened the lid—a stack of cards?

Cissy blinked several times, dumbfounded.

Very, very carefully, as if it might bite off her finger, she lifted the topmost card. She slowly turned the strong, ivory-colored paper around.

The ace of hearts.

How fitting.

Cissy frowned. How was a deck of cards supposed to help her with her marital problems?

The single ruby-red heart on the card seemed to wink at her mockingly. "Stupid thing," she muttered and shoved it back into the stack. Impatiently, she looked for an accompanying letter. Yet all that she found was an uncharacteristically short note: *My dear, I hope this will help to bring light into the darkness. Else have a little more patience with your husband. I am sure he will eventually relent. Yours, &c.*

Mrs. Chisholm obviously liked to keep at least the censor's officers in the dark. Unfortunately, Cissy could not make any sense of her message, either. She read the note a second and a third time, even held the sheet of paper against the light to see if there was any hidden message to be found that way. After all, Mrs. Chisholm had written:

Bringing light into the darkness . . . light into—

Cissy smacked her forehead. "That's it!" Hastily, she

picked up the ace of hearts once more and held it against the light coming through her window. Very faintly, a picture appeared around the heart.

The blood thudded in her ears as she started a frantic search for a candle and her tinderbox. The candle lit, she held the card against the glow. As if by magic, the image appeared, strong and clear: a man and a woman on a bed and—

Cissy's breath caught. Her stomach somersaulted.

The woman sat on the man and, with their clothes pushed out of the way, she had . . . impaled herself on him.

The image trembled.

Cissy licked her suddenly dry lips. This was certainly most improper again, but she couldn't help staring in helpless fascination. She could see the hair around the woman's secret place. Her round breasts with puckered nipples were bared, and she was smiling down at the man beneath her.

Human intercourse, she was happy to see, appeared to be much nicer than the mating of sheep. Cissy's breathing quickened.

She imagined baring herself thus for Fenris, spreading her legs wide while she sat on his lap, with this . . . part of him deep inside her. Would he look at her like the man in the picture looked at his woman? Her face flamed. "Oh my," she whispered.

Nevertheless, she took up the next card . . . and the next . . . and the next. And on each she saw that mysterious act which could make two bodies one, that act in all its curious variations—people making love on beds or chairs, even hanging from trees, with the men sitting beneath the women, or lying above or behind or kneeling or standing. She saw women proudly displaying their bodies, taking delight in what they were doing.

As if in answer, Cissy's breasts tingled and heat pooled

low in her belly. Yet it was the queen of spades that made her moan softly: smiling serenely, the queen leaned on a table, her thighs and belly bared. And between her legs sat a man and he . . .

With a groan, Cissy let herself fall back against the pillows. Breathing heavily, she pressed the queen of spades to her heart. With wide eyes she stared up at the canopy while the blood hummed in her veins.

Was she the most awful wanton for wishing to share this same kind of intimacy with her husband? She remembered the sight of his naked torso, all that pale, smooth skin stretched taut over hard muscle. How her fingers had itched to slide through the springy dark hair on his chest. Perhaps even through that intriguing whorl around his navel.

Her breath hitched, and she turned her hot face into the pillow.

She would have to pursue him, to go to him, to undress herself, stand naked in front of him. How could she cross this line of propriety without feeling shame?

Cissy bit her lip.

You've been given this one chance at happiness. Do you want to let it slip through your fingers because you're afraid to side-step social conventions?

She rolled onto her back.

Very slowly, her hand curled into a fist.

She would get her wedding night. She would brave the demon wolf. After all, all that was needed to transform the fairy tale beast into an adorable prince, was a kiss.

Just a simple kiss.

CHAPTER FIFTEEN

If she had hoped for a quick solution to her problem, Cissy was disappointed: after two weeks she still had had no opportunity to test her newly gained knowledge. The snow had started to thaw and had left the world in shades of muddy gray. Only the forest stood as dark and forbidding as ever.

Woodsolitude,
brings joy to me . . .

Or not.

Cissy grimaced. Actually, she was quite sick of it. She carelessly threw the book she was reading on her bed; it was late at night, almost time to extinguish the lights. Another day spent reading. If she continued at this pace, she would have gone through the whole Wolfenbach library before summer.

She sighed.

Another day spent without once seeing her husband. As much as she appreciated the contents of his library, she would have preferred to actually see *him* once in a while.

A knock on the door announced her maid, come to inquire whether she needed anything else for the night. *Only my husband,* Cissy thought wryly. "No, thank you, Marie, there's nothing."

Yet instead of leaving the room, the maid hesitated and shuffled her feet. "*Gnädige Frau,* I . . . um . . ." A soft blush appeared on her cheeks.

"Yes, what is it?"

Marie twisted her fingers. "I've meant to ask you if I could have a free afternoon on Thursday, *gnädige Frau.* It's the start of the carnival and I wanted to go to town and watch the parade of the *Hemdklunker.*"

"The *Hemdklunker?*" Her interest roused, Cissy leaned forward. "What are these?"

"Everybody dresses in a white nightgown and nightcap and powders his face with flour." Marie took a step toward the bed. "And then there's a big parade." She smoothed her hands over her skirt. "It is great fun . . ."

"Of course!" And because Cissy loved to discover new things, she asked, "Will you let me go with you? We can take the gig."

"Actually I meant to walk—"

"To walk?" Cissy gaped at her. "Won't that take terribly long?" It took over an hour to get to Kirchwalden by carriage!

Her maid shook her head. "Not if we take the footpath."

"Through the forest?" A prickling sense of excitement filled Cissy. Here at last it was: an adventure to break the monotony of her days.

And thus, the following Thursday, shortly after midday, the two young women set out on their way down to the valley. The path dived deep into the forest, and the dark trees closed in on them. The air was filled with the scent of wet earth and rotting leaves. Sometimes a small animal rustled in the underbush or a bird chirped overhead. In the distance Cissy could hear the gurgling of a small stream, and it almost seemed to her as if time itself had stopped in the musty twilight of the woods.

What joy to me,
Woodsolitude.

And who knew what they would find beyond the next bend? The castle of Eckbert the Fair and his Bertha? The gingerbread house from *Hansel and Gretel?* Cissy giggled. After the winter and the thaw, the gingerbread would be all soaked and mushy. Not the nicest of abodes, even for a witch.

Marie threw her a strange look. "Are you all right, *gnädige Frau?*"

"Oh, yes. Yes." Cissy grinned. She had insisted that both of them wore nightgowns over their outer clothes and nightcaps instead of bonnets. After all, she wanted to be authentic.

It took not quite an hour to reach Kirchwalden, yet the walk through the fresh, crisp air energized Cissy. She nearly burst with her eagerness to see and experience new things. She was not disappointed: the streets of the small town teemed with cheerful bustle. Everywhere were people in nightgowns and flour-pale faces, but Cissy also spotted other, more eerie disguises: faces hidden behind grotesque wooden masks and dark hoods. At the sight, a chill ran down her spine. Then she forgot all about these other masks, as she heard the sweet ring of small bells on the donkey ears of a jester's cap, the clatter of wooden rattles and the sharp slaps of blown-up pigs' bladders. The air hummed with the sound of innumerable voices and laughter, so much laughter.

"Oh, this is wonderful, Marie!" Cissy exclaimed, a little breathless with excitement. Laughing, she looked around—but her maid had disappeared.

Cissy frowned. She glanced this way and that, stood on

tiptoe for a better view. Yet the features of the faces all around her were obscured by flour. They formed an indistinguishable sea of white planes with wide open, laughing red mouths.

"Ah, well . . ." Cissy shrugged. She slipped through the crowd and worked her way forward to the market. From a street trader, she bought an apple glazed with red, sticky sweetness, which melted on her tongue and stuck to her teeth and lips. And when finally the parade of the *Hemdklunker* marched by with a din and much clattering, she laughed and cheered and clapped with the rest of the crowd. Afterwards, she drifted along through the masses, gaping with amazement and utterly enchanted. However, the sight of a golden head made her halt. For a moment she thought it must be Leopold von Wolfenbach—but what could he want in Kirchwalden?

The slap of a pig's bladder on her cheek made her forget all about her brother-in-law. She winced. But almost immediately, she heard the boisterous shout, "For good luck! For good luck!" Rubbing her cheek, she smiled again—and chuckled as she saw the flour now clinging to her mitten.

Only slowly did she become aware that the daylight had begun to wane. With a jolt, she finally realized it must be much later than she had thought. It was more than time to be on her way back to the castle, for darkness would fall much sooner in the forest.

As she pushed through the crowd, she was struck by the increased frenzy she could feel all around her. The smell of alcohol and human sweat saturated the air. Why had she not noticed before that the numbers of white *Hemdklunker* had dwindled? More people in colorful costumes surrounded her now, and wooden masks. Long-nosed, with leering grins or feral snarls.

Sharp ridges were the wooden cheekbones. The masks muffled the voices and lent them a strangely hollow sound.

A fight broke out on the street before her. Fists flew.

The breath caught in Cissy's throat. With her heart beating madly, she quickly slipped onto a sidestreet. For a while the hustle and bustle continued, then the crowd gradually thinned. Cissy lengthened her steps. She hoped Marie would be all right. But then, her maid had lived here all of her life; she would know how to deal with this.

On the other side of the street, the door to an inn opened and a pair of drunken men tumbled down the stairs. To the delight of the people around them, they rolled through the mud before they finally managed to get to their feet.

Cissy slipped past them unnoticed. She threw a look over a shoulder. Some way behind her she could detect a trio of particularily nasty wooden masks. Devils, demons, whatnot. Shuddering a little, she again quickened her strides.

Well, really, her worries were probably for nothing. These were just the normal, boisterous celebrations of a small town. Back at their small assemblies in Yorkshire, old Squire Elrich had always fallen into a drunken stupor before half the evening was over. With his head sunk back, he had lounged in a chair for the rest of the time, snoring loudly and displaying his rows of black, rotten teeth for all to see.

Cissy couldn't help chuckling at the memory.

And woe be to him who had dared to disturb Squire Elrich's sleep! The best thing the unfortunate could hope for was getting the man's heavy walking stick smacked over his head. And at one of Mrs. Quirking's musicales Elrich had actually thrown her good china vase at the piano player. It had probably been the shortest musicale in the history of mankind.

Oh yes. Celia grinned. Squire Elrich would have liked the carnival in Kirchwalden!

She reached the last house in the street, which dwindled down to a muddy path through a meadow. The forest loomed darkly some way before her. Cissy heaved a sigh of relief.

The din of the crowd had receded; this part of the town was almost deserted for now. She cast a look behind her . . . and froze. The way was deserted apart from that trio of tall, masked figures. And they were much closer than before.

Surely they didn't . . . wouldn't . . .

Cissy started to walk a little faster. Her heart hammered against her ribs, and her breath wheezed through her nose. She darted another glance over her shoulder. Nearer still.

"Oh no!" She took a deep breath and . . . bumped into a solid, muscular body.

She shrieked.

"What the hell do you think you're doing down here?" her husband asked in his most frigid tones.

Gasping, Cissy pressed a hand against her racing heart. "W-what?" A most unsettling habit this, for a man to pop out of thin air.

"And these . . ." His eyes narrowing, Fenris looked beyond her to the masked trio. With a swish, he drew a glinting sword and stepped around her toward them. "Go and look for some other entertainment," he growled.

Cissy turned. The masked figures had stopped at some distance—and small wonder, for Fenris stood in an agressive stance, his legs apart, his shoulders slightly crouched, like a wolf ready to pounce. The fading sunlight glinted on his sword. How curious, Cissy thought numbly; her husband didn't even need a wooden mask to look like a demon. He bristled with barely leashed violence.

She blinked. *A sword?*

The masks slowly swung to and fro as the men regarded him, dumbstruck. "Eh," one of them finally protested, "we found her first!"

Fenris's muscles tensed. "Oh really? Care to discuss the point further?" Cissy could well picture him giving them a wolfish smile. His blade danced through the air, softly swishing in a graceful, deadly arch.

The trio stared.

Perhaps it was the aggressive power he emanated, or perhaps it was the fact that he had a sword and they had not. "Bah. Too much trouble for a silly chit," one of them finally mumbled. The others muttered their agreements and backed away. Then they shrugged, turned, and sauntered back to the town.

Cissy heaved a sigh of relief. "Well, that was—"

Snarling a violent oath, Fenris thrust his blade back into the sheath hanging at his side. Whirling, he grabbed her arm and dragged her on into the forest.

"W-what—"

"Shut up!" His grip tightened painfully. "How could you have been so damn stupid to go to town today? Have the crows picked out your brains?"

"I—"

"And what the hell are you wearing?" He scanned her body and his eyes nearly popped out of his head. "Have you completely taken leave of your senses?" he yelled. "To run around in a bloody nightgown when the bloody town is swarming with bloody drunkards?"

Annoyance replaced her gratitude. How dare he treat her like this? Especially when she never saw him. "I—"

"And what's this? A bloody nightcap?" He yanked it off her head and flung it into the forest.

"Hey, that was—"

"A bloody nightcap when it's still so chilly? Do you want your ears to fall off with the cold?" He fumbled with his coat and drew out a woolen cap, which he proceeded to plunk on her head.

Cissy tried to ward him off. "This is much too warm. We're walking and—"

"Leave it on!" he snarled at her. And with his chest heaving, he actually bared his teeth.

Cissy blinked.

Perhaps he had the rabies? She opened her mouth. Closed it again. "Well," she finally said. "Where have you come from, anyway? And with a sword on top of it!"

Which, she realized, was a mistake, because it set him off all over again. So he dragged her on and snarled and shouted about how he had gone to search for his ninny-brained wife because, like any normal human with some brains, he had known that carnival spelled trouble and that stupid little chits from the other side of the world had better stay away from it.

"And how should *I* have known?" she yelled back, all her anger and frustration finally bubbling over. "When Mr. High-and-Mighty never deigns to show his face in my presence and goes skulking on the ramparts instead? I thought it would be *fun*, when Marie told me about this day—"

They stopped again. "And where is your maid now?" Fenris rounded on her.

"Er . . ." Cissy blinked rapidly. He was so near that she could smell the warm scent coming off his body. Sandalwood and musky sweat—how utterly distracting! It reminded her of the kiss they had shared, of resting her head in his lap. Of the cards she had kept hidden in one of the drawers of her dresser. She heaved a dreamy little sigh.

"What? *What?*"

Her eyes snapped open. Did he *have* to be so loud? "I . . . um . . . lost her."

"You lost her!" Fenris threw up his hands, nearly dislocating her arm. "God, you're even more stupid than I thought!" He turned and walked on. "I guess Marie can take care of herself," he muttered darkly. "After all, *she's* got some brains."

Cissy had finally had enough. She dug in her heels and wrenched her arm free. "Why do you have to be so mean?" she shouted at him. With grim satisfaction she watched his eyes widen in surprise at her attack. "Yes, I wanted to have some adventure, some fun! Is that so bad? And yes, I learnt my lesson, thank you very much. But do you have to rub it in? Do you have to harp on and on and on? Can't you just . . ." She bit her lip. "I know it could've been ugly, yes, I know that now. So can't you just . . . I mean . . ." Her voice trailed away as she realized that she was all alone in the forest with her husband. A husband who clearly cared on some level about her. And thanks to her cards, she knew that there were possibilities. . . . Given, it was a little bit cold, but she was willing to make some small sacrifices. Perhaps she should just try a different strategy with her spouse.

She cocked her head to the side and gave him a pleading look through her lashes. "Hug me?" she whispered. "And perhaps kiss me better, and—"

He gave her a look of utter disgust and stamped farther up the hill.

Cissy stared after him. After a long moment, she took a deep breath and exhaled noisily. "Well, I guess not." Apparently, danger would not further intimacy with the demon wolf. Instead it made him mad as hell. "Drat."

With a sigh, she went to follow him back to his den.

CHAPTER SIXTEEN

Some more weeks passed, and finally Cissy's patience with her bugbearish husband snapped. He couldn't just be nice and sweet one day and go snarling at her the next. Or buy her the sweetest present and then avoid her like the plague. Or rescue her and immediately afterwards start yelling at her like a madman. No, she wouldn't put up with the antics of this demon wolf any longer!

When she thought about the moments when he had been tender and protective, when he had kissed her with such sweetness, her heart always melted with longing. *This* was the man she wanted. This was how their marriage could work—and she *wanted* it to work. She simply had to force the demon wolf to cooperate.

It was, Cissy thought, very simple: she needed a plan. How to seduce your husband in ten easy steps. Thanks to Mrs. Chisholm's present, she already knew a little about steps five through ten. And she knew that Step Two—getting undressed; Step Three—getting your husband undressed; and Step Four—getting into bed, were not really obligatory. Indeed, if the cards were to be believed, one never fully undressed for these matters. Why, all the men wore at least shirts . . . even if they actually made it into a bed!

This point of her ponderings always left Cissy rather dissatisfied. For she remembered the sight of her husband's naked chest and the intriguing whorl of hair around his navel with much fondness. How was she supposed to properly admire his chest when he was wearing a shirt?

She wondered whether the shirt was somehow negotiable.

Yet before she could put Step Three into action, she needed to take care of Step One—getting hold of your husband. Thus, one afternoon she went to the library and chose a strategically favorable window seat that overlooked the courtyard. There she settled down with a book and awaited her husband's return from his daily ride. She lost herself in the adventures of Peter Schlemihl, who sold his shadow to the devil for a magical purse producing unheard-of riches. She grimaced. Her husband's snooty brother would probably sell his shadow, too, if it would lead him to the dratted Wolfenbach Hoard.

Cissy snorted.

If it had ever existed, the Wolfenbach ancestor must have hidden it so well that his descendants would never find it. A little bit like a squirrel hiding its nuts. Only, no young trees would ever sprout from gemstones and gold.

Chuckling, she read on.

An hour or two later, she finally heard the clatter of horse hooves down in the courtyard. She leaned forward and looked outside.

Fenris had not bothered to wear a hat, so the sunlight made his tousled hair shimmer like raven wings. The wind had stained his cheeks with ruddy color, and for once he looked almost carefree and happy. Cissy watched Johann walk outside. As soon as the valet reached up to help his master dismount, Fenris's expression changed. The happiness dimmed, the sparkle of carefree joy died. Leaning heavily on his valet, he slid out of his saddle and to the ground, before he took the crutches Johann had brought.

Cissy's heart contracted as she watched. Like a bird whose wings had been clipped and broken, her husband hobbled over the cobblestones.

Cissy touched her fingertips to the window as he walked up to the door and disappeared inside. Uncertainly, she bit her lip. Perhaps she should set her plan into motion on another day, at another time. She looked down at her book. Should she follow Peter Schlemihl's story and find out to which wondrous lands his seven-league boots would carry him? It seemed . . . safer.

Listlessly, she turned the page. From Tibet through Asia to Africa Peter went, following the course of the sun to Egypt and the pyramids. Cissy sighed.

Twirling a loose strand of hair around her finger, she wondered whether it was really true that Napoleon's soldiers had cut off the nose of the Sphinx. If the Sphinx had to lose her nose, why couldn't it have simply broken off and dropped onto that detestable little Frenchman? It would have spared many people a whole lot of grief.

She thought of her husband, who surely carried an enormous burden.

She looked down at her book. "Drat it all!" She closed it with a snap and sprang up. She was heartily sick of Peter Schlemihl and his story. How could anybody be so bird-witted as to sell his shadow and not think about the consequences? And how could any groom be such a pea-goose as to try and evade his wedding night?

"Men!" Cissy muttered darkly as she went to put the book back on its shelf. A woman wouldn't have been so feebleminded as to sell any old man in gray her shadow for a purse! Ha! A mere purse? No, a woman would have taken the mandrake and thus would have secured for herself not only great riches, but also love and happiness. But no, the nodcock male had to go for the obvious. Snorting, Cissy stomped out of the library. Well, she would show her husband that a woman went for it all. Yes, she had married him to keep this castle and probably wouldn't have married him at all if not for her father's will. Who would want to marry a snarling demon wolf? But . . .

She frowned.

Of course, he could be a rather *sweet* demon wolf at times. Like when he had done battle with the ribbons for the Christmas tree. He had been so utterly adorable. And later, when he had kissed her . . .

Her steps faltered. She touched her mouth, remembered the feeling of his lips on hers. She sighed dreamily. *Beautiful.*

But still, it had been just a little kiss, which was now only a pale memory. And Cissy had enough of pale memories and little kisses. She wanted it all! She wanted friendship and company, and yes, the joys and delights that Mrs. Chisholm's cards promised.

Determinedly, she marched up the stairs to her husband's room. Taking a deep breath, she raised her hand and knocked at the door. There was no answer.

She cocked her head to the side and knocked again. Though she listened carefully, there was still no answer.

Cissy chewed on her lower lip. She looked up and down the hallway.

"All right," she murmured. "Three time's lucky." And she knocked again.

No answer.

Cissy chewed on her lip some more. Then she sniffed and wriggled her nose. "But he *must* be in there!"

Without her volition, her hand came to rest on the doorhandle. The next moment, the door swung open with a loud creak.

Cissy winced. Here was another door that needed to be taken care of. But first . . .

Carefully, she took a step forward and peeked into the room. It was dark-panelled, with a frieze depicting a hunting scene on the upper third of the wall. Lush, red Persian rugs covered the stone tiles on the floor. In the corner was the obligatory hunter-green tiled stove. When she had last been in this room, after Fenris's fall, she had had neither time nor inclination to take it all in. But now . . .

Cissy took another tiny step forward.

Now she could also see the enormous four-poster bed with drapes of dark green velvet.

Her husband, however, was nowhere to be seen. Unless . . .

Another tiny step and Cissy could peek around the door.

Unless he hid in the enormous wardrobe. Which she doubted. He was, after all, not a *total* lumpkin.

From a small doorway on the other side of the bed came the sounds of splashing water.

It was, she knew, terribly naughty to enter other people's rooms without being invited, and yet the temptation proved too great. He was, after all, her husband.

Cissy tiptoed fully into the room and closed the door behind her to shut out any witnesses of her indiscretion. Though what witnesses there might be in this almost deserted castle was anybody's guess.

The door screeched in protest.

Drat! She closed her eyes.

"Johann, is that you?" came the muffled voice of her husband from the other room, amidst more splashing of water.

She grimaced. *No, not exactly.* She opened her eyes again, rubbed her nose. *Courage, Celia. Courage.*

She crept forward, toward the intriguing doorway.

Another step . . . and another . . . around the bed . . . My, wasn't it large?

Shivering a little, Cissy thought of the intriguing possibilities a large bed provided. Like the ace of diamonds. Or the eight of spades. Or . . . the two of clubs!

"Oh my!" she breathed as hot tingles spread through her body.

Hastily, she took another step forward and came to an abrupt halt in the doorway. Her mouth fell open. Her right hand reached up and covered her frantically thumping heart.

For in front of her, her husband stood with his back turned to her, and all he was wearing were his tight moleskin riding trousers and his wooden leg. Muscles bunched and flowed in his shoulders and back as he sponged himself down. His skin glistened wetly, while sweat and dust still clogged his hair. At his nape, the strands lay damply against the skin.

Utterly fascinated, Cissy watched how a droplet of water fell onto a shoulder blade. For a moment it hovered there like a tiny diamond, then Fenris moved, his muscles rippled, and the water slid down toward the groove of his backbone, gained momentum, swept along tiny drops clinging to his skin, slithered down and down and disappeared into the waistband of his trousers.

Cissy drew in a much needed breath of air. *Oh my!*

"Johann?"

Starting wildy, she couldn't prevent a tiny squeak

from escaping. Fenris's head snapped around. His green eyes widened.

Nervously, she lifted her hand and wriggled her fingers in what she hoped looked to be a friendly wave. "Um, it's me," she croaked.

His eyes narrowed.

Uh-oh.

In order to evade his burning gaze, she dropped her eyes. They came to rest on a powerful pectoral covered by curly black hair. In between hung glittering drops of water, and a dark brown nipple shyly peeped out as if in greeting.

Cissy licked her suddenly dry lips.

Fenris fully turned toward her, hands on his hips, and water pelted the floor from the sponge he held in his right hand. "What do you want?"

She heard the exasperation in his voice, but just then, water collected on one damp curl, formed a large, shimmering drop and . . .

Cissy held her breath.

Gracefully it slid into the interesting little groove below his ribs, trembled indecisively before it gave in and rolled down over the dips and bumps of his tightly muscled belly. With avid fascination she followed the drop's journey. And then, there it was: the intriguing little whorl of hair around the sweet indentation of his navel.

Oooh my. Cissy gave a happy sigh. Her skin prickled deliciously. Butterflies fluttered in her stomach. Dear heavens, she was certain she could look at this alluring, silky trail of hair forever and never tire of the sight.

Fenris cleared his throat. "Are you here for a freak show?" he asked.

Cissy flinched and only then became aware of what exactly she was doing. Her face flaming, she slowly raised her eyes back to his. They were blazing with anger, and dark color stained his cheeks. He looked . . .

"What?" he snapped.

Drat, the growling demon wolf was back! She squeezed her eyes shut.

"Have I provided enough freakish entertainment for you?" he continued. His breathing had turned harsh.

"No, no, it wasn't . . ." Her voice trailed away as she became aware how her answer could be misconstrued. She blinked. Given the furious twisting of his lips, her words *had* been misconstrued. Helplessly, she stared at him. "It isn't what you think."

"No?" Aggressively, he widened his stance and stared back at her. "What is it, then?" A muscle jumped in his cheek. Yes, he looked exactly like a wolf ready to pounce.

Cissy swallowed. "I . . . um. I thought—"

"Yes?"

"Er . . ." She bit her lip. This was probably not the best moment to tell her husband she wanted to have her wicked way with him. Or him to have his with her. Together. In his wonderfully large bed.

Don't think of the bed!

"I . . . um . . ." Her fingers drummed against her thigh, while her thoughts raced. ". . . Um . . ." She gave him a false, bright smile.

"Has the cat got your tongue?" he growled, clearly unimpressed.

Her smile fell. She sighed. Perhaps she should go and find Schlemihl's gray man and sell him her shadow for the mandrake. Love and happiness would automatically be hers, and she wouldn't be forced to stand in front of her husband like a namby-pampy noddy-pole. However, she suspected little gray men keen on other people's shadows were not easily come by. So it was back to dealing with the demon wolf.

Cissy sniffed. "I came here to ask you . . ." No, she really couldn't mention her plan of seduction. But then inspiration finally struck. "An alfresco luncheon!" She beamed at him.

His brows drew together in puzzlement. "I beg your pardon?"

"A luncheon. Outside." In her excitement, she bobbed up and down on the balls of her feet. "Tomorrow."

If anything, his puzzlement increased. "You haven't had an accident, have you?" He eyed her suspiciously.

"Me? No. Why?" She shook her head. "I . . . um . . . you know, the past few days have been so nice and sunny and I thought"—she rubbed her nose—"how nice it would be for us to drive out together and have a luncheon."

He shifted his weight, at last became aware that his sponge dripped water onto the floor, put it back into the bowl behind him. Slowly he turned back to her.

She smiled. "What do you think?" Oh, it was a most wonderful idea, and her heart fluttered in her chest with the excitement of it all.

"A luncheon?" He raised his brows. "*Outside*? At this time of year?"

"Och, we can take a thick wooly blanket. Just think of it—a picnic!" On a nice, sunny clearing in the forest. Uninvited, the picture of the eight of clubs rose in front of her inner eye: a couple lying together outside under a large tree. She imagined Fenris leaning over her, rucking up her skirts, his large hands traveling over her thighs while she lay back among the crisp aroma of crushed pine needles . . .

Cissy raised her shoulders as a delicious shiver raced down her back. What an awful wanton she was! But it was probably all right because, after all, he was her husband. "What do you say?" she asked throatily.

He gave her a look as if he suspected she were raving mad.

She tried another tack. "I would so enjoy driving out. I haven't seen that much of the forest yet, you know? And after what happened the last time I ventured out . . . Oh, please, Fenris, say yes!"

He stared at her a moment longer before he finally nodded his head. "It would be all right, I believe."

Joy bubbled up inside her. "Of course, it would!" She laughed at him—and became aware all over again how very delicious he looked with all that expanse of glistening damp skin on display. Her breath caught in her throat. God, how utterly beautiful he was!

And suddenly she was certain she didn't need a little gray man and his mandrake in order to gain happiness. Yes, she firmly believed it was here, within her reach.

Her heart light, she stepped toward her husband. Supporting herself with a hand on his shoulder, she lifted on tiptoe and pressed a fleeting kiss onto the corner of his mouth. "Thank you," she whispered, breathing in the warm smell of him: sandalwood with a lingering hint of musky sweat.

Before temptation could overcome her again, she quickly stepped back. But she couldn't stop smiling. "Would tomorrow suit you? I will tell Cook to prepare something for us, shall I?" With her hand on the door frame, she allowed herself a last look at her husband and at his dumbstruck expression. "I am so looking forward to it!"

And then, before the demon wolf had a chance to reappear, she danced out of the room.

"Why the hell did I let myself be talked into this?" Fenris sat on his bed and tore at his hair. "This is madness! Sheer madness!"

Johann issued some grunts while he folded clothes.

Fenris turned toward him. "It *is* madness," he insisted. "Whyever would she want ..." He shook his head. "It isn't right that I should ..." He took a deep breath. "Hell! If only she hadn't caught me by surprise!" Irritated, he glowered at his valet, who valiantly tried to smother his chuckles.

"She suddenly just stood in the door?"

"Yes! Stood there and stared at me, and I swear to you, her eyes nearly popped out!" Angrily Fenris rubbed his leg, where the straps had chafed the skin.

"Well, that's a good thing, isn't it?" This time, the other man openly grinned.

Fenris bundled up a shirt and threw it at him. "Of course not!" Groaning, he bent forward and buried his hands in his hair. "She's a bloody innocent, Johann. What right do I have to ... taint her?"

"You are her husband."

Her husband. He remembered how she had looked on their wedding day; the sight had taken his breath away. And when she had held his hand—for a moment pride had swelled his chest. Yet reality had a nasty habit of catching up with a man. The thought of undressing in front of her ... Heavens, having seen utter disgust in one woman's eyes was quite enough! Or worse—what if it were pity he detected in her eyes? He wouldn't be able to bear it. The thought alone made his skin crawl. "I should never have married her."

"Rubbish! Would you have wanted to see her married to your brother instead?"

Fenris looked up sharply. "Of course not!" He still shuddered to think what could have happened if he hadn't come upon Leo and Celia that night. If he hadn't wandered the hallways and walked past her room to be at least in that way near her.

"Then why can't you give it a chance?" Johann asked smugly. "Have this picnic and see what happens." He raised his brows. "Who knows, you might even enjoy yourself." He grinned.

"Oh, all right." Fenris sighed in defeat. "I'll do it."

She expected to have to persuade him all over again the next day, but surprisingly, in the early hours of the afternoon, Fenris sent Johann down to the stables for the old rickety gig. In many ways, Cissy reflected, her life had not changed all that much since England: she was still driven around in antique carriages and wore mostly the same old clothes she had worn back at her father's. Back at home.

Frowning, she slipped into her spencer jacket before securing the ribbons of her bonnet under her chin.

Back at home . . .

She moved her shoulders, looked around her cozy room, at the floral pattern on the ceiling, the stout little stove in the corner, the shelf with her old and new books, the massive four-poster bed with the light, diaphanous drapes. Her old blanket presented a nice, cheerful contrast to the dark wood and the gray stone.

She enjoyed the humming of the forest and the whispering of the castle at night, when old wooden beams creaked and the wind whistled softly in the cracks in the stone. She liked watching the moon rise over the remains of the big tower and listening to the song of the bells down in the valley that drifted up with the wind. And she truly loved the castle with its quaint staircases and doorways, beautiful tapestries and old paintings, dark with age. She loved traipsing to the grandfather clock at twelve o'clock to watch the King of Dwarves appear and see the transformation of his beloved princess. Yes, she loved witnessing their moment of happiness, when anything seemed to be possible.

With wonder, Cissy realized that "home" was no longer her father's house in England, but this, her castle. And she would make sure that love and happiness would be hers—even without a mandrake!

She laughed a little in delight and skipped downstairs to collect a basket with food and a thick blanket from Cook. When she stepped outside into the courtyard a few minutes later, her husband already stood beside the gig and checked the fastenings of the harness, while Johann looked the vehicle over to make sure it would survive another outing.

A smile on her face, Cissy stopped to observe the two men working side by side. From the way they moved together, it became clear that they had done similar tasks numerous times before. They might be master and servant, but they also made a perfect team.

Johann looked up and spotted her. He made a slight bow. *"Gnädige Frau."*

At this, Fenris half turned toward her, his face expressionless.

Uh-oh. She lifted her hand and waved. She would not let him spoil her mood—or her grand plan. "A good day to you," she said. Beaming at the two men, she ambled up to them. "Isn't it a most gorgeous day for an outing?"

"Wonderful for sitting in the mud," her husband muttered. Apparently, he no longer regarded favorably the idea of an alfresco luncheon. Yet he had not cried off.

Johann's lips twitched. He caught her staring at him, and hastily squatted down as if to check the carriage wheel.

"Fiddle-faddle!" She made an airy movement with her hand. "We have lovely food and a thick blanket." She concentrated her smile on her husband, silently daring him to contradict her.

Fenris crossed his arms in front of his chest and raised

an eyebrow. "Does one not normally take chairs for this sort of outing?"

Cissy suppressed the urge to roll her eyes. "Perhaps you should have brought your nonexistent dog cart, so we could have stuffed stools under the seat," she told him sweetly. Mimicking him, she raised both brows.

For a moment he stared at her, his face utterly devoid of expression, before he abruptly turned away. He cleared his throat. "Well, if that's all, we probably should be on our way. Right?" He threw a questioning look over his shoulder.

"Right." She bowed her head and smiled to herself. If she was not mistaken, her big, bad wolf had just turned away because he had cracked a smile. Heavens, just to think of it: the master of Wolfenbach cracking a smile! What a scandal! Like a brilliant, shimmering bubble, joy rose inside her. Perhaps she wouldn't need an old mandrake to gain happiness.

She let Johann take the picnic basket and stow it in the middle of the footrest. Then he handed her onto the box seat, while Fenris swung himself up from the other side. "All settled?" He threaded the reins through the fingers of his left hand and took up a small whip with the other.

"Perfectly." *Oh yes*, she thought smugly. *More than perfectly, in fact.* For the narrow seat of their vehicle forced her husband to sit so close to her that his shoulder rubbed hers with his every movement.

Fenris nodded to Johann and let the whip crack above the horse's back. The gig rumbled down the ward, across the bridge, and soon they were in the forest.

"Any place you would particularly like to see?" He kept his voice coolly polite, yet from the corner of her eyes she could see how he regarded her from the corner of his own.

Biting her lip to keep from smiling, she thrust her nose in the air. "Not at all." She cocked her head to the side and blinked at him. "Why don't you surprise me?"

His lips twitched. One corner of his mouth lifted. Yet quickly he had himself under control again. Politely, he inclined his head. "As you wish."

Oh my. She raised her hand to her fluttering heart. A demon wolf impersonating a lap dog. It promised excitement and perhaps a little bit of danger, and she was determined to enjoy herself to the utmost.

Several minutes later, however, she started to question the wisdom of her grand picnic idea. For the farther they drove, the more she wondered whether he had chosen this route with the purpose to frighten her off. He had led them into the depths of a dark coniferous forest where trees rose forbiddingly and shut out all sunlight. Here and there, gray spongey lichen covered the bark of the trees and fat mushrooms covered stumps. Their little gig rattled over stones and gnarled roots pushing through the ground. Cissy could almost see a little girl with a red cape skipping merrily along between the trees on her way to her grandmother's house.

As Little Red Riding Hood now entered the woods, she met the wolf. But Little Red Riding Hood didn't know what a bad animal he was, and was not afraid of him. . . .

Cissy shot a look to the wolf at her side. She wasn't afraid of *him* either, but . . . Nervously, she gnawed on her lower lip. The prospect before her was a bit daunting, considering.

She frowned and threw another glance at her husband. He did not wear a hat, so the sunbeams falling through the roof of green overhead created shimmering highlights in his dark hair and made it gleam. He concentrated on the path ahead, handled the reins with competent ease. She wondered whether he knew how much assurance he radiated. While most of the time he seemed to be on the defensive, he now wore a relaxed expression. It made him look younger, smoothed the harsh lines that bracketed his mouth. And that mouth . . .

His mouth looked more relaxed, the lips more sensual. More approachable.

Cissy licked her lips.

More kissable.

Heat rushed up into her face, and hastily she lowered her head. She could not help thinking about his lips and how they had moved over hers when he had kissed her. They had felt soft and strong at once. And when he had kissed her hand, they had been hungry. Masterful. As if he had wanted to devour her.

And the bad wolf jumped out of bed and devoured poor Little Red Riding Hood. . . .

Cissy shook her head, yet she could not stop wondering what it would be like to be devoured by this particular wolf. To have him strip her of all social conventions, all daytime façades, and to consume her entirely. She shot him a glance from the corner of her eyes and suppressed a shudder.

Fenris finally halted the gig on a small, sun-filled clearing where a large boulder sat amidst the grass like a fat little troll. *A troll?* Cissy smiled at her fancy. Her father would have been appalled: trolls were creatures of the northern countries. She watched how her husband gracefully slid off the box seat. He turned around and looked at her.

"I hope this is to your liking," he said. He leaned his hip against the moss-covered rock and crossed his arms in front of his chest. It was a nice chest, to be sure, broad and muscled.

Cissy swallowed hard. She remembered how she had

uncovered that chest when he had lain unconscious, the
satin-soft feeling of his warm skin over the hard steel of
the muscles beneath. The crisp black hair that had tickled her fingers while she had opened the buttons of his
shirt. The utterly adorable hair around his navel.

"Celia?"

His deep, raspy voice snatched Cissy out of her
reverie, her memories—erotic memories. Heat flamed
up in her face, and she quickly dismounted, nearly stumbling as her feet hit the ground.

"Fine," she said, and tried not to notice how his brows
shot up. "A nice place this is. Very nice. Quite suitable
for a picnic, is it not? Oh, well, I say that is why you have
picked it, but still . . ." She was babbling like a fool! "It is
very nice. Lovely."

Be quiet. Quiet!

She gave him her gayest smile, smiled and smiled until her cheeks hurt. "Shall I spread the blanket next to
that stone . . . rock? And the horse—oh, the horse. I—"

"You can sling the reins over that low branch over
there." He narrowed his eyes. "You are not nervous, are
you? After all, this was your idea."

"Me? Nervous?" *I squeak like a mouse,* she thought with
disgust, and forced herself to laugh even more gaily
than she had smiled. "Of course not." *Food. Think of the
food,* she admonished herself sternly. He had already
taken out the basket Cook had prepared for them.

Cissy took a deep breath and then went to secure the
horse, smiling, always smiling. She carried the large,
bulky blanket over to where her husband stood, tall and
lean like a greyhound.

"A nice spring outing we will have," she chattered
while she spread the blanket. He sat down and leaned
against the boulder. She knelt, keeping the basket between them. "And a nice day—sunny, almost warm." He

helped her to unwrap the small parcels of food. "Yes, rather warm for spring, don't you think?" His warm fingers brushed against hers when they both reached for the same plate, and all breath seemed to rush from her. "I . . . I am quite surprised, I have to admit," she choked out, "I would not have thought it would ever get warm again after this winter. But now it is and . . . and . . ." She looked up.

His green eyes twinkled. "Here." He held out a pewter tankard. "Have some wine."

Embarrassed, Cissy stuck her nose into the tankard. *I am sure he just wants to silence me.*

But then he said, "Have you read any of Grimm's treatises? Tell me, what do you think of his theories on folk literature?" And because his father, too, was a scholar of mythology and history, it was a joy to discuss the latest theories and developments with Fenris. All the time he was solicitous and courteous, passed her plates with cold chicken and rosted pork and filled up her tankard again and again. The wine must have relaxed him, too, for after they had eaten all bits and crumbs, he held out an inviting hand. "Come here, Celia. Let us sit together and enjoy this lovely day."

Surprised but pleased, she scooted over to him and allowed him to draw her into his arms so that she sat with her back against his chest. His hands rested over hers on her stomach, and his fingers painted fiery little circles on her skin.

"Much better," he sighed. His warm breath tickled the suddenly sensitive shell of her ear, making her shiver. "Are you cold?"

"No." How breathless she sounded. "No . . . just . . ." When he rubbed his cheek against her hair, she froze.

"Mmm. I like this." Oh, yes, he had definitely had too much wine! He would have never touched her like this when sober; she was sure of it. "You have been a little jumpy today, haven't you?"

"J-jumpy?"

"Mmhm." His arms tightened around her. "Like a wild doe. But now I have you. . . ."

He could not have given her a better opening. So she gathered all her courage and blurted out, "Well, yes, I wanted to talk to you about that."

"Hm?"

His hands were so large and dark against her own.

Cissy swallowed. "About our marriage, that is. The . . . the consummation . . ."

She felt his body tense behind her, and his arms fell away from her. "What about the consummation?" he said. He used his most chilling tones.

"Fenris." She half turned to look at him. His expression had become shuttered and remote, while his eyes had darkened dramatically. In anger? "Fenris, please . . ." Without volition her hand rose to cup his strong, stubborn jaw. "I have been wondering why our marriage is not consummated yet. I . . ." Once again, she felt the heat rise in her face, but doggedly she went on: "As I understand it, for this, legs are not really . . . necessary."

"As you *understand*?" he sneered. When she would have shrunk away from his sarcasm, his hand came up to shut around her wrist like a vise, his fingers biting into her soft flesh. "And what do you know about the consummation of marriages? What would my lovely wife know about coupling?"

Oh, how wonderful. It was back to the demon wolf.

Cissy averted her face and bit her lip to keep from crying. Bawling like a baby would not help her, even if, with a few words, all the joy seemed to have been sucked out of the day. "You're coarse," she choked, while she tried in vain to free her wrist.

"Have you had a merry go with the stable lad back at home?" he asked. Such an ugly tone; she had never heard it from him before.

"No."

"Has he touched you like this . . . ?" His free hand groped her breast. "Made you hot and panting?"

"No!" The more she fought, the tighter his fingers gripped her.

"Have you two had a merry go among the hay bales, is that it?"

Cissy choked. Heavens, Fenris was an utter dimwit! Anger swept away her dismay. Her head jerked up. "Don't be ridiculous!" she spat. "What would I want with a man of nearly sixty?" That, she saw with satisfaction, surprised him.

"Oh," he said, the ugliness leaving his face. Then his eyes narrowed. "Well, what then? How would a gently bred young lady like you know of such things?"

Cissy rolled her eyes. "We lived in the country, for heaven's sake! And besides, if you must know, there are books and such!" She glared at him, willing him to wither under her gaze.

All he did, however, was blink. "Books and such." His grip on her wrist relaxed.

"Yes." Thinking about Mrs. Chisholm's cards, she felt heat rise in her face and ducked her head.

His thumb rubbed over the pulse in her wrist. "What exactly do you mean by 'and such'?" There was no more anger in his voice, only mild interest.

Cissy shivered a little as the callused pad of his thumb drew another circle over her sensitive skin. She bit her lip as, unbidden, the pictures from the cards rose in front of her inner eye: *a couple in a cornfield, her breasts bared and pouting, the skirts rucked up over her hips. She sat with her legs spread wide, so his hands could—*

"Celia?"

She stared at his hand around her wrist and imagined . . . imagined . . .

He let go of her wrist and put two fingers under her chin. With gentle pressure he lifted her head. "What did you mean by 'and such'?" he repeated, and she thought she could see a glimmer of something new in his eyes.

She licked her lips. "Cards," she murmured.

One black brow shot up.

"Um . . ." Her face glowed and she very much wanted to pack their things and drive home again. This outing had been a stupid idea. A really, really stupid idea.

She took a deep breath. "Adeckoferoticcards," she said.

"A deck of erotic cards?" His second eyebrow joined the first. "Ahhh, how very interesting. I did not know such things would . . . appeal to you." His body relaxed, and a rare full smile flitted over his face. Instead of gripping and groping her, his hand settled on his left leg. In a probably unconscious gesture, he rubbed the stump as if the amputation hurt. And with a pang of remorse, Cissy suddenly understood his earlier anger and the hateful words.

She touched his arm and searched his face, feeling the need to comfort him somehow. "Fenris . . ."

His lips curved. "You have to show it to me sometime," he said. And then he bent his head to capture her lips with his own.

The kiss started like their first, soft and sweet. But then his tongue slid hotly into her mouth, entwined with hers, and it was as if the world fell away. Cissy felt a curious tug in her stomach, as if he did not just caress her tongue, but her insides, too. She lifted her body a little and moaned.

"Mmmm." He drew back and nibbled on her lips. "You wanted to talk about the consummation of our marriage," he growled between nibbles. "What did you have in mind?" He took her lower lip between his teeth and tugged.

"Oooh." Her back curved like a bow so that her breasts pressed against his chest. "I wanted to seduce you," she admitted breathlessly—and could have bitten off her tongue the next moment. Heavens! The wine must have befuddled her brain. "Er . . ."

With deft fingers he opened the buttons of her spencer jacket. Then his hand glided up from her waist until it cupped one breast. "How interesting." His kisses became more intense. "Let's do that later. For now . . ." He drew the back of his hand over the upper swell of her breasts and suddenly her brains were addled by more than the wine. She thought she heard him mutter something unflattering about stays, but the blood hummed so loudly in her ears and her breasts tingled so deliciously that she couldn't quite be sure.

"Ooooh."

"You like that, don't you?" His lips slid down her throat, and his tongue was like fire on her skin. "Do you know what *I* would like?"

His moist breath fanned over her, making her gasp. Cissy slung one arm around his head and buried her fingers in his thick hair. "What?" Now she finally understood why some of the people on Mrs. Chisholm's cards had loony smiles on their faces.

"I'd like to experiment a little." He looked up so that he could meet her gaze. "Will you let me?" His fingers still played with her breast, gently kneading her flesh.

Cissy stared at him, willing the sensual fog to clear from her brain. *Tip-tap,* his fingers moved against her. His eyes were darker than usual, and there was a slash of color high across his cheeks. His lips seemed somehow fuller, his expression almost vulnerable.

Will you let me? he had asked. But what he had meant was, *Will you trust me?*

Hope blossomed in her chest, a warm glow that seemed to fill her being. She gave him a wide smile. "Yes," she murmured. "Oh, yes." And she closed the distance between them to kiss him.

She heard a chuckle rumble in his chest. "So much enthusiasm." She wriggled against him, and he groaned a little. "Let me—perhaps I haven't quite lost my touch after all," she heard him mutter. His finger slipped under the neckline of her dress and into the dimple between her breasts. "So eager," he breathed, and kissed her neck, licked her collarbone.

"Mmmm." She arched against him. "Fenris . . ." And felt how his fingers became bolder in response.

"Sweet Celia, so sweet . . . Let me . . ." Gently he turned her so that her back rested against his chest. His hands covered her breasts. "See how perfectly they fit into my palms?" he murmured against her ear. "How I've longed to touch your bare skin."

Cissy quivered at his words.

His mouth played with her earlobe. "I've imagined what it would be like to touch you. At first your skin will be soft and cool like silk." His hands stroked down her belly. "And here it'll be as white as milk."

With a sigh, she pressed her shoulders against him and lifted her middle a little. Even through the material of her dress she could feel the heat of his body, surrounding her, enveloping her. She felt as if her body would slowly melt.

"And then"—his voice dropped deeper and turned hoarse—"it will heat to my touch until it will be all covered in sweet dew."

Cissy's skin prickled with the images he evoked. "The heat is already there," she gasped. It made her a little afraid, the way her body felt, so strange and new, as if it were no longer her own. She hadn't expected that, this curious new vulnerability.

His fingers bit into her waist. For a moment, his breathing faltered, before he laughed a little unsteadily. "You are a delight, my sweet." He pressed a kiss onto the crown of her head.

"My insides are melting," she told him, panting. She dropped her head against his shoulder and closed her eyes. Her face burned. "I am afraid," she admitted on a whisper, and shuddered, half with fear, half with delight.

Fenris hugged her to him and rained soft kisses onto her neck and shoulders. "Don't be, my sweet wife. There's no need, no need whatsoever. . . ." His voice changed, became low and sweet and tempting, flowed over her like caramel sauce. "Let me show you. . . ."

She lay against his chest, her eyes still closed, and let him pull up her skirts, let him touch her thighs with butterfly-like strokes. The muscles in her legs quivered under his fingers. But his gentleness increased her fear, for quite suddenly she was afraid she would lose herself in him, that he would wrap her up, overwhelm her, make her lose a bit of her soul.

Her eyes flew open. She saw how pale her thighs were, his dark hands on them a sharp contrast. How could these be her legs? Miss Celia Fussell did not lie in forests like a wanton with her legs spread wide and the sun shining on the thatch of hair there.

"Fenris," she gasped.

And then she noticed the pulse that had started in her flesh. And the dampness.

Panic made her heart flutter.

"Fenris!"

She tried to sit up straight, to close her legs.

"Hmm?" But his fingers were already touching her,

and all thoughts of escape flew from Cissy's mind. She could only lie back in his arms and gasp and sigh and moan, and let the feelings wash over her in rolling waves, until with a scream, she was pulled under and drowned in pleasure while her husband held her securely in his arms, one of his hands resting big and warm between her legs.

Afterwards, when sanity returned, and with it propriety and her sense of shame, she could not meet his eye. Nothing had prepared her for this. The cards had shown nothing about the danger of losing one's self, losing a little bit of one's soul to the man who had touched her.

And quite suddenly, the crisp spring air felt bitter cold. Shivering, she rearranged her skirts so they fell over her knees, her ankles, over all the places his fingers had caressed.

"I think," he said, "it is time to head back home."

They spent the drive to the castle in awkward silence, and as soon as they had reached the inner ward, Cissy fled inside, afraid of the things she might have awakened.

CHAPTER SEVENTEEN

The light of the single candle was reflected by the glass in the window, a ghostly flame in a sea of darkness. It quivered in the soft draft, its golden halo dancing over the walls and painted ceiling.

Cissy sat alone in the golden light and slowly combed out her hair, the gentle swooshing of her brush and her breath the only sounds in the room. She remembered how her breathing had quickened that afternoon when pleasure had heated her blood. She remembered the sounds she had made then, the pants and moans, the sweet ache in her body, the hard wall of her husband's chest behind her, supporting her, and his arms around her, strong and sure. He'd been a safe haven where she could come unravelled, where her world could splinter and be put together again.

Let the birds sing, diddle, diddle,
And the lambs play,
We shall be safe, diddle, diddle,
out of harm's way.

Yet eventually they had left the clearing and returned to real life. And here, she was not free to pursue this joyful pleasure, but was bound by social conventions and restrictions like a bird in its cage, fluttering its wings in vain against the bars. A proper young lady did not writhe in her husband's arms among the green grass, did not invite male hands to touch her flesh, did not crave the magic his body could provide. Yet she did.

> *I heard one say, diddle, diddle,*
> *Since I came hither,*
> *That you and I, diddle, diddle,*
> *must lie together.*

How could she be so wanton as to go to him, to go to his chamber, to his bed. . . . Cissy closed her eyes and painfully swallowed. How could she venture into the unknown, untutored? She would only stumble and fall. Oh yes, she had studied Mrs. Chisholm's cards, had even pursued her husband, had imagined . . . all kinds of things. But the reality—the reality had been so different, so overwhelming, so overpowering. She had felt too vulnerable. As if she had been about to give him a part of her soul. Stupidly, she had never thought beyond the act itself, and had only wanted to forge a connection with her husband. It had never occurred to her that it could change her as well, that it would change the way she thought and felt, change her innermost being.

And now that she knew . . .

Cissy opened her eyes and stared at the pale flame in the window. It was bitter, this realization that, in the end, she lacked both courage and skill.

"Another night perhaps," she whispered. She lifted the brush and ran it through her hair once again. Down and down, it glided easily through the silken brown strands. Down and down, she let herself be hypnotized by its strokes.

A knock on her door made her start.

Her skin prickled and her fingers trembled when she reached for her robe. Her voice came out as a croak. "Y-yes?"

The door swung open and revealed the tall figure of her husband leaning nonchalantly against the frame, arms crossed upon his chest. The breath caught in her throat.

"I daresay," he said. "Here you are." His eyes glinted devilishly as he looked around the room. "A cozy place you have here." His gaze returned to her, and he lifted one eyebrow as if in silent challenge. "May I come in?"

What ho! what ho! thy door undo;
Art watching or asleepe?
My love, dost yet remember me,
And dost thou laugh or weepe?

To remember a stanza from Bürger's "Lenore," who was abducted by her husband's ghost, at that moment was rather unfortunate. Cissy suppressed a shiver. *Drat.* With emphasized carlessness she lifted one shoulder. "Of course," she murmured. She watched how he ducked his head as he stepped into the room and shut the door behind him. The click of the latch sounded unnaturally loud in the silent night.

Candlelight flickered over his face and tinged his skin golden. He seemed too tall for her small chamber, and his shadow sprang up and stretched to the ceiling, swallowing the delicate floral pattern.

Nervously, Cissy licked her lips. She felt like the little goats in the Grimms' fairy tale when they realized the big, bad wolf had stepped over their threshold. Unfortunately, there was no grandfather clock in her room where she might hide. So she just lifted her chin a notch higher and watched him as he looked around the room once more.

Tap-dam, tap-dam, his steps sounded on the ancient tiles. *Tap-dam, tap-dam, tap-dam.*

"I seem to recall a bargain we struck this afternoon," he announced to the shelf where she kept her books.

He was still wearing his waistcoat, shirt and trousers, and Cissy, only scantily clad in her thin nightgown and even thinner robe, felt at a distinct disadvantage. She cleared her throat. "A bargain?"

"Well . . ." He threw her a look over his shoulder. "More like a promise on your part. A nice selection of books you keep here."

Cissy forced herself to sit straight and still, even though her skin prickled as if a hundred ants were crawling over her body. "Thank you. But you already know I like books."

Tap-dam, tap-dam. "Yes, yes, I know. We talked about books some time ago, didn't we?" *Tap-dam, tap-dam.* "Gosh, is that stove really green? One wouldn't have guessed with all the dust and—"

"You spoke of a promise," she interrupted. Better to be impolite than to eventually scream with supressed nerves. Or than to whack him over the head in late retribution for the cobwebs and the rodent skeleton she had encountered in this very room all that time ago.

"Ah, yes, the promise." He turned to her. "I seem to recall . . . Did you not promise to . . ." His voice trailed away.

"Yes?" The word came out rather impatient, and Fenris, the ill-mannered lout, had the nerve to grin as she started to squirm on her seat.

"Well, how shall I put it?" He tapped his forefinger against his chin. "Did you not promise me an . . . um . . .

attack on my virtue?" At her incredulous gasp, his grin widened. "Seduction. Did you not want to seduce me, my pretty wife?"

Cissy jumped to her feet. He was outrageous! But oh, how her body quivered and trembled as she recalled the feeling of his warm, large hands on her flesh, cupping her breasts, touching her between her legs. "I . . ." *Seduction?* How his fingers had teased her, slipped inside her. Cissy felt her cheeks flame. "I . . ."

He put his hands on his hips, and his teeth gleamed in the candlelight. "Yes, indeed—seduction. I distinctly remember you promised to seduce me." He cocked his head to the side. "I hope you have not changed your mind."

"I . . ." Yes, he looked most definitely like the big bad wolf, about to gobble up the small, hapless goat. Involuntarily, Cissy took a step back. "I . . ."

"I really hope you won't go back on your promise." Slowly, steadily, he advanced, a dangerous gleam in his eyes. "Because, you see, my dear,"—he smiled then, a winning, charming smile, which did not fool her for one bit—"I was looking forward to it." His voice dropped to an intimate growl, which snaked out and wound around her, ensnared her. It reminded her how he had crooned encouragements into her ear when she had burned up under his skillful fingers, when she had moaned and panted and . . .

Cissy put her hands against her burning cheeks.

How was one supposed to deal with this? With one's memories? With one's own wantonness?

And still he advanced, Fenris, that dangerous, dangerous wolf, who could only be bound by dwarves' chains and who would eventually swallow the sun. But first, he seemed determined to swallow her.

Cissy gulped. Didn't she want that? Her body called out to be consumed.

Alas, the floor was old, the tiles worn out by many feet and made crooked by time. The knowing smile was wiped off her husband's face as he tripped and stumbled and nearly fell.

Cissy cried out and rushed forward to grab his arm and to steady him. With a bitter oath, he wrenched his arm free and stumbled to the bed, where he sat down heavily. His breathing harsh, he drooped forward and buried his face in his hands.

"God, what a fool I am," she heard him mutter, his voice so different from before. When he finally looked up, he seemed to have aged ten years. His face was haggard and the grooves around his mouth more deeply etched. "Such a stupid fool," he murmured, his eyes burning into hers. "I should not have come here tonight."

His words and the bitterness in his tone loosened Cissy's paralysis, and she went to him. Her heart ached at his defeated expression as he looked up at her. "No," she whispered. "No. Not a fool, never a fool—my wolf." She leaned forward and brushed her lips over his, hesitantly at first, but then his hand came up and around her neck and held her fast while his mouth opened under hers. This was no tender, gentle kiss, but a hard onslaught, tasting of desperation. His tongue invaded her mouth, his free hand gripped her waist and he pulled her roughly between his legs. And it was this roughness which excited her, this urgency with which his fingers kneaded her soft flesh.

Passion flared between them, and suddenly there was no more room to worry about wantonness. It was as if in the arms of this man she lost all sense of propriety. All Cissy could think about was the burning desire to feel his skin against hers. She tugged at his shirt, fumbled with the buttons of his waistcoat and helped him to push the robe off her shoulders. And all the while his lips moved under hers, their mouths moved together, hot breath mingled, seared her lungs.

She could not wait until he had divested himself of his shirt and waistcoat. Instead she spread them open and splayed her hands over his chest, tunneled her fingers through the springy dark hair there. Oh yes, how she had dreamt of doing that! He groaned, and his muscles tensed. His hand lifted to cup one of her breasts in imitation of what she did to him. How exquisite a feeling, his large, hard hand over her vulnerable softness! When his thumb roughly rubbed her nipple, a shaft of quicksilver delight shot through her and exploded in the secret place between her legs.

As her hand glided over his belly, she felt the ridges of his sculpted muscle. They bunched under her touch, and her fingers tingled with pleasure. When Fenris started to place hot, open-mouthed kisses against the tender skin of her throat, her body melted. It seemed only natural to slide her hand to the waistband of his trousers and lower, where his erection pressed up against the material. He had brought her so much pleasure this afternoon, and she wanted to touch him in the same intimate way, to return his intimate gift. The heat of him almost seared her skin when she tentatively closed her fingers around him. Like a small animal, his penis moved against her palm.

"No!"

He suddenly grabbed her wrist tight enough to leave bruises.

"No," he repeated, his breathing harsh. Dumbfounded, Cissy stared at his heaving chest, where beads of sweat glistened in the curly black hair. He shook her, and there was anger in his voice.

Anger and something else.

"Not out of pity!" he growled hoarsely. "I don't want you to touch me just because you pity me!"

She looked up then and met his gaze. His eyes burned, and for once his face was stripped naked of all mask. His torment and desperation were there for her to see. His terrible, terrible fear of rejection.

Leopold's taunting words echoed through her mind. All that vileness: How much had Fenris overheard? And what had his snooty brother thrown at him on earlier occasions? For how long had this festered inside Fenris?

Her heart clenched with compassion, and tears welled up in her eyes. Naïvely she had thought a kiss enough to release this beast from his evil spell. Only now did she see it was not nearly enough. What he needed would demand so much more courage than a simple kiss, even though none of the kisses they had shared could be called simple. The desire between them ran deep, and Cissy counted on that.

She took a deep breath and, as she slowly expelled the air, she cast away the last remains of her maidenly shyness. Between them, there was no room for it. Not here. Not now. Not when she needed to teach him how well he was desired.

Slowly, she lifted her free hand to cradle his cheek. "Pity?" she repeated, her voice strong and steady. Her thumb caressed his stubbly skin. "There is no pity."

For a long time, he simply stared at her, his expression so lost that her heart ached for him. Then he shook his head, dislodging her hand. *"No!"* he said wildly. "No!"

"No pity, Fenris," she insisted, and again laid her fingers against his cheek.

"No!" It was as if he could not understand that he could be desired.

"Never pity." Slowly, very slowly, she leaned forward and kissed him. This time the kiss was tender and sweet, just the merest brush of her lips. "No pity, Fenris," she repeated against his cheek, and rained butterfly kisses against his temple, his brow, his eyelids. When she lifted her head a little, he gazed at her, his heart in his eyes. He looked like a small boy, yearning for something unreachable.

She smiled a little. "Don't you know that?" Her fingers played with the hair over his ear, while her thumb drew soothing circles on his temple. The intensity with which he hung on her every word was endearing—and heartbreaking. "Don't you know, my wolf?" she whispered against the corner of his mouth, blinking away sudden tears. Her hand glided around his head, her fingers sinking deep into his thick, wavy hair when she tenderly cupped the back of his skull.

"Your hair is black and shiny like raven wings." She pressed her lips to his temple before she kissed the crown of his head. "Softer than silk," she murmured throatily and let her mouth slide to his ear. "Mmm." Gently, she closed her teeth over his earlobe. "Your skin is like velvet here. Like the skin of a peach."

She kissed her way down the strong column of his throat, deeply inhaling the scent of him: sandalwood and woodsmoke, overlaid by a hint of muskiness. She licked the little hollow at the base of his throat, smiling against his skin when she heard his sharp intake of breath. "You taste like the sea, wild and salty."

"Celia . . ."

"And your shoulders are wide." She eased her hand under his shirt and over his shoulder, digging her fingers into the beautifully rounded muscle. "Wide like the wings of an eagle." She pushed the shirt down his arm and admired the elegant shape of this part of his body. His upper arm was hairless, leaving the lovely bulge of muscle fully revealed to her view. "I like this," she told him, and rubbed her fingertips in little circles over his biceps. "A sign of your strength and power." His arm flexed, and she threw him a mischievous smile.

"Of course, I also like your chest." She splayed her hand over one of his pectorals. "It's so wide and broad. Like a horse's."

"A horse's?" His voice sounded rusty, as if he hadn't used it in years.

"All right." With a little laugh, she pressed a quick kiss on his chin. "Like a bear's. It's hairy like a bear's, too. Silky soft hair." She ruffled the black curls. "And these." With her forefinger she nudged one of his tiny nipples. "They remind me of small copper coins." She watched how his nipple pebbled under her touch.

He groaned, as if she were wrenching his heart out. "What exactly are you doing?" he asked in a strangled voice. A muscle in his jaw jumped as he clenched his teeth. His eyes flashed. Yes, this was the ferocious wolf Fenris, whom only dwarves' chains could bind. But Cissy would make sure that this wolf's fetters would be unlocked.

She rained playful, tiny kisses on the hard line of his jaw. "Why, I'm only keeping my promise."

"Promise?" His grip around her wrist tightened.

"Yes, my promise." She chuckled at his question. "I promised to seduce you, don't you remember?"

She managed not to wince as his fingers spasmed around her wrist. Instead, she placed a soft kiss against the corner of his mouth. "Could you let go of my wrist? You're hurting me."

Immediately contrite, he hastily released her. "I . . . I apologize." His eyes flickered, as if with panic. "This is madness. I . . . I shouldn't have come. I'm not . . . You're not . . ."

"Shhh." She put her finger over his lips. He looked up at her, and again he wore that lost expression, which once more brought tears to her eyes. "Shhh, sweeting, shhh." She replaced her finger with her mouth, opening his lips with hers because she knew how everything else became unimportant when they kissed. How the world fell away and left them in a small cocoon of desire.

Her hands moved up to cup his face, and she felt his arms come around her, drawing her against him. "Don't think, Fenris," she whispered against his lips. "Don't think. Just feel." She smoothed her hands over his shoulders. *"Feel."*

And again, desire exploded between them. She cherished him with hands and lips, placed kisses on his shoulders and his chest, while his hands roamed over her back and kneaded her bottom. He groaned against her neck when he pressed her tighter against his body, so that the bulge of his erection came to rest between her legs. This time, when her hand wandered down his belly, he did not stop her. Teasingly, she slipped a finger under the waistband of his trousers and ran it over his hips. His gasp and the quivering of his muscles made her chuckle in delight.

"Vixen!" he rasped, and captured her mouth with his, chewing on her lower lip until she felt giddy with wanting him.

Quickly and boldly, she opened the fastening of his trousers. She looked down and, somewhere between shock and awe, saw his penis spring free. "You're not wearing any drawers!"

Fenris licked the side of her neck, causing her to shiver with pleasure. They had switched positions again: now he was the bold one. "Of course not. They have the habit of getting in the way of seduction." He sucked her soft skin between his teeth, and with a small moan she leaned against him.

She cupped him tentatively. "Oooh, your skin is even

softer here," she murmured with appreciation. "But it's also hard. Hard and soft, like a shaft of velvet over a rod of steel." And against her palm he became even harder.

With a groan, he closed his fingers over hers, showing her how to grip and stroke him. "Do you want me to lose my mind?" he asked.

"Yes, exactly." She smiled and caressed him, loving the feel of him in her hand, how he grew longer, how the blood pulsed against her palm. "Am I succeeding?"

"God, yes. *Yes!*" he panted. His eyes closed. His head fell back.

With wonder and tenderness Cissy watched him, saw his gleaming chest heave with each breath and the expression of blissful rapture that appeared on his face. She loved the heavy, lusty smell of him, and the little sounds he made at the back of his throat. His Adam's apple bobbed so endearingly when he swallowed that she couldn't resist leaning forward and running the tip of her tongue over it.

It was then that Fenris snapped.

The feel of her small, soft hands on him—fondling him, playing with him—was torture and heaven at once. Each caress tugged at his heart and soul until Fenris thought he would go mad with wanting her, needing her.

The last woman who had touched him like this had been a common whore—one who had lusted after his money and not his body. She hadn't been able to hide her grimace of distate when he had shed his trousers. He had already been too far gone by then, lost in a haze of need and lust, but he had shagged her hard in retribution. Left marks on her body. Rode her like a wild stallion, brutally bucking into her. He had departed feeling sullied.

He had been sick in the bushes on his way home, later

had scrubbed his skin raw to wash the smell and touch of the woman off his body, to expurgate his own violent lust. After the episode he had never given in to his lust again. He hadn't touched a woman in years, hadn't even touched himself, had felt only disgust—the same disgust he knew women must feel at the sight of him.

Except for his wife, it seemed.

Still, a voice whispered in his head, *what right does the King of Dwarves have to—*

But the thought was lost as he gasped under another particularly crafty caress. His wife's answering chuckle seemed sweeter than any music. Her flowery perfume wafted around him, mingled with the scent of arousal, his and hers. He remembered the feeling of her treasure trove in his hand this afternoon, how hot and wet she had been for him. God, so wet! A shudder of delight ran through his body, and the memory combined with the reality of her hands on his body dried out his mouth. He swallowed convulsively, and then—

Dear God!

He felt her warm damp breath against his throat, followed by her tongue licking over his Adam's apple.

Fenris groaned. His body jerked. The shaft of lust running through him was so intense he thought his heart would pop right out of his chest. Like a dark wave, passion and desire engulfed him and drew him under, erased all rational thought but one: to possess this woman in every way possible for man.

His eyes snapped open. He grabbed her arms, stopped her caresses. His mouth devoured hers. As she met him boldly, he felt his lust surge up even more. Their tongues intertwined while he ran his hands over her body.

He dimly registered the sound of ripping material, but foremost in his mind was the feeling of her naked flesh against him, dewy with wanting him, desiring him. He groaned into her mouth, swallowed in turn her little pants and moans.

It was no effort at all to hoist her up and lie her on the bed. The sight of her pale flesh against the white linen was enough to bring his blood to the point of boiling. And her eyes—dear heaven! Her eyes when she watched him get rid of his clothes: hot and hungry eyes, they devoured him whole. Even when he snapped the straps around his stump loose. Even then. Dear God, even then.

But what right does the King of Dwarves have to—

He fell into the bed beside her, into the arms she yearningly held out. Her hands ran over his body, her fingers dancing over its hard ridges while he lost himself in her softness. "I need you," he growled, his voice barely recognizable even to himself. "So much. You don't know how much. I can't wait, I—"

Her teeth nibbling at his earlobe made him shudder. "Then come to me," she whispered throatily. "Come to me, my wolf."

"I . . ." His trembling fingers found the secret haven between her legs, overflowing for him, welcoming him, sucking his finger into that searingly hot sheath. Panting, she bucked against his hand.

"Come to me, Fenris, come to me now," she begged him. "Come, my wolf. Come." Her hips moved sinuously against him, urging him on, and with something akin to a sob, he complied.

He rolled her onto her back and came up between her legs, spread wide for him, leaving her open and vulnerable. Her trust and acceptance humbled him and made his eyes prick. God, he had no right, no right whatsoever.

Yet the next moment her fingers dug into his buttocks. "Now, Fenris, *now!*" she commanded, her voice rough with urgency.

Need ran like a firestorm through his body. Her obvious desire for him erased all thought and reason. He gripped her hips, tilted them up and, with one sure, long stroke slid home.

Underneath him, she winced and held her breath.

"Sweetheart?" His arms trembled as he held himself above her, still.

But then she smiled a little and reached up to draw him down, down, into her, her hands moving over his back while he moved inside her. Her legs locked around his waist, drawing him in, making them one, their bodies blurred. She moved with him, around him, once, twice, he rocked against the cradle of her hips. Once, twice; her nails scraped over his buttocks, her whispered endearments tickled in his ear, and deep inside her, his world fractured. He exploded.

He gasped and shuddered, safely cradled in her arms. Her hands stroked his shoulder, his hair, while she pressed her lips to his temple, his cheek, his throat, crooning to him, praising him.

Fenris felt as if he had been catapulted out of his body right into Heaven. But when slowly—so slowly—he came back to himself, he was still in her arms, hot and sweaty, his heart a large drum in his ears. He dimly registered that he was crushing his wife into the mattress and tried to roll off her. But his body was slow to obey. His limbs moved only sluggishly, as if he were drugged. His mind was befuddled, yet somehow he seemed to remember that his wife, his sweet, brave wife, had not cried out in pleasure as she had done this afternoon. She had not finished.

He tried to open his eyes and focus on her. "I . . ." He licked his lips, wanted to apologize, yet it was all a daze.

His mind did not seem to function well, for all thoughts slipped through his fingers like nimble little fish, much too fast for him. "I . . ."

"Shh, my wolf." Her sweet voice. She petted his hair. "Shhh. Come here." She helped him to roll over and tugged the bedcovers up over them both. Blissful warmth enveloped him and his mind slipped away a little bit further. His wife's voice seemed to come from a great distance, hovering in the air. "Come here, my wolf. Come." She drew his head down to her soft breasts, and with the sound of her voice in his ears and the sweet scent of her in his nose, he fell asleep in her arms.

CHAPTER EIGHTEEN

Cissy woke in the gray hours of the morning, the time between night and day when the world was bleached of all color. Her husband's eyes were just two dark shadows, yet his teeth flashed white in a smile. Leaning on one elbow, he lounged beside her, sleek and gray in the waning night.

When she languidly stretched the sleep from her limbs, her thigh brushed against his. The feeling of his hairy male skin rasping against her made her shudder delicately.

"Have you been awake for long?" she whispered.

"Not long." Another smile quirked his lips. He reached out and trailed his forefinger over her naked shoulder. "I enjoy watching you when you sleep." His finger traced the upper slopes of her breasts and lazily slipped into the valley between.

Cissy swallowed. "Do you?"

He laughed. "I even more enjoy watching you when you are awake." He nudged the bedcover with his wrist so that it fell back to reveal her breasts. Her nipples were already puckered and tingling and awaiting his touch. He readily complied, leaning closer and bestowing a gentle kiss on one upthrust peak. Cissy gasped.

As easy as that, she felt tingles spread through her whole body. It was the most curious thing, really, the way her husband made her feel.

"I meant to apologize for last night," he murmured against her skin, kissing his way from one breast to the other.

"Apologize?" Abruptly, the pleasant sensations vanished and were replaced by apprehension. All at once he seemed vulnerable, and as if to physically shield him, Cissy put her hand on his neck, burying her fingers in his wavy black hair. "Why ever would you want to apologize?"

A rueful smile twisted his lips as he looked at her. "Because I behaved like an oaf, selfishly taking my own pleasure." He sighed and rested his forehead against hers. "And not giving you anything back. I would have had your first time be different."

"Oh." Relief flooded her—and a warm rush of tenderness. Her hand stroked down to cup his cheek. "But there was plenty of pleasure for me."

He closed his eyes and leaned into her touch. "You are very generous. And yet you did not . . . finish. I should have been more patient." A hint of bitterness crept into his voice. "Instead, I . . . You deserved more, so much more."

Cissy searched his face, watched how his features briefly contorted as if he were in pain. And perhaps he was—not due to some external wound, but to inner torment. Last night she had hoped it banished forever. However, this was not a fairy tale; this beast would not be released from its evil spell simply by a kiss. He still needed loving, so much more loving. . . .

Loving?

Her heart gave a peculiar lurch.

In her heart she had known it for some time. Yet it had happened so gradually, she had almost not noticed. It had begun at the first sight of him, when he had stood in the hall downstairs, his hair tousled, his face darker than thunder. Such a disgruntled beast he had been, so angry his isolation had been breached by a stranger.

Over the weeks and months it had grown, this feeling inside her, while she had caught glimpses of the man beneath the beast: when he had made his body a shield for her against the violence of his brother, when he had gamely stamped through the snow in search of the Christmas tree. He had made her heart melt when he had fumbled to tie silky ribbons into lopsided bows, and he had made her chuckle when he had given her that gothic novel—the *Castle of Wolfenbach*,—as a Christmas present.

Yet only glimpses, these.

His soul was still not healed, the beast not yet redeemed.

Her palm rubbed over his cheek, making his lashes flutter open. Surprise flickered upon his face. Cissy smiled. Surely there was enough loving in her heart.

"There was plenty of pleasure for me," she insisted, her tone gentle. "So much joy when I touched you—and when you touched me." She watched his eyes widen at her frankness, and her smile deepened. All lingering shyness was swept away by the assurance that this was right for her, that this was the place where she belonged. "So much joy, Fenris. And I did finish yesterday afternoon, if you remember."

"I remember," he mumbled, quiet.

"See? So it was only fair—one finish for me and one for you."

He blinked several times, then his expression changed. "Ahh." With a smothered laugh he turned his face into her palm and nibbled on her tender flesh, grinning when she squirmed in surprise. "Perhaps we should have another go, then, and see if we can manage to finish together." He raised an eyebrow.

"Perhaps." She aimed at nonchalance, even though the thought of "more" made her heart accelerate.

"Good, then." And he proceeded to place hot, open-mouthed kisses on her collarbone. Already she felt herself melting against him. But almost immediately he raised his head. When suddenly cold air whispered over her damp skin, she shivered and murmured in protest.

Soothingly, he tugged the bedcover a bit higher, kept one hand cupped around her breast. "I seem to remember that you mentioned a deck of cards this afternoon."

"Cards?" she echoed, utterly distracted by his kneading fingers and the thumb brushing over her nipple. "Hmmmm?" Sighing, she closed her eyes and arched against his hand. But to gain her attention, Fenris pinched her nipple, hard. She sucked in a breath. Her eyes flew open—and she found him grinning down on her. At that moment, he looked impossibly young, and her heart flipped over.

He waggled his brows. "*Erotic* cards."

She blinked. "Oh." She blinked again. "Oh, that."

"Would you show them to me?"

"Show them . . ."

"Mmhm." He bent his head to nibble on her earlobe while he continued to run his thumb teasingly over her aroused breast. "Please?" he breathed against her neck, his hot, damp breath nearly making her moan.

How could she deny him? Vividly she remembered his jealousy and anger when he had thought she had slept with some other man. Did he feel threatened by this, too? Seeking to reassure him, she slung her arms around his smooth, broad shoulders and hugged him close.

He came willingly into the embrace, and once more she enjoyed how he fit against her, as if their bodies had been made for each other. When their legs tangled, his stump brushed along her thigh. At that, profound sadness washed over her: that he had had to endure this, that he'd had to go through it alone, all alone, for twelve long years.

He stroked her hair and played with the long strands that clung to his fingers. Cissy buried her face in the hollow of his shoulder and breathed in his unique scent: sweet sandalwood, overlaid by the muskiness of their lovemaking of a few hours ago. She closed her eyes and smiled against his shoulder. His symmetry might be disturbed, but not destroyed, never destroyed. And they fit well together.

Turning her head a little, she pressed a kiss against one stubbly cheek. "If you want to look at my cards, we need a bit of light," she whispered.

"As my lady wishes," he whispered back. Before he rolled off her, he captured her lips in a searing kiss, his tongue whirling hotly through her mouth. When he finally raised his head, he was grinning again. "To keep you warm."

With a giggle, she shoved at his shoulder so she could wriggle out underneath him and leave the warmth of the bed. Immediately, gooseflesh took her skin. "Brrr." She rubbed her arms.

Behind her, she heard her husband chuckle. "Oh dear, I see my warming-up technique leaves something to be desired."

She looked back over her shoulder and caught him ogling her bare behind from where he lay among the rumpled pillows. She raised her brows in mock severity. "Enjoying yourself?"

His teeth flashed. "With you, always."

Joy rose inside her like a golden bubble. He was quite wrong, she found: his warming-up technique left nothing to be desired.

She went to her chest of drawers, and at the same time she heard him rummaging for the flint box. When she turned, her small package of cards in hand, soft candlelight had enshrouded the bed and transformed Fenris's skin into molten gold.

He watched as she walked toward him, and under his gentle scrutiny she felt herself blush. Who would have thought this a few months ago: that she would ever walk around a room stark naked while Fenris von Wolfenbach watched, this smoky, hot look in his eyes promising undreamt of delights?

When he saw the fiery color suffusing her skin, his lips twisted in a tender smile. "Have I already told you how beautiful you are?" he asked. He reached out a hand.

By now Cissy felt as if her cheeks were on fire. She placed her hand in his, and his warm, strong fingers closed around hers. With a gentle tug, he drew her to his side. With his free hand he flipped back the cover so she could slip back inside.

"Beautiful, but freezing," he laughed, as her icy limbs brushed against him. "Come here." He wrapped her in both the cover and his arms.

"Mmmm." She snuggled against him, luxuriating in the heat his body radiated. "The cards." She held out the stack.

"Oh yes, the cards." He kissed her wrist before he took them. Leaning on his elbow above her, he opened the box, and ivory-colored cards rained on the duvet. Clearly puzzled, he fetched up the ace of spades. "Didn't you say it was an *erotic* deck?" He turned the card around. Frowning, he glanced at Cissy, who tried to smother her giggles with a hand over her mouth. "Have you been pulling my leg, sweet wife? This is a normal, plain ace of spades, as erotic as a broomstick."

At his consternation, she burst out laughing. She took the card. "You have to hold it against the light." She proceeded to show him, and as if by magic, the card revealed its secret.

Fenris's jaw dropped. "Holy cow!"

"As erotic as a broomstick, hm?" Cissy asked, amused.

Together they looked at the picture, which was of a man and a woman coupling on a settee. The man lay against a fat red pillow, his trousers down around his knees, while the woman, her skirts drawn up to display her bare bottom, lay on top of him, pierced by his large member.

"Holy cow," Fenris repeated, clearly thunderstruck.

Cissy giggled. A disconcerted beast was quite a novelty. "Rather . . . um . . . enlightening, don't you think?" she asked innocently.

He shot her a dark look.

She batted her lashes.

"Minx," he growled, and reached for the next card, the nine of hearts. A naked woman lounged on a chair, while in front of her, down on his knees, a man teased her cleft with his finger. "Ah. Proper supplication," Fenris commented.

Beside him, Cissy shifted. A rather extraordinary feeling this, her husband's hot body pressed against her, while they looked at these erotic little pictures together.

Reaching for another card, he threw her a look, his eyes glinting with sudden devilry, as if he knew that a pulse had begun to throb between her legs. "Have you looked at all of them?" he wanted to know.

This time the card showed a woman on her knees before a soldier, sucking on his manhood.

"Ye-es."

On the next card, the king of diamonds's enormous penis sprung up from among his loosened clothes. Fenris arched a brow. "Impressive," was his dry comment. "If somewhat crooked. Don't you think so?" His gaze returned to Cissy's, pierced her.

Blood heated her cheeks. "Hm." She fought hard not to squirm under his scrutiny.

His gaze shifted away as he chose another card. The seven of clubs: another settee, another couple. "Do you look at them often?" Fenris asked, his tone almost disinterested. But there was still that glint in his eyes.

Cissy swallowed. By now, her whole body tingled most uncomfortably. "Sometimes," she croaked.

"Ah." He sounded as if he had made a profound discovery. He turned the five of hearts to the light. "A nice one, that."

Two women, this time; naked and kissing, and one of them was fondling the sex of the other, while in the background a man stood by and watched.

Cissy swallowed. The duvet rasped painfully over her puckered nipples. She bit her lower lip in the vain hope the tingling would stop.

Her husband's gaze swiveled back to capture hers, like an eagle capturing its prey. Smiling, he leaned down. "And what do you feel when you look at them, my sweet?"

At the sound of his voice, dark and smooth like hot cocoa, Cissy felt the muscles in her stomach contract and a rush of scalding heat between her legs. She sucked in a sharp breath. "I . . . I . . ."

He nuzzled the hollow under her jaw. "Does it make you shiver and tingle?" His tongue rasped over the soft column of her throat. Ecstatic, Cissy closed her eyes and arched her neck to give him better access. "Does it make you hot, so hot . . . ?" His teeth closed over her tender skin in the gentlest of bites. *"Hot,"* he breathed.

Cissy moaned. "Y-y-yes . . ."

"Does it? Does it indeed?" He stopped kissing her, and she thought she would die.

"Fenris!" She opened her eyes.

"That's a nice one, too." He held up another card. This time, the grin he gave her was decidedly wolfish. "A very nice one, the queen of spades."

The queen of spades.

Cissy ran her tongue over suddenly dry lips.

His eyes fastened on that tiny movement. "A very, *very* nice one," he rasped. He raised his eyes to hers, daring her. "Don't you want to look at it?"

Temptation, that voice. It flowed over her like warm syrup, so smooth and tempting.

"I . . ." Of course she knew what she would find when she looked at the picture. "I . . ."

"Go on," he invited, his eyes smoky and smoldering. "Look at it," he whispered. "Look to your delight. Let the heat spread through your body."

Helplessly, she followed his gaze as his eyes turned to the queen of spades, which he held flat between his fore and middle fingers. Flat, so the light glinted off the card, but didn't yet reveal its secret.

"Behold"—a flick of his thumb and the card sprang to life—"the queen."

The woman leaned nonchalantly against a small green table as if she did not care that her skirts were rucked up to her waist, revealing her rounded belly and thighs. And on the floor between her legs sat a man who . . . who . . .

"And what do you feel when you look at *this*?" Fenris whispered against her ear, making her shiver helplessly. "Can you feel the heat?" His lips caressed her temple. "So much heat . . ."

It was burning her up, the heat. A fire raged through her veins.

Transfixed, Cissy stared at the little queen of spades, at the man who sat between her legs and—

"Here." Fenris pressed the card into her nerveless fingers. "Look at it, will you? Look at her delight, Cissy."

Now free, his hand slipped under the duvet. She sucked in a breath as it reached her breasts, brushed over her aching nipples. Darts of delight nipped at her nerve endings.

"Fenris . . ."

"Just look." He kissed her temple. "Look at her. So much delight, Cissy." His hand stroked her quivering belly, and she had to bite her lip to prevent herself from screaming. "A true queen, isn't she? Just look at her, my sweet. Look."

His fingers brushed over the springy hair at the apex of her thighs, while she stared at the card, at the woman who stood so proudly and at the man who orally pleasured her.

One of Fenris's fingers found the little nub between her legs and flicked. Cissy moaned loudly. Her eyes fell closed. Her back arched, and she pressed herself against his fingers.

"Do you feel the heat, my sweet? Do you?"

"Yes," she whimpered. "*Yes.*"

His finger slid deeper, sinking into her. "Ahh, and how wet it makes you." Sultry satisfaction rang in his voice. "So wet you're overflowing."

She could feel his finger moving inside her, in and out, sliding easily through her moist heat. She panted. Surely this was too much. Nobody could feel so much and still live.

"Look at the queen, Cissy. Do you think she is as wet as you?" His deep, dark voice flowed over her, added to her delight, and she whimpered again.

Abruptly, his fingers disappeared, leaving her empty and aching. So empty, she could have wept. She blinked and looked at him as he loomed above her. "Don't . . . don't stop," she begged.

He raised her hand holding the card. "Look at the queen, Cissy. *Look* at her."

Almost sobbing, she complied.

"Beautiful, is she not?" With tender hands he stroked the damp strands of hair out of her face. "Can you imagine what she feels?"

"Fenris, *please!*" Her whole body ached for his touch.

The flame of the candle flickered, making the woman on the card shudder wildly.

Cissy shivered. "Please, Fenris, please. . . ."

He stared down at her, his eyes darker than she had ever seen them. Frantically, she reached up to stroke his cheek, his chin. "Fenris, please. Please, I beg you. I . . ."

A dark, dangerous smile lifted his lips. "Shall I show you?"

"I— What?"

His gaze flickered to the card. "Will you let me . . . ?" His voice trailed delicately away.

He would . . . ?

Cissy gasped. She felt as if she were burning up from inside.

"Yes or no, my sweet?" His lips roamed her face, raining kisses on her brows, her nose, her cheeks, her lips. But it was not enough. Not nearly enough.

Shuddering, she let her head fall back and closed her eyes. "Oh, yes," she breathed. "Yes."

He took her mouth with his, branded her with his tongue. "As you wish," he finally said, his voice hoarse. And a heartbeat later, the cover was ripped aside, her scattered cards rustling like the wings of little birds.

Cool air washed over Cissy's hot body, but only for a moment, then his mouth was there, nibbling on her collarbone, tracing the outline of her breasts and then—

yes!—kissing his way down her stomach. She moaned as his tongue dipped into her belly button, whirled around. Her thighs fell open.

Against the black of her closed lids she saw the queen of spades, proudly displaying her nakedness. The man sitting at her feet, licking her, licking . . . Fenris!

Cissy screamed.

His tongue flicked over her again and again, ran teasingly up and down her folds and dipped into her wetness. And as he sucked on her, he catapulted her right into the sky and made her fly.

She felt his hands clamp around her waist as she thrashed helplessly on the bed, moaning his name.

And he licked, and licked, like the man on the picture. He licked until the sky exploded into a thousand stars, raining down on her.

Cissy's scream echoed in the room, but still Fenris did not cease, and she could not evade his tongue, even though she whimpered and begged. He licked and teased and a second wave washed over her . . . and another . . . and another . . . until she lay in his arms, damp and limp, and thought she had surely died with so much pleasure.

His hands stroked her in gentle circles, soothing the tremors which still wracked her body. "The most beautiful thing I have ever seen," she heard him whisper. He nuzzled her ear, traced its outline with his tongue.

Then, when she was still lying boneless against the pillows, he gently turned her around so she was facing away from him. He wrapped his arms around her and drew her back against his chest, slick with sweat. She could feel his erection against the small of her back, so hot he must surely burn her skin. And then he lifted her leg a little and in one smooth thrust slipped inside her.

It was enough to rouse her from her languidness and

make shafts of fire pierce her body once more. "Ahh," she groaned. Her head fell back against his shoulder.

"Do you like that?" he murmured, his breath a warm caress against her ear, while he flexed his hips and slowly moved inside her.

"Mmmm." Her sigh ended in a moan, as his hand found her breast. She wriggled her bottom against him.

A soft laugh drifted over her cheek. "I gather that means you like it."

This time, their loving was slow and dreamy. He moved without haste, his hands tender on her body. His warmth surrounded her, flowed into her, until the barriers between their bodies blurred and the pleasure swept over their heads like a dark wave. They floated in it, and it gently carried them over into sleep while they were still joined: she wrapped in his arms, he embedded deep inside her.

So deep he must surely touch her heart.

INTERLUDE

The happiness soaked through them until they fairly hummed with it. They remembered such happiness from ages past when they had been filled with joy. Would the joy return to them now, brighter than sunshine? Would there be enough happiness to chase away the shadows, to break the ice of desolation?

They hoped and waited.

Sometimes a tiny spark was enough to ignite a mighty fire.

CHAPTER NINETEEN

The second time Cissy woke, it was to sunshine and birdsong—and to a cold, empty space next to her in bed.

Fenris had opened one of the windows, and the fresh, crisp morning air had already chased away the scent of their lovemaking. A feeling of loss stabbed at her heart, as sharp as any knife. And fear. Was he embarrassed that her maid might come in and smell it, their passion, the joy they had found and shared? All at once, tears pricked in her eyes.

She turned her face into the pillow where his head had rested. His scent still clung to the linen, and greedily she inhaled it. *Wolf, my wolf.* She sighed.

For a moment, she lay limp, then she rubbed her cheek over the pillow and remembered the moments she had hugged him to her, when she had buried her face in the hollow of his shoulder. She remembered the weight of him when he had moved inside her body, and the even more delicious heaviness of him after he had orgasmed that first time. He had lain so still she might have thought he had died had it not been for the thundering of his heart against hers. He had smelled so sharp and sweet, of joy and love. Love—

Cissy rubbed at her eyes.

How she would have loved to wake up with him to a new morning. How she would have loved to hug him to her once more, to feel his living warmth, his strength and gentleness. To feel how well their bodies fit together, so very well.

Frowning, she sat up. Why *wasn't* he here with her?

Something pricked at her thigh, and when she reached down to remove whatever had caused the little sting, she found the knave of clubs smirking back at her. In fact, her cards lay scattered all around the bed, showing their shiny, innocent daytime faces. Cissy looked from them to the burnt-down candle beside her bed.

"It's no use pretending last night hasn't happened," she told the knave of clubs grimly. "So you can just stop." She scrambled up and retrieved her cards.

Yet one was missing. One was . . .

She found the queen of spades under her pillow, slightly crumpled but still smiling serenely. Cissy pressed the card against her heart. "You and I, we both know what happened last night," she whispered to the queen. "And we will hold on to it. Yes, we will."

Cissy did not bother to wait for Marie, but donned her wrap stays over her chemise and chose a simple morning dress. She splashed some cold water into her face and quickly combed out her hair. After braiding it tightly, she pinned it up and deemed herself respectable enough to confront her husband.

She took a deep breath.

He would know, just like her, that her simple, respectable appearance was a daytime façade, too. In his arms she had become a wanton, had been naked and had lost all decorum. And yet, she refused to be ashamed, for there had been so much joy and pleasure.

And love.

For a moment, she had to close her eyes. But yes, that too. Love.

She picked up the queen. "I will not feel shame for something so beautiful," she told the card before she slipped it into her pocket. Determined, she walked out of her room and started to search for her husband.

She found him in his study, deeply engrossed in his account ledgers. Cissy's heart softened as she stood unnoticed in the door and watched how he ran his hand through his hair, making it stick up in all directions. Concentration tightened his features, and had created a wrinkle between his brows. *So he just has work to do.* She felt an overwhelming urge to kiss the wrinkle away, to smoothe her fingers over his face and chase away all that tension once more.

Smiling tenderly, she stepped fully into the room. "Good morning, sweetheart," she said.

Clearly startled, he looked up. The line between his brows deepened even more. A muscle jumped in his jaw. "I've got work to do," he finally said curtly, and busied himself with his papers once more.

Cissy's steps faltered. But hadn't she thought this herself last night: that it would need much loving to fully redeem the beast?

"You were not there when I woke up," she said. She heard how plaintive the words sounded, and her fingers curled into fists at her sides. Still, she continued, even though it cost her some pride. "I missed you," she added softly.

"As I said, I've got work to do." His voice was even more distant than before, and this time he wouldn't even look up at her.

Cissy licked her dry lips. She had to work hard at making her voice sound cheerful. "But surely you've got time for breakfast? It would be lovely if we could have breakfast together and—"

"I've already told you, I've got work to do," he snarled. Cissy flinched, for he sounded nothing like the man who had lain in her arms the night before. "You aren't deaf, are you?"

She gasped. Last night she had given all of herself to this man, who was now treating her like an inconvenient nuisance. Cissy's nails dug into her palms, hoping the pain would distract her from the hot prickling of her eyes. "I thought after we shared something so beautiful last night, that—"

Fenris looked up, and she couldn't go on. There was no sparkle in his eyes, no twinkle of heat. They were flat and dead.

"Last night was . . ."—something had happened to his voice, and he had to swallow hard before he continued, his voice frosty—". . . a pleasant distraction."

Pain blossomed in Cissy's chest. Such terrible, terrible pain, as if he had shot a dart into her breast, and her heart's blood was now running freely down her body to stain the carpet like her virgin's blood had stained the linen sheets. She had given all of herself . . . and he did not care.

She lifted her chin a notch. *Courage.* "If you see it like this . . ." But then her voice wobbled. She could not go on. She whirled and fled the room so he would not see the tears on her cheeks.

Fenris leaned his head against the bookshelf and closed his eyes, his body aching with weariness. Last night had been . . . How to describe an experience where he had felt blessed and cherished for the first time in years? In

Cissy's arms he had become reborn. Her ardor and desire had almost led him to believe that he could become strong and whole again. A man instead of a cripple.

A bitter laugh escaped him.

No, that was why he'd been forced to be cruel just now. For, of course the King of Dwarves had no business courting the Fairy Princess in the first place. Her beauty was far too removed from his ugliness. All he would achieve was to drag her down into his darkness. And this he refused to do. He was filled with too much bitterness, was too twisted inside out. All these years of loneliness had eaten away at his soul until he was more beast than man.

It had been a mistake to let himself be overwhelmed by her sweetness. He had been charmed by her intelligence and humor. Foolishly, he had brought her a present because he had thought it would make her smile—and God knew, he craved her smiles. Foolishly, selfishly, he had not been able to resist stealing a few sweet kisses, had not been able to resist touching her until his damned lust had blown away all common sense. Until he had forgotten what he was.

A cripple . . . a freak . . . half a man.

His brother had been right: It would be a miserable marriage bed indeed for Celia. He would only taint her with his ugliness. And he was not beast enough to want that.

No, it was better to stay away from the Fairy Princess.

For the King of Dwarves, there were only dreams—impossible, foolish dreams—never to be reached in real life.

He would not forget again.

Days and weeks passed, and her husband evaded Cissy like sand running through her fingers. If, by chance, she happened to come across him on her wanderings through the silent castle, the soft whistle of the wind her only conpanion, he stopped and stared as if he were seeing a ghost. His features would shift, turn to stone, and he would hastily walk away, his uneven steps echoing in the hallway.

Yet even then she saw the man she loved. She watched the smooth flow of the muscles in his back and remembered the feeling of them under her hands when he had moved above her, inside her, when their bodies had melted to become one. Her skin prickled, yearning for his touch. Her whole body ached for him, for the delight he had brought her, and for the feeling of shelter and protection she had found in his arms.

But even sharper than this pain in her body was the pain in her heart. It cried out for him, cried and cried in vain.

So she wandered the hallways and roamed the ramparts, accompanied by the lonely song of the wind through the trees. Dark and impenetrable, the forest spread around the castle, and the village at the foot of the hill seemed far, far away and so small it could have been a child's toy.

On some days Cissy could almost pretend to be the only living thing in the castle. An enchanted princeess kept prisoner by the gargoyles looming above, springing up from the stone, their twisted faces forever frozen in ugly snarls. Then she wrapped her old, black pelisse tighter around herself, for the wind seemed to blow colder, mocking her hopes and dreams.

Lavenders green, diddle diddle,
Lavenders blue,
You must love me, diddle diddle,
Because I love you.

Cissy closed her eyes against the sudden hot sting of tears. *Life is not a fairy tale,* her brother had told her, and in these bleak, dark moments she despaired that there would ever be a happy ending for her, and she thought she would gladly sell her shadow for even a little bit of joy. But, no. She would forever roam the castle, sad and lonely, while the forest grew dense and thick around her so escape would become impossible. The wind sang in the trees, the same song forevermore, unchanging as the roar of the sea. And she was just a small pebble, thrown this way and that by forces far greater than herself.

It seemed to Cissy as if a whisper ran through the stones beneath her feet. When she was walking through these ancient rooms and hallways, the tapestries on the walls seemed to spring to life, green vines reached out off the fabric, unicorns bowed their horns toward her. An unseen breeze seemed to lift the clothes of the human figures as they turned their heads to stare after her.

And today, when she came to the great grandfather clock with its fantastic figures, the Sheep Princess regarded her stoically.

The clock struck five.

Cissy watched the lower screen slide aside to reveal the busy dwarves in their mine. *Click-clack, click-clack, click-clack.* Always busy, always working, unchanging like the song of the wind in the trees. The eight on the face of the clock turned inward; the King of Dwarves appeared at the window and shot his beloved yearning looks. The enchanted princess might have smiled a little, but she remained a sheep, gray and wooly.

Cissy blinked. *I don't want to remain a sheep forever,* she thought. *No, I don't.* She reached inside her pocket and drew out the queen of spades, which she had been carrying around ever since the confrontation with her hus-

band. The little queen leaned on her table and smiled at
Cissy. When Cissy held up the card, she could just discern the outline of the man sitting between the queen's
legs, and the triangle of the hair over the queen's sex.

Cissy looked from the card to the closed door of Fenris's study. The lion's den, Leopold had once called it.
But Leopold was an odious nidget. His brother was not a
dangerous monster. Fenris had touched and kissed her
just like the man in the picture. He had made her
queen. And queens had power.

Unlike fairy princesses.

Unlike fairy princess sheep.

Taking a deep breath, Cissy straightenend her shoulders and curled her fingers around the queen of spades,
as if some of the queen's power would thus spring over
to her. *Well, I'm certainly not going to mope around like a
ninny-brained daftie any longer, so he can just deal with it!*
Her head held high, she marched to the door of the
study, knocked once and entered. The door clicked shut
behind her. Fenris raised his head.

When he saw who had intruded, something flickered
over his face, a yearning, a softness that made him look
vulnerable. But the next moment, the expression was
gone and his features were cast in stone once more.

"What do you want?" he asked.

"I want to talk to you," Cissy said calmly, even though
her heart hammered in her ears and drummed in her
throat, threatening to drone out everything else.

Fenris held up the letter he had been reading and
studied it intently. "Talk? I don't see what we have to talk
about." He somehow seemed leaner than a few days ago,
as if all the tension emanating from him had stretched
tight the flesh over his bones.

Cissy's skin prickled, and she had to take another
deep breath to be able to continue. "Well, for one thing

I was wondering why you no longer visit me." She had tried to make herself sound nonchalant and flip, yet her words had come out yearning. *Pitiful,* she thought in disgust.

"Visit?" He frowned.

One corner of the queen of spades dug into the soft flesh of her thumb. "At *night,*" Cissy hastened to clarify. She gulped. "To share my bed."

He froze. Slowly, ever so slowly, he turned his head toward her. His gaze raked her up and down. "Do I understand you correctly?" His voice sounded strange, as if he were choking. "You're asking me why I don't come to your bed?"

Despite the heat flaming in Cissy's cheeks, she nodded. "Yes."

Incredulity was written all over his face. "To fuck you?" His eyes burned into hers.

Her cheeks heated even more. So, the snarling demon wolf was well and truly back. "Yes," she said, and refused to look away.

Growling an oath, he whirled and strode to the window. His head bent, he braced his hands against the window frame. "You're asking me why I don't come to you at night to fuck you?" His voice was muffled. He shook his head. *"Himmel!"*

Cissy watched how his shoulders heaved with his rasping breaths. Then he straightened and slapped his hands against the stone. He turned, and for once his eyes burnt with some unspoken emotion. "Well . . . I . . ." When words seemed to fail him, he exploded. "Because I don't want to molest you again!" He stared at her, his chest heaving like that of a horse ridden much too far.

Cissy's eyes widened. "Molest?" she whispered. *He thinks . . . ?* A powerful rush of emotion overwhelmed

her, and she hurried toward his desk. "But Fenris, Fenris, you didn't . . ." She felt tears dripping over her
cheeks, and impatiently, she wiped them away with the
back of her hand. "You thought . . ." Joy exploded in her
veins, made her dizzy. She laughed. "Oh, sweeting, how
could you have thought . . ." She looked at him tenderly.
"You didn't 'molest' me, Fenris. There was joy for me—
so much joy and pleasure." She opened her hand and
put the queen of spades on his table. "Don't you remember? So much joy!" She sniffled, wiped her nose.

Yet the expressions of relief she had expected did not
come. Instead he stared at the card on his table as if it
were a poisonous viper. With horror she watched how
his face lost all expression. When he looked from the
card to her, his eyes were bleak and dead. Then he
turned toward the window once more.

"There was so much joy, Fenris," she whispered,
pleaded with him.

"Why can't you let it be?" he asked harshly. "Why are
you doing this to yourself?"

"What? I don't understand." Her throat hurt. Awkwardly, she wiped her hand over her wet cheeks.
"Fenris—"

"Damn you!" His hands slapped against the stone
wall. She started. An icy shiver raced down her spine.

"Fenris—"

"I wished to spare you, but you—" Again, he slapped
his hands against the stone before he turned around.
His expression strangely calm, he lifted his chin to a
haughty angle and crossed his arms in front of his chest.
"If you must know, that encounter did nothing for me."

Everything in Cissy went still. "What are you saying?"

He raised an arrogant brow. "There might have been
joy for you, but I found the whole experience utterly
boring." He shrugged. "I didn't want to be so crass as to

say this to your face, but since you insist . . ." His voice trailed away. Another shrug.

Somewhere inside her, trembling started. The demon wolf she would have been able to handle. But this? She took a step back. "It was all a lie?"

He heaved an exaggerated sigh. "It is understandable that an innocent virgin would blow such a thing totally out of proportion."

She took another step back. "You did not enjoy . . ."

"Well, I guess, it was not *too* bad, not for having been with an innocent like you."

Her trembling reached outward. A violent shudder wracked her body.

"You shouldn't take this so hard, you know," he continued in the same hateful, bored voice. "It was all right, I guess. Just . . ." His mouth twisted. "Just not for me."

A sob caught in Cissy's throat. Pressing her hand against her mouth to hold it back, she whirled and ran blindly out of the room.

When the door banged closed behind her, Fenris flinched. He remained standing in the same posture a few moments more before his shoulders finally sagged. Wearily, he passed his hand over his eyes.

Then he looked at the card, which still lay on the table. Unperturbed by the drama that had been going on, the little printed queen smiled up at him. Very slowly, he reached down and ran a gentle finger over her daytime face.

INTERLUDE

The man prowled the ramparts while unseeing eyes followed his progress. His bitterness churned in their hearts, as it had for so many years. That bitterness, that pain had become his companions on his lonely wanderings through the castle. No other companions than these. Always alone.

They understood his bitterness and pain.

They understood the fear that prevented him from reaching out when happiness became possible.

For a little moment it had seemed possible.

For a little moment . . .

But that fear had been greater, older, more powerful. And now, together with him, they mourned the loss of that one chance at happiness, and the pain which nearly buckled his knees twisted their hearts of stone.

Alone. Forever.

CHAPTER TWENTY

To stay away from him was easy. It was a big castle, after all. Sometimes days would pass before she even caught a glimpse of him. Yet at night, when she looked out the window, she would often see the flickering light of his lantern on the ramparts below her. Then she couldn't help herself, couldn't help following its progress until it disappeared around the next bend. And her heart would weep the tears she did not allow her eyes to shed.

Though she tried, she couldn't forget that night he had been hers, the night he hadn't walked the ramparts, but had lain in her arms, had cradled her safely. But— oh, it had all been an illusion! The protectiveness, the tenderness, the passion: he had repudiated it all.

Mrs. Chisholm wrote soothing letters, said to give him time.

Time? Cissy laughed bitterly. She had given him all the time in the world, and in the span of one night she had given him all of herself, her body and soul, and he had found the experience "utterly boring."

Yet whenever she tried to hate him for what he had

done to her, she would see the flickering light of his lantern, a testimony of his lonely wanderings through the castle. He was a beast prowling his cage, never, ever able to escape.

Just as I am doomed to be the enchanted princess, Cissy thought, and leaned her forehead against the cool stone. And now she couldn't even go back. There was no return to her old life, no chance of ever being plain Cissy Fussell again. For better or worse, she was Celia von Wolfenbach. This was her castle. This was her fairy tale.

Easter approached. Together with all the women in the household of the old *Graf,* Cissy was busy dyeing paper and cutting it in thin strips. These were given to the young townspeople, and on the morning of Palm Sunday the young men carried high stakes adorned with crowns of colorful paper strips in the procession.

The family of Wolfenbach walked behind the priest and the wooden palm mule with the server swinging the incense. The sweet, bewitching smell mingled with the crisp aroma of spring as the procession moved from the marketplace to St. Margaretha's. Yet, neither incense nor the heralding spring could erase the scent of sandalwood emanating from the man walking beside Cissy, his head bent and his mouth cast in a tight line as he maneuvered the uneven cobblestones. He was so near, she only needed to reach out to touch him, to slip her fingers into his hand, to intertwine them with his and offer him comfort and reassurance. But . . .

I found the whole experience utterly boring.

Cissy blinked away the sudden sting of tears. No, he would not want her comfort, even though he clearly looked miserable. It was obvious he didn't want to be here, where the people stared at him and whispered behind their hands, where small children gaped at him as if they expected he would pounce and devour them at any moment. Yet tradition and the duties of family demanded of him to be here, to stumble over cobblestones with the whole town watching.

Not for the first time, Cissy wondered why he insisted on flaunting his disability like this, wondered whether he saw it as a punishment for a young boy joining the war against Napoleon and thus throwing his family into disgrace. As a punishment for the wish to fight for the freedom of his country.

As she followed the cross to St. Margaretha's, Cissy's heart clenched with the desperate urge to again take her husband into her arms and make his pain go away. To banish the beast forever. Instead she bowed her head so nobody would see the tears in her eyes.

The Holy Week saw her go to the Villa Wolfenbach. There she helped boiling and coloring eggs, while Cook and her kitchen maid were busy baking Easter pretzels. The *Gräfin* showed Cissy how to apply delicate patterns of wax on the fragile eggshell before letting the egg slide into some liquid color. Best of all, Cissy liked the shades of dark pink that birch bark produced. She loved rubbing a sheen of grease over the eggs and making the colors more brilliant.

And she loved the beautiful mass at St. Margaretha's on Easter night, when the whole church was immersed in darkness before the procession of the priest and the servers carried light into the darkness and heralded new hope for the world.

But, of course, there was no hope for the Castle of Wolfenbach.

Cissy sighed while the church rang with the halleluja. But then the flame that was given from candle to candle ignited the candle she was holding, and she felt as if the light also blossomed inside her heart. By the time she stepped outside and found the blazing bonfire in the churchyard, a smile lit her face.

The crisp, fresh night air stung her cheeks, and she watched the sparks from the bonfire shooting up toward the stars in the sky. All around her the churchyard hummed with the happy chatter of the folk of Kirchwalden talking to their friends and neighbors. For a moment the German voices all blended together, an unintelligible buzzing, swelling up and down in volume. It was like the song of the sea. The song of the forest.

Cissy searched the crowd until she found the familiar figure on the other side of the fire doing his best to blend into the shadows. She watched how the firelight flickered over that face she had kissed and caressed, how it lent him a diabolical appearance. With the fire between them, they stared at each other. *So near, yet so far apart.*

She could not avert her eyes. Instead, she drank in the sight of him, tall and lean, black hair slightly tousled by the breeze.

She remembered how she had woken up beside him long before dawn, when the world had been rendered a gray, colorless place. A place where all boundaries blurred. She remembered the feeling of his skin against hers, the rasp of his springy body hair. How good he had felt. How right it had been to take him in her arms.

What would he do now if I hugged him? Cissy wondered bitterly. How naïve she had been to believe a single night could redeem the beast. Or even a whole lifetime.

I found the whole experience utterly boring.

A dagger into her heart.

And he had known it.

Determined, she turned away and went over to her mother-in-law to help hand out colored eggs and pretzels. Children ran squealing around the fire. One of the innkeepers produced a pot of hot mulled wine to go with the pretzels and eggs. A festive, happy air seized the gathering. Lent was finally over.

Suddenly, another figure separated from the crowd. The firelight glinted on his golden blond hair, and his green eyes twinkled merrily as he stood before her.

"Happy Easter, *Liebchen*," Leopold von Wolfenbach said, his thumbs thrust into the pockets of his waistcoat. "Happy to see me?" He didn't wait for her answer, but leaned over to greet his mother and kiss her on the cheek.

"Where have you been, Leo?" The reprimand in the voice of the *Gräfin* was unmistakable.

He just shrugged and grinned. "Here and there. There and here." Casually, he cast a look around. "And where is my big brother, so happily married? Ah, there he is." He raised his hand as if in greeting, then abruptly focused on Cissy once more, his eyes boring into hers. "Why is he not at your side, *Liebchen*?" He gave her a knowing smirk. "Trouble in paradise already?"

When Cissy refused to answer, he shot a look at his mother, who was busy giving more pretzels to the children. Obviously reassured that she wouldn't notice, he leaned toward Cissy and trailed a familiar finger down her arm.

She jerked away. "Stop it!" she hissed.

Leo just chuckled. "Have you ever wondered if you might have married the wrong brother?" Ever so slowly he turned his head, willing her to follow his gaze and look upon his brother on the other side of the fire. Fenris stood very still. He was watching them intently.

Smiling, Leopold caressed Cissy's cheek. As she tried to turn her head away, he held her fast, her chin caught between his thumb and forefinger. "You don't want to make a scene, sister dear, do you?" he whispered into

her ear. "Think of how it would ruin the atmosphere."
He rubbed his thumb over her skin. "What a pity it
would be. Now, tell me: if my dear brother is over there,
and you are here, and I am here with you, don't you
think that says you must have married the wrong
brother?" He lowered his voice to an intimate purr.
"Don't you think so, *Liebchen?*"

Anger choked Cissy. "I would have rather given the castle to the vultures of the Altertumsverein than marry you!"

Laughing, Leo let his hand fall away from her face.
He threw another look at his brother and his lips lifted
in a smirk. He was undeterred. "Tomorrow evening they
will light another fire and they will dance around it." His
voice was a soft, disgusting caress against her ear. "Does
your husband dance well, *Liebchen?*"

For a moment she simply stared at him, too angry for
words. His smile widened, widened, until he gave a short
cough of laughter.

"Leopold!" his mother suddenly hissed. "Behave
yourself!"

The people standing around them stared, then smiled
good-naturedly. The youngest son of the *Graf,* the town's
golden boy—he was back, and that was reason to rejoice.

Cissy cast a look at her husband. Shadows danced over
his face and made his expression impossible to discern.
In all likelihood, his features were frozen into stone as
they always were when he didn't want people to know his
thoughts or feelings.

Come to me, my wolf, she summoned silently. *Oh, please,
come to me!* But of course, he did not budge.

Wiping his eyes, Leopold chuckled. "It's not as if I
didn't warn you," he continued, clearly not caring that
his mother and half the town could hear what he was
saying.

Did he feel so sure of himself that he thought he

could slight his brother in public? With all the world to hear and snicker? A hot wave of anger rushed through Cissy and made her forget all caution.

"Oh yes." Steadily she advanced on him until they stood toe to toe. "Yes, you warned me. You warned me what a von Wolfenbach could be." She cocked her head to the side, then switched to English. "You've shown me perfectly what a sniveling little bastard *you* are." She gave him a pleasant smile. "You've shown that your brother is much more of a man than you could ever be." And with satisfaction, she watched the dull color rise in his cheeks, how his triumphant expression changed to a sulky pout.

"You want to make me believe you're happy with my brother, that cripple?" he snarled in English. "For what kind of fool do you take me? Tell me, have you yet found out how much more they shot off than his leg?"

Shaking her head, she stepped back. "You're disgusting."

"Yes? Well, my dear brother's first fiancée obviously thought the same about him. When he came back from the war"—his eyes glittered maliciously—"all shot to pieces. And how could anybody fault her for it—that she would want a real man instead of a cripple?"

Everything in Cissy went cold. Her basket with the pretzels fell to the ground. "His first fiancée?" she whispered.

Leopold laughed, a hateful, triumphant laugh. "So he hasn't told you about her either?" His laughter became louder, wilder. "She did the only sensible thing, ran off to marry another man." Wearing a satisfied expression, he stroked his thumb along his jaw. "I have to say that she did well for herself. . . ." Abruptly he turned and gave his brother a wave. "Hey, Fenris," he shouted, falling back into German. "Greetings from the Contessa Czerny. She said to give you her congratulations on your nuptials."

At his shout, the whole crowd fell silent. Their gazes moved back and forth between the two brothers—one with a shining golden halo like St. George about to slay the evil dragon; the other looking like the devil himself, dark and menacing.

A grin split golden Leopold's face, and he licked his lips as if he were a cat who'd just swallowed all the cream. "Yes, greetings from the Contessa Czerny. And I have to say . . . ,"—the grin widened—"she's just as *lovely* as always." He let his tongue curl suggestively around his lips once more, before laughing and walking away.

"God, what has gotten into the boy?" the *Gräfin* moaned. Her husband put a comforting arm around her shoulders.

Cissy, however, kept her gaze trained on Leo. She saw how a young girl timidly stepped into his path and touched his arm. With a snarl, he twisted and continued to stride off into the night. Clearly miserable, the girl clasped her hands around her elbows. When she turned, she caught Cissy watching her. She blushed a painful red and hastily disappeared into the crowd.

Cissy frowned.

Marie, her maidservant? Whatever did Marie want from Leopold von Wolfenbach?

On the drive home, her husband broodingly lounged on his side of the carriage and didn't spare Cissy a glance. Silence surrounded them like a shroud, with the clacking of the horses' hooves and the crunching of the wheels on the road the only sounds.

"I didn't invite your brother to talk to me," Cissy finally said when she couldn't stand the silence any longer.

Fenris just continued to stare out of the window. Not even a flutter of his lashes betrayed that he had heard.

She tapped her foot on the floor. "You must have seen that."

He still gave no answer.

Cissy crossed her arms in front of her chest and glared at him. She snorted. "You must have seen that even from where you stood." Narrowing her eyes, she remembered how she had wished he would come to her aid. But no, she had been forced to deal alone with his brother. "Like a pillar of salt," she added nastily. "Stonestruck, as if you'd seen Medusa herself."

She waited another moment, then she threw up her arms. "Gad, what is *with* you? Your parents are such sweet people! Whatever have they done to produce such sons? One is a cad, the other a dunderhead! How wonderful!"

That, she saw with satisfaction, finally got to him—his jaw tightened and a muscle in his cheek jumped. She gave another snort for dramatic effect and, arms crossed, leaned back and watched what her husband would do next.

For a moment he continued to smolder in silence. Then he snapped around so abruptly Cissy started. "Don't you think I know what I am, what I have done to my parents?" he hissed. Fury and frustration sparked from his eyes.

Instant remorse tightened Cissy's stomach. "That's not what I meant," she said. Imploringly, she leaned forward. "That's not what I meant at all, Fenris."

"I *know* what you meant," he snarled. Angrily he knocked against the front of the coach. "Perhaps you married the wrong brother!"

Cissy gasped with outrage. "Do you really think I would have wanted to marry your creepy, spoiled brat of a brother?"

The carriage came to a squeaking halt. Fenris reached to open the door. "I saw the way he looked at you," he threw at her over his shoulder.

"The way *he* looked at *me*?" Cissy couldn't believe what she was hearing. "And what about me? I would have happily pushed the lout into the fire, if you must know." She watched him get out of the carriage. "What do you think you're doing? You can't just leave in the middle of an argument!"

He threw her one of his stony glances. "I am going to ride on the box seat." And the door clicked shut.

Angrily, Cissy shot forward and fumbled with the window. She pulled it down and thrust her head out. "You're such a crack-brained dunderhead, Fenris von Wolfenbach!" she yelled in English. "I hope you freeze your behind off on your beloved box seat!" And with an unladylike curse, she shut the window and fell back onto the seat, just as the carriage rumbled into motion once more.

"He's such a buffleheaded bumpkin! A daft bugbear, that's what he is!" She sniffed.

Yet slowly her anger evaporated. With a sigh, she closed her eyes and hung her head. When had her life become such a mess?

God, how tired she was! How she yearned for the safety of an embrace! She yearned to walk into her father's study and bury her head against his housecoat, while his heart thumped steadily against her ear as if in reassurance. She yearned for the feeling of his hand stroking her hair, for the scent of pipesmoke, for the deep rumble of his laughter. . . .

A dark wave of grief washed over her. She pressed her lips tightly together against the sobs that rose in her throat.

She was alone.

All alone.

By the time the carriage rumbled into the courtyard of the castle, Cissy had managed to regain her composure and to dry her tears. The carriage door opened, but surprisingly, it was Johann who helped her down. "Are you all right, *gnädige Frau?*" He gave her a look full of concern.

"Yes. Yes, I am." Distractedly, she gazed around the courtyard.

"He has already gone upstairs," the valet said softly.

"What?" She stared at him, felt her eyes widen.

"My master. He has already"—he cleared his throat—"retired for the night."

Cissy blinked. "Yes. Of course. He would." What else had she expected? And still this repeated rejection stung bitterly. She took a deep breath and forced a smile onto her lips. "Thank you, Johann. And happy Easter."

Yet when she turned to go inside, the valet put a hand on her arm. Questioning, she looked back at him. He searched her face. "I know it's not my place, but . . . are you sure you are all right, *gnädige Frau?*" He hesitated. "I saw you talking to the young master. . . ."

Cissy gave an amused snort, though she was touched by his concern. "Johann, half of Kirchwalden—no, make that *all* of Kirchwalden saw me talking to Leopold von Wolfenbach tonight." She shrugged. "He is a nuisance, and I wish he would stay away from us."

"He has always been obsessed with the castle."

She wrinkled her nose. "I assume he's been more obsessed with the legendary Wolfenbach Hoard." She rolled her eyes, making the valet chuckle.

"Yes, I assume that is true," he conceded. "I didn't want to keep you, *gnädige Frau.* I was just concerned." His honest brown eyes regarded her solemnly.

This time, Cissy didn't have to force a smile. She patted his arm. "I know. And I thank you for it. I . . ." She frowned, remembering something Leopold had said.

"Actually, Johann, I was wondering: what is so special about the Contessa Czerny?"

The valet's expression darkened dramatically.

"Leopold mentioned her tonight," Cissy continued slowly, watching his reaction. "And . . . yes, when he first arrived here, he mentioned her, too. And it was like . . ." Feeling suddenly vulnerable, she turned her head away and shrugged a shoulder. Briefly, she closed her eyes. *But no . . . I don't want to remain a sheep forever.* Determination lent her courage, and she looked back to Johann, looked him straight into the eye. "What is the Contessa Czerny to my husband, Johann? Is it true that she was his fiancée?"

The valet sighed and rubbed his neck. "I wish I weren't the one to tell you this, *gnädige Frau.*"

Cissy stared at him. "Well, I haven't got that many options, have I? My husband isn't talking to me at the moment, and when he does, all he does is snarl." She raised her eyebrows. "So?"

For a moment Johann stared at her, slack-mouthed, then he gave a laugh. "God bless you, *gnädige Frau.*" He immediately sobered. "I understand that before he ran away to join the British army, my master was indeed engaged to marry the Contessa Czerny." Awkwardly, he cleared his throat. "I understand that he was very much in love with her."

In love. Cissy closed her eyes and swallowed hard. For the first time, she noticed the bite of the crisp night air. "But his need to fight for the freedom of his country was stronger," she whispered.

"Yes. Yes, that's true." Johann's voice was gruff, and he cleared his throat once more. "Apparently, he asked her to wait for him. Or at least he thought she would wait for him. When we were lying in the field together, he would sometimes talk of her, and I think it was his thoughts of her that got him through the ugliness of it all."

Blinking back tears, Cissy looked up at the dark sky, searching for familiar formations. She needed something to ground her. "What happened?"

There was a rustle of clothes as Johann shifted his weight. "Apparently, she . . . balked," he said uncomfortably. "When the family of Wolfenbach lost their privileges, she must have thought she deserved better. And she searched for a new husband."

"And finally became the Contessa Czerny."

"Yes. My master didn't know. Until he returned to Kirchwalden, he didn't know. He thought . . . hoped . . ." The valet's voice trailed away.

Cissy turned back to him. Johann's face was set in grim lines.

"He had so hoped," he said grimly. "But she wasn't there. And when he was sent back, while he lay nearly dying without his leg, she returned all the letters he had written to her, all the presents he had given. She sent them all back with the words that he should never come near her again so the sight of him would not disgust her."

Cissy gasped. "Oh my God," she moaned. She could only too well imagine his despair and pain. "How could she do something like that?"

A cynical smile twisted Johann's mouth. "If I should venture a guess: because she was very much in love with the title and the money, but not with the man. Just as she is in love with her current title and wealth, but not with her husband." He scratched his ear. "I beg your pardon, *gnädige Frau*, but the Contessa Czerny's extramarital affairs are always fodder for the gossipmongers."

"Oh my." Cissy's mouth went dry. "And Leopold von Wolfenbach is one of her *beaux*, is he not? That is what he's rubbing Fenris's face in at every chance he gets." White-hot fury nearly choked her. "The snivelling cur! I should have pushed him into the fire after all!"

And suddenly, so much made sense, most importantly her husband's strange behavior. Why he was keeping his distance. And yet . . .

She had already given him all of herself, and it hadn't been enough to break the curse.

Cissy shivered.

Though she finally understood the game, she had already lost all her trump cards. There was nothing left. The realization was a bitter pain that sliced her heart. She doubted she had ever really had a chance to win this particular game.

She took a deep breath, then smiled weakly at the valet. "Thank you, Johann. You have helped me greatly. Thank you. And good night."

She thought she saw something like compassion in his gentle brown eyes before he bowed. "Good night, *gnädige Frau.*"

CHAPTER TWENTY-ONE

Weeks passed, and while Cissy now never saw her husband during the day, his nightly wanderings on the ramparts did not cease. Whenever she spotted the flickering light of his lantern, a curious, painful mixture of anger and regret, longing and compassion—and love, so much love; always love—would fill her. It cut her to pieces.

Sometimes she wanted to go to him and whack him over the head in the hope it would right his addled brain. Given the obstinacy of her demon wolf, she very much doubted violence would do the trick. Instead, she spent her days overseeing the spring cleaning, making sure that all the rooms were refurbished, that the furniture was waxed, and the tapestries mended.

On Wednesdays she went to the market in Kirchwalden with the kitchenmaid. She loved the hustle and bustle of the market, loved strolling from stall to stall and choosing fresh vegetables, fruit and meat for the kitchen of the castle. And it was there, in the market of the little town on a sunny spring day, that the footman of the Villa Wolfenbach came to find her.

When she spotted the disconcerted man, the smile left Cissy's face. "What is it, Franz?" she asked.

"*Gnädige Frau . . .*" Sharp lines bracketed Franz's mouth. "Something dreadful has happened. The young Herr von Wolfenbach, your husband, has had an accident."

"Oh my God." A droning sound filled Cissy's ears. The noises of the market receded in the background, were blended out in a rush. "What . . ."

"You need to come, *gnädige Frau*. They've brought him back to the castle. Graf and Gräfin von Wolfenbach are already on their way and the doctor has been sent for as well."

"Yes. Yes, of course," Cissy murmured. God, it would take them an hour to walk back to the castle! An hour! How much could happen in that time!

Never before had the path up the hill seemed so long, even though Cissy was walking so fast she soon had left the little kitchenmaid behind. The forest closed darkly around her, the trees humming amongst themselves, looming over her.

Cissy shook her head. On and on she ran. By the time she stumbled over the wooden bridge and up the ward, sweat drenched her clothes. Her heart hammered frantically in her chest. *Oh, my wolf, my wolf . . .*

In the Great Hall she found Frau Häberle huddled on a chair. "Oh *gnädige Frau*, it's the most dreadful thing!" the old woman wailed as she caught sight of Cissy. "The poor young master!" With a white handkerchief she dabbed at the corners of her red-rimmed eyes.

With flying fingers, Cissy unbuttoned her spencer. "Where is he?"

"They brought him upstairs to his room. The doctor's there with him." Frau Häberle took the spencer and

Cissy's bonnet. "Oh, he looked such a fright when they brought him in! Pale as death and blood everywhere!"

Pale as death?

An icy hand gripped Cissy's heart and squeezed her lungs tight. Breathing became difficult.

"Oh, *gnädige Frau*, whatever shall we do if the young master . . . Oh, *gnädige Frau!*" Frau Häberle buried her face in her handkerchief. "The poor young master," she sobbed. "Pale as a corpse, he was!"

Impossibly fast, the ice spread through Cissy's whole body, numbing her limbs, freezing her soul. She caught her breath.

He couldn't.

He wouldn't.

"No," she muttered. "No." And louder. "*No!* He cannot." Her eyes burned. One night. He had been hers for only one night. She wanted more, so much more.

Wide-eyed, the housekeeper stared.

Cissy clenched her hands into fists. "I have to see him!" Abruptly, she turned and walked toward the stairs, faster and faster, until she almost ran. It seemed to her that her feet never touched the steps at all. It hardly mattered, anyway. She would have walked barefoot through broken glass or through burning coals, if need be. If only he was there to await her. Alive.

Alive.

As she was rushing down the corridor to the master suite, Johann came out of the room carrying a bowl of bloodied water. Cissy's stomach turned over.

"*Gnädige Frau—*"

She didn't pay him any heed, but brushed past him to the room he had just exited. The first thing she saw was the doctor, clad all in black, leaning over the bed like a vulture.

A sob rose in Cissy's throat. She stumbled into the room . . . and into the arms of her mother-in-law.

"Liebes—"

But she couldn't tear her gaze away from the doctor leaning over the bed, half-concealing the still form of a man, her love, her husband.

"Fenris," Cissy whispered painfully. *"Fenris."*

With surprising strength, the *Gräfin* dug her fingers into Cissy's shoulders. "Alive, my dear. Badly bruised and scraped, but alive." Tears glittered in the eyes of the older woman. "The doctor is just putting on the last bandage."

Endless minutes passed before the doctor finally stepped back from the bed and Cissy could hurry forward. When she caught sight of her husband, her hands flew up to cover her mouth. His face was leeched of all color, his skin waxen. Deep grooves of pain bracketed his mouth, and his beautiful lips were chafed and cracked. A bandage ran around his head. Underneath the blankets, his big body was still and lifeless, all its intense vibrancy gone.

Tears blurred Cissy's vision. "Fenris!" She fell to her knees beside the bed and reached for his hand. His fingers—his long, elegant fingers, which had touched her with so much tenderness during that one night— were icy-cold. "Oh, dear God." Desperately she pressed a kiss onto his knuckles and held his hand against her cheek. "Oh, Fenris." Tears trickled down her face, dripped from her nose and chin.

His lashes fluttered.

Cissy blinked. "Fenris?" With the back of her free hand, she rubbed the wetness from her face. "Can you hear me, sweetheart?" She gripped his hand tightly.

His eyes cracked open, his lashes fluttered once, twice; then he opened his eyes wide. They were fogged and almost black with pain, his gaze at first slightly unfocused. "Hurts . . ." he murmured.

Without conscious thought, only eager to soothe him, Cissy reached out and cupped his cheek in her hand. "Yes, I know. I know," she crooned to him, her thumb stroking his cold skin.

"You took a nasty bump on the head, *gnädiger Herr*."

The doctor leaned over Cissy's shoulder. Her head whipped around to stare at him. She had completely forgotten the presence of other people in the room.

"Your horse must have shied at something and thrown you," the doctor continued, not unkindly. "Thank God, the clever animal came running home and let people know that there was something not right."

Fenris frowned. "I seem to remember . . . There was a shot," he murmured.

"There you go, my dear!" his father's voice boomed from the foot of the bed, where he and his wife stood arm in arm, their eyes fastened on their son. "It must have been a hunter, then. Somewhere nearby."

"A hunter? Yes." Fenris closed his eyes, the line between his brows deepening. He groaned softly. "Did I split my skull?" He licked his dry lips. Sweat beaded on his forehead. "It feels like I split my skull."

"No!" Cissy gripped his hand again. "No. You'll be all right." Her heart wrenched at the sight of his pain. "Fit as a fiddle," she promised, and pressed his hand to her heart.

His eyes shot open. He looked at her as if he had only now become aware of her presence. His mouth twisted into an ugly sneer. "Really? Pity for you, then." He breathed heavily and his voice faltered. His lashes drifted close. "Just think about it," he murmured. "You'd have the castle all to yourself."

Cissy dropped his hand as if he had burnt her. Despair

pierced her heart, that he could think something like that of her. "No!" she cried, and leaned over him. "It's not the bloody castle I want! Do you hear me? Fenris? *Fenris!*"

"It is no good, my lady." The doctor's hand on her shoulder held her back. "He's lost consciousness once more."

"I . . ." Cissy turned her stricken face to him and then to her in-laws. "I wouldn't . . . never . . ." How could he have said something like that?

"Oh, we know, my dear." The *Gräfin* hurried around the bed and took Cissy into her arms. "We know, my dear. Fenris is . . . distraught."

"I wanted to make this all work, but he—"

"We know, my dear, believe me, we know." Her mother-in-law stroked her hair. "My son has become a master at pushing people away. He scares everybody off when they come too close. Don't you know? Haven't you guessed?" When Cissy looked up at her, the older woman wiped the tears from her cheeks. "Ever since he came home from the war, Fenris has feared intimacy. Human warmth scares him, because he fears more pain." Her face contorted. "Of course, he doesn't realize that this way, his heart and soul will eventually freeze and turn to stone." She gave Cissy a sad smile. "We had so hoped . . ."

"Anna," the *Graf* said.

She threw her husband a long look. "You are quite right, my dear. This is neither the time nor the place." She looked back at Cissy. "The most important thing right now is to see that Fenris gets well again, isn't it?"

"Yes." Cissy clasped her hands over her heart. "Yes."

The doctor, packing his instruments into his bag, turned. "Somebody needs to stay with young Herr von

Wolfenbach throughout the night. He needs to be roused at intervals. A head wound combined with deep sleep is dangerous." He looked at the still form of the man in the bed. Worry creased his round face, and he no longer resembled a vulture; he was just a tired old man. "Some patients slip off into an even deeper sleep, one from which no human can ever awake them."

Pale as a corpse already . . .

Cissy shuddered. "I will sit with him," she said quickly.

The doctor blinked, surprise written on his face. "I'm sure a servant could—"

A servant? A *servant* sitting with Fenris, while she went to sleep? Abandon him when he was at his weakest? Determined, she shook her head. "No. I will sit with him. Would you like to stay the night?" she asked her parents-in-law. "I will tell the servants to prepare a room for you. Johann?" The valet had returned some time ago and now hovered on the threshold.

"Yes, *gnädige Frau*. It will be done immediately." He bowed and left the room.

Her heart heavy, Cissy threw another look at the still figure of her husband. His dark lashes lay in sooty half-circles against his cheekbones. Despite the dark shadow of his beard on his skin, he looked impossibly young and vulnerable. So vulnerable it broke her heart.

For a precious moment, she cupped the side of his face in her hand. *I want to protect you, my darling. To see to it that no harm ever comes to you again.*

Around her, the old walls of the castle sighed and whispered, and all at once, she felt a burst of strength flowing through her. Straightening her shoulders, she stepped back from the bed and took a deep breath. She could and would do this. She was a princess, not a sheep.

She made sure that her parents-in-law were settled comfortably in a guestroom and that dinner would be prepared for them. She saw the doctor to the door and pressed his hand in heartfelt thanks. He promised to call again the next day. And later, when she sat at her husband's bed with her old book of Grimms' fairy tales on her lap, she had plenty of time to study him and to think about what his mother had said.

Like Bearskin in the fairy tale, Fenris had grown claws that frightened people away. Yet underneath the ugly bearskin he was still a man, and his goodness shone through. Time and time again, Fenris had unwittingly given her proof of his good heart. Now she had to convince him it was time to shed the bearskin. And the claws.

She reached out to stroke his hair.

My wolf.

She remembered the old tale of the woman who made clothes for the wolf-man until he came to her hearth and put his head into her lap. *It's time to come into the warmth, my wolf. Don't you know it's cold outside? But my house is warm and there's a place for you there. Waiting for you.* Cissy leaned forward and pressed her lips to Fenris's forehead. "Just as I'll be waiting for you, my darling," she murmured.

A sound from the door made her whip her head around.

"I'm sorry to disturb you, *gnädige Frau,*" Johann said, looking abashed. His face was gaunt, and the skin around his eyes smudged with fatigue. It reminded Cissy of the valet's loyalty to her husband. For more than twelve years, Johann had served his master, and now he, too, would be worried about Fenris. She gave him a smile.

"It is all right. What is it?"

He closed the door behind him and came nearer. For a long moment he stared down at Fenris. Something like pain flittered over his face. "He looks so . . ."

"I know." Cissy clasped her hands over the book in her lap. "As if all his vitality has been snuffed out." She swallowed hard. She remembered how he had moved in her arms that one night. How he had risen above her, dark and magnificent, his body brimming with energy. And so alive.

Dear God, so alive.

Cissy drew an unsteady breath. "It hurts to see him like this." She blinked the moisture from her eyes before she raised them to his valet. He regarded her gravely, then surprised her by taking her hand and pressing it briefly.

"Don't worry, *gnädige Frau*. My master has survived worse than this. And the doctor said he will recover soon, did he not?"

"Yes. Yes, you're right." She sniffled, then wiped the back of her hands across her eyes. "Of course." She gave him a watery smile. "Why have you come, Johann?"

"*Gnädige Frau.*" He dropped to his knees in front of her. "Do you remember the other . . . *accident?*" He gave the word a peculiar emphasis. "The incident on the staircase." He searched her face.

A slither of ice whispered over Cissy's back. The accident which hadn't been an accident. She bit her lip and nodded.

"You saw how the wood broke, didn't you, my lady?"

"The break which wasn't a break," she said softly.

"No wood breaks that cleanly." Johann's gaze was intense. "Think about it, *gnädige Frau*. Wouldn't it have been perfect: a lonely lane, a shying horse—who knows what might have spooked it?"

The candlelight danced over the walls and made strange shadows flicker in and out of existence in the corners of the room. Very slowly Cissy said, "A shot in the air leaves no trace. A simple accident. Accidents happen."

"Whereas a shot into a man's head or chest—"

"Doesn't look like an accident at all," she finished for him. She caught her breath. "Do you think . . . ?"

Johann bowed his head. "With your permission, in the morning I would like to go back to the place where we found the master."

She licked her suddenly dry lips. Who would want to kill her husband? "Go back? But a shot in the air leaves no trace. . . ."

He looked up. "But a man standing on the muddy ground in the forest does." He raised his brows.

A murderer lurking between bushes? Fenris's daily tour of the land was well known, after all. If he had not survived the fall, nobody would have known of the shot. "Yes," she whispered. "Yes." Johann must discover the truth.

The valet stood and bowed his head once more. "Thank you," he said. He reached into the pocket of his waistcoat. "There is another thing. I found this while taking off the clothes the master wore today."

He held out a card and Cissy froze. On the card, a little woman leaned nonchalantly against a green table, a secret smile on her lips.

The queen of spades. The card she had given him when she had confronted him that time in his study, when he had claimed their night of passion meant nothing to him.

Her hand clutched her throat. "Where . . ."

"He carried it in the inner pocket of his jacket." The

valet regarded her with kind eyes. "I thought it must be something precious to him."

The queen of spades?

Precious?

Tears welled up in Cissy's eyes. "Thank you, Johann," she said huskily, and took the card from him. "Thank you. I will give it back to him."

He searched her face, then smiled. "I thought you would, milady. Good night." With that, he bowed and left the room.

Cissy clutched the card.

Something precious.

Her heart pounded in her ears. With trembling fingers, she turned the card into the light and watched the hidden picture appear: the man who sat between the queen's bare legs and licked her. Just like Fenris had done.

Something precious.

Cissy looked from the card to her sleeping husband. The wave of tenderness which swamped her was too much, too intense. Tears trickled over her cheeks. She cried a bit, then laughed and wiped the tears away. "My clever wolf," she whispered. "So you've already come to my hearth and hoped I wouldn't notice." She sniffled. "You think you're such a clever devil, don't you? But I've found you out." *And this time I will never let you go. You won't be able to divert me with one of your silly smokescreens, either, no matter how much you should huff and puff. No, this time we are going to look at the heart of the matter.*

Smiling, she threw the queen of spades a kiss, then opened her book and read until it was time to rouse him. Grumbling, he opened his eyes. When he saw who was leaning over him, his expression darkened. "Whatever are *you* doing here?" His glare was magnificent, yet his croaking voice spoiled the effect.

"Hm, let me see." Cissy pretended to ponder while she fetched him something to drink. "You are my husband. You received a nasty bump on the head. Now you're bedridden and need some loving tender care." She turned to him and raised her brows. "Whatever do you *think* I'm doing here?"

Dark color splashed his cheeks. She decided to ignore the accompanying scowl, and held out the cup.

"What is it?" he asked suspiciously.

Cissy rolled her eyes. Really! You would have thought he was a boy of six, not a grown man. Outwardly, she smiled. "Camomile tea."

If possible, his scowl darkened. "Do you really think I'd drink something that looks like horse piss?" he snapped—or rather, croaked. He huddled into the bedlinen.

Cissy tapped her foot on the floor. The demon wolf was sharpening his claws again? It would do him no good. She narrowed her eyes and shoved the cup at him. "Drink it! Or do I have to hold your nose and pour the stuff down your throat?"

It gave her great satisfaction to see his eyes widen. It was an even greater satisfaction to watch him drink the tea, even if he kept muttering under his breath. When he was done and she had put the cup away, she sat down on the chair beside the bed once more. While she carefully smoothed her skirts, she watched him from under lowered lashes. The bedcovers had slipped down to reveal a large discoloration on his shoulder. Her heart clenched with a longing to put her lips there, to kiss it all better.

Taking a deep breath, she took the queen of spades from her book and held it out to him. "Johann found this in your jacket."

He glanced at it. His eyes rose from the little queen to

Cissy's face. Abruptly he turned his head away, but not before she saw his expression, his desperate yearning and vulnerability.

The cords in his throat moved as he swallowed. "I must have found it somewhere, picked it up, put it in my pocket and forgotten all about it," he murmured, still keeping his eyes averted.

Cissy stared at him. She looked down at the card, watched how the candlelight danced over its surface and revealed short glimpses of the queen and her lover. She looked back at her husband, at the angry bruise on his shoulder.

"You're such a liar, Fenris," she finally said.

"What?" He jerked around, coming half up on his elbow, and stared at her, his eyes a little wild. He breathed heavily, as if he had run for miles. But when she reached out to touch him, he flinched as if she would strike him.

"No."

"Fenris—"

"No!" He fell back onto the bed and groaned a little as his body protested. "No." He threw his arm over his face, shielding his eyes.

Cissy watched how his chest moved up and down with his harsh breath. She remembered what Johann had said: *"I thought it must be something precious to him."*

"You did not keep it by accident," she said quietly.

He laughed, a painful, rasping sound, muffled against his arm. Or perhaps it had been a sob.

"Don't you understand?" he asked. He took the arm away to look at her. "Why do you still not . . ." He paused, and his eyes glittered feverishly. "God! Don't you know how *unworthy* I feel? The last woman I lay with was a whore, no less, because my betrothed . . ." He gave a bitter snort. "Ten years ago I last lay with a woman, and she was a goddamned whore. And even *she* couldn't hide her disgust at the sight of my body." Pain spasmed through his features, and he closed his eyes as if he could no longer endure the sight of her. "Don't you know how I wish . . . how I wish . . ." His Adam's apple moved convulsively. The desperation that laced his voice cut into her heart. "How I wish," he continued in a hoarse whisper, "that I could have met you before this happened." His fist struck the stump hiding underneath the blankets. "When I was still whole and sound—a man instead of a cripple." His voice broke.

Cissy thought her heart would surely break, too.

How could he consider himself less than a man? That his body could repel her?

"Fenris . . ."

He gave a heartwrenchingly unsteady laugh. His face briefly contorted before he looked at her again. "That foolish King of Dwarves," he whispered. "What right does he have to court the Fairy Princess?" Wetness clung to his eyelashes.

Dear God, why hadn't she understood earlier? He was utterly convinced he was doomed to roam the ramparts of the castle like the beast in a fairy tale, without any hope of redemption.

Her eyes were stinging as she slid from the chair onto the bed. "Fenris . . ." She touched his shoulder, the crown of his head, desperate to soothe his inner torment. "Oh, Fenris, darling, don't you see? Life is not a fairy tale. We are not kings of dwarves or fairy princesses—"

His expression hardened, and he twisted away from her touch. "And yet I will only drag you down into my darkness, and that I won't do, Celia. I won't!" His gaze roamed her face. As if he couldn't help himself, his hand rose and he ran the back of his forefinger down her cheek. "Don't cry, my sweet," he whispered. "It is better for you. I have already wrecked the lives of my parents. And my brother . . . Do you know how close we once were? When we were still children, he always trailed after me like a little puppy dog . . ." He swallowed hard. "And then I went and destroyed everything. How I must disgust them." His voice wavered. "I disgust myself. So it is only fitting, is it not, that I should have destroyed myself, too, and been shot into a cripple." He stared at her, his eyes very green.

Cissy's breath caught in her throat. "No, Fenris, no." She leaned forward and cupped his face in her hands. "How can you even think such a thing? You don't disgust your parents, and you most certainly don't disgust me." She shook her head. "Nothing could be further from the truth. *This*"—she put her hand on his bad leg, squeezed it through the blanket and did not care that tears streamed down her face and dropped onto him— "has shaped you into the man you are today, the man I fell in love with. It doesn't make you less. It makes you *more*. So much more, Fenris."

He searched her face. "What did you say?" he whispered. Blindly, he groped for her hand. His fingers slipped into hers and clung. And more strongly: "What did you say?"

Cissy blinked away her tears. With her free hand she stroked his face over and over, wishing to erase his bewildered look. She leaned over him and pressed a light kiss onto his forehead. "I *love* you, Fenris. I love you very much. I *want* you very much. There hasn't been a day in the past months when my body didn't long for yours."

He stared at her for a long moment, then his eyes

filled with tears. Reaching out to her like a drowning man might, he turned over until his head came to rest in her lap. Then he broke down. Cissy slung her arms around him while violent sobs wracked his body. She stroked his hair and back, rubbing softly between his shoulder blades.

"Hush, sweeting, hush," she crooned to him. "Everything will be all right."

He tightened his arms around her waist and held on to her as if she were his anchor in a stormy sea. And indeed, a terrible storm raged in him as all his pain and despair, all his insecurities burst forth for her to see. Yet her loving touch and voice had the power to lead him through the storm into safe harbor.

When he finally calmed down, he turned his head a little to the side. "God knows I'm not good enough for you," he said quietly.

"Hush!" Cissy lightly clapped his arm in admonishment. "What rubbish you talk, dearheart." She leaned over, sheltering him with her body. She kissed his hair, his temple, then put her cheek on his head, mindful of his bandage. "Don't you know you've been my hero ever since you rescued me from that bat?" she said lightly.

He gave a choked laugh, just as she had hoped. "Oh yes, let's not forget the bat. Does it count like killing a dragon, do you think?"

"I'm sure it does." She smiled against his hair. "Bats have wings, don't they?"

He laughed again, then drew his arms from her waist and turned onto his back. Cissy straightened to give him room. With his head still resting in her lap, he looked up at her, his face for once stripped bare of all masks. A rush of tenderness filled her with warmth, and she gently wiped at the traces of tears on his cheeks. He took her hand and placed a kiss into her palm.

Their gazes locked. She saw how clear his eyes were, how untroubled, though the last remnants of tears still spiked his lashes. A radiant smile spread over his face, transforming him into a younger self.

" 'A celuy que pluys eyme en mounde,' " he quoted slowly. To her whom I love most in all the world.

Cissy's breath caught and her eyes widened, and wonder filled her heart. His voice became soft and lilting, as much a caress as his gaze which held on to hers.

"Saluz od treyé amour
With grace and joye and alle honour,
Dulcissima."
I greet you and send you love
With grace and joy and all honor,
sweetest lady.

Again he kissed her palm, closing his eyes, as if to savor her taste and smell. "I love you very much, my sweet Cissy," he said against her skin.

Joy filled her, and love. So much love it could encompass the whole world. She stroked his head, then leaned over him and touched her mouth to his. Their lips clung and parted. Their breath flowed between them and mingled, became one. She felt his arm around her shoulders, a sweet weight, while his hand stroked the back of her neck. And Cissy knew that both of them had reached the safe harbor, and that she hadn't needed any powers from a mandrake to gain happiness.

"Will you stay with me?" he whispered.

"You know I will. The whole night and always."

He fell asleep with his head still on her lap while she

watched over him and remembered the story of the wolf at the woman's hearth.

She smiled and tousled the dark hair of her wolf and guided him through the night.

INTERLUDE

A new emotion dripped into the stone.

They pricked up their ears and listened how it trick-led through the ancient walls. Slowly, slowly, like thick syrup, but, oh, clearer than sunshine and sweeter than honey.

They rumbled amongst themselves, joyful, and basked in its warmth.

Yes, they had known this, felt it from the first.

Their whispers floated through the darkened corri-dors, soaked the castle.

And they knew . . .

All of them knew . . .

They wouldn't let anybody take this warmth from them again.

CHAPTER TWENTY-TWO

When Cissy woke up, specks of dust were dancing in the sunbeams falling into the room. The wind carried the sweet song of the bells of St. Margaretha's up from the valley, where they merrily chimed the Angelus.

Angelus Domini nuntiavit Mariae et concepit de Spiritu Sancto.

Cissy looked down at Fenris's head in her lap, his nape exposed and vulnerable. His sides moved with deep, even breaths. Her heart swelling, she gently covered his nape with her hand and let her fingers play with his hair.

With a sigh, he turned his head a little and nuzzled his nose into her skirt before lying his cheek onto her thigh once more. She regarded his profile, the dark, sooty lashes resting in half circles against his cheek, which was no longer deathly pale but flushed from sleep. But there were still dark circles under his eyes, and the lines of pain around his mouth had not yet fully disappeared. And yet . . . and yet sleep again made him look much younger than he was. Cissy could easily envision the small boy he had been. She carefully ran the back of her hand over his cheek, let his stubble rasp her knuckles.

Down in the valley, the bells still sang of the creation of a new life, and with a sense of wonder Cissy put her hand on her stomach. Someday she would be carrying Fenris's child. She imagined her belly swelling underneath her hand, growing round with new life. A child, created with sweetness and joy and love. A child to bring the castle to life again, to fill it with happiness and banish the beasts of the past. A small boy, with dark hair and sooty lashes, one who would grow into a gangly youngster with a devil-may-care smile. But always, always it would be a child well loved.

Smiling, Cissy studied her sleeping husband. With gentle fingers she brushed at his forehead, then leaned down to press a kiss against his cheek. "I love you," she whispered.

He made a sound deep in his throat, like the purr of a big cat, and the corners of his mouth lifted. "Nuff you," he mumbled, and his arms closed tightly around her waist. He sighed, and his breaths deepened once more.

A delighted smile spread over Cissy's face. "You are such a darling man," she told him softly. "How could you stand being a snarling demon wolf for so long?" She petted his nape and his shoulders, mindful of his injuries.

At the creaking of the door, her head whipped around. In an unconsciously protective gesture, she looped her arms around Fenris's shoulders.

"I beg your pardon, *gnädige Frau*," Johann said. "I wasn't sure whether you would already be awake." His hair was windblown, and he was wearing what looked like a riding cape.

She waved him inside. Sudden anxiety swamped her and formed a hard knot in the pit of her stomach. "Have you been out? Have you found anything?"

Johann bowed his head and turned his cap around in his hands. "I think so. But I believe it would be better if you could come and see for yourself." He looked up to meet her gaze. "Should this need to be testified to in front of a judge . . ."—a hint of ruddy color stained his cheeks—"your word would carry more weight than mine, *gnädige Frau.*"

The wind whispered in the trees and tugged at her hair as Celia rode down the muddy country lane at the valet's side. Like wooly sheep did the wide Yorkshire moors, clouds dotted the bright blue sky. Bird song filled the fresh, crisp air—and yet Cissy could not suppress the shiver that coursed through her. Danger lurked beneath the idyll, and it seemed to her that the dark swaying trees wanted to tell her of the evil that was hidden in their midst. *Murderer, murderer, murderer.*

She caught Johann watching her. "What is it?"

Narrowing his eyes, the valet looked ahead over fields and meadows and the thick, dark forest on their right. "I've been thinking . . ." He cleared his throat, looked back at her. "About who might want to kill Fenris."

"Yes?" She inclined her head.

"Who would have a motive."

"Yes."

The breeze seemed a little colder than before. Perhaps Johann felt it, too, for he remained silent several moments before he finally continued, very quietly. "I could think of only one person."

Near to them, a blackbird rose into the sky, scolding loudly as a magpie came flying over from the forest. Another blackbird joined in. Cissy blinked.

With a shake of her head, she turned her attention back to Johann. "Do you really think he would do it?"

The valet shrugged. "He would be the only one to gain if my master died."

"Do you think he wants to inherit the title?" Cissy frowned. "I would have thought he'd be keener on money."

"The Wolfenbach Hoard?"

She rolled her eyes. "That hoax! But he wouldn't get the castle. It would come into my sole possession." She had learned that from the family solicitor.

Johann raised his brows. "Perhaps he doesn't know."

"Perhaps not." Cissy shivered. She remembered the night the bat had invaded her room and he had come across her in the hallway. She remembered his stale breath wafting over her cheek. How the sunny, charming façade had given way to an arrogant, violent insolence. When the two brothers had faced each other, she had thought of a golden St. George and a dark Merlin, devil's spawn. But outward appearances were *so* misleading. Mrs. Chisholm had noticed long before her.

All is not gold that glitters.

Johann brought his horse to a halt. "We've arrived," he said. He dismounted. Holding the reins in one hand, he went over and offered Cissy his other to help her dismount.

But she could not stop staring at the strip of country lane, where her husband had laid hurt and unconscious. *Oh, my wolf, my wolf.* All of a sudden tears clogged her throat, burnt her eyes. How very easily she could have lost him.

"Gnädige Frau?" Johann prompted softly.

Taking a deep breath, Cissy lifted her leg over the lower pommel of her saddle and slid down to the ground. She looked around and found the place ideal for an ambush: the forest spread out and reached almost down to the road, and yet a man could stand un-detected in the underbrush here, she supposed.

She flexed her fingers. Inside her gloves they were icy-cold.

"Where?" she asked quietly.

After looping the reins over the twigs of a bush, Jo-hann led her a few steps into the forest. "A person can hide here quite undected by people on the road." He echoed her earlier thoughts. "If you remember, we had a bit of rain yesterday morning. In the afternoon the ground was still a little wet." He pointed to several foot-steps on the ground. Most of them were smudged, as if somebody had impatiently walked up and down, but there was one deeper, clearer set.

Eagerly, Cissy squatted down to take a closer look.

"Ah, yes. Here he must have waited," Johann com-mented behind her.

Frowning, she extended a fingertip and traced the outline of the tracks. "There must be something wrong with heel of this boot. See? A little corner of it is miss-ing." She glanced up at the valet.

He nodded. "I've noticed that, too, *gnädige Frau*. That was the reason I asked you to come here—as I said, in case this needs to be testified to."

"Wouldn't we need the boots for that, as well?" As Cissy rose, a momentary dizziness overcame her. Her hand reached out for the support of the nearest tree, but Johann's hand shot out to grip her elbow.

"*Gnädige Frau,* are you all right?" Concerned, he peered into her face.

She took a deep breath. "Yes. Yes, I am." She gave him a quick smile and let go of the fir tree. "I—eww . . ." Gri-macing, she inspected her gloves. "Resin." She rubbed her fingers together. "That won't be easy to . . ." Her voice trailed away as something occurred to her. Hastily, she raised her eyes to meet the valet's.

He nodded.

"All the trunks here are slightly resinous. It's likely he touched one of them. So . . ."

"We need his boots and the clothes," Cissy finished. She gazed at the road where her husband had ridden, unsuspecting of what awaited him.

Cissy's throat grew tight, and she had to swallow hard before she could continue. "That bastard." Quite suddenly, a thin veil of red slipped down over the edges of her vision. "That *bloody* bastard!" she whispered fiercely. "I'm going to rip his heart out and feed it to the dogs!" She turned to look at the valet. "We will stop him, Johann. We will stop that despicable cur and make sure he will never harm anyone even again!"

Johann blinked. "Yes, *gnädige Frau.*"

"Yes." Cissy nodded emphatically. She marched back toward the road. "But we need the boots and the clothes to prove it was him." Just then she became aware that the valet wasn't following her. She turned and found him still standing in the same spot.

She frowned. "Is something wrong, Johann?"

He cleared his throat. "Not at all, *gnädige Frau.*" He hurried to catch up with her. "It just . . ." He coughed. "It just occurred to me that the Wolves of Wolfenbach will have to hurry if they want to avenge this wrong themselves." Flushing, he ducked his head and busied himself sorting out the reins of their horses.

The Wolves of Wolfenbach? Cissy's frown deepened. Now where had she heard that before? In that novel Fenris had given her? Shaking her head, she pushed the thought aside to concentrate on more pressing matters. "We need his boots and his clothes." She tapped her finger against her chin. "But how?" How to catch the mouse?

The play's the thing,
Wherein I'll catch the conscience of the . . . brother.

Cissy let Johann help her up onto her horse. She settled in her saddle and took up the reins. She watched him getting into the saddle himself. Looking up, he met her gaze and questioningly raised his brows.

"*Gnädige Frau?*"

"We're going to lure him back to Wolfenbach," she said. And then she pressed her left leg to nudge the horse into motion.

Later that morning, Cissy wrote a letter to Leopold, asking for his help because his brother, her husband, had taken a nasty fall and was likely to die; Fenris had told her how close they had once been, and she hoped Leopold would forget their differences and return to Wolfenbach. How could she run such a large castle all on her own? Her dear parents-in-law were so distraught they were of no help. She needed a strong male hand to guide Wolfenbach through this crisis.

She carefully sanded and sealed the letter, then handed it to the valet. "When will he get this, Johann?"

"This evening."

"So we can expect him tomorrow morning." She folded her hands on the desk in front of her. "We should make sure the *Graf* and *Gräfin* have gone home by then."

"Yes, *gnädige Frau.*"

"It would be too cruel." She thought what it would mean to his parents when their son's unscrupulous behavior would be revealed. "Do you think he might be innocent?"

The valet cocked his head to the side and seemed to ponder her question. "Do you?"

She thought of Peter Schlemihl, the fool who had

sold his shadow for a purse of money. How far would Leopold von Wolfenbach go? Would he sell his brother? In the Bible, Jacob's sons had sold *their* brother just because they were jealous of him. Leopold blamed Fenris for ruining their family.

"We will see, won't we?"

INTERLUDE

In the darkest hours of the night, when everybody in the castle slept and for once no flickering light was walking the ramparts, a shudder ran through the stone. They flexed their muscles, tested their strength. Sparks of power sprang from pinnacle to pinnacle, spanned the circumference of the castle. And then the power turned inward, raced up and down the walls, saturated the stone until the whole castle hummed with it.

And then . . .

All settled down.

All watched.

All waited.

They had spun their deadly web of power. Now they stood guard to protect, where only hours ago they had failed to do so.

They would not fail again.

CHAPTER TWENTY-THREE

The demon wolf was back. Bristling and gloriously naked, he sat on his bed and glowered at her. Cissy crossed her arms in front of her chest and tapped her foot on the floor.

"No. Absolutely not."

"Yes," he growled.

"No."

He sent her a last withering glance, then bent to pick up his wooden stick from the floor.

"You are such a mutthead," she told him in English.

With angry, jerky motions he secured the straps around his thigh.

"A total hoddypoll!"

He tested the stick by stumping several times on the ground.

Cissy narrowed her eyes. "An addle-brained daftie!"

Obviously satisfied, he reached for the pair of trousers Johann had put on the bed earlier before wisely fleeing from the room.

Cissy winced as a large, blackish purple discoloration became visible on her husband's upper back. Sighing, she let her arms fall to her sides. "Fenris . . ."

His head snapped up. "Does it turn you on to watch this?" he asked nastily.

She rolled her eyes, no longer hurt by it. "And a bugbear on top of everything else." He was a bugbear because he hated feeling like a weakling, never mind that he had almost been killed two days ago. She took a step forward. "Fenris," she repeated.

He put the trousers aside and reached for the white shirt instead. Roughly, he jerked it over his head. When his face reappeared, his hair was even more tousled than before, lending him a hint of vulnerability despite his mood. The sight tugged at Cissy's heart.

Quickly she closed the space between them and dropped to her knees in front of him. "Fenris . . ." She put her hands on his thighs. In an unconsciously soothing gesture she rubbed her palms over his hairy skin, loving the feel of those hard muscles under her hands. "Fenris, I swear, you're a total bird-witted dodo," she said, yet without the heat of a few moments before.

He gave her his darkest scowl.

In answer, she lightly dug her fingers into his thighs. "Sweeting, you took the nastiest fall so recently."

"Thank you for reminding me," he snapped. "Can I finish dressing?"

"You're a frightful bugbear."

"That doesn't seem to impress you."

She couldn't help smiling at his disgruntled tone. "Of course not." She reached up to caress his clean-shaven jaw. "You're *my* bugbear." She pressed her lips to his cheek, petted his neck and shoulder. "You had a nasty fall and bumped your head," she murmured into his ear.

"You could have died." Shuddering, she closed her eyes and hugged him. "Why can't you just stay in bed and rest for a little while longer?"

He held himself stiff in her arms. "Because I'm not an invalid."

She sighed. "No, you're a bugbear. We've already established the fact." She lightly clapped his shoulder and pulled back to search his face.

Under furrowed brows, dark green eyes glowered back at her.

Clicking her tongue, she cupped his stubborn jaw between her hands. Beneath her fingertips, the muscles tightened. "You know, you really leave me no other option. . . ." She leaned forward and kissed him properly, with just enough tongue to make tingles of delight race through her body.

His arms came up to close around her shoulders. His knees opened to form a V, and with a small groan, he drew her in between and against his body. Restlessly his hands roamed her back, and his mouth opened wide under hers. Forceful strokes of his tongue against hers made her shiver and moan. As if in answer, his hold tightened until her breasts were crushed flat against his chest.

Cissy gripped his upper arms. She felt as if she were hovering on the rim of an abyss. Dizzy. She gasped.

Oh yes, kissing most certainly dispelled the horrid bugbear.

His mouth trailed feverish kisses over her cheek, down the side of her neck. At the same time, his teeth grazed the sensitive flesh between her neck and shoulder, his hands gripped her bottom and lifted her against his surging erection.

"Oh my." She sighed against his shoulder and inhaled the wonderful scent of him—sandalwood and Fenris.

He growled against her neck and moved his pelvis.

It was delightful, sensuous, delicious—and totally wrong, given his condition.

She swatted at his arm. "Oh, no you don't."

He growled some more and sucked a little of her skin between his teeth. Oh yes, he was very good at what he was doing. She couldn't help arching her neck a little to give him better access. The suckling intensified.

He seemed bent on leaving a big enough lovebite that she would have to wear a shawl for a week. At the same time, his swollen sex burned against her belly, so hot that she could feel it even through her dress and chemise.

"I should've worn my long stays today," she complained in jest.

He chuckled, the puffs of his breath a delicious tickle.

She rubbed her cheek against his. "It's delightful to know the bump on your head hasn't had any serious consequences for other body parts."

More chuckles rumbled from his chest, vibrated sweetly against her chestbone. Smiling, she stroked his sides. "But we can't possibly. The doctor said you needed rest."

Fenris said something rude about the doctor, which made her laugh. He harrumphed and loosened his hold a fraction.

"Yes, you're quite a frightful bugbear," she said again. She pressed a teasing kiss against the hollow under his jaw before leaning her forehead against his.

His green eyes regarded her intently. "What I've been wondering is," he said in German, his voice husky, "why you insist calling me names in English—bugbear, bugaboo, beloved—when most of the time I don't even know what you're calling me."

Cissy dissolved into laughter.

"I mean," he continued, "what is the purpose of calling me names I don't understand?" His caressed her nape. "A 'bird-witted dodo'? That's a stylistic faux pas of the highest order."

She buried her face against his shoulder to smother her mirth.

"A pleonasm." His hand trailed languid strokes up and down her backbone. "Have you heard of them?"

"Mmhm."

"Quite shocking, isn't it?"

"Quite," she gasped between giggles. But then her hilarity slowly faded. With a hiccup, she turned her head so her cheek rested on his shoulder. For a moment she was silent. "I love you," she finally murmured.

She felt him press a kiss onto her hair. "I love you, too."

Cissy sighed. "Even if you are more stubborn than a mule." She straightened and regarded him solemnly. "You know that you don't need to prove to me what a wonderful, tough fellow you are." It seemed important to say.

"I know that."

"Hm." She pushed out her lower lip. "But you plan to get up nonetheless, don't you?"

"I do." Fenris gently rubbed his nose against hers.

"When you get dizzy and fall flat on your face, I will tell everybody to leave you lying in a heap on the floor," she warned.

He laughed and stole a swift kiss from her. "Do that."

She wrinkled her nose at him. "Nigmenog."

She left Fenris sitting in his study with a book and a steaming mug of caramel-colored coffee. However, she suspected that as soon as she left, he would bury his nose in his ledgers instead, even though she had threatened his life and limbs should he do so. It had cut her heart to see him walking down the stairs without his usual grace and fluidity. His movements were stiff and awkward, which was hardly surprising given that his body was black and blue.

"A total hoddypoll," she muttered darkly.

How she would have loved to spend the whole day in bed beside him, just holding him in her arms, feeling his big body rest heavily against hers, just as he had done during that one night so long ago. She wanted to clasp him in her arms and never let him go again.

But no, it was not to be.

And she had a trap to bait.

With a weary sigh she went and checked on her parents-in-law, who had settled down in the drawing room. Despite her urgings, they had refused to leave the castle. The *Gräfin* had especially insisted on staying, until her firstborn was mended. And now . . . Now it was too late. Now the *Graf* was reading the newspaper, the sunlight glinting on the rims of his glasses, and his wife had a piece of embroidery on her lap. It should have been a scene of perfect domestic contentment, had it not been for the restlessness that gripped Cissy, the knowledge of the dark undercurrents waiting to bubble up to the surface and destroy all pretense.

She went to find Johann, who stood on the remains of the tower and scanned the road leading to Wolfenbach. Beside him, a gargoyle jutted out of the crumbled wall. Time had gnawed at its face and rendered its stony features indistinguishable. One pointed ear was missing, as was the greater part of the snout. The wings, which had once sprung up from the muscular shoulders, were gone, a sacrifice of bygone ages. A sense of loss overcame Cissy, and it seemed perfectly and sadly in tune with what was to come.

With a sigh, she stepped up to the valet, resting her hand on the gargoyle's head. "Johann . . ."

He turned around. When he saw her, he briefly inclined his head.

"Anything?"

"No. Nothing." With narrowed eyes he gazed toward the road. "Is the master well?"

Cissy snorted. Recalling the scene in Fenris's room, she was torn between amusement and exasperation. "Och, he sits in his study and is probably about to fall face-first into his account books."

Johann coughed delicately. From the way his lips twitched, she knew he was attempting to stifle laughter.

"Which would serve him absolutely right for being such a mulish fellow," she finished.

This time, the valet couldn't help laughing aloud.

Cissy rolled her eyes, but she joined in. "Oh dear, he is so, so stubborn!" She wiped her eyes, and, shaking her head, let her gaze wander over the forest.

As always, the dark green sea of fir trees seemed impenetrable. It would swallow sunlight and transform it into a green, shadowy haze. All was possible in such a forest. It was a place where witches dwelled and the big bad wolf lay in wait for foolish little girls. A place where a man would lie in wait for an opportunity to bring death to his own brother.

All lingering amusement fled, and Cissy shuddered. Her fingers tightened on the head of the gargoyle. "Oh, Johann, do you believe everything will turn out all right?"

The valet was silent a moment, and the humming of the trees filled her senses, whispered to her of danger and betrayal. What had the inhabitants of Wolfenbach felt in bygone ages when their castle had come under siege? Had they, too, stood on the top of this tower and listened to the song of the forest, apprehension in their hearts? Or had they felt safe in the knowledge Wolfenbach's mighty walls could withstand any foe?

She had no such solace. This time they would invite the enemy into the castle, would allow him to pass through the gates unhindered.

"Legend says," the valet began slowly, "that in days of old a Wolfenbach once spared a she-wolf and her cubs when he was out to hunt. In gratitude when she finally died, many years later, the animal sent its spirit into the castle. Wolfenbach has been under the protection of the Wolves ever since."

The Wolves of Wolfenbach.

Cissy now remembered how Leopold had told her his version of the story during one of their tours of the castle all those months ago. How easily she had let herself be dazzled by his golden looks and charming dimple. But all is not gold that glitters.

She smiled bitterly. Oh yes, she well knew that by now. Just as she knew life was not a fairy tale, that there were no knights in shining armor, no fairy godmothers, no gray men who sold mandrakes and magic purses. Nothing to protect the good and innocent.

Wearily, she shook her head. "It's just a story, Johann. It's not real. If it were real, they would have . . ." Her voice trembled, and she had to bite her lip hard as the memory of Fenris's black and blue body threatened to overwhelm her. "Wouldn't they have protected my husband as somebody sawed through his wooden leg, as somebody tried to kill him two days ago?"

Johann nodded. "I quite agree, *gnädige Frau.* And yet, ever since the Wolves were said to have come to the castle, no siege has been successful. There are stories how attackers were pelted with stones that mysteriously fell out of the walls; how they got entangled in thorns, were attacked by crows . . ." He shrugged. "The stories might be true or not, who knows? But what I've been thinking about . . ." He took a deep breath. "If the younger Herr von Wolfenbach is really behind the accident, if we unmask him—what will it cost his family?"

"Yes. I know." Cissy's eyes started to prickle. She blinked rapidly. "And yet we need to stop him."

"Exactly." Johann crossed his arms in front of his chest. "Back . . . during the war, Fen—" He caught himself. "Herr von Wolfenbach saved my life." His jaw hardened and his tone became firm. "Wolves or no wolves, I won't let any more harm come to him."

The way he stood there, his stance wide, his broad shoulders coiled with restless tension, Cissy was forcefully reminded that this was no ordinary valet. He had once been a soldier, had killed other men—and would kill again if forced to do so. There was no doubt he would guard Fenris with his life.

For a moment longer she stood silently with him, side by side with this loyal warrior ready to protect the family he served. Yes, danger lurked all around, but wolves or no wolves, the halls of Wolfenbach would not be usurped easily.

Her hand lightly stroked the shoulders of the gargoyle, over the stumps of its wings. The castle might have paid tribute to the old hag Time, which was the mightiest opponent of them all, strong enough to subdue even a god. But desite all this, Wolfenbach still wouldn't easily be beaten.

Cissy took a deep breath. "Let me know when he arrives."

Johann inclined his head. "Of course, *gnädige Frau*."

Long after midday, he finally arrived at the castle.

When Johann appeared in the door to the drawing room, Cissy's nerves were so tightly strung that she couldn't help the sigh of relief that escaped her. Finally, it had begun. She excused herself from her parents-in-law.

"He's come on horseback," the valet told her as they hurried down the stairs.

"So it seems we're lucky." Her thoughts raced. "A bath! He will want a bath first to wash off the dust of the road."

Johann shook his head. "A bath takes too long to prepare. A sponge bath. But perhaps he will want his riding habit cleaned."

"Oh yes, yes. He still keeps a change of clothes here at the castle, doesn't he?"

"Indeed."

They had almost reached the Great Hall. Cissy's gaze flickered over the tapestry with the hunting scene, where that Fräulein von Wolfenbach had immortalized her vow of love. *Te amo.*

Johann opened the door to the hall. "I will take care of the bath and everything else." The clothes. To gain the proof of the betrayal.

"And the rest shall be my play," she agreed. She would see the trap snap shut, would catch the mouse.

The valet's face was taut with tension, but he nodded.

"Let the game begin," Cissy whispered as she slipped into the hall. Behind her, the door clicked shut. She was on her own.

A moment of dizziness overcame her. She shook her head.

Let the game begin. . . .

As she went through the hall, a strange calmness filled her—as if the world retreated a step in order to allow her to focus on the moment and what needed to be done. Each sound and each color became brilliantly clear until there was no more room left for emotions, for doubt or apprehension.

Let the game begin.

She stood at the window and waited for Leopold to ride into the courtyard before she stepped onto the gallery outside. With measured steps she walked down the wooden stairs to greet her brother-in-law. She watched him dismount with fluid grace and give the reins of his horse to their young stableboy, who had come up from the stables with him.

Golden curls protruded from under Leopold's dusty hat. As he turned, she saw his cheeks were ruddy from the wind. "My dear." He rushed toward her, picked up her hands and bestowed fervent kisses upon her knuckles. "I came as soon as I could." Pressing her hands against his chest, he searched her face with an air of true worry.

St. George, come to save the damsel in distress, Cissy thought cynically. Her lips lifted in a polite smile. "Thank you for coming."

"I . . ." He licked his lips. "Is Fenris . . . ?"

She lowered her head demurely. "He took a most ghastly fall." A mere whisper, one which became a distressed maiden.

"Oh. I . . ." He cleared his throat, patted her hands. "What a horrid affair."

"Indeed." For a moment, the urge to throttle him then and there threatened to overwhelm her. But it would not do, so she forced herself to keep her voice calm and even as she continued.

"Do come inside. I am sure you must wish for some refreshment after your journey." She led him up the hall, where a disconcerted Rambach was already waiting with a tray and something to drink. He radiated disapproval.

Leopold downed his glass of wine, and Cissy subtly shook her head at the butler. The old man frowned, and she wondered at the wisdom of keeping her plan between Johann and herself.

"Would you like to freshen up before you see Fenris?" she asked.

"Well . . ." Leopold lowered his glass. "Perhaps I should go and see my brother first." Again, he cleared his throat. "Given his condition."

Oh, such solicitude, when the villain had not only called his brother a cripple but also tried to kill him.

Gritting her teeth, Cissy forced herself to smile and proceeded to talk him into retiring to his room for a bit. By the time she had ushered him out of the hall, Rambach's eyes were as round as saucers, yet luckily the man had kept his mouth shut. Still, Cissy had no doubt he would go straight to the *Graf* and *Gräfin*. Or worse, to his master.

Time was running out. The trap needed to be sprung before her parents-in-law came face-to-face with their youngest son. Before Fenris stumbled upon him.

With barely veiled impatience, Cissy accompanied Leopold to his room. She even tolerated it when he took her hand and put it in the crook of his arm. By the door to his bedchamber, Johann took over and offered his services as valet. Cissy shared a glance with him as Leopold stepped over the threshold. Barely discernible, the valet inclined his head. Releasing her breath, Cissy took a step back. The door closed.

She bit her lip. The game was under way.

While she waited for Johann to reappear, she started pacing up and down the corridor. She did not dare to leave her post for fear of coming across her in-laws. Had Rambach already told them of Leopold's arrival? Surely he must have, and at this point she did not want to give any explanations. She briefly closed her eyes.

Neither did she want to have to deal with an angry demon wolf right now.

She sighed. If her and Johann's suspicions turned out

to be true, Fenris would be devastated. He had always tried to find excuses for his brother's behavior. Even when Leopold had thrown the vilest insults at him, he had tried to find excuses. His brother had furthered the undermining of Fenris's sense of worth, but Fenris had thought it to be his just punishment.

Damn Leopold. Damn the sniveling little bastard. Scowling fiercely, Cissy stamped up and down the hallway.

The door to Leopold's room finally opened and Johann emerged, with an armful of clothes and holding a pair of boots. She flew toward him. "And?"

"Shh." Hastily, he closed the door. With a twist of his hand, he turned the boots around for her inspection.

Hardly daring to breathe, she leaned closer.

"Right boot," he said tonelessly.

And there it was: the heel had one corner nipped off. This was the boot whose owner had stood in the underbrush and fired a shot to make her husband's horse shy.

Air escaped Cissy's lungs in a noisy puff. Yes, she had suspected it, known it, but still, the proof was like a punch in her stomach. How could any man be so greedy as to attempt to kill his own brother?

"We've got him," Johann said quietly. "There's also a spot that looks like resin on his coat." He smiled wryly. "It's a good thing he doesn't have a manservant to take care of such things."

"Yes." She nodded mechanically. "Yes, of course." Again, her thoughts were racing. God, what would his family say? What would it do to her husband?

At the sound of approaching footsteps, her head snapped around in apprehension and she took a step away from Fenris's valet. Catching sight of the person coming hesitantly toward them, she frowned. "Marie, what are you doing here?"

The girl blushed. "I . . ." She gulped. But then she shook the hair out of her face and thrust the pitcher she was carrying forward. "I'm bringing warm water for Master Leopold."

"Warm water?" Johann's voice sharpened. "Nobody sent for more water."

Marie looked from one of them to the other. Her tongue snaked out to lick her lips. "Cook told me to bring it."

"Did she? Well, I can assure you that Master Leopold has enough warm water already. You can bring it back downstairs."

"Oh no!" Desperation rang in the maid's voice. "I . . ." But under Johann's stern gaze, her voice trailed away. The muscles in her throat worked as she swallowed. "But . . . but . . . Cook . . . She will be so angry when I come downstairs with the pitcher again. She will think I'm tardy and . . . well . . ." She turned to Cissy. "Oh, *gnädige Frau,*" she wailed, "she will tell Frau Häberle, who will surely fire me."

Cissy stared at her. "Because you didn't bring a pitcher of water to this room?" she said very slowly. The maid seemed awfully determined to get into that room. "But she cannot fire you; you are in my employ. There's no need for you to bring—" A memory popped into her mind, brilliantly clear.

Cruelly clear.

The last piece of the puzzle had fallen into place.

"This is not about delivering a pitcher of water. Is it, Marie?"

The girl's eyes widened in alarm as her mistress took a step toward her. "W-what?" She backed away, but Cissy followed relentlessly.

"This is about getting to Leopold von Wolfenbach."

Yes, Cissy recalled Marie stepping up to Leopold in

the flickering light of the Easter fire. Touching his arm with that strange kind of familiarity, though being shrugged off.

"What has he told you, Marie? What kind of lies has he fed you?"

White as a sheet, the girl continued to stumble backward. "I . . . I have no idea what you are t-talking about."

"No?" Cissy raised her brows and gave a thin smile. "Well, then, let's find out." And with that she grabbed the maid's arm. She didn't care that Marie flinched, or that she flailed her arms and the pitcher crashed onto the floor. Mercilessly, she dragged the girl away.

"Gnädige Frau!" Johann rushed after her.

"We're going to the kitchen," Cissy informed him grimly. "To hear what Cook has to say."

"I didn't do anything wrong," Marie sobbed. "Oh help! *Help!*"

Cissy tightened her grip on the girl's arm as she marched her down the stairs. "You can scream as much as you want, my dear, but nobody will hear you. That's the beauty of these old castles—the walls are quite thick."

"Johann." Red blotches appeared on Marie's face, and tears streamed down her cheeks. "Help me, Johann. She is mad. Mad!" The girl gave a few heartbreaking whimpers.

Cissy gritted her teeth. "On the contrary," she growled. "I've never been more lucid in my life."

"Gnädige Frau . . ." Worry laced the valet's voice. He hastened after her.

"Why don't you help me, Johann?" Marie screamed. "She's mad!"

"Stop making such a noise," Cissy hissed. "Johann, you go and take care of my brother-in-law. He'll want help with his dressing." She pushed Marie down the narrow staircase to the servants' quarters. "Go! You too, Johann."

"As you wish." The valet threw her a last worried glance before disappearing upstairs again.

Barely reining in her anger, Cissy strode downstairs after her maid. She opened the kitchen door and, grabbing Marie's arm once more, propelled her into the cook's realm.

The three senior servants were sitting around a small table, and they scrambled to their feet when their mistress suddenly appeared. *"Gnädige Frau!"* Astonishment and something very much like guilt registered on their faces, especially Rambach's.

They've probably been talking about their mistress, who welcomed the master's awful brother to the castle. Ha! If only they knew!

"Now, Marie," Cissy said grimly, "let us ask Cook whether she has sent you upstairs with a pitcher of water."

Beside her, Marie sniffled pitifully.

Her eyes the size of saucers, the cook looked from one woman to the other. "With a pitcher of water? Whatever for, *gnädige Frau?*"

The sniffling halted. The breath caught in Marie's throat, became a hiccup. But then she sobbed even louder than before. "Oh, you m-must help me! Herr Rambach! Oh p-please! She's . . . she's a m-madwoman!" She wanted to take a step forward, yet Cissy held her fast.

"A madwoman?" With that, Cissy's control finally snapped. Two days ago her husband had almost died in the mud of a country lane, and this girl dared to call her a madwoman? Cold fury descended. With a snarl, she shoved Marie against the wall, not caring about the maid's shrieks or the other servants' scandalized gasps. She pressed Marie's shoulders against the cold stone and pierced her with her gaze. "A madwoman? Let's talk about why you brought this pitcher of water upstairs."

"I w-was sent to bring w-warm water f-for M-master Leopold," her maid sobbed.

"Try again. Cook already said she didn't send you. Frau Häberle, did *you* send Marie upstairs with warm water?"

"No, *gnädige Frau,*" came the weak reply.

Her wide eyes swimming in tears, Marie stared at her mistress. Cissy didn't once avert her gaze, and she continued asking:

"Rambach, did *you* send Marie upstairs?"

The old man cleared his throat. "No, *gnädige Frau.*"

She lifted her brows. "Who sent you then, Marie?"

The girl's eyes widened even further. Fear flickered in their depths. "I . . ."

"Didn't you come upstairs for some altogether different reason? Didn't you want to go and talk to Leopold von Wolfenbach?"

"No! *No!*" Her voice rising to a hysterical pitch, Marie shook her head wildly. "No!"

Cissy slapped her hands flat against the stone on both sides of Marie's head. "Liar! Didn't you come to see him? *Didn't you?*"

Shaking her head, Marie hid her face in her hands and cried.

"What lies did he tell you, Marie? What lies? What did he promise you?"

"N-nothing . . ."

"So you did it all for nothing? For what kind of fool do you take me? What, Marie, *what?*" Again Cissy slapped her hands against the stone, making the girl flinch. "Answer me!"

"*Gnädige Frau . . .*" The butler put a hand on her shoulder, but Cissy shook him off.

"Not now, Rambach. Marie!"

Her maid lifted her blotched, tear-stained face. "I did nothing wrong!" she screamed. "After what your husband did, Master Leopold should become the rightful heir!"

"Oh really?" Cissy took a step back.

"Marie, how can you say such a thing?" the housekeeper said, her voice trembling.

Marie wiped her hand across her wet cheeks. "Because it's true," she spat, and her face twisted into a mask of hate. "He ruined the whole family! He had no right to come back afterwards! It should have all been Leopold's!"

The three older servants gasped in unison.

"Leopold's?" Cissy echoed, her voice strangely calm, even though icy fury burned like acid through her body. "Now, isn't this interesting?"

Marie's eyes flickered from person to person, her chest heaving with uneven breaths. Cissy watched how the blood drained from her face as the girl realized she had just betrayed herself. Her mouth opened and closed, yet no sound emerged.

As if in a dream, Cissy felt cold rage overtake her. She turned and spotted the big knife lying on Cook's kitchen table. Very slowly, she reached out. Her fingers closed around the handle, so cool against her hot skin. And the next moment the razor sharp edge rested against the vulnerable flesh of Marie's throat. The maid lost all remaining color, turned ashen, her eyes bulging.

"Now, what exactly did he promise you?" Cissy asked, still in that calm voice, which seemed to come from far away. Somehow, it didn't seem to be her voice at all.

The air whistled through Marie's nose. No sound came from any of the other servants.

Cissy pressed the knife a little closer against the skin. *"Talk."* A drop of blood appeared. It ran into the hollow at the base of the girl's throat. For the blink of an eye, it hung there, red and glittering, like an exotic gemstone, then it slipped down and was soaked up by the neckline of Marie's dress.

All of a sudden, Cissy's maid talked very fast. "He'll take me away, to Town. He'll buy me dresses and jewelry and we'll live there. In Town. He will take care of me, he said."

"By making you his mistress?"

"*No!* He'll marry me." Marie licked her lips. "He'll marry me. Yes, he said that."

Cissy shook her head. "How can you be so stupid? He will never do anything like that."

"You don't understand!" Marie's eyes glittered feverishly. She pressed forward, and another drop of blood ran down her pale throat. "How can you, with a husband like yours? He *loves* me. Yes, he does!" Her voice rose. "I'll be his wife!"

A wave of sadness washed through Cissy. She had trusted Marie. She had counted on the girl's loyalty. Her hand holding the knife fell to her side, and she took a step back. "How long has this been going on?" she asked.

Color came and went in the maid's face. Then she tossed her head back and told Cissy defiantly, "Since his first visit."

"God!" Cissy gave a sound: half snort, half laugh. "He cavorted with you while he was courting me? Probably right after coming straight from Contessa Czerny's bed. What a . . ." A new thought occurred to her, and her eyes narrowed. "The accident on the stairs. That was you, wasn't it?"

"I—"

"Oh, I already know it wasn't an accident. Somebody sawed into my husband's wooden leg so it would break sometime that day. It couldn't have been Leopold, because he was away in Freiburg. But he had *you*." Cissy arched her eyebrow.

A smothered sound came from behind her. As she looked over her shoulder, the three head servants stared back, stricken. Frau Häberle pressed one hand against her mouth, while the cook's eyes were swimming in tears. Rambach looked as if he had aged ten years in the past quarter of an hour. With shock and disbelief written across his face, he slowly shook his head.

Cissy turned her attention back to Marie, who pressed her lips together in a mutinous line.

"What has my husband done to you that would justify the things you did? That you listened to Leopold's lies and even took part in this treachery?"

The maid flinched a little, but remained silent.

The door to the kitchen was thrown open. *"Gnädige Frau!"* Out of breath, Johann stumbled into the room, the bundle with Leopold's clothes in his arm. "You must come. He has gone to the drawing room to see his parents."

Marie's head whipped around. She stared at the valet, her face stricken. "No!" she whispered.

Cissy snorted. "Oh, yes. And as for you . . ." Once more she backed Marie against the wall and gave her an unpleasant smile. "I will give you half an hour to pack your things and leave this castle. I should call the constable, but since Leopold obviously turned your head . . ." She shrugged. Then she hardened her voice again. "Yet, should I ever see you again near Wolfenbach or in Kirchwalden"—she cocked her head to the side—"I will kill you myself."

The girl jumped. Fear showed on her face, in her eyes, and Cissy smiled in satisfaction. "Frau Häberle, will you please go with Marie and watch her pack her things? We wouldn't want her to pack more than is hers."

"Of course, *gnädige Frau.*"

Slowly, Cissy turned her head toward the woman and nodded. "Thank you." With great care, she put her knife back on the table, then walked out of the room past a gaping Johann.

Dizziness assaulted her on the stairs. Yet immediately her husband's trustworthy valet was at her side and supported her with a hand under her elbow. She thanked him and gave him a wan smile. "I didn't think I had it in me to be so . . . so . . ."

"Protective?" he offered.

"Violent. I could have killed her. I really wanted to, for what she did to Fenris."

Johann shrugged. "Protective," he said. "If you forgive my saying so, *gnädige Frau,* but I've always thought only a very special kind of woman would do for my master."

Cissy stopped so abruptly that the valet nearly bumped into her. She turned. "I'm not special."

He gave her a crooked smile. "Oh yes, you are. That's the beauty of it, *gnädige Frau.*" He gestured upward. "The drawing room?"

Cissy gathered her skirts and hurried upstairs. At the prospect before her, she felt slightly sick. The encounter with Marie had left her shaken; she still couldn't quite fathom how her maid could have betrayed her trust like that.

She halted in hallway outside the drawing room. "We're doing the right thing, aren't we?" she asked, her hand on the door handle.

"Yes, *gnädige Frau.*" Johann's voice was as steady as a

rock. "We *are* doing the right thing. If we don't reveal Master Leopold's deviousness now, who knows what might happen? The next time, his plan might succeed."

"You're absolutely right."

Straightening her shoulders, Cissy took a deep breath and pushed the door open. Beyond, several pairs of eyes swiveled around to gaze at her, and Cissy was dismayed to find her husband had joined his family. At the sight of her, the faces of the Wolfenbach family registered different degrees of anger and annoyance.

"What are you doing in the drawing room?" she asked her husband.

Fenris's face flushed, and his eyes glittered dangerously. "What am *I* doing in the drawing room? What is *he* doing here?" He pointed to his brother. "Is it true that you invited him to Wolfenbach?"

Cissy stood very still. "Indeed it is." At her back she could feel Johann's reassuring presence. Her husband's eyes flickered from her to his valet. She saw how his expression slightly relaxed, and astonishment replaced some of his anger. His brow furrowed in an unspoken question.

Steadily, she met his gaze. *Please, trust me in this.*

Leopold snorted. "You let me think he was dying!" he spat. "What kind of joke is this?"

"Indeed, my dear, this is a very strange ruse, I must say," the old *Graf* spoke up.

Fenris slowly crossed his arms upon his chest. His eyes narrowed.

"Is it?" Cissy focused on Leopold and let a small smile play around her lips. She looked him up and down. "Yes, I let you believe your brother was dying." She lifted her brows. "For isn't that what you hoped to hear?"

"W-what?" Leopold spluttered.

"I say!" Both the *Graf* and the *Gräfin* shook their heads in disbelief.

The *Graf's* face turned purple. "What kind of rubbish is this?" he thundered.

"Indeed!" Leopold fumbled with his necktie. "Totally . . . ridiculous."

Cissy threw a glance at her husband to gauge his reaction. Not surprisingly, his face had frozen into its familiar, stony mask. Not even a flicker of an eyelid betrayed what he was thinking.

A wave of fresh anger assaulted Cissy. "Oh, is it ridiculous?" she asked archly, shifting her attention back to her brother-in-law. "How interesting. Weren't you the one who told my maid the title and everything should one day be rightfully yours? That Fenris had no right to come back after the war? Hm?"

Leo paled. "Y-your maid?" He rolled his shoulders and worked up some blustery indignation. "Ha! What would I care about a silly chit of a servant girl?" He waggled his finger. "If I were you I'd . . . I'd be careful about such false allegations, sister!"

"Indeed, Celia." The *Gräfin* touched a corner of her handkerchief to her eyes. Her voice, though, was cold. "You are most definitely going too far!"

Cissy shrugged, but she didn't take her eyes off Leopold. *Oh, little mousie, no matter how you run and keep trying to wriggle out of it, the trap has already closed behind you.* And how the thought filled her with grim satisfaction.

"Quite so." Tossing his head back, Leopold puffed himself up. "I don't even know the girl."

Cissy gave a laugh. "Oh, come on, *brother.*" She lifted her brow. "After all, you seduced her." With mock playfulness she batted her lashes at him.

Leopold gasped like a fish on dry land.

"Which you did while you were still courting me, did you not?" Cissy continued relentlessly. Her voice was sweeter than honey. "And how practical for you: after all, you needed somebody to saw into Fenris's wooden leg so he would eventually fall and look like a fool." She cocked her head to the side and nodded knowingly.

Gasping, the *Gräfin* fell back on the settee.

"Is this true, son?" the *Graf* inquired, his voice tremulous.

Leopold just stared at Cissy, slack-jawed.

"For as you've already told me—*us*—on an earlier occasion, such a fall would prove perfectly what poor husband material your brother makes. A 'cripple.' Wasn't that the gist of your little speech?"

A wave of deepest red rushed up from beneath the folds of Leopold's cravat. "You . . . you . . ." She wouldn't have been surprised if foam had formed in his mouth.

Again, Cissy flicked her gaze to her husband. His eyes had been glued to his brother, but now, as if he felt her looking at him, he turned to her. A muscle jumped in his jaw. How she longed to rush to him and take him in her arms!

"You wanted to get the castle so you could finally search for the fantastic Wolfenbach Hoard and become rich beyond your wildest dreams," she accused Leopold quietly, her gaze still on her husband. "But your plan did not work. I chose your brother."

At that, Fenris's features fractionally softened.

She felt her lips curve a little in response. "Yes, I chose your brother. Bad for you." And as her voice hardened, her eyes switched back to Leopold. "And so you tried something else. A lonely country lane, anything can happen there—a horse might shy, a rider might fall . . ."—she widened her eyes—"and die."

Leopold's temper snapped. "You little bitch!" He took

a few menacing steps toward her. "You shut up! That was an accident!" His face distorted into an ugly grimace. "An accident!"

Unperturbed, Cissy stared back at him. "An accident?" She gave a delicate snort. "You call it an accident? You standing in the underbrush, firing a shot into the air so your brother's horse would bolt and your brother might crack his skull on a stone? What a most interesting definition!"

"I did no such thing!" Leopold yelled, his face mottled.

Fenris frowned. "A shot in the air?" he asked, his voice gruff. "Why not shoot me?"

"Oh, that's easy. It wouldn't have looked like an accident then." Coldness touched her heart while she calmly disected the plot to destroy him. Cissy folded her hands in front of her to still their sudden trembling.

Looking like an irate bull, Leopold breathed noisily through his nose. "You've got no proof of this." He turned to his parents. "You can't possibly believe her. I did no such things. She is a raving lunatic."

"How interesting. Marie said exactly the same thing," Cissy exclaimed with false brightness. "Of course we've got proof. Johann?" He handed her the boots. "Johann and I, we went back to the place of the so-called 'accident' and found that somebody had stood in the underbrush waiting for Fenris. Somebody whose right riding boot has a broken heel." She turned the boots around. "Just like Leopold's right boot has a broken heel."

For a moment the silence in the drawing room was absolute.

Leopold started laughing. "Yes! Yes, I did it!" He threw his hands up. "I did it! Because then Wolfenbach would belong to me!" He regarded his brother with glittering eyes. "You should've never come back from the war. You should've snuffed it on one of these battlefields you were so eager to see!" A little bit of saliva ran down from the corner of his mouth. "You ruined our whole family! They took away all our privileges!"

With an expression of utter weariness, his father wiped a hand across his forehead. "God, Leopold. The titled families in this country have been steadily losing their privileges ever since 1803."

"But not the land!"

The *Graf* sighed heavily. "We still have enough land left to live in comfort."

"Ha! He brought dishonor over the name of our family!" Leopold spat. "Don't you care about this at all?"

"Actually . . ." Cissy stepped up to her husband and took his hand. As the reassuring warmth of his fingers engulfed hers, she relaxed a little. "Attempted fratricide versus fighting for the freedom of one's country and all of Europe? What do you think is the more dishonorable, hm? Besides, you would have needed to kill me, too. The castle still would have belonged to me. Or do you think I would have married you? Never!" She leaned her head against Fenris's shoulder and felt him tighten his hold of her hand.

"Tough luck for you, is it not, little brother?" Fenris asked softly. "It would have all been for naught."

Leopold gritted his teeth. "You bastard," he growled. "If it hadn't been for this little bitch—"

"That is quite enough!" his father cut in. His mother was crying silently into her handkerchief.

Cissy's heart contracted in sympathy. "Oh, Anna," she murmured. She slid her fingers out of Fenris's hand and hurried toward the settee. Yet before she could reach it, a rough hand gripped her arm and hauled her backwards.

"What a pretty show of sympathy." Leopold's breath whispered intimately against her ear, while he pressed her against his body. A click sounded close, then cool metal was pressed against her temple. "You should have told my brother's lackey to check my pockets, *Liebchen*. Then he might have found this pretty toy."

"Leopold!"

Cissy did not know from whom the shout had come, because the blood was roaring too loudly in her ears. Icy fear coursed through her, while her heart throbbed frantically against her ribs. Her gaze swiveled around the room and came to rest on her husband. She hardly recognized him.

"Let her go at once," Fenris snarled. Menace rolled off him in waves, and never had she seen such fury in his eyes. His features had tightened, his eyes narrowed, until he looked ready to rip Leopold's throat out.

His brother only chuckled. His breath puffed against Cissy's cheek, and she shuddered in disgust. Another chuckle, then his taunting voice: "Oh, no you don't, big brother. You will stay where you are—or would you like to watch your wife's brains sprayed all over the wall?" With the barrel of the pistol he caressed her ear, her temple. "I would be sorry to do it, of course, but—"

"Don't you dare!" Fenris roared. Johann gripped his arm when he would have lunged forward.

"Leopold," the *Gräfin* pleaded, tears streaming down her face. "Don't do this. Let Celia go."

"Oh, I will, Mother dear. I will. In time." Abruptly, his tone changed. "Get me my horse," he snapped. "And no tricks."

Anna stared at him, stricken, her face turning even whiter than before.

"You bastard!" Fenris growled.

"Johann?" The *Graf*'s voice was devoid of intonation. "Go to the stables and bring Leopold's horse."

"Yes, Johann, do," Leopold mocked. "And make it fast."

The valet threw a worried glance at Cissy, then leaned

forward to whisper something in Fenris's ear before he hurried out of the room. For a moment, the silence was absolute.

The arm around Cissy's middle tightened. "How cozy this is—is it not, *Liebchen?*" Leopold brushed his lips against her temple, laughed when she couldn't suppress another shudder. "And now we will all follow dear Johann at a leisurely pace." He continued to issue instructions and herded them out of the room, down the staircase and into the courtyard. "The perfect set-up for a family farewell."

The wind whistled sharply around the nooks and crannies of the castle. The gargoyles stared at them with dead stone eyes. Cissy swallowed hard. The time that passed until Johann finally came back with the horse seemed endless.

"I will kill you for this," Fenris forced out between gritted teeth.

"I don't think so. Not while I am holding a loaded pistol against your wife's head. And here's trustworthy Johann. Well done, Johann, well done." Leopold took a few steps forward and dragged Cissy with him. "It seems the time has come to say *adieu.* Shall we give them something to remember me by, *Liebchen?*" Before Cissy knew what was happening, he roughly forced her chin up and pressed a hard kiss onto her lips. With a laugh, he finally shoved her away and swung himself up into the saddle.

Cissy stumbled and would have fallen, but Fenris caught her in his arms. He enveloped her in a fierce hug. "Are you all right?" he whispered against her temple.

She nodded.

"Touching," Leopold commented. "I would advise you not to send anybody after me." His lips lifted into a feral smile. "This time I wouldn't shoot into the air." With a last glance at his family, he urged his horse on.

"May you all rot in hell!" The next moment, he was out in the ward.

"Dear God," the *Graf* muttered. "Dear God."

Pressing her handkerchief tighter against her face, his wife hunched over, her pain so intense it nearly broke Cissy's heart. She pressed her cheek against Fenris's chest and closed her eyes. How she would have wanted to spare them this!

Cissy heaved a sigh. She could only hope that Leopold had left their lives forever.

INTERLUDE

With stony eyes they watched as he rode down the ward, followed his progress.

Hatred coiled inside them, and a ripple of power whispered through the ancient walls of the castle.

And then . . . they pounced.

The horse whinnied shrilly in fear, but they did not want the horse. It raced out of the castle and disappeared into the forest.

Unperturbed, the trees hummed amongst themselves. After all, they had known the secret of Wolfenbach for centuries.

CHAPTER TWENTY-FOUR

Wearily the family trudged back into the drawing room, where the *Gräfin* sank onto one of the settees, still crying silently.

"I am sorry," Cissy said softly.

The *Graf* shook his head. "Don't be, my dear. Don't be. I am only glad that he didn't harm you. To imagine . . ." He rubbed his hand over his face before he went to sit down on the other side of his wife. He took her in his arms. "My poor sweetheart. Who would have thought it?"

"Well . . ." Fenris grimaced wryly. "In one point Leo was right, though." He shrugged. "I did ruin the family when I ran away to join the British army."

His mother lifted her tear-stained face. "Fenris Ferdinand, don't you dare talk such utter rubbish!" Despite her tears, her voice rang strong and clear. "It was only right that somebody tried to stop that mad little Frenchman! My dear boy, don't you know how proud we are of you?"

Her husband cleared his throat and nodded.

Fenris stared at his parents. And while his brother's vile tirades against him had never effected any show of emotion, he now visibly paled. He licked his lips. "But I didn't just lose you your privileges. I lost you your other son."

"Don't be foolish," the *Gräfin* said sharply. She wiped her nose. "Leopold managed to do that quite on his own."

"Oh." For once, Fenris seemed at a genuine loss for words. He shifted his weight. "Well . . ." He awkwardly lifted his shoulders.

"My dear boy." His mother stood and went to him. She smiled a little as she did, tears swimming in her eyes. She rubbed his cheek, and then she reached up to draw his head down so she could press a kiss to his forehead.

Cissy ducked her head and averted her gaze. The exchange between mother and son seemed too intimate for her to witness. She heard them murmur among themselves, and then more loudly: "I think we should retire," Fenris said, the tiredness in his voice unmistakable. "The doctor might have been right about the bedrest after all. And Celia . . ." He turned his head to look at her.

Cissy's heart ached for him. Weariness had etched deep lines in his face, and he was pale beneath his tan. Yet, when their gazes met, his expression softened.

"Celia should rest, too."

"Oh yes, she should." The *Gräfin* looked at her intently. "What an ordeal this must have been for you, my dear. You are sure you are all right?"

Cissy nodded. "I am perfectly fine," she reassured her.

Fenris raised a brow. "Will you help me upstairs?"

"Yes. Yes, of course." She was with him in an instant, slipping her arm around his waist. His warmth seeped through her clothes, and she could feel the play of his muscles when he lifted his arm to settle it over her shoulders. She found the solid weight of it deeply reassuring.

The *Gräfin* gave them a trembling smile. "God bless you, my children." She kissed Cissy's cheek. "I know you will take good care of him," she murmured.

Cissy and Fenris left the room, and Fenris's breath fanned her temple. His movements were stiff and lacking their usual fluidity, but it was enough to finally have him alone at her side.

On the stairs his steps faltered, and he bowed his head. His fingers gripped the banister so tightly his knucklebones pressed white against the skin. Cissy stood beside him and studied his profile. She rubbed her hand slowly up and down his back in wordless comfort.

Finally he released his breath in a long sigh. "I didn't know," he said, without looking at her.

"Didn't know what, my wolf?"

His turbulent green eyes met her gaze. "That he hated me quite that much."

"I know." She touched his shoulder.

A shudder ran through him. "My little brother . . ." His voice broke.

"Oh, my wolf." Reaching up, she drew his head down into the curve of her neck, slipped her arms around his shoulders and hugged him hard. "I am sorry," she murmured, and stroked his hair. "I am so sorry, sweeting." She kissed his temple.

He took a deep, shivery breath before he drew back to wipe his eyes. "And my parents . . . God." He rubbed his hands over his face.

"It's not your fault, Fenris."

"One could most certainly argue with that."

"You heard what they said."

He snorted. "I did. And still . . ." A muscle jumped in his cheek as he locked his jaw. "All these years I thought . . . I thought . . ." His throat worked, and the sight of it wrenched her heart. Her arm slipped back around his waist to offer the comfort of her softness and warmth. For a moment, he leaned his forehead on the crown of her head. "I thought they secretly held it against me that I ran away," he murmured, his voice muffled against her hair. "We never talked. I thought . . . I was sure they regarded it as dishonor."

Her fingers squeezed firm flesh. "Because your brother spouted all that nonsense? Ah, how wrong you were."

His body was warm and alive under her hands. Wonderfully alive. A reminder of how near she had come to losing him. How precious their time on earth was, and how short and fragile a human life.

Carpe diem.

Seize the day.

Cissy smiled a little. "Sometimes it helps to talk," she whispered into his ear. "Don't always be so eager to turn into a horrible demon wolf."

A frown marred his forehead, and he lifted his face. "Demon wolf?"

"Fenris—the frightful wolf who is going to eat the sun." She stroked his cheek, which was faintly shadowed with new stubble.

He looked at her blandly. "I've never had any intention to eat the sun."

"Good." She rose on tiptoe and pressed a kiss onto his jaw. "Because I wouldn't let you." She let her breath tickle his ear and got the rumble of a chuckle in response. His arms closed around her and caught her against him, and it was then that she knew that the beast had indeed been redeemed, and everything would be fine for them.

"Come," he whispered to her. "Come with me."

Together they went upstairs, and while they walked the curving stairs and twisting hallways, a feeling of deep peace filled Cissy.

Fenris stopped only once: at the old grandfather clock with the enchanted princess. He pressed a kiss on the crown of Cissy's head before he stepped away from her. His hand on the latch of the glass door, he half-turned to Cissy, as if inviting her to share a secret. Silent and unmoving, the Fairy Princess observed them from above.

Suddenly, Fenris lifted the latch and opened the door. When his long finger touched the hand of the clock, Cissy knew what he would do, and all at once her heart was beating hard and fast against her ribs.

She watched how he turned the hand, turned and turned, until the clock struck twelve. Below, the screen slid aside to reveal the industrious dwarves, hacking at the stone down in their mines. *Click-clack, click-clack, click-clack.* Up on the face of the clock, the Roman eight turned inward, opening the window for the King of Dwarves, who looked yearningly toward his beloved above.

After the last stroke had sounded, the sweet little melody began. To the tinkling of the music, the sheep transformed into the Fairy Princess. . . .

Fenris stopped the clock.

Cocking his head to one side, he shot a shy glance at Cissy, a hint of red darkening his cheeks. "Today they shall be happy," he said softly, and her heart opened wide to draw him in and never let him go. "Because fairy tales can come true."

Arm in arm they went to his room, but when Cissy wanted to step back upon reaching the door, he pulled her inside and slid the bolt closed.

"Fenris!" she protested.

"Hm?" With short, efficient movements, he opened the lacings of his shirt and pulled it over his head, wincing a little. Sunlight flooded the room and played over the muscles of his chest and arms, shimmered on the fine hairs of his chest and on the lovely whorl around his navel. A bolt of desire contracted Cissy's stomach, and her heart almost jumped right out of her chest.

"What are you doing?" she whispered breathlessly.

With a thud, he sat down on the bed and pulled the boot off his foot. "What does it look like?" He glanced up, his eyes glittering hotly.

She swallowed hard. "The doctor said you need quiet and rest."

The grin he gave her was decidedly roguish. "Oh, but *I* intend to be quiet. It is you who makes all that noise." His voice dropped to a sensual purr. "All those little moans and groans . . ."

Cissy felt a blush burning on her face, yet at the same time his deep, husky voice and the wicked words made another heat rise in her body. A pulse started in the secret place between her legs, which he had kissed and licked and . . .

Cissy sighed. Her body seemed to melt.

"Yes, exactly," Fenris murmured throatily. "*These* little pants and sighs, and that beautiful scream when you finally come and clamp down on me."

Cissy bit her lip to prevent herself from whimpering at the erotic memories he evoked. "You . . . you need rest. The doctor said . . ." His hot gaze devoured her, and her nipples tightened in response, rubbing painfully against the restraints of her stays.

"I need you," her husband rasped. "I need to feel you in my arms, to know that you're real. That you're well."

With an effort, Cissy concentrated on the instructions they had been given. "The doctor said you shouldn't be doing anything strenuous."

"Strenuous?" One raven-black brow shot up. "So I will

just lie back, like this." He sank against the pillows. The muscles in his stomach rippled delightfully. "And you will do all the work."

Entranced, Cissy stepped nearer. "Me?"

"Oh, yes. Surely there must be something about this in your cards? What about the five of clubs? The eight of spades? The—"

"Ace of hearts." The first card she had looked at on her campaign to seduce her husband. She took another step toward him, charmed and aroused in equal measure.

"Ahh. How fitting." One corner of his mouth twitched, while his gaze roved over her face. "Then, will you come? To ease my pain." With the back of his hand he stroked lightly over the bulge in his trousers. "You cannot want me to remain in pain?"

"No," she breathed.

Their eyes met, clung.

He held out his hand. "Then come," he said, his voice sure and strong. "Come, Cissy. Celia von Wolfenbach." And he gave her one of his rare full smiles, which lit up his face and would forever capture her heart.

Without hesitation, she took the last step and put her hand in his. His long, strong fingers closed around hers, and he drew her to him so she could kiss the smile off his face.

She would see that smile she loved so well often in the years to come as the bond between them grew stronger and the laughter of their children filled the castle with happiness. More happiness than either of them had believed to be possible.

They never heard from Leopold again, nor did they ever find any treasure of gold among the stones of the castle. Yet what they found together was worth more than all the treasures of the earth, and none of them ever again questioned fairy tales.

> *Lavender blue, diddle diddle,*
> *And roses red,*
> *When I am king, diddle, diddle,*
> *you shall be queen.*
> *Who told you so, diddle diddle,*
> *who told you so?*
> *'Twas mine own heart, diddle, diddle,*
> *that told me so.*

POSTLUDE

Nobody ever counted the gargoyles, so nobody would ever know they had sucked up he who had no heart into the stone. Nobody would ever find the twisted face high up on the wall, just as no one had found the other enemies who had been absorbed and found a home there. Only the north wind, blowing harshly, visited this corner of the castle and whispered over the gnarled stone, stone which stayed cold and unmoved forevermore.

No, nobody ever counted gargoyles.

Nobody would ever know their secret. They basked in the sun and rumbled among themselves of love and laughter, and over the years the happiness of the humans they were guarding filled them to the brim.

Created at the dawn of time to protect humanity, the ancient warriors have been nearly forgotten, though magic lives on in vampires, werewolves, the Celtic Sidhe, and other beings. But now one of their own has turned rogue, and the world is again in desperate need of the

IMMORTALS

CHRISTINE FEEHAN

DARK GOLD

Alexandria Houton will sacrifice anything—even her life—to protect her orphaned little brother. But when both encounter unspeakable evil in the swirling San Francisco mists, Alex can only cry to heaven for their deliverance . . .

And out of the darkness swoops Aidan Savage, a golden being more powerful, more mysterious, than any other creature of the night. But is Aidan a miracle . . . or a monster? Alex's salvation . . . or her sin? If she surrenders to Aidan's savage, unearthly seduction will Alex truly save her brother? Or sacrifice more than her life?

WRIT ON WATER

Melanie Jackson

Chloe is having visions, visions of her upcoming assignment to photograph tombs in Virginia. She has the Sight, just like her Gran, the witch.

But Gran hasn't taught her anything about her gift, and Chloe is at a loss. The horrible things she sees: What do they mean? Are they real? Can she stop them? She is in a new place with no allies—at least, none that she knows. MacGregor Patrick is charming, but is his kindly nature a charade? His son Rory is handsome as sin, but angelic features can hide diabolic intent. There is no one she can trust, and her enemies wish her name to be…*Writ on Water*.

Blood Moon

✠ ✠ ✠

Dawn Thompson

Jon Hyde-White is changed. Soon he will cease to be an earl's second son and become a ravening monster. Already lust grows, begging him to drink blood—and the blood of his fiancée Cassandra Thorpe will be sweetest of all. Is that not why the blasphemous creature Sebastian bursts upon them from the London shadows? But Sebastian's evil task remains incomplete, and neither Jon nor Cassandra is beyond hope. One chance remains—in faraway Moldavia, in a secret brotherhood, in an ancient ritual and in the power of love.

SIGN OF THE WOLF

ELAINE BARBIERI

It is an eerie howling in the night that only she can hear. As always, tragedy soon follows. This time, Letty Wolf will obey the teachings of her Kiowa heritage and bring back to New York her three estranged daughters…before it is too late.

Raised in fancy Eastern boarding schools, Letty's daughter Meredith is determined to return to Texas. Once there she is caught up in a whirlwind of mayhem. The only calm in the storm is Trace Stringer, who tracked Meredith down with a summons from her mother. In Trace's arms, Meredith begins to believe love might be possible, even for her.
